ICE PRINCESS
LUCKY STRIKERS HOCKEY ROMANCE

LIA BEVANS

COPYRIGHT

This is a work of fiction. Similarities to real people, places or events are entirely coincidental.

ICE MECHANIC
Copyright © 2025 Lia Bevans
Written by Lia Bevans
Edited by Jalulu Editing
Cover by Nisa Sanchez

CHAPTER ONE

REBEL

If I leave this world, it will be in a shroud of pink. In a pink coffin. Beneath a pink tombstone, stained with the words *'Rebel Hart, she was many things, but invisible wasn't one of them'*.

As I stalk into Carol Kinsey's enormous barn, several heads swivel to look at me. Three ladies in particular glare at me, as if they'd want nothing more than to bury me in the pink casket of my dreams.

I smile tauntingly at Marjorie White, who scoffs and returns to her task of wrapping a row of rusty bleachers in dainty, white cloth.

Her two henchwomen barricade themselves on either side of the bleachers' entrance. Time is against me or I might have considered running up to their human blockade, just to see what they'd do in response.

Continuing on my way, I ignore the whistles that erupt as I pass crew members doing last minute preparations on their monster trucks. The raucous calls are nothing but background noise.

Just then, I spot a frantic man huffing through the barn's southern entrance. He's wearing a T-shirt bearing the name 'Scooby's Nightmare Staff'. I take out my phone and double-check the email April forwarded to me.

Scooby's Nightmare.

Yup. It's my client—Rodney Howard.

The red-faced man stops in front of me, breathing hard enough that I wonder if he needs an inhaler.

"Are you the one from Pink Garage?" He stares pointedly at the pink over-alls covering my pure white undershirt. "Tell me it's you."

I like this guy already.

Normally, I'd have to introduce myself as the mechanic. And when I do, I'm either laughed out of the room or I'm forced to do an entire song and dance about why and how I'm qualified to fix a car.

"Yes, it's me," I say simply.

He starts fast-walking to the exits. "This way."

I keep up with him, trying not to let the waves and waves of anxiety on his shoulders affect my own psyche. Whatever's causing him to respond with *this* much desperation will only cloud my judgement.

Remain calm, Rebel.

As we move, I pull my hair into a high ponytail and secure it with a clip. "Did you call a welding team?"

"They just got here," he explains.

"I'll double-check their equipment before we get started. I don't want us to run out of rods before the roll cage is secured. If everything's set, we'll begin welding. If not, I'll have to ask you to find what we need."

"Anything. Just let me know." He rubs his head as if he has a terrible headache. "It's our first out-of-state show and we had no idea about the adjusted roll cage dimensions. My assistant must have missed the email or…" He huffs out another breath. "Anyway, what matters is getting this done before the preliminaries in an hour. If we don't, we'll be disqualified."

Once we're outside of the main arena, he takes a sharp left to one of the outpost barns on the property.

The nearby trees applaud our brisk trot and offer a bit of shade from the blistering sunshine. The smell of freshly turned mulch fills my nose.

The Kinsey's apple orchard is *the* biggest, and arguably, the most beautiful in all of Lucky Falls. During harvest time, the air is alive with the scent of ripe apples and during planting time, tractors rumble as they prepare the soil.

My history with the Kinsey family is bittersweet, but their apple orchard holds pleasant memories.

I see a pickup parked outside the outpost. The welding machine is still tucked in the bed. I shield my eyes with a hand, squinting past the sun's glare in order to make out the model of the machine.

That'll do. But why hasn't it been unloaded?

I stalk ahead of the client and enter the outpost. There are five men standing around a bright green monster truck with the words 'Scooby's Nightmare' emblazoned on the side in a graphic font.

Dazzled, I take a moment to admire the machine.

While some monster trucks are just rusty hubs with fancy paint slapped on them, Scooby's Nightmare is a total beauty. The wheels are the size of tractor wheels and are so new, they carry the scent of rubber. The chassis is fabricated from scratch to match the suspension.

It's clear the client spent a pretty penny on this masterpiece.

"Well, I'll *be*. Rebel is that you?"

I turn to the voice and come face-to-face with Clifford Davoe, an old high school classmate.

"Cliff." My eyebrows shoot up. "Fancy seeing *you* here."

"Girl, how have you been?"

I smile tightly as Clifford's eyes drag up and down my body.

"Still the beauty of Lucky Falls, huh?" He gives me another, obvious once-over and then glances at his crew. "This girl had *all* the seniors eating out of her hand. Everyone was gunning to date the bell of Cornblue High." Clifford ambles over, arms outstretched. "Come give me a hug, girl."

I step back. "It's good to see you, Cliff, but let's save our catching up until after we get Scooby's Nightmare up to scratch."

The smile teeters on his face and he flashes me a look of annoyance.

Frankly, I don't care. I've long out-grown being called 'girl' by men my own age. Besides, we're here to get a job done, not to shoot the breeze.

"Let's unload the machine," I say, moving toward the truck. "How many lengths of the iron rod did you bring, Cliff?"

"Doesn't matter. I'm afraid there's no salvaging this." Cliff nods to the monster truck, his demeanor a tad cold.

Mr. Rodney gasps. "What do you mean? Can't we adjust the roll cage to meet the competition standards?"

"Uh-uh." Cliff shakes his head. "The cage is supposed to protect the driver if the vehicle turns over. It's specific to the frame of your truck. You'll need to order the part from the manufacturer."

Mr. Rodney's eyes nearly pop out of his head. "The manufacturer? Even if I got in touch with them today, it would take weeks to ship out. The competition starts in an hour. We don't have time for that."

"Cliff, the roll cage can be welded," I speak up.

"Yeah." Cliff crosses his hairy arms. "But to get the right specifications, it'll take three months and way more materials than we have at the shop right now."

Mr. Rodney staggers back.

I turn to the old man in concern. "Mr. Rodney, are you okay?"

"My son's coming to the arena today," he whispers,

massaging his throat. "We've been estranged since his mother's passing, but I reached out to him about the competition…"

My heart twists in my chest. I can practically *feel* how badly Mr. Rodney needs this.

"Forgive me. I'm rambling." His chest caves in with a sad exhale. "Maybe this is a sign that he's better off without me."

My bottom lip trembles.

If my rolling stone of a father had cared *half* as much as Mr. Rodney, he wouldn't have walked out on me and mom.

Mr. Rodney swallows hard. "If it can't be helped, it can't be helped. I'm sorry to waste everyone's time."

"No," I say firmly.

Every eye darts my way.

Resolve surging in my heart, I motion to the monster truck, "I'll work on the dimensions and find a design that's both secure and safe for the driver."

Cliff snorts.

I ignore him. "Mr. Rodney, I already suspected the roll cage would be difficult to build. That's why I asked you to contact a welding team. I believe we can get this done by the preliminary judging."

Mr. Rodney looks up at me with hope filling his dark brown eyes. "Is there anything I can do?"

"See if the organizers of the show can judge Scooby's Nightmare last. If not, do your best to switch with someone later in the lineup. The more time we have, the better."

"Great idea. I'll make it happen." Mr. Rodney leaves the barn with a few of his assistants trailing behind him.

Cliff swaggers up to me, a smirk on his lips. I've seen that expression a million times before and I know exactly what it means:

You shouldn't waste your pretty face on hard labor.
Can someone who looks like you really be that smart?
Awww, it's cute that you think you can fix this.

I motion to one of Cliff's men. "Bring out your welding

machine and your tools. I'll decide on the design of the roll cage after I see the materials we have here."

The worker's eyes swing to his boss, waiting for direction.

I look at Cliff too.

His amused expression annoys me. *'Get the machine and get to work, Cliff! We don't have time for this!'* is what I want to say.

Instead, I smile prettily. "Is there a problem, Cliff?"

"Rebel, anyone with half a brain could tell that there's no fabricating a roll cage in an hour."

My eyes narrow.

Cliff raises both hands. "I'm not saying this because you're a woman. Don't get me wrong." He moves toward me, his tone slipping into that of a father coaxing a wailing toddler. "Why don't we call Mr. Rodney back and tell him to drop out of this competition, then you and I can go grab a drink?"

"Alright, I'll call him," I say easily.

Cliff chuckles and shoots his crew an 'I told you so' grin.

Lifting my phone, I tap out the number and wait for the client to answer.

"Hello?" Rodney croaks.

"Mr. Rodney, the current welding crew is unwilling to cooperate. I'd like to bring my own guys here? Is that okay with you?"

"Y-yes, of course. Anything to get it done in time."

Never taking my eyes off Cliff's face, I hang up. "Cliff, you're fired."

His smile collapses into a hard frown. "What the—"

I stop his angry tirade by speaking louder. "Get your things and get out now. I have a job to do."

"I'm not going anywhere."

"And I'm not going to repeat myself." I shift my focus to my phone so I can call another company. I already have someone in mind. The welding crew that April and I use at The Pink Garage is ideal. We've got a good rapport with them and at least they won't question my judgement.

As I'm dialing my colleague's number, Cliff grabs my arm.

I whip my head up, glaring at his fingers.

His spittle flies when he says, "You were always like this, Rebel. Acting all high and mighty when you're nothing but a pretty face from the trailer park."

My lips tighten into a firm line, but it's not because of his words. I've been called 'trailer trash' all my life. Cliff would have to try harder to hurt me.

My eyes slide down to my phone.

Fifty five minutes left.

Restlessness pours into me and makes my fingers jittery. We're working against the clock here. I don't have time for his temper tantrum.

"Let me go, Cliff."

He yanks me forward instead so I collide with his chest.

None of his crew members come to my aid. Not that I expect them to turn against their own boss.

I'm on my own.

I struggle to free my arm from the bigger man, but he's got a rock-hard grip. I claw at his hand with my fingernails. "Let go!"

Cliff snarls at me, his bruised ego turning him into something ugly. "I bet you could get away with anything thanks to that pretty face of yours. Well, sorry. I'm no longer one of those losers from Cornblue who worships you. I won't let *anyone* disrespect me. Much less a woman like you."

Fear skitters down my throat as his fingers tighten on me.

My voice trembles, "Cliff, I said let—"

Something whistles through the air. I see a black blur come dangerously close to Cliff's face. A moment later, it thunks to the ground by his feet.

Cliff yelps. "What was that?"

I scan the disc on the floor.

It's a hockey puck.

At that moment, a low voice rumbles from the doorway. "Let her go or the next shot *won't* miss."

CHAPTER TWO

GUNNER

CLIFFORD DAVOE'S FACE TURNS PURPLE WITH FURY AND HE FLINGS Rebel's hand down, storming toward me with a snarl.

"You're asking for a beating, Kinsey."

I swing the old, busted hockey stick over my shoulder like a baseball bat.

Clifford's workmen take threatening steps toward me. I deliver a warning glare. It's a look that needs no words and the crew shirk back, glancing at each other with uncertainty.

Clifford nears me and I toss the hockey stick to the ground, preparing for a fight.

It's a toss-up for who'll get the bigger beating.

I've gotten my fair share of bloody lips and raw knuckles on the ice, but Cliff's become a lot brawnier since high school. Besides that, he's got a skull so thick, he could probably crush cement with it.

I don't expect to walk out of here without a bruise.

But before Clifford and his beer paunch can reach me, a streak of pink cuts in front of his path.

In a clipped voice, Rebel says, "If you're going to start a brawl, do it *out* of my way. I'm too busy for all the caveman grunting."

Clifford stops in his tracks.

I freeze too.

Rebel's not looking at either of us.

Long, pink fingernails wrap around her cell phone as she speaks into the device. "Hey, Dalton. Yeah, are you and your crew available today? Oh, that's perfect. Can you come down to the Kinsey farm? Dalton, you lifesaver!"

Sunshine wraps around her soft blonde hair like a halo and the fitted pink over-alls hug her willowy figure.

My heart does a strange double-tap, a symptom I've only experienced in Rebel Hart's presence. It's one of the many reasons I make it a point *not* to be in the same room with the woman.

Grunting, I rub my chest.

Cliff's shadow falls on me. I glance up and find the jerk watching me with a glib smile.

He looks pointedly at where Rebel walked away and then focuses on me again. "Guess *you* haven't changed since high school either, Kinsey."

I stare at him, expressionless. "Are you going to leave on your own, Davoe? Or do you need to be escorted off the property?"

A shadow falls over Clifford's face and he spits to the side. "You're lucky you're on your own turf, *Prince* Kinsey. If your dad weren't the sheriff…"

I advance on him, seeing his eyes widen at my sudden movement. "If my dad wasn't the sheriff, it would have been my fist and not a hockey puck coming at you."

Clifford grins, showing off his big, yellow teeth. "You think Rebel will thank you for this? She won't. She's got a truckload of losers just like you who can't see nothing but her pretty face. It's because of guys like you," he juts his finger in my chest, "that she thinks she's something special."

I stare at him, my lips curling up in a mocking smile. *Idiot.*

"You think I'm funny, Kinsey?" Clifford barks out a laugh, but it's not one of amusement. He looks down at his fists as if he's trying his best to control his arm. "You and that arrogant, *punchable* face."

I applaud Cliff's effort, but I'd give that insult a two out of ten. As a Kinsey, I've been called worse things.

"Clifford, you're still here?" Rebel says, appearing in the doorway again with her cell phone hanging from her right hand. In a crisp voice, she demands, "Why haven't you left yet? My crew is coming in fifteen."

I flinch. With a tone like that, she's poking at a bear. Does she not understand how unhinged Clifford is?

"I was just leaving," Clifford snarls. He knocks into my shoulder as he passes by and hisses in my ear. "Better keep close to home, *Prince* Kinsey. Venture too far, and mommy and daddy won't be there to save you from me."

Well, since we're exchanging advice…

I whisper too. "Put your hands on Rebel again, and not even my dad can save *you* from *me*."

Clifford scowls. He and his workmen give me dark looks as they file out.

The welder's truck coughs to life. I spin around to see a cloud of sand whip up over the tires. A moment later, Clifford peals away from the farm.

"I suppose I should thank you," Rebel mutters, passing me by while tapping on her phone. The scent of her perfume mixes with the engine oil and brake fluid coming from the monster truck to my right.

She's real close to me. Close enough that I can see the sparkly, pink clip in her hair wink in the sun.

A jumble of words spring to my lips.

Are you okay?

Did you hurt your arm?

Clifford's an idiot. Whatever he said, don't let it get to you.

But, as usual, the sentiment gets stuck behind my lips and can't seem to find a way out.

Instead, all I say is, "You don't have to thank—"

"Great. Then I won't."

She skates past me to the monster truck. Gripping the gasket on the front, she pulls herself up.

I lurch forward on instinct, my arms extended to help her. But she doesn't need my help and scrambles up to the cabin of the monster truck with ease.

I'm promptly ignored as she dislocates something inside the cabin and starts sketching on a notepad.

Hesitant to leave and not sure why, I rub the back of my neck. "Do you need help?"

She pointedly ignores me, her ponytail swinging back and forth like a pendulum as she sets the notepad down and crawls across the monster truck's hood with the grace of Jane after ten years and five kids with Tarzan.

I'm not wanted here. Her frosty silence is ten times louder than the warning shot of a well-oiled rifle.

Still, I stick around like a sore thumb.

But it's not because I *want* to be here.

It's just in case Clifford comes back. I'm a gentleman and I can't in good conscience, walk away without ensuring her safety.

Awkwardly, I retreat to the wall where dad keeps a bunch of my old hockey gear. I'm glad that, when Cliff was harassing Rebel, I saw a hockey stick and not something more dangerous. I have no idea what came over me back there, but I know it would have ended badly if my weapon of choice was something sharper.

My phone rings.

Mom.

I put the cell phone to my ear.

"Gunner Kinsey, did you get lost in your own backyard?

Earlier, you insisted you weren't interested in the show. Then Marge and the girls came over and you suddenly changed your mind. We've been waiting ages for your help with the tent."

"I'm on my way," I say quietly.

Mom hangs up and I close my eyes, recalling what brought me to the barn.

"I saw that Hart girl," Marjorie had whispered to mom in the kitchen earlier. *"You don't think she'd dare to show her face at a Kinsey event when her little garage and Stewart's auto shop have all but declared war?"*

Thanks to my mother's gossiping best friend, I was able to stop Clifford Davoe from doing something stupid. All in all, it was worth the tongue lashing from mom.

As I walk to the door, the sound of fabric rustling and the thud of feet smacking the ground erupts behind me.

"Kinsey, wait," Rebel says.

I tuck my surprise behind a bland expression.

Rebel chews on her lush bottom lip. They're the softest, pinkest hue, just like her clothes and hair clip. Blue eyes, like two ocean pools, dart up to look at me and then dart away as if she can't stand the sight.

"Thank you," she says abruptly.

My eyes widen.

She digs the toe of her pink sneakers into the scattered hay littering the barn floor and admits, "You helped me out. With Cliff, I mean… earlier." She clears her throat. "I don't like owing people… not that I owe you anything more than this. A thanks is all you'll get…" She pins her lips shut, squeezes her eyes closed and then takes a breath.

Ba-thump. Ba-thump.

I rub my chest.

"Thank you… Kinsey," Rebel says earnestly.

I try to swallow and realize that my throat has gone completely dry. The symptoms worsen as Rebel stands there, looking at me with those summer-sky eyes.

Ba-thump. Ba-thump.

With a nod and a swift turn, I leave her behind.

My steps are slow at first.

And then I move faster and faster until I'm running like a loon.

When I'm a good distance away, I stop and catch my breath.

Ba-thump. Ba-thump.

My pulse is racing, and it's not from the run.

Before heading in, I dial the number of the hospital and set an appointment to see the cardiologist bright and early on Monday.

CHAPTER
THREE

REBEL

After Gunner leaves, I go in search of a water hose to wash my mouth. Fair is fair and I wouldn't have gotten out of that situation with Cliff on my own.

But why did it have to be Gunner who came to my rescue?

He's the last person I want to be around. He's a Kinsey, and thus, he's my enemy by default, but beyond that... I just don't like him. Simple as that.

Before I can find a hose, a familiar truck lurches to a stop in the sandy yard.

Dalton and his crew are here.

I usher them into the barn.

"What's the plan, Hart?" Dalton asks, setting his tool box down with a serious expression.

I smile at the question. Dalton has no sky-high ego I need to stroke nor does he have a propensity for asking me out for drinks—what with him being happily married and a father of twins.

Talk about a breath of fresh air.

We get right to work.

At first, my calculations are slightly off and we scratch our heads, trying to figure out how to substitute the materials we don't have.

After talking it over, I realize we can bend the iron rods using a unique welding method that I researched online. Dalton has no experience with it, but after showing him the video and talking him through the process, he gets it done.

The hour mark passes.

Anxiety causes sweat to bead on the back of my neck. My undershirt sticks to my chest like a second skin.

We're out of time and we're only three quarters done.

I check in with Rodney. To my relief, he was able to switch with another contestant.

"I was just about to call and inform you," he says. "How are things on your end?"

I observe the frantic activity happening around the monster truck. Everyone is scrambling to pull this one off. "We're… getting there."

"That sounds less than promising," Rodney says nervously. "But I won't distract you. Keep me updated."

I promise him that I will. After hanging up with Rodney, I focus on directing the welders.

Machinery whirrs. Orange sparks fly. Iron rods get sliced and diced.

We're moving as fast as we can, but each glance at the clock makes me wince.

I don't think we can make it.

"It's not fitting in the slot, boss," one of Dalton's workmen says.

Dalton rubs the back of his neck. His face is covered with black grease stains. "I think we should call it now, Rebel. You said we had an hour. It's been twenty minutes past that time."

"We can't give up."

Dalton gives me a pitiful look.

"The specifications are right. I double—no, I triple checked it," I murmur, rubbing my chin as I stare at the roll cage.

Dalton grips the iron rods. "The cage isn't secure. It'll slide out under pressure. The judges won't pass this at the preliminaries."

I stare at the ground in thought and my gaze lands on my tennis shoes. I notice the little plastic edges on the ends of my shoe laces and an idea comes to me.

"Dalton, do you have anything rubbery?"

"Rubbery?" He blinks.

"No, you probably don't." My eyes roam the barn until I notice his portable table. "Wait, we can work with plastic too." I point to the rubber ends secured to the legs of the table. "If we weld this material down to the rods," I whip my hand in a back and forth motion, "it can act like a cap—"

Dalton's eyes widen. "That keeps the roll cage in place."

"Yes!"

"I'm on it." Dalton springs into action. With his quick work we set the roll cage in place. It fits perfectly in the monster truck's cabin.

Scooby's Nightmare is ready for the preliminaries just in the nick of time.

"Thank you. *Thank you,*" Mr. Rodney says earnestly as his crew wheels the monster truck out of the barn. He shakes my hand like his life depends on it. "This means so much to me."

"I hope everything works out between you and your son."

"You'll stay for the competition, won't you? I'd like to introduce you to my son if I can."

"I wasn't planning to. And I'm not really dressed for it." I gesture to my dirty overalls and vest. Though I wore gloves when handling the equipment, there's still dirt on my fingers too. I need a bath.

"If you can't make the competition, at least swing by for the donors' luncheon afterwards."

"I, uh…" I reach into my overalls where I keep my pink,

beaded bangles. "That's not really for crew members. It's only for the donors."

"Nonsense. Come as my guest."

I shake my head.

"Then at least let me treat you and the crew to lunch."

"If you want to treat the crew, you can talk to Dalton. But it's fine. Really."

Mr. Rodney is already handing out a generous fee to The Pink Garage for our emergency service. To take a penny more from him would be robbery.

"Mr. Rodney," one of his assistants points to the exit, "we need to go."

"Not until our star mechanic agrees to attend the luncheon." Rodney pleads, "Even if you simply take a plate and go, I'd be satisfied."

The assistant bounces from one leg to another, anxiety carved into his face.

"Fine." I give in. "I'll swing by during the luncheon."

Mr. Rodney breaks into a large smile and allows his assistant to whisk him away.

Since my work is done, I ask Dalton for a ride back to my studio. He heartily agrees and banishes his workmen to the bed of the truck so I can have the backseat to myself.

On the way to my place, I call my best friend.

April answers on the third ring. "Hey, Rebel. How'd it go?"

"We got it done," I say, melting into the busted leather seats, "but it wasn't easy."

"Told you you were the right person for the job."

"You probably would have done it in an hour," I mutter good-naturedly. April went to a vocational school renown for its auto repair program. She's continued to study and attend certification classes every year.

The woman is a genius.

I, on the other hand, went to an unremarkable vocational

school and have far less certifications. Sometimes, I wonder if April only keeps me around because of our friendship.

"Don't be ridiculous," April insists. "You're incredibly resourceful. You can fabricate a new part for a vehicle with just your imagination and the materials you have on hand. I don't have your level of creativity. Today's emergency would have been impossible for anyone but you."

My smile grows. "This much flattery will get you *everywhere*, April."

"I'm only speaking the truth. You know I can't lie." She laughs. "What are you doing later?"

"Why? Aren't you busy getting ready for your date with Chance?"

"We're going out after his training, so I'm free for lunch. Do you want to come with me to the Tuna?"

"You've been eating at the Tuna more often lately," I observe.

"I can't explain it, but the food tastes so much better now that I'm not running into Evan anymore."

I laugh. April's ex-boyfriend is a *huge* fan of Chance McLanely. He couldn't handle seeing April happy and in love with his hockey hero, so he moved another town over and joined a mechanic shop there.

"A burger from The Tipsy Tuna sounds amazing," I moan, "but I can't. I'm going to the Kinsey's luncheon and I need to shower and do my hair first."

There's a beat of silence.

"I'm sorry. I think I just heard you say you were attending something thrown by the Kinseys."

"I don't plan to stay. Our client begged me to show my face, so I will."

"Do you need backup?"

"From those grouchy ladies? No, I can handle it."

However, when I return to the Kinsey farm, dressed in a long, pink summer dress with spaghetti straps, I start to wish I'd taken April up on her offer.

"What is *she* doing here?" Rosalie Davis whispers loud enough that I can hear her from the dessert table.

Rosalie's sister, Cecilia, cuts me a dark look. "That's obvious. She probably flirted with one of the men to get a ticket."

I reach for the lemon tart.

Their conversation follows me.

"Look at her shoes. Aren't they from last year's clearance rack?"

"Doesn't she know it's tacky to wear all pink? Is she a toddler?"

More laughter rings out.

My fingers tighten on the dessert plate. The more the Davis sisters poke at me, the more difficult it is to keep my mouth shut.

Yet, defending myself will only play right into their hands.

Should I just leave?

"Excuse me," a voice says.

I look up and find a tall, lean man with closely-cropped hair and intelligent brown eyes hidden behind delicate round glasses. He looks at me with an eyebrow arched, as if we should know each other.

"Is it good?" he asks.

"W-what?"

"The lemon tart, is it good?"

"Uh, yeah." I offer a polite but tense smile.

He takes a bite of one and makes a face. "Oh, that's bitter. You two." He waves to the Davis sisters.

They jolt in surprise.

"Have some," the stranger says. "They're as bitter as the both of you combined."

Cecilia coughs in embarrassment while her sister pouts and stalks off.

I fight my laughter. "You shouldn't have done that. They'll hold a grudge."

"I hold grudges too. We'll see which one of us lasts the longest."

This time, I can't hold it back. I do laugh out loud.

A charming smile grows on his face. He offers a hand. "I'm Benjamin, but my friends call me Benji."

"Rebel."

"Rebel? Is that your actual name?"

"My mother was in a very 'female empowerment' stage of her life when she had me."

He chuckles.

I smile too.

"Well, Rebel," Benjamin leans in, "I hope you weren't too hurt by anything those nasty women said."

"On the contrary, I know I look amazing when they start screeching."

His eyes shine with interest as he looks me over. "They should have screeched a little harder."

I snort out another laugh. Something about Benjamin's clumsy attempt at flirting is endearing to me.

He clears his throat, blushing a little. "Having a good time? Aside from the jealous heckling?"

"The food is good. I do like it tart." I take another bite of the pastry.

"But the company is dreadful." Benji laughs softly. "Present company not included." His brown eyes dart around. "I've never liked these things."

"I haven't attended enough of them to know whether I like it or not." I look at the three bleachers in the middle of the arena that's shrouded in white. The sign on the pillar says 'Reserved for the Lucky Falls's Lady Luck Society'.

Benji shakes his head, "It's a world I know too well. Trust me. You don't want to be a part of it."

My eyes narrow on the high society tables. At the women who smile and laugh and clink champagne glasses. At the women who hold so much power over Lucky Falls.

"What if *I* do?"

"Huh?" Benji startles.

"What if I want to be a part of that world?" I ask, staring at the VIP tables in thought.

Benjamin inhales sharply, but before he can ask me anything, a voice rings out. "*There* you are!"

Mr. Rodney appears in front of us.

"And look, you found our star mechanic. Let me make the introductions. Benji, this is the lovely lady I was telling you about."

Benji stares at me with astonished eyes. "*She's* the mechanic?"

I glance between Mr. Rodney and Benji. "Wait… is this…?"

Mr. Rodney brandishes his hand in a proud wave. "Yes, *this* is my son."

CHAPTER
FOUR

GUNNER

Rebel has never smiled at me the way she's smiling at that stodgy-looking man in the glasses and suit.

I dislike him already. Who wears a suit to a monster truck competition?

There's another, older man with them now. He's touching the arm of the one with the glasses and Rebel is nodding, looking between the both of them with a pleased expression.

The older guy says something that makes her grin genuinely.

Rebel Hart has many smiles and most of them are just a stretch of her pretty lips to show off her white teeth. There's no feeling behind those plastic smiles, no warmth, it's just that she's so pleasant to look at, any smile of hers seems convincing.

But when her eyes crinkle like that... yup.

The older man must be someone she genuinely likes. Her eyes toward him are full of friendly affection.

Best case scenario—they're her uncle and cousin.

No, that's not right either. The glasses guy is *not* looking at

Rebel like he's related to her. In fact, he's staring at her as if he's seeing his future rolling out in front of him in high definition.

Rebel, covering her mouth with glee after he proposes. Rebel, walking down the aisle to him in a white dress. Rebel, announcing she's pregnant with their first child—a boy who wears the same dumb glasses straight out of the womb...

"Whoa," a feminine voice says. "Careful, Gunner. You were about to break that champagne flute with your bare hands." Pale hands cover mine. A moment later, the cup I'm holding is removed from me.

I meet a pair of familiar eyes that belong to my ex-girlfriend.

Stunned, I step back.

Victoria sets my cup on one of the standing tables. "Since when did you drink champagne?"

I don't.

Earlier, I overheard Rosalie and Cecilia Davis tearing into Rebel and headed over there. But that square in the suit got there first. To hide my original intentions, I swerved left and pretended I was getting champagne from the table.

"Aren't you going to ask me when I got back to town?" Victoria arches a brow.

I glance away.

"As talkative as ever, aren't you?" Laughter crackles through her words. "Believe it or not, it's really good to see you, Gunner. I missed you."

Rather than answer, I stretch past her, grab the champagne again and knock the entire glass back.

Tastes like carbonated water.

Laughter trickles from Rebel's side of the barn.

There are conversations all around and country music pouring from the speakers but, somehow, Rebel's delight cuts through the noise. It's like the bell mom used to ring for lunch on the farm, a pealing sound I would hear even if I was in the farthest parts of the orchard.

What on earth could that boring guy be saying to make her laugh like that?

Victoria seems determined to keep talking to me, despite my lack of interest. "I hear congratulations are in order, by the way. The Lucky Strikers are headed to the play-offs. Not that the town expected any less."

I flick my eyes down to her.

She smirks a little harder when I finally look her way. "Yeah, I kept up with the team. You're doing really well with Chance McLanely in the lineup. Not that the team wasn't doing well before. You were a great captain. It's because of the foundation you built that Chance could come in, acting like a hero."

It's an empty and unnecessary consolation. When Chance first rolled into town, I despised him. But after everything we've been through as a team—not to mention him ditching the pros and coming all the way back to Lucky Falls to play with us, I'd pretty much take a bullet for him.

Plus, reality can't be argued with. If it wasn't for Chance's relationship with April, his girlfriend, he'd be tearing up the ice in a way bigger city. The guy's in a totally different league than us.

"Really? Still nothing? Even though I'm talking about hockey? Your favorite subject ever?"

I frown at Victoria. Since when was hockey my favorite subject?

"If you keep quiet like this, Gunner, I'm going to take advantage," Victoria says with a mischievous smile.

My eyes narrow slightly.

"Like," she steps closer and lowers her voice, "will you go out with me this Friday? If you say nothing, that means yes."

I open my mouth to disagree when mom comes trailing in, "Victoria! You made it!"

"Carol! It's so good to see you!" My ex girlfriend squeezes my mother tight and the two of them exchange a bunch of words that mean absolutely nothing.

What facial masks are you using? You look so young, Carol!
Darling, I'm just trying to keep up with you! I love the hair!

I tune them out and notice that Rebel and the suit are walking away. Are they leaving together? Is he taking her home? Or worse… taking her out for a date?

There's no reason I should care this much. Despite growing up together, Rebel's been doing her own thing since as long as I can remember. And it's not like I've cared one way or another what she does with her dating life.

But who the heck is that guy?

"Mom," I mumble, eyes still on Rebel. "Weren't you going to give a speech before the food was served?"

"Oh, right." She squeezes Victoria's hand. "I'll be right back, sweetie. I've got Lady Luck Society duties." Mom waddles to the front of the large tent and knocks on a microphone hooked up to a speaker. "Yoo-hoo!"

Rebel and the guy stop in their tracks and turn to look at mom.

Success.

"I hope ya'll have been enjoying the desserts. Before we serve the food, I wanted to say a few words."

The suit gestures for Rebel to continue their walk to the exits, but she shakes her head and I nearly cave in half from relief.

"Thank you *so* much to everyone for coming and for being such big supporters of our Lady Luck Society. If you don't know, the Lady Luck Society or just 'the Ladies' for short, are a group of highly esteemed, community-oriented, and dare I say… extremely *beautiful…*"

That earns a hoot from my dad, who's standing at the front of the crowd with a beer bottle in hand.

"… townsfolk." Mom smiles at his antics. "We started this community with the park beautification initiative, planting trees and flowers in the park to spruce things up. After that brutal storm in '95, we donated fifty baskets of food and toiletries to the families surrounding the area."

The people around me all nod at the memory.

"And then, after years of moving with our own efforts and finances, we were recognized by the Lucky Falls city council and given a yearly grant to help with community projects. Thank you, Mayor Kinsey."

My uncle, Kit, lifts his drink in acknowledgement.

"Since then, the support from the community has been overwhelming. As most of you already know, a portion of the entrance fee from today's competition will be donated to the Lady Luck Society to be put to good use."

Cheers go up from the crowd.

Mom smiles heartily. "Thank you all for your continued support. Please enjoy the luncheon as a small token of our appreciation. Now, we'll ask Pastor Derrick to say grace and after that, we can dig in!"

Everyone bows their heads while Pastor Derrick takes the mike.

After, mom flits over to me. "Victoria, come sit with us."

I twist around and realize Victoria had been sticking around me this entire time.

"At the Ladies table?" Victoria's voice turns high-pitched with excitement. "Really?"

Mom winks.

"Are you coming too, Gunner?" Victoria asks.

"Yes, come sit with us, son." Mom subtly juts her chin at Victoria and wiggles her eyebrows.

I look away, searching for Rebel.

She's not in the crowd.

Where'd she go?

I whip my head back and forth. Did she leave already?

"Come on, son. Your mother's hungry." Mom loops an arm around my elbow. With me on one side and Victoria on the other, she steers us to the Ladies' table.

The other Ladies are already present and giggling together.

The mean Davis sisters who were rude to Rebel earlier are there too.

At the sight of their heavily made-up faces, my stomach turns. The last thing I want to do is sit and eat with them.

"Mom, I've got practice," I whisper in my mother's ear, hoping that'll be my 'Get Out of Jail Free' card.

But my card is rejected.

Mom frowns at me. "Gunner, you promised you'd be at my disposal to help with the event today. Is hockey worth more to you than your mother?"

I flinch. How am I supposed to win an argument like that?

"Come. Sit here." Mom plunks me down next to Victoria and then runs away grinning like a child who just dropped a Mento's mint into a shaken soda bottle.

"Hey, Gunner." Cecilia wiggles her fingers at me.

Her sister giggles. "Hi, Gunner. I'd be happy to fix you a plate?"

Victoria's smile turns brittle at their offers.

I sigh from deep in my chest, already feeling a headache. How much longer do I have to put up with this?

Suddenly, I hear a chair scrape against the ground and the entire table snaps into silence.

I look up and my entire skeleton jumps inside my skin when I see Rebel wrapping her delicate hands around a chair. She taps the back of the chair twice with a pink-painted fingernail. The wind picks up and stirs the hem of her long, pink dress.

Smiling breezily, she tilts her head and asks, "Is this seat taken?"

CHAPTER
FIVE

REBEL

IF LOOKS COULD KILL, I'D BE DEAD FIVE TIMES OVER.

In fact, I'm pretty sure if looks were a pickup truck with four-wheel drive, the Lady Luck Society would ram me down like an armadillo crossing the road, stop, put their car in reverse and run me over again.

Not one woman around the table is happy to see me dragging out a chair and preparing to sit.

"Darling," the leader of the Ladies and the highly respected matron of the Kinsey family herself—Carol Kinsey gives me a tight, polite smile, "I'm afraid that one's taken."

"That's fine." I grab a chair from a nearby table, drag it over and fall into it.

Carol Kinsey has the most polite cold shoulder in town, but she can't hide her distaste totally. Her mouth tightens like someone forced her to suck on the ripest lemon they could find.

Twitters of disapproval rise from the others.

I toss a saccharine-sweet smile at each of them, but my confidence falters when I see Gunner at the table. With his tattoos and dark hair, Gunner looks like a vampire prince in the middle of a bright, colorful flower field—albeit a poisonous flower field.

I dismiss him with a flick of my gaze. No matter how quiet and edgy Gunner wishes to be, he is—first and foremost—a Kinsey. And by birth, he has a seat around this table, whether he likes it or not.

I, on the other hand, have no birthright whatsoever. Everything I have, I've worked hard for and now, I'm ready to work harder than I ever have in my entire life.

"I like sitting at the table with you ladies," I tell Carol Kinsey. "It almost makes me want to do this more often."

My words are a poison-tipped arrow with one target. I know the threat will bother them.

"What is that supposed to mean?" Marjorie White spits. The woman has dark hair and a perpetual scowl etched into her face. That scowl gets deeper, and more wrinkly whenever she sees me.

Her dislike for me started when her eldest son, Buddy, rented an entire restaurant just to ask me out.

I said no.

And later found out that Buddy had stolen the money from his mother in order to pay for his wasted grand gesture.

Rather than blame her son, the little thief, Marjorie put the blame on me.

In a way, I understand her. Right or wrong, in this town—it's family over everything.

That's partly why the Lady Luck Society—once a well-intentioned community service club—turned into a wealth-flaunting, ego-stroking, status symbol for the powerful families in Lucky Falls.

Carol tilts her chin up. "Rebel, why don't you stop the antics and tell us what you want?" *'So you can leave'* is the silent but very obvious end to that statement.

I lean forward. "Did you hear that the community wellness building on the southside of town had a broken pipe since last

Tuesday? The kids have been doing after school programs next to moldy walls and buckets of water."

Carol frowns.

"What about the park where little Shelly Jenkins had to get a tetanus shot after scraping her elbow on that broken swing? Oh, and the road to the farms out west is full of pot holes so deep, falling into one takes you on a journey to the center of the earth."

Gunner makes a choked sound that resembles laughter, but when I look over, his eyes are as bored as always.

Marjorie stares pointedly at me. "The riff-raff on that side of town have no idea how to take care of anything. It'd be a waste to spend any more time or money on the southside community buildings. You should know since you're—"

Carol lifts a hand.

Marjorie bites back her words.

"Since I'm what?" I tilt my head and say what they're all thinking. "From the trailer park?"

The Davis sisters twitter.

Marjorie pulls her lips into her mouth in glee.

Carol clears her throat. "Rebel, you're mistaken. The Lady Luck Society is not responsible for the projects you mentioned. Maybe take it up with the city council. *We*," she makes a circle that includes the Ladies but does not include me, "are not the ones you need to speak to."

I look at all the chilly faces around the table. No one cares. They really, genuinely, don't give a hoot.

Carol Kinsey leans forward, her short, black hair swooping in front of her eyes. "How about this? I'll pass along a message to my brother that you have some concerns and you two can talk about the changes you'd like to make in *your* community."

I stiffen.

There it is.

Us vs. them.

The trailer park residents, the blue-collar workers, the poor, struggling farmers who don't have half the legacy or financial power that the Kinseys do—we're not acknowledged as a part of this town.

I've seen it all my life. Felt it more keenly than most.

But it's never been more obvious than now.

My fingers curl into fists beneath the table.

I had no intentions of stepping into this perfume-spritzed pile of dog doo-doo today. My original plan was to keep my head down and work independently as I've always done.

But after hearing Carol's high and mighty recount of the Lady Luck Society's history, righteous indignation burned inside me.

I couldn't stay still.

It was impossible.

And now, I'm getting the urge to do something foolish.

Calm down, Rebel.

My pulse hammers in my veins. I have no plan. I came over here on impulse and it would be best to leave, regroup and return to my quiet life, in my quiet corner of town, far away from the Kinseys.

That's the smart thing to do.

But then Marjorie White opens her big mouth and says to the Davis sisters, "Can you believe that? I almost thought she was here to join the Lady Luck Society."

The other women snicker as if the thought is completely and totally bonkers.

And that's when I snap.

"Why can't I?"

Carol arches a brow in surprise as if to say 'oh, you're still here?'

The fire in my heart burns brighter. "Why can't I join the Lady Luck Society?"

Carol smiles patiently, as if I'm a struggling student she has to spend extra time to teach after school. "Rebel, if this is about the community center across town, I already said—"

"I'd like to join."

"Join what?" Carol says in a measured tone.

"The Lady Luck Society."

There's a beat of silence.

Suddenly, Marjorie and the Davis sisters burst out laughing.

Carol's lips twitch as well, but she's more adept at controlling it. "I'm afraid we're not opening the club to new members at this time. Now, if you'll excuse us, this is a private, Lady Luck Society *only* table. So if you'll just—"

I turn my attention to the woman beside Carol. "Victoria Pierce."

She startles and glances up at me.

I rest my elbow on the table and set my chin in my palm. "When did you get back? I didn't know you were already a member of the Ladies."

My eyes are on Victoria, but my words are for Carol.

"Well, I… I…" Victoria's mouth falls open and then slams shut.

I don't mean to put her on the spot since I don't know her. She was two years ahead of me in school and one of the most popular girls at Cornblue, so we didn't interact much.

However, fair is fair. Everyone here knows that Victoria was not a member of the club before she left for law school and yet, she's sitting here with them.

Carol puts a hand over Victoria's and rises slowly. Her eyes are hard as flint and I can tell she's about to take the kid gloves off.

"Rebel, the Lady Luck Society takes many things into consideration, including family background. Your mother does hard, honest work around town. However, Victoria's family is not on the same level as yours for you to compare yourself to her."

Carol's words prick my heart and angry tears spring to my eyes.

The older woman pats Victoria's hand comfortingly. "Besides, Victoria is practically family. She and Gunner were almost engaged before she left for college. There's no need for her to go through the rigid process. Certain privileges are given to the girlfriends and wives of the Kinseys."

I drop my hands into my lap.

My shoulders tighten.

My chest burns.

I want to argue, but I remember that my mother still works for the Kinseys. *'They're the boss, Rebel,'* mom always told me, growing up, *'if you want to go far, make the Kinsey's happy'*.

Though I don't agree with that, mom still does. I already took a risk coming over here to speak my mind. I don't want to push Carol so far that she retaliates against my mother.

The ladies watch me with satisfied smirks.

Humiliation burns my ears red.

Carol's got me pinned against the proverbial wall. I'm done for. There's nothing I can do except withdraw and lick my wounds while they all laugh at me.

In the midst of my chaotic emotions, I feel a shadow standing behind my chair. Gunner is there, his eyes on his mom.

In a deep, rough voice, he says, "If that's the case, there shouldn't be a problem with Rebel joining you."

"S-son," Carol's eyes dart back and forth, "what do you mean by that? She's not—"

Gunner plants his hands on each of my shoulders, tugs me to my feet and says in that quiet, frosty way of his, "Rebel and I are dating."

CHAPTER SIX

GUNNER

The words feel so good leaving my mouth that I wonder if I've been waiting for this moment all my life.

Rebel reels away, glaring at me with fire in her ice-blue eyes.

Horrified shock spills across the faces of the Ladies, but I'm… calm.

I place a hand to my chest and realize that there are no heart skips. My pulse is hammering steadily as it's supposed to.

In fact, I feel downright *alive.*

"Gunner?" Mom clutches her cheek as if she's been slapped.

"You said it yourself, mom." I nod to Rebel. "Certain privileges are given to the wives and girlfriends of the Kinseys. I just wanted you to know who those privileges rightly belong to."

Marjorie's jaw smashes to the floor.

I straighten my shoulders. "Rebel and I—"

"Uh…" Mom slumps over the table and groans in pain.

I jump into action, racing to her side. "Mom?"

"I think I need to lie down."

"I'll get you some water," I offer.

"No." Mom's grip tightens on my arm. "Take me home."

"Carol…" Rebel's soft voice trembles through the air.

My eyes flash to her. She's staring at mom, her blue eyes brimming with concern and guilt.

Sensing that she's blaming herself, I tell Rebel, "She's fine. I've got her. You can go home."

Rebel flinches and I realize those words came out wrong.

"I'll come by later," I tell her, softening my tone.

She nods, grabs her purse and walks to the exits.

I'm relieved that she didn't argue. I'd hate for Rebel to stick around, waiting for news of mom's condition, and get verbally lashed by the Ladies.

"Carol, are you okay?" Victoria murmurs, rubbing my mom's shoulders.

Marjorie and the Davis sisters crowd around her too.

Mom shakes her head pitifully, but her mouth curves up at the edges and a part of me thinks she's loving all the attention.

"Wait up, Rebel," a man says in the distance.

I glance up and see the suit from earlier chasing Rebel down. He says something to her and then walks with her outside.

Frustration nips at me, yet there's nothing I can do but watch. I can't abandon my mother—even if I'm half-convinced she's just putting on a show.

Dad skates to a stop in front of us, his eyes searching mom's frantically. "Sweetheart, what's wrong?"

"It's too stuffy in here." Mom pulls at her collar.

"We're under a tent." I point to the giant canopy mom rented. At that moment, a rough breeze blows through the party area, further proving my point.

Mom gives me the stink eye. "I know what I feel, Gunner."

"This way, honey. Let's get you to the house." Dad coos to her, "What happened? You seemed perfectly fine earlier."

"It's all because of that *horrid* girl," Marjorie whines, keeping up with mom while holding her purse. "That Rebel Hart, she—"

"Thanks, Marjorie." I snatch mom's purse away from Marjorie, effectively cutting off any reason she has to follow us.

Dad, mom and I use a shortcut, cutting through a path that takes us to the edge of the orchard.

At home, I open the screen door for them, and dad helps mom into the living room. He deposits her gently into the sofa, fussing over her.

"Tell me what you need, Carol. Should we call Dr. Mark?"

Mom shakes her head.

Dad notices her massaging her temple. "I'll run up and get the headache medication."

"We put the meds in the car, remember? They're in the extra first aid kit in the pickup."

Dad frowns. "The truck is parked all the way at the northern entrance. Gunner, keep an eye on your mom while I run and get the medicine."

I nod.

The moment the screen door slaps shut behind my father, mom's face smoothes out. She straightens, cranes her neck to peer through the window and then looks at me. "You want to explain yourself, young man?"

"What happened to your headache?"

"I asked first."

"It's exactly as I said. Rebel and I are dating."

She barks out a dry laugh. "I've never seen you *talk* to that girl. And now you're suddenly dating?"

I nod sharply.

"Since when?"

I fold my arms over my chest and think about it.

"You don't know? You announced such a ridiculous lie without even thinking of such details?"

"What matters is that we're dating now."

Mom pinches her lips together. "Son, you've never been impulsive. Why on earth would you..." Her words trail off and she talks to herself like she's working through a complicated math problem. "Yes, you've always had a soft spot for the less fortunate. Your father and I raised you to have a generous, giving heart. But what I don't understand is why you'd say such a thing in front of poor Victoria?"

My eyes narrow slightly. Why is mom mentioning Victoria?

"Don't act as if you don't know why she came back to Lucky Falls. She had several job offers back in the city. Her career would have taken off if she hadn't turned those opportunities down."

I frown. *That's not my responsibility.*

"I don't know how you left things when you broke up with her, but it was obviously not clear to her that your intentions were with someone else."

My lips remain pressed together. I've already said what I needed to. Mom can talk circles around me all she wants.

Mom studies my face and, when I say nothing, she changes tactics.

This time, her voice is coaxing. "Gunner, I'm your mother. I want what's best for you. You were happy with Victoria, weren't you? You two would have continued dating if she hadn't left to study."

"Victoria and I are just friends."

"You dated her for three years," mom insists. "That's more than friendship."

My eyes lift to the ceiling as I try to find the words that will convince my mother.

Mom gets tired of my silence and spits out, "Fine. Date other people. But not her."

"Why not?"

"Gunner," mom's voice rings with exasperation, "I said nothing when you tossed your business degree and went to work for your uncle's hardware store, stocking shelves. I said nothing when you got all those tattoos."

She waves to the ink that's hidden beneath my black, long-sleeved shirt.

"I didn't say anything when you spent all your time playing with the hockey team instead of settling down and marrying a nice girl. I figured you'd find your way eventually. You've always been a sensitive child. Maybe you just needed more time."

Mom shakes her head, causing her bob to swish around her cheeks. "But I was wrong. Today shows that I should have been guiding you with a stricter hand."

"I don't need your guidance or your permission to date someone."

Her eyes flash with hurt. "Really? Is that how you feel? After all the years I raised you… is that all you can say to me?"

I rub my forehead. Again, it seems like I said the wrong thing.

This is why I keep quiet.

Mom exhales in frustration. "That girl won't fit in with us, Gunner. You heard what she said about the Ladies. She has no respect for everything I've built, everything this family stands for."

My eyes slide away. Rebel made several points in her speech that I agreed with, but Mom is *definitely* not open to hearing how the Lady Luck Society has been disproportionately focused on one side of town while ignoring the other.

"And she's in a fight with several of our family members too. Your Uncle Stewart is *livid* about those ladies at the Pink Garage. They stole all his customers!" Mom wags a finger. "And that Rebel-one especially is said to flirt with every two-legged male who walks into her shop, married or otherwise."

"Let me guess," I growl, "Did you hear that from Marjorie?"

Mom tilts her chin up. "I neither confirm nor deny that."

I scoff and shake my head.

"Where there's smoke there's fire. Can you seriously tell me that girl doesn't use her beauty to her advantage? Who's to say she's not using you for the Kinsey name?"

"Trust me," I mutter, "Rebel wants nothing to do with the Kinsey name."

Mom dramatically grips the back of her neck, launching into a familiar spiel about how hard it is to be a mother. In the middle of her dramatic performance, my phone buzzes with a message.

REBEL: *How's your mom?*

I look up, observing mom's one-woman monologue about the discomfort she had while pregnant with me, how she thought she wouldn't survive the fourteen-hour labor, and how I came out at ten pounds and two ounces at birth.

ME: *She's doing better.*

REBEL: *We need to talk. Meet me at the treehouse.*

Dad comes back with the first aid kit and I leave mom to his care.

On my way out the door, I think about what I'll say to Rebel. Given how she responded at the table, she wasn't happy about hearing that we're dating now. There's no way she'll want to go along with being my girlfriend.

And that's probably for the best.

It can't be her. Mom's voice is on a loop in my ears. *It can't be her.*

I know that more than anyone.

But as I near the treehouse, I find myself reluctant to apologize or take the words back.

CHAPTER SEVEN

REBEL

Gunner clears the forest line on the edge of the Kinsey property and moves toward me at a sedate pace. He's always been frustratingly even-keeled, compared to his more dramatic mother.

But this is no time to be calm.

Marjorie and her cohorts couldn't keep a secret to save their lives. By now, the entire town must have heard that we're dating.

It's my worst nightmare come to life.

He needs to fix this.

I wait impatiently for him to get closer, shifting my weight from one leg to the other. Gunner stops in front of me, his hands in his pockets.

I straighten to my full height. "Gunner, what was… why did you…" I grit my teeth in frustration. "I don't even know where to start."

The prince of Lucky Falls says nothing. He just stares at me like I'm a car with a stalled engine.

Rubbing the crown of my forehead briskly, I mutter, "Is your mom really okay?"

He nods.

"Good. That's... that's good." The Kinseys are *the worst*, but I would hate to be responsible for Carol Kinsey getting hurt. Reassured, I fold my arms over my chest, "I'll hear your explanation now."

He arches a brow as if to say *what do you mean?*

"You told the Ladies we were dating," I point out flatly.

"I did." Gunner's voice is incredibly deep and quite soulful for someone as quiet as he is. However, he doesn't sound apologetic at all.

"You..." I point to him. "And me?"

He nods.

"Are dating?" I hiss.

Another nod.

"When were you going to inform *me* of that?"

"That's what this conversation is for."

I look up at the treehouse, at a loss for words. *What on earth is going on right now?* "I don't understand. Are you ordering me to date you?"

He squints into the distance. "I'd call it more of a negotiation."

"You must be joking." I release a frustrated breath and rake my fingers through my hair. "But even if you aren't, my answer is no. I'm not interested in you nor will I ever be interested in you. Even if you were the last man on earth, I wouldn't date you. Even if I was cursed to be alone and miserable for the rest of my life, I wouldn't choose you. I'd rather chew on a box of radiator caps than be your girlfriend. Is that clear enough?"

His gaze on me remains steady and unwavering. "I'm not interested in dating you either."

I throw my hands up. "Then *why* did you say that?"

He just stares at me.

"Fine. I don't need an explanation or an apology. Just go back to your mom and the other ladies and clarify that we have nothing to do with each other."

"No."

"No?"

He nods decisively *I said what I said.*

"Gunner Ezekiel Kinsey, have you lost your mi—"

Gunner steps toward me.

I shuffle back on instinct.

He stops and, for a brief moment, looks hurt by my retreat. But what does he expect? Gunner is a big guy. That long-sleeved, black shirt he's wearing can't hide his impressive muscles or the ink peeping out at his wrists.

He could break me in half if he so chose. Since we're mortal enemies and his family pretty much run this town, he could easily get away with my murder.

Heart hammering in my chest, I declare, "If you don't tell your mom the truth, I'll tell her myself."

Turning sharply, I walk away.

"I'm surprised you asked to meet at the treehouse," Gunner says to my back.

I freeze.

He adds, "You and I used to play here, remember?"

"Did we? I totally forgot." I scratch behind my ear.

It's an unfortunate stain in my memory. Believe it or not, there was a time when I looked forward to tagging along with my mom to the Kinseys' farm. A time when I thought I might one day marry Gunner Kinsey. A time that's a lot simpler than now.

"Back then, I even had a nickname for you," Gunner says.

My insides coil tight. *Don't. Don't you dare…*

"Bell."

I swerve around, heated. "Why are you bringing that up now?"

Gunner's eyes lift briefly to meet mine. I startle at the eye contact. His irises are a pale, *pale* blue. Like all the vibrancy was strained from the sky and only the faintest thread of color remained.

There's something otherworldly about those eyes. Which is probably why the fangirls in town swear he's some kind of fairy prince from another realm.

"So much time has passed, it seems like a dream," Gunner says steadily. "But there was a moment when we didn't hate each other."

"Yeah, when I was five." I stomp up to him and gesture between the two of us. "If you haven't noticed, your family and I are mortal enemies. Have been since I was a kid. And *you* stopped talking to *me* first. This is the longest conversation we've had in years."

Rather than answer me, he looks at the treehouse. The structure is made of logs and held together with enough rope and nails to keep it sitting tight in a hurricane. The tree leaves nearby formed a natural roof, but it's overgrown and unkept, ivy trailing down the sides. The small balcony that wraps around the entire structure is filled with fallen leaves and debris.

Silence washes between us as we stare at the eyesore. It's a perfect parallel for me and Gunner. Whatever affection I had as a child for him is as abandoned as this old spot.

"I can get you a seat at the table," Gunner offers. "My mom is a woman of her word. She might regret what she said at the party, but it's out there now. She'll honor her promise to let you into the Society."

"I have my own plan." Sure, that plan involves joining the knitting society, networking with the ladies there, finding a recommender, and then jumping through a bunch of hoops but…

"Rebel—"

"I don't need you," I insist. "I'll figure it out on my own."

He frowns at me. "You're being stubborn."

"Kind of comes with the name."

"Let me help you."

"Why?"

"Because I don't like it either," he says.

My eyes shift to Gunner again.

"The way only one side of town gets help and attention." He frowns as if it really bothers him. "The way the Ladies talked to you, none of it. A lot of my teammates are from the southside. They find time to train for hockey *and* go to work at the factory after the games. They didn't grow up like me, but they're good people. They don't deserve to be discriminated against."

My eyes shift between his. "*You* care about fairness and justice?"

"You asked me why I did it." He shrugs.

I chew on my bottom lip, considering my options. On the one hand, I can continue pricking my hands and eventually join the knitting club so I can ask around for a recommender.

Or I can take the golden ticket and skip right into the Lady Luck Society.

Silently, I weigh my hatred for Gunner Kinsey against my desire to join the Ladies. It's a tempting offer, but can I really put my disgust aside and convince the town that I'm dating a Kinsey? It's a well-known fact that Gunner and I can't stand each other.

Plus, I don't expect Stewart Kinsey or Carol Kinsey to sit back and do nothing when they see me parading around with Gunner.

The giant hockey player draws closer to me and, this time, I don't step back. "Come on, Rebel," he whispers, "this is your chance to use a Kinsey to get what you want. Are you really going to pass that up?"

When he puts it like that…

I do relish the thought of torturing the Kinseys with the fact that I'm dating their golden child.

But more than that, there's so much good I could do at the Society. Once I start bringing attention to the people, roads, and buildings that need the most help, it'll all be worth it.

Trying my best to hide my growing interest, I face Gunner. "You said you brought me here to negotiate. What did you mean by that?"

"If you and I start dating, we need to go all-in."

I frown at the term. "What does that mean?"

His eyes dart to my lips. My heart starts thudding. Is he going to ask for a kiss?

"You'll need to smile at me."

I'm so astonished, that I can only stare at him for a second. "Smile? Seriously? That's it?"

He nods.

I bare my teeth in what I know is probably the ugliest smile in my arsenal. "There."

"Not like that."

"How then?"

Slowly, Gunner reaches out. The pad of his thumb brushes against the corner of my eye. It's a whisper soft touch and yet my heart thumps wildly.

"The smile that reaches your eyes." He runs his thumb back and forth. "It doesn't have to be today or tomorrow, but eventually, give me that one."

CHAPTER EIGHT

GUNNER

Sweat drips from the edges of my hair and trails down my forehead. I adjust my grip on the hockey stick and lean my weight back to maneuver around the orange cones.

Thwack!

The sound of the puck slashing into the net echoes through the empty stadium. I make three shots at a rapid-fire clip, adjusting my balance to increase speed.

"When did *you* get here?" Chance's voice reverberates over the ice.

I straighten and nod in welcome. "You think you're the only one who comes to training early and leaves last?"

"It's not a competition." Chance chuckles. "Unless it is. Because I'd win for sure."

My lips rise imperceptibly. No matter how close we are, as athletes, we turn everything into a fight for number one.

"Whoa." Chance's eyes fall on the pucks in the goal. "Something going on?"

I hesitate and then I shake my head. What exactly do I tell

him? *As of two hours ago, I'm a taken man. My girlfriend's the prettiest girl in town. She still hates my guts and would like nothing more than to set me on fire, but we're in a serious relationship.*

Have I mentioned that my mom hates her and now I'll be stuck between a rock and a hard place for as long as we're together?

"Gun?" Chance arches a brow.

"I'm fine," I grumble.

A grin stretches across Chance's face. "Anything you want to share with the class?"

"Yeah, Scooby's Nightmare won today's meet." I fish the pucks out of the goalie net.

"That's not what I heard." Chance sings. His smile widens and I kind of wish we were enemies again, so I had an excuse to punch him.

"Then you heard wrong." I skate past him, focusing on collecting the pucks.

Chance's skates shred ice as he speeds in front of me and smacks my back joyfully. "How'd you do it, man?"

"Do what?"

"Keep you and Rebel a secret. April was *blindsided* when she read the texts in the neighborhood group chat."

"Then that's between her and Rebel."

"But I took up for you. I told her I knew you had feelings for Rebel."

I look up quickly, my eyebrows bunching in question.

Chance helps me gather the pucks. "I think it was a few weeks ago? Back when I was leaving Lucky Falls and I asked your permission to hire a lawyer to investigate your uncle…" Chance stops and looks over his shoulder at me, checking my face.

I give him a subtle nod.

After I heard what Uncle Stewart did to April, I understood why Chance was outraged. A part of me is glad that someone else is making a move to put him in check.

Uncle Stewart is a bad apple in our family, but he's still

family. I learned at a young age that, when it comes to our family's secrets, my hands are tied.

"Anyway," Chance clears his throat, "I saw the way you looked at Rebel when she came in to The Tipsy Tuna."

Balancing my hands on the top of the hockey stick, I grumble, "How did I look at her?"

"You were staring at every move she made. And you even smiled when she walked in."

"I smiled?" I stick a finger in my chest. "*I* did?"

"Your entire face kind of..." Chance pauses in thought. "I don't know how to explain. You... melted."

I laugh out loud.

Chance smirks. "What's so funny?"

"You need to get your eyes checked." Skating briskly, I gather the rest of the pucks and send them skittering back to the neutral zone. "I'm telling you this because Rebel will probably tell April anyway."

"What?" Chance holds his breath. "Did I misunderstand something?"

"Big time. Rebel and I aren't really dating." I shake my head.

"What?" Chance's voice reverberates through the entire arena.

"We're just pretending to so she can join the Lady Luck Society."

"The Lucky *what* now?"

I roll my eyes. "It's a community service group... the point is, we're not really together. She hates me and that goes both ways." I stick my finger in his face. "So don't go around saying things like 'I melt' around her."

Chance blinks a couple times, processing what I just told him.

At that moment, the door to the arena bangs open and the rest of the team march in. Loud laughter and conversation immediately liven up the air.

I tuck my chin against my chest to hide my growing smile. While I love my family, the Kinsey name is a heavy chain around my neck. Sometimes, it's difficult to tell if anyone sees *me* when they look at me.

But when I started playing hockey with the Lucky Strikers, it felt like I'd found home. We were connected by our obsession with hockey and our desire to win. I was finally a part of something due to my own merit. It's one of the reasons I was so affected when Chance took my captain spot on the team.

"There he is! The man of the hour!" Theilan hoists his hockey stick in the air like a trophy.

Watson starts singing *'For He's A Jolly Good Fellow'* and the other guys join in, singing so robustly that Max pokes his head out of a window in the second floor admin section to see what the racket's about.

"What's going on?" our team manager yells.

Chance looks at Max with a shrug.

Theilan spins around to yell at our team manager, "Gunner and Rebel are dating."

"That's nice," Max says. "What does that have to do with you guys?"

Watson shakes his head. "You and Chance didn't grow up in Lucky Falls, so you don't know. But Rebel Hart is a legend around here."

"Rebel Hart?" Max snorts.

I frown at him.

The team manager looks at me in surprise. "Is her last name actually Heart? As in 'Brave Heart'?"

"It's Hart without the 'e'," I grumble. "H-A-R-T."

Theilan protests, "Nah, spell that correctly. It's Rebel K-I-N-S-E-Y now."

Laughter breaks out from the team.

I roll my eyes.

If they knew how hard I had to work just to get Rebel to *pretend* to date me, they'd know the likelihood of her changing her last name to Kinsey is as good as aliens descending on Lucky Falls and playing against us on the ice.

"My older brother told me this once," Theilan's voice drips with a gossipy undertone, "that so many guys were leaving her love letters and trying to get with her, that it started fights in PE and on the basketball court. Even the teachers had to get involved."

Chance swings around, his eyes wide. "Is that true?"

I squirm. "There were only a few fights…"

Chance's eyes double in size.

Watson takes up the story. "From then on, Rebel swore that she'd never date a guy from Lucky Falls. She's only ever dated out-of-towners. No matter how hard anyone tried, she'd turn them down flat."

At first, I open my mouth to argue but, on second thought, I wonder if they have a point. I didn't notice before, but each time I heard of Rebel dating someone, it wasn't a native of our town.

"I should have known that if anyone in Lucky Falls could do it, it would be a Kinsey." Theilan points to me and starts applauding.

Max purses his lips, impressed. "Not bad, Kinsey."

"It's not like that," I mutter.

But no one hears me nor do they care.

I give Chance a helpless look.

He clears his throat and motions to the team. "Enough chit-chat. Where's coach? Everyone's got so much energy today that I'll suggest we do suicide drills."

Groans break out from the guys.

I hold back my laughter when Theilan begs, "Are you punishing us for being single?"

"Yeah, now that you two have girlfriends, you're ganging up on us," Watson whines.

"I'm happily single." Renthrow pats Watson on the shoulder. "Leave Gunner alone and let's get started. I have to hurry home."

"Why? Is Gordie sick?" Theilan asks, straightening immediately.

I pay attention too. Gordie is Renthrow's baby girl and, by default, the niece of every member on the team.

Renthrow nods gravely.

Theilan claps his hands together loud enough to wake the dead. "Come on, boys. Let's get this started. Gordie needs some chicken soup and a bed time story."

The boys scramble to change and get on the ice where coach runs us through a harsh set of drills. By the time we're finished with practice, everyone's wrung out and panting.

"I think Coach wants to kill us," Theilan groans, dragging himself off the ice and onto a bench.

Watson guzzles a bottle of water.

I move over to Renthrow. "Do you need anything for Gordie?"

He shakes his head. "I already asked Mauve to make some chicken soup. I'll swing by The Tipsy Tuna to pick it up before heading home."

"I can do that."

He shakes his head. "It's alright, but I appreciate the offer."

I nod.

Renthrow nods back.

Limping to the showers, I open my locker door and reach for my gym bag. At that moment, I hear a buzzing sound and check my phone.

The moment I see the name rolling across the screen, my blood runs cold.

UNCLE STEWART: *Heard you're dating the Hart girl.*
UNCLE STEWART: *That better be a joke.*

CHAPTER
NINE

REBEL

The drive from the Kinseys to the neighborhood where I grew up is a long one. With every mile, I notice a sharp difference in my surroundings.

Even the sky changes, turning from a cheerful blue to a sunset red firing across the horizon.

With the sky ablaze and the buildings ahead growing more and more decrepit, I feel like I'm driving out of a dazzling, utopian world into a dark and hopeless apocalypse.

But it's not *all* bad.

Children play on a basketball court happily. The basketball net was lost or stolen ages ago, but that doesn't stop the game or the laughter.

An abandoned lot filled with garbage sits next to the old pharmacy where Abe Jenkins has been handing out lollipops to little kids since before I was born.

My perusal lands on a pack of dogs. I screech to a stop as the wild canines prowl the neighborhood, on the hunt for trash bins they can tear into and scatter across the streets.

Okay.

So even if there are pockets of good in my community, there's no hiding the fact that we're the abandoned people of Lucky Falls.

There are no wide, spacious parks, nor upscale boutiques or fancy restaurants out here.

And there definitely aren't any Victorian-style houses surrounded by lakes, beautifully maintained apple orchards or acres and acres of family land worth millions.

The houses are small and huddled together, boundary lines protected by rusty, chain link fences—no white picket fence to be seen. Paper thin walls separate one family from another, so that if a couple argues, the people in the house next door can hear every word.

I take a right, pointing my car to the trailer park. As the sun streaks low in the sky, I roll to a stop and peer out the windshield.

Mom's in the front yard, taking clothes off the line. She's got a bandana wrapped around her head, as always. The holes in her oversized T-shirt are hidden by a threadbare apron. The slippers on her feet are so worn, it's only duct tape and a prayer keeping them together.

Mom wraps her fingers around a shirt on the line, tests to see if it's dry and then plops it into her basket.

Annoyed, I throw my car door open and lumber across the yard. "Mom!"

She looks up, startled. "Rebel?"

"Why are you still hanging out your clothes? I already paid the hardware store for your washer and dryer. It should have been delivered by now."

"I told Robert Kinsey to keep the money you paid as store credit. You can buy other things you need with it."

"Mom…" I groan.

"I don't have space in the trailer for that." Mom shakes her head at me. "I'm perfectly fine doing things the way I always do them."

"You work so hard, and you're getting older. You should relax when you get home."

"I don't mind hard work. Idle hands are…"

"… the devil's playground. Yeah, yeah. Let me help." I squeeze the clothes pin at the top and release the blouse held between its teeth.

Mom watches me closely.

I unpin a pair of rough work pants and a jacket next, pretending not to notice.

"Are you really going to make me ask?"

"Ask what?" I release a wash rag from the clothesline.

Mom snaps it out of my hand. Excitement hums in her voice. "You're dating Gunner Kinsey!"

I wince. "News travels fast."

"Why didn't you tell me?"

"I don't want to talk about it."

Mom wags a finger. "You're always like this. You never discuss boys with me."

"I don't need to add to the conversation. Boys talk about me enough as it is," I grumble.

"Well, for what it's worth, I approve. Gunner Kinsey is a fine young man. So quiet and steady. He treats his mama well too. Oh dear, his mama." Mom touches her lips, her face turning white. "What did Carol say when she heard about this?"

I open my mouth to answer.

Mom waves a hand to stop me. "It doesn't matter. I've been working for the Kinseys all my life. They know us well. Our family might not have much, but we've got our dignity and our name. That's worth more than gold." She smiles shakily. "Money can't buy a good reputation, you know."

"Do you really think the Kinseys care about things like dignity and a good reputation?" I snort.

Mom licks her lips. "E-even so, Gunner was brave enough to tell his mother about your relationship, that means he's serious about you. He wouldn't have done that if he would easily change his mind now, would he?"

"Mom—"

She gasps suddenly. "What if you two get married? You'll be a Kinsey! My daughter... a Kinsey." The tail of the bandana wiggles as mom shakes her head in delight.

"Why are you so happy?"

She stops to look at me. "What do you mean?"

"You know how the Kinseys see us. They think we're beneath them. Why would we want to be family with people like that?"

"Rebel..."

"Do you love the Kinseys so much you'd trade your daughter to them?"

Mom's eyelashes flutter.

I glance away, trying to calm my emotions.

Mom's voice sounds tentative. "Are you okay, Rebel? Did Carol say something to you when she found out about you and Gunner?"

"No, mom. She welcomed me to the family with open arms."

"Really?"

I was being sarcastic, but I feel bad seeing how happy mom is to hear that.

She bounces on her feet. "Oh that's so *lovely* to hear!"

Awkwardly, I add, "Yeah, Carol loves me so much, she even invited me to join the Lady Luck Society."

Mom covers her mouth. "No! Are you serious!" She grabs my hand and brings it to her lips. "*My* baby... is one of the Ladies?"

I'm twisting the truth quite a bit, but I'd rather see my mother smile than hammer her with reality.

"I'm so happy for you, Rebel!" Mom pats my hand. As she does, I catch sight of her knuckles. They're laced with scratches and cuts from years of working on the Kinsey farm.

Sadness weighs my heart down like a rock sinking to the ocean floor. A knot of emotion in my throat, I bend down, hoist the basket of clean clothes to my hip and carry it inside the trailer.

The living area is neat and tidy. *'The Lord won't bless you with a bigger house if you don't take care of the one you got'* is what mom used to tell me growing up.

Unfortunately, I'm still waiting for the promised blessing. Mom faithfully plucks the weeds around the trailer, scrubs the cement blocks holding it up, and wipes every wooden surface that collects dust, but she still hasn't been granted a new home.

"You want some tea, sweetie?" Mom moves past me to the tiny kitchen.

I shake my head and sit on the sofa. Mom's home-making skills are so impressive, it's impossible to tell we're in a double wide. She hung pretty curtains over the windows, the kitchen cupboards are stained white, and the old gas stove looks practically new.

My studio was built five years ago, but my house looks far less cozy than hers does.

Mom comes over while the kettle heats up. She pats my knee. "Tell me the story of how you and Gunner got together."

"I," my mind goes blank, "there was nothing to it, really."

"Come on, Rebel. Throw your mama a bone. It's been years since I've been on a date. Let me live through you."

Eyelashes fluttering, I give it a shot. "I guess… uh… we were just… talking about how we used to play together on the farm."

"Oh, yes! You two went *everywhere* together. You were Gunner's little shadow. And he doted on you too. What did he used to call you?" Mom taps her chin. "It was 'Bell', I think. Just the sweetest."

I force a smile. *Yeah, mm-hm. So sweet, I could choke on it.*

"What happened next?" Mom leans forward.

"Well…" My eyes dart back and forth. "After that, he stepped closer…"

Mom's eyes widen expectantly.

"He touched my face…" My heart quickens at the memory.

"And?"

"And told me he wanted to see my smile."

"That's so romantic!" Mom coos. "Oh, Rebel, sweetie, you're blushing. Do you like Gunner that much?"

I cup my cheek with my hand. "I'm not blushing. It's just hot in here."

"It's not *that* hot," mom teases.

Feeling exposed, I change the subject. Mom prattles happily about her day and I'm free from discussing my relationship with Gunner Kinsey.

As the night winds down, I say my goodbyes.

"Bring Gunner with you next time," mom says, waving from the front steps.

"I'll try," I tell her. But it's hard to imagine the distinguished, golden child of the Kinseys stepping into our humble trailer.

The car hums beneath me as I drive away from the trailer park. Today has been absolutely draining, but I don't want to be alone right now. My thoughts are a mess and I need my best friend's help to sort them out.

I stop at April's place on the way home.

To my surprise, April is waiting up for me, along with Chance and May—April's college-aged sister.

I freeze in the doorway, my eyes darting from one face to the next. "Am I in trouble?"

April shakes her head slowly. "Rebel Eleanor Hart."

I step back.

April stomps toward me. She's wearing a white T-shirt beneath a navy jumper. Her straight brown hair is pulled back into a ponytail. Her green eyes spark with disapproval.

I wince. "Can you save the scolding till after I get a hug. It's been a really long day."

"Humph." April wraps her arms around me and squeezes. "I can imagine." My best friend runs a hand down my back in comfort. "Are you okay? Chance told me everything."

I ease back. "Everything?"

"Yeah, everything," April says with a nod.

"Gunner told me at training today," Chance explains. "He says you two can't stand each other, but you're faking a relationship for a good cause."

"Gunner said that?" I breathe out.

April studies me closely.

I'm too tired to fix my expression or to work through why I feel so betrayed. My eyes sink to the ground. Gunner asked me to smile at him. Why did he make that stupid comment about my smile if he hates me so much?

"Rebel?" April touches my arm.

"It's exactly as Chance said," I speak to the floor. "I agreed to be Gunner's girlfriend so I can join the Lady Luck Society."

April pulls her lips into her mouth as if she's forcing herself not to share her true thoughts. An awkward silence falls on the room.

"I think that's *great!*" May skips to me, her eyes bright with excitement. "Chance and April started as a fake couple too and look at them now."

"Gunner and I are *not* like that. Believe me." I hike my purse strap over my head and toss it in the couch.

"What do you mean? You're insanely pretty and he's so hot. Why wouldn't you be together?"

April scolds her little sister. "May, there's more to a healthy relationship than being good-looking."

"I *know* that. I'm just saying. It doesn't hurt."

"Something still isn't adding up," April murmurs.

Everyone in the room turns to look at her.

"I understand why *you'd* want to join the Lady Luck Society, but what's in it for Gunner?" April folds her arms across her chest. "Why would he do that for you if he hates you so much?"

"He wants the Lady Luck Society to change too," I answer flatly.

April rubs her chin, not buying it.

May offers, "There could be another reason. Like he's trying to stop his family from marrying him off? I heard the Kinseys still believe in arranged marriages."

"It could be simpler than that." Chance shrugs. "Maybe Gunner doesn't hate you as much as you thought, Rebel."

I shake my head. "You didn't grow up in Lucky Falls, Chance. Gunner Kinsey has made it abundantly clear that he doesn't like me. We grew up together, but he never talked to me, even when we were in high school. And his eyes are always so cold and arrogant when they look at me."

May insists, "But that doesn't mean—"

"May," I sink into the sofa and tilt my head back, "I can tell when a guy likes me. Guys have been confessing their love for me since elementary school. Trust me…"

The smile that reaches your eyes.

"…Gunner Kinsey and I…"

Give me that one.

"… are never going to be real."

CHAPTER
TEN

GUNNER

Uncle Stewart's texts bother me to the point that I can't sleep.

I run a hand down my face groggily and notice the time on my alarm clock.

1:15 AM.

I have early morning training, a shift at the hardware store, and then our first game of the play-offs later tonight. This isn't the time to be tossing and turning in bed.

Thirty minutes later, I give up.

Sleep is *not* going to happen for me.

With a sigh, I push myself to a sitting position, rake my fingers through my hair and then head downstairs.

I'm surprised to see dad behind the counter, stirring a pot of tea.

His eyebrows rise in tandem when he sees me approaching. "Couldn't sleep either?"

I nod and then point at the cup. "Mom?"

"I, uh, think yesterday's announcement was a bit too much

for her. I figured a cup of chamomile tea would help calm her nerves."

"Is she *that* upset?"

"Upset isn't the word I'd use." Dad rubs the back of his neck. "She's just overthinking things a bit. Change is hard for her. You know that. She wants her family close to her and introducing anything new could mean an unwanted change."

I nod in understanding. I originally wanted to move near the stadium so it would be easier to go to and from practice, but mom got wind of it and begged me to stay on the property. She offered to renovate the studio above the garage to give me 'my own space'.

I couldn't tell her no.

Moving around my dad, I open the fridge and notice that it's packed with leftovers from the luncheon earlier. The cherry pie on the top left corner is calling my name, but so is the banana cream pudding.

"I've got to get this tea to your mother but son I've been wanting to tell you this all day…" Dad waits for me to look up before he says, "Your mother and I trust your decisions. Whoever you bring home, we want you to be happy."

I nod.

"Does Rebel make you happy?" Dad asks, scanning my face.

Happy?

I think about how angry I was when Clifford Davoe grabbed her hand in the barn. Fury had spurted from every pore and I couldn't hold myself back.

I think of how upset I was when the suit at the luncheon kept staring at her. How annoyed I was when she smiled at him. How scared I was when Uncle Stewart sent me those texts, demanding to know if the rumors about me and Rebel are true.

"I don't know." I admit to my father.

His eyes widen in alarm. "She… doesn't make you happy?"

"No, she does," I amend quickly. That's what a real boyfriend would say in this situation.

"But...?" Dad prods.

I close the fridge door and face him. "It's strange, dad. I worry a lot. I get upset. Stupid things annoy me."

Dad's lips inch up into a slow, knowing smile.

"I'm not violent, but I want to punch other guys just for touching her. I'm not emotional, but it bothers me when she says one thing and her eyes say another."

Dad sets the tea down on the counter, draws up a chair and watches me with that smile growing and growing.

"What else?"

I avoid his eyes. "Nothing. That's it. She drives me crazy."

He leans forward, his wedding ring glinting in the soft kitchen lights. "Does the thought of her getting hurt make your heart stop beating and your hands get clammy?"

I nod slowly, thinking about Uncle Stewart's texts.

"You hate making a fuss, but you find yourself acting more and more out of character when you're with her?"

"Yes. That's exactly it."

Dad scoops up mom's tea and lumbers to his feet. "In the upstairs closet, where we keep the comforters. To the left."

I frown. *What?*

"Your great-grandma Elda's ring. I stashed it there when we were doing construction and never moved it back."

"R-ring?" I blink rapidly.

"Give your mom some time and be patient with her. She's got a good heart. I'm sure she'll see what you see in Rebel eventually."

I jolt back. "Dad, no. I don't need a ring—"

"Good night, son." He raises the cup in salute.

"No, dad. Listen—"

I watch helplessly as he carries mom's tea down the hall and to the right. Their bedroom door closes softly in the stillness.

Realizing that I'm no longer hungry, I retreat to my studio too and fall into bed. But dad's words run in circles around my head and I barely get any sleep.

I'm still thinking about it during early morning training, later at my uncle's hardware store, and when I drive over to The Tipsy Tuna for a late lunch.

What on earth did I say to make dad think I was THAT serious about Rebel? Is it obvious that I don't hate her as much as she thinks I do?

As I knock back my glass of sweet tea and crunch thoughtfully on the ice cubes, the object of my thoughts breezes through the door.

"Hi, Rebel!" Mauve yells from behind the bar.

"Looks like in here's full," Rebel says, her eyes skipping over the tables. "Guess I'll take today's lunch to go."

Mauve points a dark hand at my corner of the restaurant. "No, need. Your boyfriend's at that table over there. You can sit with him."

Rebel's thick blonde hair spins around her shoulders as she turns to take me in.

I swallow hard and sit up straighter.

"Let me get you an extra mat and coaster," Mauve says.

"Thanks, Mauve." Rebel follows the plump, older woman to my table.

"Your usual, Rebel?" Mauve asks, setting the mat down across from me.

"Yes, please. And I'll have a root beer float too."

"Ooh, are you celebrating something?"

Rebel sighs in exhaustion. "I need a sugar rush. April and I have been doing interviews all morning. It hasn't been going well."

"Interviews?" I ask.

Rebel glances at me and her eyes go dim. "The shop is extremely busy these days. We can't keep up with demand, so we need more mechanics in the bay."

Mauve offers a consoling nod. "I'm sorry to hear that. I'll be right out with your orders."

Rebel smiles sweetly at Mauve but, as soon as the older woman leaves our table, she turns frosty.

Lips tightening into a straight line, she shuffles around her purse. Her thick, blonde hair swings down to hide most of her face.

My heart picks up speed as I mentally trace the slope of her nose down to her lips. They're shinier today, like twin flower petals heavy after a gentle rain. Her jumper is half-unzipped, revealing a white tank top underneath. A grease stain sits on her cheek and I want to wipe it off so badly that my fingers quake.

I pull my hands beneath the table so I don't give in to the impulse.

Ba-thump. Ba-thump.

My Adam's apple bobs. Why is my heart misbehaving again?

Rebel pulls a pink bottle of hand sanitizer from her purse and squeezes a dollop into her palm. When she notices me watching, she freezes.

"Want some?"

I pull my hand back at first, afraid that I'll tremble too much. I'm normally steady and unflappable, but I don't feel like myself when I'm in front of her.

"Whatever," Rebel says when I retreat. "But just know that people are watching."

I glance around and notice the locals ducking behind their menus and whispering while sneaking peeks at us.

I offer my hand.

She shares out the sanitizer and says, "I get it. You'd rather not eat with me. But this kind of comes with the territory, don't you think?"

My eyebrows hike. *What?* When did I say I didn't want to eat with her? All I did was reject her hand sanitizer. How did it turn into her glaring at me like that?

Rebel whisks her dainty hands together. "I didn't want to crash your lunch either, but if I avoided you, Mauve would find it weird." She nods decisively. "However, this is awkward and uncomfortable for me too. So when she brings the food, I'll make an excuse to leave and eat in my car."

"You'd rather eat in your car than share a table with me?"

"I'd rather eat next to a garbage dump in the middle of a volcano." Rebel's harsh words are delivered with another one of her fake smiles. "Does that answer your question?"

The ring is behind the comforter. Dad's voice returns to me and I almost laugh out loud.

The likelihood of Rebel and I getting married is so low, only a hockey puck would be able to limbo under it.

The woman is infuriating to the infinite degree.

My jaw flexes. "If you're uncomfortable with me, I can leave first. You can have the table."

"No, I'll leave," Rebel insists.

I get up.

She does too.

"Stay," I tell her. "I can eat at the stadium anyway."

"No, you were here first. You should stay."

"Where are you two going?" Mauve asks, approaching us with two trays in hand.

"Yeah," a low, familiar voice says.

I stiffen as my Uncle Stewart steps out from behind Mauve and towers over our table. "I was just thinking I should join my nephew and his girlfriend for lunch."

CHAPTER
ELEVEN

REBEL

I'D RATHER SWIM IN A SHARK-INFESTED OCEAN DURING MY MONTHLY than sit for a meal with Stewart Kinsey.

He made his disdain for us at The Pink Garage abundantly clear. So clear, in fact, that Chance set up a security system at the garage to keep an eye on April when she's locking up at night.

I do think that's overkill. My mom worked for Stewart Kinsey in between planting and harvesting season at the apple orchard. I grew up in his mechanic shop, so I mean this when I say...

Stewart Kinsey is a grimy, selfish, manipulative human being.

I despise his creepy smiles, suggestive comments and, I will *never* forgive his outrageous 'advice' to April after her ex cheated on her. However, he never crossed the line with my mother or me.

Not that it means anything.

Kinsey may not have done anything illegal, but I doubt that's for lack of trying. He's a ticking time bomb. The question isn't if, but *when* the explosion happens and who'll be in his path when it does.

"Maybe another time, Uncle Stewart," Gunner growls.

I swing around to watch my fake boyfriend.

Nothing's out of place.

Gunner's leaning back in his chair, so tall that even when he slouches he still looks intimidating. His square jaw is relaxed. Blue eyes bored as ever.

So what's with the tension I'm picking up here?

"Why not? Don't want to eat with your old uncle now that you have a pretty lady at your side?"

"Rebel and I are on a date and we'd prefer to be alone," Gunner says firmly.

Stewart's playful smile drops a smidge.

I glance between the two of them. Gunner Kinsey is as cold and hard to read as always, but there's no mistaking the warning in his tone. It sends a chill down my spine. I thought the Kinseys all loved and covered for each other.

Does Gunner know something about his uncle that I don't?

"Rebel doesn't mind." Stewart flashes me an oily smile. "She's been running around in my shop, getting underfoot since she was knee-high. Why, we're practically family."

My fingers coil into fists. "With family like you, Stewart, who needs enemies?"

Stewart Kinsey bursts out laughing.

Gunner arches a brow at me.

Mauve clears her throat. "C-come this way, Stewart. I'll see if I can find you another table."

"No need, Mauve. I'll sit with my nephew." Leaving no room for argument, Stewart pulls out the chair next to me and plants himself firmly into it.

I scoff in outrage.

What on earth does he think he's doing?

"Stewart—gah!" The chair I'm sitting on suddenly lurches to

the side. I flail my arms to keep my balance as the ground shifts underneath me and my body jerks to the left.

The chair legs scrape the floor so loudly that the entire diner stops to watch us. Pink stains my cheeks and I frantically look down at the hand gripping the underside of my chair.

My eyes drag up that pale hand, to the tattoos peeking out from Gunner's wrist, up to his neck and finally to his face. Gunner pulls me steadfastly around the table until I'm so close to him that my arm brushes his massive shoulder.

He says nothing. Not a word. And yet, the statement he made in that one move is so loud that my ears ring.

Stewart struggles to smile. "Calm down, Gunner. Do you think I'll bite your girlfriend or something?"

"Or something," Gunner mumbles.

My eyebrows fly up in surprise. There's definitely animosity between the Kinsey's. But why? It can't be because of someone as irrelevant as me.

Stewart turns to Mauve. "I'll have a burger with onion rings, Mauve. Burn the onions and hold the ketchup. You know how I like it."

"Let me set these down first and I'll put in that order for you," Mauve says, her eyes darting between me, Gunner and Stewart.

As Mauve sets down plate after plate filled with delicious burgers and fries, my stomach turns. It was hard enough eating with one Kinsey. Now, I've got two in my sight. They're multiplying like cockroaches.

Stewart moves his hand in a circular motion. "Don't worry about me. Eat up!"

Gunner grumpily chomps on a French fry.

I don't think I can stomach a bite of food, but I came here for a rootbeer float and I'm not going to let Stewart Kinsey take that simple, sugar-rush pleasure from me.

Gripping my straw, I drink so fast that pain slices through my head.

I wince.

Gunner pounces on me like I sawed my leg off and blood is spurting everywhere. He says nothing, but his frantic eyes and hands on either side of my head scream his concern.

"I'm fine," I mumble, squeezing my eyes shut. "It's just brain freeze."

He pushes his glass of water across to me.

Under normal circumstances, I'd never drink from his cup. But even enemies join together in times of war.

So I take a sip.

Much better.

"So, Rebel," Stewart says in a conversational tone, "I heard your little garage is looking for employees."

"You heard right," I say, drinking my root beer more slowly.

Gunner keeps a close eye on me and, when he determines that I'll no longer try to freeze my brain circuits with ice cream and soda, he relaxes again.

Stewart snatches one of Gunner's fries. "Interviews going well?"

I raise my chin. "We've gotten a few applications."

"Any good ones?"

I stiffen.

Stewart is totally oblivious and chomps happily. "Word on the street says you got a bunch of clueless kids who don't know the engine from the radiator. The only decent technicians who applied were..." He cracks his filthy mouth open and cackles. "You know, now that I think of it, they were the ones who couldn't hack it at mine."

Annoyance skates up my body. "Finding technicians that fit our vision at The Pink Garage takes time. April and I aren't in a rush."

"No, no. Of course not. But let me give you a word of advice."

I scowl. "I really don't need it."

Stewart lifts a fry and shakes it at me. "Businesses need a

solid foundation. Every time you turn a customer away, you're sending them to the competition. Why? Because no matter how famous a mechanic is, if he's not available to fix your car, he's not that good of a mechanic." Stewart raises both hands in mock apology. "I'm sorry. That mechanic might be a 'she' or a 'he'. I know how sensitive you ladies are about these things."

I'm holding onto self-restraint for dear life, but something inside me snaps at his condescending words.

Shooting to my feet, I glare down at him, "You know what Kinsey? You—"

"Should take your food to go," Gunner says in a calm, still voice.

Both Stewart and I whip around to take him in, but the younger Kinsey isn't looking at either of us. He's staring at Mauve who's just tottering to the table with Kinsey's burger.

"I'm sorry, Mauve. Make that burger to go," Gunner adds, flashing her a solemn look.

Stewart's eyes widen and his nostrils flare. "Don't be acting too big for your breeches, boy. I'm still your uncle. You still need to show me some respect."

"I'm allowing you to take your food and walk away on your own. That's showing plenty of respect, Uncle."

Stewart's face turns red, all the way to the tips of his ears.

My heart climbs to my throat and pounds so hard, I'm sure everyone in The Tuna can hear it.

Neither of the men move. For a long, tense second, I wonder what Stewart's going to do. I doubt they're going to fight. Gunner is Carol Kinsey's son. Someone of his nobility would never get into a physical altercation with family in public.

And though Stewart isn't that refined, he's got eyes. Gunner isn't loud, but he doesn't need to be. His six-foot-five height and giant muscles do all the shouting for him.

Stewart laughs bitterly. "I'll let you two have your privacy then."

Gunner nods. "Thank you, Unc."

Stewart slides his tongue over his top teeth, hesitates for a moment and stomps away, his steps rattling the floor as he goes.

Mauve winces and hurries after him.

What just happened?

I remain standing. Stewart's gone, but my emotions are still raging high.

"Sit, Rebel," Gunner says in a voice that's so gentle, it's hard to believe he was so rough with his uncle only a few seconds ago.

I ignore him.

Gunner wraps his fingers around my wrist to tug me down. His grip is careful and, again, I'm struck by the tender way he's approaching me compared to the firm way he'd handled his uncle.

I fall into my seat, seesawing between indignation at Stewart and shock at Gunner standing up for me.

He pushes my plate forward. "Eat something."

"I'm not hungry anymore," I mumble, glancing away from him.

Gunner takes fries, empties it out on my plate and sprays my ketchup over it in a heart-shape, exactly the way I do it for myself.

Surprise ricochets through my chest as he nudges the plate toward me again. My eyes dart down to the plate and back to him. How does he know I eat my fries like that?

"I won't talk about my family or the mechanic shop," Gunner says, quietly setting a knife and fork in front of me. "I won't speak at all. It'll be like I'm not even here."

Giving in to his request, I take a small bite of my burger and then another.

But Gunner doesn't keep his promise. Because, though he doesn't say a word to me all through the meal, I'm keenly aware that he's here.

CHAPTER
TWELVE

GUNNER

After the plates are cleared and I pay the bill, I walk Rebel to her car. The sunshine bounces against her blonde hair, turning the strands into spun gold. Her eyes dart to me, a spell-binding blend of cornflower blue with flecks of green.

Awkwardly, she looks away and fiddles with her purse.

She's angry. And I can't blame her.

Uncle Stewart approached us with one goal—to rattle her. Every word that left his mouth was a hockey puck to the gut, intended to make Rebel doubt her abilities as a mechanic and a business owner.

An uncomfortable feeling presses into my chest. The more I think about what happened, the more annoyed I am that I didn't speak up earlier.

After everything he's done to April and Rebel, the decent thing would be to leave them alone now.

Is that why you're holding Rebel hostage in a fake relationship? Are you doing the decent thing?

I clench my jaw.

"This is me," Rebel says quietly.

I look up and realize we're standing in front of her car. Without a word, I nod my goodbye and turn to leave.

"Gunner."

I face her.

Rebel chews nervously on her plump bottom lip. "I, uh, I'm coming to the game tonight. Just a heads-up."

Of course she is. Half of Lucky Falls is showing up tonight. We won't be home much during the play-offs, so this is the only chance the town has to catch a game live. No one's going to miss it.

But why is Rebel telling me that now? Does she need something?

"I'll get you the family tickets," I tell her, figuring that's what she's asking for.

Rebel's eyes widen. "What? No. I'm going with April, so I don't need... no."

Alright then.

Rebel fiddles with her car keys, opens her mouth and then slams it shut. With abrupt movements, she opens her car door.

I turn to go.

Suddenly, she slams it shut and stomps over to me. "Why did you do that?"

I arch a brow. "Do what?"

"Chase your uncle out? I could have handled myself. You didn't need to step in."

I catch my breath as I fall into those fierce blue eyes. They're surrounded by thick lashes, delicate arched eyebrows, and set in a peaches-and-cream complexion. It's unfair how beautiful she is. Even though I should regret ruining her lunch today, I can't.

I enjoyed eating with her.

I'd do it again.

"So?" Rebel folds her arms over her chest, her eyes cutting through me. "What was it? Did I look that helpless to you?"

"It wasn't about you."

"What was it about?"

I move my gaze past her. Her eyes are so incredibly blue that I can't keep ahold of my thoughts if I look directly at them.

"It was my fault."

"You're… what?" She gawks.

My fingers pull into fists. "You should feel safe when you're with me. You should feel protected. That's what a partner is supposed to do. I failed. I let my uncle stay too long at the table. I shouldn't have let him sit down in the first place."

"That's…" Rebel sputters and a slight pink dashes across her cheeks. "That's ridiculous."

"Ridiculous or not, you're my girlfriend." I step forward.

She steps back, her tennis shoes skittering across a loose rock. "Fake girlfriend."

I move in. "We're dating."

"*Fake* dating," she stresses, fiddling with the collar of her pink mechanic jumper.

"And that means you—Rebel Eleanor Hart…"

Her eyes widen when she bounces against the door of her car.

"… Are my responsibility and I will have your back."

Rebel looks up at me, her mouth slightly parted.

My eyes fasten on her lips. A fire that has no business burning spreads through my veins. My hands beg to touch her, to flatten on her back and give her the last, tiny nudge forward so nothing separates us.

But I don't move.

Neither does she.

The silence between us is heated, filled to the brim with words and desires that would never cross our lips. Our eyes don't stray an inch from each other's. The air around us thickens with a dangerous kind of heat.

I'm no stranger to a glaring Rebel Hart. But this stare down is different from the usual stubborn sneer or the disgusted looks she ordinarily flings at me.

I find myself leaning closer, drawn to that unexplainable warmth in her.

It's not like I have a choice.

Rebel Hart attracts people to her just by breathing, just by *existing*. Heads swiveled when she walked into the Tipsy Tuna earlier. I heard groans when the table she chose to sit at was mine.

It's some kind of sickness. Maybe something in the water?

Whatever it is, I've got zero immunity.

I reach out.

Rebel covers her mouth, coiling back.

My lips twitch and I continue to reach for her door. The handle makes a 'clicking' sound as it releases and the door bounces, lightly hitting her and pushing her forward.

Rebel's eyes widen to take up half her face and she twists around, sees her open door, and realizes that I had not been intending to kiss her.

The flush across her face deepens in color.

"Text me if you'd like to go to the game together," I say.

Rebel makes a garbled sound that, I assume, is supposed to be a response. Pointedly avoiding eye contact, she scrambles into her car, starts the engine and takes off, burning tire marks in the pavement.

I stagger back, taking in my first deep breath since we walked out together.

Rebel Hart thought I was going to kiss her. She was going to reject my kiss, sure. But the fact that she even thought about it...

I'm glad I wasn't the only one who felt something.

I slip a hand into my pocket, chuckling to myself.

Just then, I get a call from Max.

Surprised, I answer quickly.

"Gunner, sorry to bother you, but do you have a minute to swing by the stadium? I need your expertise."

"Yeah. Sure. Give me twenty minutes."

Since I, technically, should be at the hardware store now, I give my Uncle Robert a call first. I do most of my work via my laptop, so Uncle Robert doesn't have a problem.

A few minutes later, I pull into the stadium parking lot and head left to the admin section of the building.

Max is sitting behind his giant desk, but he's so massive, he still manages to make the desk look like a child's toy. He's somehow found a button-down shirt in his size and a pair of pants that look ready for a church service.

Usually, Max wears jerseys and sweatpants like the rest of us. I'm surprised to see him in such a formal outfit.

Since the team manager is so engrossed in what he's looking at, he doesn't notice that I'm standing in the doorway, I rap my knuckles on the door to get his attention.

His head flings up and he welcomes me in. "Gunner, you're here. Come in. Oh, and lock the door behind you."

My eyebrows hike even more. Since his first day, Max has touted an 'open door policy'. As an out-of-towner, it should have taken him way longer to gain the trust of the team. But we all quickly took to him. He's been fair and transparent with us.

A little on edge, I sit in one of the chairs facing his desk.

Max hands me a file. "I heard that you went to business school."

A strange way to start a conversation. "At a state college, but yeah."

Max waves away my words. "I don't need a Harvard law degree. But I do need some advice." He points a thick finger at the binder in my hands. "That's the financials for the stadium."

My thumb slides down the spreadsheet, comfortably reading the information. I do all the finances for my uncle's hardware store but, what's lesser known, is I also handle his investments.

I've always liked math. Numbers, unlike people, are black and white, unpretentious. They don't add up to anything more than what they are.

Through the years, I've told few others about my investment skills. If the secret ever got out, Mom would push me to take over the entire Kinsey family estate and I'd be trapped in an office for the rest of my life.

"It looks like you have a cash flow problem," I tell Max. "I'd need to see more of your portfolio to tell you anything deeper, but…" I hand the file back to him. "Ticket sales are through the roof with Chance on our team. Why is the stadium bleeding so much money?"

Max gestures to his outfit. "I drove an hour to meet with a fancy accountant this morning just for him to tell me what I already know. Our travel expenses and overhead are far more than the revenue the stadium generates." Max runs a hand over his head. "Even worse, I just lost another sponsor. That's three in a row."

The news stuns me. "Why'd they drop us? Our team's number one in the state. The Lucky Strikers are doing better than ever."

Max shakes his head. "Yeah, but we're big fish in a small pond. They're looking for a team heading for national or international stadiums."

I frown.

Max sighs. "Ever since Chance returned to us from the pros, sponsors have been getting antsy. It's one thing to be the best in a state league and have dreams of making it big. That way, you're the underdog and everyone is looking at you and rooting for you to grow." He makes a circle. "But if you're branded as the team who'd rather stay small than strive for the bigger pond, that's less of a story, less flashing lights, less money."

"Have you told Chance?"

"I don't want him to worry. He'll blame himself and the guy always does something stupid when he feels like something's his fault." Max's eyes flit to me and he says seriously, "Of course, I'd need you to keep this from the others too."

I nod. "The problem is both simple and difficult. The team needs more cash and that means we need more sponsors. Maybe we take it to the community?"

"The town is giving as much as it can. Local businesses, like your family's, are the only reason we could stay in the playoffs. But we need a big corporate sponsor. Those won't just drop out of the sky. Especially now that we're a team known for *not* wanting to go pro."

"Then let's change that," I say simply.

Max stares at me with narrowed eyes.

"Let's go pro."

He bursts out laughing. "You could be a comedian, Gunner. The way you deliver jokes with that dead-pan expression…"

"I'm not joking."

"How can we afford to go pro right now when we can't even keep the lights on?" Max wrenches a button on his shirt loose. "Making the league as a team isn't just about a 'can do spirit'." He counts off on his fingers. "First of all, we'll need to pay the team an actual living wage so you can practice *all day*. Right now, you and Watson and Renthrow have to work separate jobs to pay your own bills. The others are only this flexible because they're in college. Then, we'll need another coach because the one we have is great but… you know, the league is another level. Not to mention the league fees, the plane tickets—"

"We can do it."

Max grits his teeth. "You think it'll be easy just because you said those words in a calm voice?"

"I want to try, Max."

The excitement leaks out of my voice. Since I was a kid, it's been my dream to go pro. Chance walked away from it, but that doesn't mean he can't return to the top, this time, with us behind him.

The team manager scrutinizes my expression. "I never realized this before, but… you're… actually insane."

"I'll do everything I can." I extend my hand. "Let's take the Lucky Strikers all the way to the pros."

CHAPTER
THIRTEEN

REBEL

THE OVERHEAD FAN IN THE GARAGE MAKES A LOUD 'WHUP, WHUP' sound with every rotation. I glance at it and then adjust the standing fan behind me, turning the speed up a notch.

Nothing helps. I'm still blisteringly hot.

As a rock song rages in my headphones, I drop a car battery into place and pull out the left battery clamp from the tangle of wires.

My pink gloves are a bright contrast to the dusty, worn innards of the car. Normally, the sight of my gloves in the middle of an engine is enough to lift my spirits.

But not today.

With jerky movements, I fasten the clamp against the battery pole.

And then I freeze.

The battery needs two clamps to charge the engine.

I've got one.

Where's the other?

My mouth tightens when I realize I've misplaced the right battery pole. What on earth…

I gently tug wires out of the way so I can see better, but that causes another problem. The client took this car to so many mechanics that the wiring is a colossal mess.

Duct-tape was the previous mechanic's glue of choice. An empty plastic bottle wedged against the front of the hood keeps the battery from shaking in the engine. So many other modifications have been made. It's a mad house.

"You can't be serious," I snarl at the engine.

"What happened?" My best friend's voice pulls me from my sullen thoughts. April walks into my line of sight, wiping her hands on her navy jumper.

"I can't find the stinkin' pole."

April's eyes circle the hood of the vehicle and travel inquiringly back to me.

I point like a child tattling on a sibling. "It was there when I started. It's not there any more. Where did it go? It's not like an entire battery clamp can sprout legs and walk away."

April chews on the inside of her cheek, studying me intently.

I pretend not to notice and return to rummaging around the wires. Finally, I spot the clamp, attach it to the battery pole and wedge the plastic bottle in place to keep the battery steady.

Stomping around to the driver's door, I bend my head in, flick the key in the ignition and hear the blessed sound of the engine turning over. Next, I smack the lever beneath the steering wheel once, then twice, testing each of the lights.

The bulb I replaced works perfectly.

"It's good," April says, confirming that the job is complete.

"At least one thing is working out today," I mumble, shutting down the engine and backing away from the car.

April follows me as I storm to the sink and tear off my gloves. Lathering my hands with soap, I wash off the grime from my skin.

"Are you upset because of the interviews this morning?"

"No," I grumble. And then I add, "Well, I'm not happy that we wasted our time. We took the entire morning off, and we still couldn't find *one* decent technician."

April wilts against the sink. "I admit, it's discouraging. Not every mechanic has to love diagnosis like we do, but I wish we could find ones who were willing to learn."

"They don't understand how we make money doing things our way. Diagnosis is hard," I remind her. "Mechanics get paid for the job done, so if it takes a technician months to figure out what the problem is for *one* car, they think they'll go hungry."

"But people are willing to pay more for that kind of solution." April scrunches her nose. "I really thought that young guy from the next town over was promising."

I shake my hands out at the sink, careful not to get any splatter on April. Reaching for the pink towels folded nearby, I add, "It's better that he ghosted us. I could tell that he wouldn't respect us if he worked here."

April groans. "Why is it so hard to find a mechanic willing to work in our shop?"

"Probably because it's *our* shop."

"I refuse to believe that men won't join our garage simply because we're women. What about Dalton? He and his welding crew have no problem when we call them for work."

I open the mini-fridge and take out two cans of pink lemonade. Handing one over to her, I respond, "Dalton owns his own business so, technically, he's not working as our employee."

"You have a point."

I crack open the tab. The refreshing pink lemonade feels cool against my hand. Just inhaling the scent of the drink makes me feel a bit cooler.

"Running a business is hard," April whines. "I just want to fix cars."

"Cheers to that." I clink my can of pink lemonade against hers.

April takes a sip and sinks into the chair next to me. "It's like we can't catch a break. First, we didn't have customers because everyone was loyal to Stewart Kinsey. Now, we have *too* many customers, but no decent technician wants to work with us because of Stewart Kinsey."

"Anyone who decides to join us would be joining our war against the Kinseys. They're just protecting their own."

"I thought the public wouldn't have to choose sides since you and Gunner got together. Isn't your relationship a sign of a truce?"

I stiffen at the mention of the six-foot-five hockey menace who backed me up against my car this afternoon.

April taps her oil-stained, blistered fingers against the can. "You two might not be dating for real, but the town has no idea. You seem really natural together. Plus everyone knows you ate lunch with Gunner at The Tuna today."

"What?" I screech.

April seems surprised by my response. "Photos of you were all over the neighborhood group chat. I was waiting for you to tell me."

"Tell you what? There were no free tables, so I sat with him. It wasn't a big deal." I huff out a breath. "This town is *so* nosy. I can't believe lunch with Gunner made it to the neighborhood group chat." I plunk my pink lemonade on the ground. "I get why everyone was posting about you and Chance, but Gunner and I are normal people. What's with the town scrutiny?"

"You and Gunner are *not* normal people. He's a Kinsey. If Lucky Falls were a fairytale kingdom, he'd be the prince. And you are the most beautiful belle in the land."

"That's not true."

"It *is* true. Plus, you and Gunner are known for being enemies. Of course people are interested in how you two relate now."

"We're not the town's entertainment."

"You kind of are." April pulls down her clip and her long, straight hair spills around her shoulders. "If it makes you feel any better, at least no one is writing about how you aren't 'good enough' like they did with me and Chance. The old ladies like you and Gunner a lot. They say you have chemistry."

"Chemistry?" I guffaw. "Animosity. Hatred. Disdain. Sure, we have that. But we don't have chemistry."

As I speak, I remember Gunner leaning over me, his dark hair just begging for my fingers to run through it. His lips, firm. His gaze, *potent*. I'd been struck dumb by the look in his eyes. How did he *do* that? It's like he went to the Bad Boy School of Eye Smoldering.

Aggravated, I pick up the pink lemonade again and cough when it goes down the wrong pipe.

"Take it easy, Rebel." April pats my back until the coughing subsides.

I pinch my nose to stop the burn in my nostrils. Stupid Gunner. He keeps saying weird, confusing things.

You're my responsibility and I've got your back.

Yeah, right.

The only thing a Kinsey will do to my back is stick a knife in it.

"April," I wheeze, still recovering from my coughing fit, "I need your help."

My best friend offers me a napkin.

I take it and wipe my mouth dry. "How do you tick off your boyfriend?"

"How do I…" Her eyes narrow at me. "What?"

I made a total fool of myself because Gunner gave me the impression that he'd kiss me. The shame still makes my cheeks burn. I have to get him back for that.

But Gunner's so unflappable. I bet he could hammer his own thumb by mistake and he wouldn't holler. *That's* how unbothered he is.

"Pretend that you and Chance are in a fight. What's something that would really get under his skin?"

"Are you trying to get under Gunner's skin?"

Heat creeps to my cheeks. Why does it sound scandalous when she says it like that? "Forget it. I shouldn't have asked."

I set the pink lemonade aside and hop to my feet.

April laughs. "Did Gunner say something to upset you? Is that why you're asking?"

I shake my head and walk over to the car.

"Fine. Fine. Let me think." She jogs toward me and taps her chin in thought. "Chance is really easy-going so not much bothers him, but…"

"But?"

"He does have this weird thing about his jersey," April says.

I lean forward. "What about his jersey? Like he can't stand when it's dirty?"

A million ideas populate in my mind. I can sneak into the stadium, steal Gunner's jersey and spray it with fish oil. Better yet, if he has lucky socks or a lucky charm of some sort, I can steal it and…

"No," April corrects me, her pink lips stretching into a knowing smile. "Like he has this thing about me wearing his jersey. I think it would really tick him off if he saw me in another player's merch."

Another player's jersey?

A lightbulb goes off in my head.

"Does that help?" April watches me nervously, as if she can sense that I'm about to wreak havoc and she's not sure she made the right choice.

I nod and get back to work, while internally twirling my villain moustache and rubbing my hands together in glee.

CHAPTER FOURTEEN

GUNNER

I'm packing my gym bag with everything I'll need for the game tonight when my phone chirps beneath the covers of my bed.

At first, I dismiss it.

Then I recall telling Rebel to text me if she needs a ride to the game. When I offered, I knew deep in my heart that Rebel would rather paddle upstream with a toothbrush than get in a car with me.

However, I rush to pick up my phone on the off chance that she's taking me up on my offer.

A glance at the screen makes all the blood rush straight to my head.

It *is* Rebel.

I straighten my shirt and brush down my shaggy hair as if she's in front of me. With a deep breath, I unlock my phone and navigate to my message app.

REBEL: *I'm picking out my outfit for tonight's game.*

I stare at the message, taking it apart and looking underneath it to find a hidden meaning. Rebel doesn't strike me as the type who'd ask a guy for his opinion on her clothes. Maybe it's a test?

Determined not to fail, I type back.

ME: *Whatever you choose will look good.*

REBEL: *You mean that?*

ME: *Yeah.*

REBEL: *What are you wearing tonight? I want to coordinate our colors.*

I read and reread her message, but it makes no sense the first, second or third time. What does she mean by 'coordinate our colors'? I'll be wearing the team jersey… along with all the other Lucky Strikers.

Before I can figure out what to text back, Rebel sends me another message.

But this time, it's a picture.

She's standing in what appears to be her bedroom. Filmy pink curtains and tall white closet doors are in the background.

Her hair's twisted into two long braids with some kind of cloth woven into the braid. She's wearing a bathrobe that's exposing one of her slim shoulders. Did she just get out of the shower? My torrid brain conjures images of Rebel, water and steam.

I force those thoughts away and focus, instead, on her rosy cheekbones and soft pink lips. She's holding up a blouse and a jacket to her collar. At first, I dismiss the outfit. I meant it when I said she'll look good in whatever she wears.

I start to type back: *I like this one.*

But before I press 'send', something stops me.

Bothered, I navigate back to the picture and expand the image across my screen so I can get a better look at that jacket. Like all Lucky Striker's merch, the team's logo is stitched in the front, while the player's number is on the sleeve.

That number… it belongs to Theilan.

I swipe to Rebel's face in the picture.

There's a mischievous glint in her eyes and an edge to her smile. The evidence is written all over her face.

She's trying to rattle me.

And it's working.

A dark, heavy emotion claws through my chest. Like black sludge, it winds its way into my veins, taking hold of me in a way I've never experienced before.

Theilan is my little brother on the team, but suddenly, I have a burning desire to burn his jacket to a crisp.

At that moment, another text comes in.

This time, Rebel is making a kissy face at a mirror. She's holding up a dress and another jacket. It's the exact same type of jacket as before, but it has the name 'RENTHROW' in giant letters all the way across the back.

I hate the thought of her wearing any of those jackets. Hate it with my every breath.

My eyebrows coil until they meet in the middle of my forehead and I grip the cell phone tight. Restless, I pace up and down my room.

Another text pops in.

I don't bother opening the image. I don't want to see any more.

Annoyance rolls through my mind, stinging me with countless tiny arrows. I have no reason to be this upset about her clothing choices. Rebel and I aren't *truly* dating, and she can wear what she wants to the game.

Stay cool.

Breathe.

Just. Be. Normal.

But the problem is, I can't control myself.

At all.

Running my teeth along my bottom lip, I ignore the objective side of me and lean into the irrational.

ME: *None of those outfits do you justice.*

REBEL: *Not one of them? Are you sure?*

ME: *Dead sure.*

REBEL: *It's probably because I didn't try them on. Give me a sec.*

Try them on? As in, she'll *wear* the jacket with RENTHROW's name splayed across the back like a calling card? She'll let Theilan's jacket touch her beautiful skin?

The mere thought makes me want to toss my phone into the lake.

ME: *Don't wear a jacket tonight.*

REBEL: *But I'll be cold.*

ME: *Then wear mine.*

REBEL: *No thanks. Your jacket doesn't suit my complexion.*

I grit my teeth. It's the same dang jacket as Renthrow and Theilan's. What is she talking about?

REBEL: *I think April has an extra Chance McLanely sweatshirt I can borrow.*

Oh-ho. This woman is about to make me lose my mind.

Tired of the back and forth texting, I call Rebel directly.

She answers in a sultry voice, "Hey, Gunner. You still haven't told me which outfit you prefer."

"I'll tell you in person," I growl.

There's a beat of silence. I can imagine her eyes widening and then narrowing as she tries to get in front of whatever I'm planning.

"Shouldn't you be at the stadium early for warm-up?" Her voice cracks at the end of the statement, betraying her nerves.

"I'll swing by on my way."

"Y-you don't need to—"

"I can't tell if those outfits look good or not from a picture. I need to see it in person."

"Wait, Gunner…"

"I'll see you in ten." I hang up, zip my gym bag closed and gallop down the stairs.

Mom is in the kitchen, stirring a pot of spaghetti sauce. My instinct is to blow past her and jump right into my car, but I slow down instead.

"I'm heading to the stadium now," I announce.

"Okay," she says with an exaggerated sigh.

"Make sure you bundle up tonight."

"Mm-hm." She continues stirring the pot lethargically.

I tap my finger on the granite countertop, nod my goodbye and head outside.

Mom's affronted stare lasers into my back as I open the front door. I can tell she wants me to stick around and sooth her ruffled feathers.

Any other day and I would, just to be respectful.

But a very frustrating blonde—the most frustrating blonde in the universe actually—is waiting for me. Probably not *happily* waiting, but so what? Rebel knew what she was doing when she sent me those pictures.

On the drive over to her place, Rebel calls my phone, but I don't pick up. I'll see her in a few moments anyway and she can say whatever she wants to my face.

The sun is beginning to set as I find a parking spot in front of the realtor's office. Rebel's place is one of the three units on the second floor.

I grab the jacket I brought from home and head up there.

My boots pound up the stairs and I'm barely winded by the time I stop in front of her apartment and knock.

The door swings open as if she'd been waiting for me. She's changed out of the bathrobe and is now wearing a pink T-shirt, pink shorts and fuzzy pink slippers.

"I can't believe you drove all the way here," she snaps, folding her arms across her chest. "I'm going with a regular, non-hockey-themed jacket tonight. That's what I was calling to tell you before you raced over for nothing."

I take her hand and jerk her into the narrow hallway with me.

The door slams shut behind her.

Rebel jumps, startled. "What are you doing, Gunner? Do you

want to fight?" She holds up two fists and I almost laugh. "Let's fight. I'm not scared."

"I have never and *will* never put my hands on a woman. Lower your arms, Rebel."

A crease forms between her eyebrows. "Then why are you here?"

Rather than answer, I wrap my fingers around her wrist and tug it away from her side. Stepping so close her face is almost buried in my chest, I shrug my jacket sleeve halfway on to her elbow. Next, I slide on the other sleeve.

My hands tremble slightly while I dress her. Being this close to Rebel Hart, I can smell her perfume. It's a light, citrus scent. Probably something held in a pink perfume bottle, knowing her. I bet the fruit this flavor is based on is pink as well. Something citrusy. Grapefruit, maybe?

I shrug the jacket over her shoulders and linger for a beat longer than necessary. Finally, I step back and survey her.

My team number is proudly displayed on her sleeve.

My last name is scrawled across her back.

KINSEY.

The heavy, dark emotions retreat completely, like wild wolves running back to their cave for the night. *Perfect.*

Rebel blinks slow and steady, as if waking from a daze. And then she bristles.

"I'm not wearing this," she protests, yanking the jacket off.

"I can't force you to. But if you don't…" I shrug carelessly, "I'll be distracted all night and I'll probably miss all the shots I take and then, when they interview me after the game, I'll blame you on live television and the town will turn against you. Do you want that?"

"Gunner Kinsey, are you threatening me?"

I wiggle my phone in her face. "You threatened me first."

"You're insane."

I shrug again. It's the second time someone's accused me of

being out of my mind today and I'm starting to think they might be right.

I am insane.

Especially when it involves Rebel Hart.

As Rebel chews on her bottom lip and struggles for a comeback, I tap her nose. "See you tonight, Hart."

I make my way to the staircase and hear Rebel yell, "I hope you trip on your skates and fall flat tonight, Kinsey!"

It's the sweetest thing anyone's ever said to me.

CHAPTER
FIFTEEN

REBEL

April eyes my jacket as I ride shot gun to the stadium. She licks her lips, clears her throat and faces the road.

Seconds later, she glances at the jacket again.

I hunker lower in my seat. "Don't ask."

"I wasn't gonna."

"Don't look either."

"Kind of hard not to," my best friend mumbles, biting back a smile. "It's cute."

"It's basically handcuffs."

"That sounds like a story."

"I don't want to talk about it."

"Your plan didn't work?"

I gesture to the jacket. "Isn't it obvious?"

April snorts. "I have some news that might cheer you up. May posted a 'help wanted' ad for our garage on social media and she broadened the search outside of town."

I sit up straight. "Outside of town? Isn't that a waste of time?

Who's going to move to Lucky Falls to work at our mechanic shop?"

"Well, one person is considering it."

I arch a brow. "Are you sure it wasn't a troll or someone pulling a prank? I doubt we could attract anyone serious with an ad."

"I got in contact with them and they sent over their resume. So far, it seems legit."

"Who is he?" I ask, lowering the sun visor to reapply my lip gloss. I've been gnawing on my bottom lip the entire drive and I *know* I need to reapply.

"It wasn't a 'he'."

I freeze, the pink lipstick halfway to my face. "What?"

April bobs her head. "She's a female mechanic. She's been working at a really prominent garage in the city, but she wants a change of pace and an environment that'll respect her ideas. I'll forward her resume to your email later. She's super impressive."

"That's amazing! How soon can we meet her?"

"I made an appointment for Friday."

My stomach flips over in anticipation. I didn't let myself consider hiring a female technician. There aren't many girls who make a career out of repairing cars.

"It's too early to celebrate," April reminds me, barely holding back an excited smile of her own. "We don't know if she'll be a good fit, if she'll like our compensation package and even if she'll like Lucky Falls enough to move here. Plus, there's the issue of building a bigger mechanic bay once we actually take on more staff… so much to think about."

"Yeah, but this is the farthest we've ever gotten in the process. I think she's the one."

April laughs. "You haven't even met her."

"I've got a good feeling."

Traffic thickens as we get close to the stadium. Cars wrap around the entire block and movement slows to a snail's pace.

I glance at the long line in shock. "The Lucky Strikers must be really popular. This feels like the entire town came out tonight."

"I'm glad to see people are still coming out to support. Chance was worried they'd lose interest after he moved back."

I frown. "Lose interest? Lucky Falls is a town that loves good hockey, no matter who's on the team. Plus he's still *Chance McLanely*."

"He's Chance McLanely, the hockey player from a small team in a small town in a small league. That's a completely different title."

"Are you saying he regrets choosing and staying in Lucky Falls?" I ask tentatively.

"It's not that." She chews on her bottom lip. "I think he feels bad that everyone in the world is calling the Lucky Strikers a 'downgrade'. He really cares about the guys on the team. They put in their blood, sweat and tears to be the best at their level. But now…"

"But now, that effort looks like nothing and Chance feels responsible."

April nods and takes her time pulling the car into a parking spot. "I thought everything would work itself out after he came back…" She shakes her head. "Isn't life funny? After you achieve a goal and get what you want, you'd think everything would be perfect. But immediately after you conquer one mountain, there's another you have to climb. It's true for Chance and for our garage. The goal post just keeps moving."

"That shouldn't surprise us, April. Your dad used to say, 'the only guarantee in life is that things will change.'"

April smiles softly. "I remember that."

"I grew up watching all my friends have nice things and wishing I could afford that too. Happiness is pretty elusive for a Hart. But I've learned to be happy with a little. As long as I have my friends and family close to me, the goal post can move all it wants."

"I'm borrowing that confidence, if you don't mind," April

says, popping her car door open and joining me in front of the hood of her truck.

"Here. Take all of it." I blow her a kiss.

She laughs. "Oh, I forgot to ask. What happened with the Ladies? When's your first meeting with them?"

"I don't know. I haven't been added to a group chat, gotten a text, nothing."

April stares at me with stricken green eyes. "Oh no."

"I have a feeling Carol is going to pretend she never said anything about a Kinsey girlfriend being allowed to join."

"But everyone around that table heard you."

"Everyone at the luncheon was connected to the Kinseys. If they all pretend nothing happened, she can probably get away with never inviting me to the Society. And I'll be back at square one."

"That's awful. What are you going to do?"

I think about that question before I answer.

Last night, when I visited mom, I saw so many things in our neighborhood that need changing. The kids' basketball court. The public landfills. The street lamps with flickering light bulbs.

"I don't know yet. But I won't roll over and play dead just because they're ignoring me. I've come too far to stop now."

"I believe you can do it, Rebel. And hey, if it doesn't work out, at least you got a nice jacket out of it."

I groan and shake my head pleadingly. "Don't remind me about the jacket."

April skips in front of me, grinning like a maniac. "Whose name is on that jacket again? I suddenly can't read."

Embarrassed, I wrench the jacket off. "You know what? I don't care if Gunner misses every shot tonight. I'm not wearing this thing in public."

"Oh stop it." April tugs it back on my shoulders.

I shake my head at her, but keep the jacket on and follow the human riptide leading into the stadium's double doors.

The arena is roaring with the music blasting from the

speakers and the chatter of a massive crowd. Excitement zips through the air like bolts of lightning. Below the bleachers, the hockey players are warming up on the ice.

April and I walk confidently past the general bleachers to the reserved seats closer to the boards.

The first time April attended one of Chance's games, she was flocked by paparazzi and had to be escorted to a different seat by Bobby and Max. However, she's a pro at this now and no one bats an eye when we step into our usual row and get comfortable.

One of my favorite hockey fans is already present and seated next to her nanny.

"Hi, Gordie!" I wave brightly.

"Hi!" The little girl wiggles her fingers. "Daddy's over there."

Gordie points at Renthrow who's stretching out his legs on the ice.

"Are you excited about tonight?" I ask her.

She nods and starts chattering happily.

Renthrow's daughter is an absolute delight, and I'm not just saying that because she was named after one of the *best* hockey players of all time.

"Excuse us, excuse us," a familiar voice says.

My smile collapses when I see Carol Kinsey wiggling into the row behind us. She's not alone. Gunner's ex, and the woman who originally received permission to join the Society, is moving closely behind her.

Victoria looks like she's ready for a night on the town, as she's wearing a short black dress with heels and, surprise-surprise, she's *also* wearing a jacket with Gunner's last name.

However, her jacket shares a similar design to the one I bought with Renthrow's name. Which means she probably bought hers from the merch shop available to the public.

I can instantly tell when she notices that my jacket is different than hers. Her eyes fasten on the embossed threads and the hockey association patch on both sleeves.

She scowls so deeply that I wonder if I should offer to exchange jackets.

Who cares? She can wear Gunner's team jacket and make moon eyes at him all she wants. Heck, she can have him.

What matters isn't that Victoria still likes Gunner.

It's that Victoria is still Carol's pick for the Society.

The two ladies don't acknowledge me and, though I wish I could be just as rude, I decide to take the high road. After all, I'll need to talk to Carol Kinsey later about my admission and get details on the next meeting.

"Goodnight, Carol. Victoria," I say dryly.

April turns around too and nods in greeting.

Carol tilts her chin up and ignores me.

Victoria smiles stiffly.

None of the ladies return my greeting.

My ego stings. I hate being ignored and the fact that I went out of my way to be nice only to be disregarded scratches at me.

The game starts and I'm still so upset that I barely pay attention. That is, until Gunner commandeers the puck from his opponent in a move that would make the original Gordie proud.

Behind me, Victoria charges to her feet.

"Go, Gunner!" She yells the words as if she's channeling all her years of high school cheerleading. "That's how you do it, Gunner! Yes!"

I release a disbelieving laugh and swing my head around to stare at April.

"Can you believe her?" I mouth.

April blinks and shrugs. My best friend is way too calm about this.

Determined not to be outdone by Gunner's ex, I wait for another impressive move from Gunner. Unfortunately, the other team fights fiercely for the puck and there's not a perfect moment to out-do Victoria.

Until, finally, near the end of the second period of the game, Gunner takes a shot at the net and it goes in. The moment he scores, his teammates converge on him, tapping his helmet and his butt.

The crowd is roaring, a deafening sound that makes the entire floor tremble.

I'm on my feet, arms raised, screaming at the top of my lungs.

"Whoo! That's my boyfriend!" I twist around, pointing my arms at Gunner like an airplane marshall guiding a plane home. "That's *my* boyfriend!"

The glamorous lawyer glances away, brushing her hair back in exasperation.

That's right, Vicky. That Society seat is mine!

Satisfied that I won our little battle, I spin around again and pay attention to the action on the ice, only to see Gunner slowing down in front of the boards. His blue eyes are boring through the protective glass shield on his helmet and are steady on me.

Terror sinks its claws into my body when I realize he heard my possessive chant.

Oh no, oh no, oh no.

Frozen, I can only stand there, mouth slack and a blush tearing through my face while wishing I could sink into the benches and disappear from the face of the earth.

Thankfully, Theilan skates up to Gunner and grabs him, pushing him forward and toward the other players. It effectively breaks our staredown, and I breathe out in relief.

Until Gunner swivels his head around to look at me one more time.

My heart stops in my chest because, for a quick, furtive second, I think… Gunner Kinsey smiles at me.

CHAPTER
SIXTEEN

GUNNER

It's second intermission. Coach is yelling out plays for the final period of the game. I should really be paying attention.

Tonight's been rocky. The opposing team is on a roll, and the Lucky Strikers are on... whatever the opposite of a roll is.

Chance, especially, seems to be in his head and missing shots that he'd spot a mile away any other night. Coach is being heavy-handed with the substitutions because of it and our plays keep falling apart.

I've tried to take up the strain. After living in the same town and playing together for years, I can read the guys with a look. That familiarity is the only reason we've been able to rally this far. We're defaulting to our natural rhythm as a unit.

However, a natural rhythm and an intentional strategy are two different things. The other team is still ahead by a point and we'll need more than scatter-brained desperation to pull ahead.

I force myself to pay attention to Coach, while keeping one eye on the Jumbotron.

An image of a little girl grinning up at the camera fills the giant monitor along with the words 'HAPPY BIRTHDAY, PRINCESS'. Music is pulsing and the announcer is interacting with the crowd, leading them in the happy birthday song.

It's tradition to give fans a chance to post special messages on the main screen during the second intermission of a home game. Max didn't have a choice when he bought the Lucky Strikers.

The players aren't allowed to submit anything, since the privilege is reserved for the fans, but I begged Bobby—the stadium's all-around maintenance man—to do me a favor.

If he succeeded, the message should come up any minute now…

"Kinsey!" Coach yells my name, along with a few, choice expletives. "Are you listening to me! Get your head in the game! I can't have both you and McLanely running like chickens without heads on the ice."

"Yes, coach!" Chance and I yell in tandem.

I glance at our team captain. He's breathing hard, his head ducked and his eyes on the ground. Patting his shoulder, I get his attention and tilt my chin up in a silent 'are you okay?'

Chance pulls his lips into his mouth and nods.

Whether he's truly okay or not, I'm with coach. I hope he can get it together for the last period. We'll need him if we want to finish tonight's game with a win.

"Oh-ho! Would you look at that!" The announcer's jovial voice perks my ears and I swing around. *Congratulations to Rebel Hart on joining The Lady Luck Society!"*

Warmth spreads in my chest when I spot the announcement on the Jumbotron. There's a picture of Rebel, smiling prettily at the camera in a pink, mechanic jumpsuit. I didn't give Bobby a photo, but I'm glad he added it, so there's no mistaking who this announcement is for.

Applause sweeps through the arena.

The announcer explains, *"For those out-of-towners, the Lady Luck Society is a staple in our town. Only the most prestigious, purehearted, and worthy are allowed to join, what with it being an organi-*

zation dedicated to community service. There hasn't been a new member in over six years. Congratulations, Miss Hart!"

The audience cheers louder, after the short explanation.

I'm not in her line of sight, so I can't tell how Rebel's reacting to it. I'm hoping she likes it, if only to secure her spot with the Society.

If she doesn't like it, well, I doubt she's going to jump to the conclusion that the announcement came from me.

Mom, on the other hand, probably knows without me having to say a thing. She's always been able to sniff me out. When I get home later, there's going to be another fight and maybe some more dramatic fainting, but I was prepared for that when I asked Bobby to slip the announcement into the second intermission.

"That you?" Chance asks, pointing to the Jumbotron.

I shrug.

A brief smile tugs across Chance's face, but he doesn't say anything more about it.

The photo changes to an announcement of a couple celebrating their twenty-fifth anniversary and I can finally focus on the last of coach's directions.

The buzzer sounds and we're back on the ice. Chance is in the game and I offer him my fist. Whatever's causing this drought tonight doesn't matter to me. I still believe he can overcome it.

He knocks his knuckles against mine in a determined fist bump and then skates into position.

At the drop of the puck, he takes off like a bullet. I'm glad to see that fire back in his eyes. It's not long before he assists Theilan in scoring a point.

We're in the game now.

The problem is that the other team lit a fire of their own. We're now tied and the finish line is in sight, but their defense is like a solid brick wall.

Coach doesn't call any more substitutions and I realize that tonight's game is riding on every player currently on the ice.

This is it.

Chance and I pass each other and he makes a gesture with his hands. He's going all in with an attack.

My heart slams against my chest in anticipation. This is the part of hockey I love. When all the odds are stacked against me. Pulling through in a time like this requires one thing. And it isn't my family name or my family connections. It's my skills on the ice.

I nod.

Theilan takes control of the puck and passes to Chance. I watch the other team swarm him, skating over the blue line.

I get into position waiting for the right moment to charge.

The clock counts down to the seconds.

We don't have time for this *not* to work.

The goalie is locked in on Chance.

Before the other team's wingers can converge on him, he passes to me and skates into position. I defend the puck and pass back to him just as he takes aim for the net.

The sweet sound of the puck colliding with synthetic fiber fills my ears.

Yes!

The arena comes alive with shouts of victory but, I can hear one voice much louder than the others. I swing around to the reserved section where Rebel is. I can just make out her light peach-pink blouse beneath my jacket from this distance. She's on her feet, screaming along with the rest of the fans, her hands in the air.

The world fades around the edges. I feel this strange sense of deja vu. As if I've been in this exact moment before, hearing Rebel's screams echoing over the ice.

I'm all the way across the stadium. We're on opposite ends of the rink, actually. There's no reason I should feel this way.

I mean, unless Rebel Hart got surgery to turn her voice into a megaphone.

Or…

Unless…

I've always been listening for her voice after a game.

The revelation takes me by surprise, but I don't have time to dwell on it as I'm jolted into a team huddle. We all dogpile on top of Chance. The guy's probably a pancake beneath our bodies.

We finally let up to give Chance air. He barrels straight for me, slinging an arm over my shoulder.

"You read me, Kinsey. How'd you understand that sign? We haven't practiced it before."

I shrug again. Back when Chance first came to the team, he challenged me to a game and beat me so badly that I limped home with my tail tucked between my legs. Right after he humiliated me, he let it slip that he'd studied our tapes.

Two could play that game and I decided to study his tapes too. Not just for entertainment, but to really learn how he played so I could beat him the next time we took to the ice for a showdown.

The more I watched Chance's plays, the more I learned how he thought on the ice. He had a temper, sure. And he hated being pushed into the boards. The guy was a hot head.

But he was also loyal. He looked out for his teammates, didn't hog the puck, and was fast to shift plays when the situation called for it.

My intense dislike slowly turned into a grudging admiration.

"I'm not letting you get away that easy, Kinsey. You gotta tell me." Chance playfully hooks his arm around my neck as we skate to the player's bench.

Thankfully, he's distracted by Theilan, Watson and Renthrow. The guys are talking about the game and raving about the last play.

The coach does *not* look happy that we went off-script, but I know he's on his way out so it doesn't bother me.

I take off my helmet and grab my bottle of water. As I sip, I glance at the section where Rebel sat during the game. The bleachers are emptying out. Rebel's probably lost among the masses who are heading home.

If I know her, she's probably running to be the first through the gate. I doubt she wants to see me right now. Not with the way she was blushing after I caught her yelling *'my boyfriend'* over and over.

The memory feels just as good as the win tonight.

I really enjoyed hearing her say that.

A lot.

The adrenaline fades from my veins while I move through the after-game routine.

Reporters are clamoring for an interview. Chance takes most of the questions, which I'm extremely grateful for. Prancing around in front of the press is the worst part of hockey for me.

When I'm asked specific questions, I offer the lines I've rehearsed a million times over, making sure to give praise to the entire team for any win of my own.

Then, finally, the frenzy is over and we jog back to the lockers where most of the team is congregated. Theilan is chatty, as usual, but most of the other guys are tuckered out. We came out the victors tonight, but that battle felt ten times harder than usual.

"Guys," Chance says, clearing his throat as he steps forward. "About tonight, I'm sorry."

Everyone's head whips around to look at him.

It's so quiet, a pin could drop.

"I've been overthinking a lot of things since I came back to the team. For some reason, the pressure here feels ten times heavier than it did in the league."

Watson grins. "That's because you care about us."

"Yeah, actually giving a crap messes with you," Theilan agrees.

Renthrow nods. "I felt the same way with Gordie. Every decision felt so important. I second-guessed myself a lot."

Chance seems to appreciate that because he nods at Renthrow.

"What's important is that you came through." Theilan pats Chance on the back. "And even if you didn't, we would have still had your back."

Chance blinks a bit as if he's trying not to get emotional. He opens his mouth to speak and then clears his throat instead.

I silently move toward him and squeeze his shoulder in support.

The entire team gets up to give Chance a hearty smack on his shoulders, chest and back. Rumbles of 'it's okay' and 'you're good, man' fill the entire locker room.

Watson breaks the sober moment by teasing, "Enough with the sappy stuff. Go take a shower, McLanely. And don't worry. This time, we *won't* steal your clothes."

Guffaws break out as we all think about our prank on Chance when he first got here.

He smirks. "Hey, I promise I'm not stealing *your* clothes either."

I chuckle and head over to my gym bag, extracting a pair of sweatpants, underwear and a fresh jersey.

After I've showered and changed, I walk out of the locker room with Chance. The other guys are going to The Tuna to celebrate and Renthrow is, of course, going home to his daughter. So we're the only two heading up this way.

The stadium is completely empty except for Bobby who's running the Zamboni. He waves to us from the ice and congratulates us on the win.

"Thanks, Bobby!" Chance yells.

I lift my hand in acknowledgment.

"Are you and Rebel hanging out after this?" Chance asks, checking his phone. Probably to message April.

I shake my head.

"Do you want me to ask April to invite her to the Tuna

tonight?" He grins and nudges me with an elbow. "I can sacrifice a date night to help you out."

I'm considering the idea when I hear a familiar voice call out, "Gunner."

Rebel walks toward me, her ponytail swishing behind her. My gaze tracks down her body as she gets closer, taking in her slender figure swallowed up by my jacket and her long, long legs in the gray leggings and sneakers. I've never seen a woman in Lucky Strikers merch and tennis shoes look so enticing in my life.

I'm so occupied with Rebel that I don't notice her eyes twitching weirdly to the side. When I finally do, it's too late.

My mother emerges from the shadows like a villain in a low budget film. Her eyes are as hard as marbles and she lifts her chin stiffly.

"Hello, *son*," mom says, her voice sending a shiver down my spine.

"Hi, Gunner," Victoria says, walking beside mom. "Great game tonight."

I swallow hard.

This can't be good.

CHAPTER SEVENTEEN

REBEL

CHANCE READS THE TENSION IN THE DARK, EMPTY LOBBY RIGHT AWAY and makes a break for it, mumbling about being late for a date with April.

I wish I could follow him.
But I'm stuck here.
With Carol Kinsey.
And Victoria.

I can't decide who between the two women I dislike the most. Carol—for her snobbishness, her disdain for anyone who doesn't own a significant piece of land in Lucky Falls and her obvious favoritism when it comes to Lady Luck Society members?

Or Victoria for… well, for being Gunner's ex.

That's as far as her list goes for now, but I'm sure I can rack up more reasons to despise her once I get to know her. After all, she's real close to Carol Kinsey. The two women must be more alike than not.

"*Honey*, what took you so long?" I chirp, slipping my hands around Gunner's giant bicep.

His eyes widen and he jerks back as if he's seeing a ghost.

I reach for him again and pull him back to me, baring my teeth at him while my eyes scream *'play along'*.

His eyebrows cinch together. Not necessarily the look of a man in love with his girlfriend.

Well, too bad.

I don't like this either, but I don't have a choice. As the saying goes, the enemy of my enemy is my friend.

"Son," Carol steps forward, each step light and graceful, "I reserved a table at a restaurant in the city to celebrate your first win of the playoffs. Your father's working the night shift, but he'll meet us there."

"You didn't need to reserve a table," Gunner says. "I'd rather celebrate quietly."

"But what would be the fun in that?" Carol coos, her mouth tilted into a tight but firm smile.

Oh, she's good.

Someone published my Lady Luck Society membership on the Jumbotron. Since the entire town was here, it was basically like a debutant ball for a nervous teenager of one—me.

I didn't turn around to look at Carol or Victoria during the announcement, but I *felt* the negative energy coming off them.

Carol was *livid*. Right after, she asked what I was doing after the game tonight. I couldn't exactly tell her that I planned on going home, setting myself a strawberry bubble bath and drinking strawberry wine while binge-watching Netflix.

I lied that I was celebrating with Gunner and she invited me out to a family dinner with them.

Except this 'family dinner' also includes Victoria.

I have no idea when Gunner's ex became a Kinsey. Maybe there was a secret adoption? I don't know, but I recognize a trap when I see one.

"It's okay if I go, but Rebel must be tired," Gunner says, his cold eyes dropping to me. "Go home first."

My muscles tighten and it takes every thread of self-restraint I have to keep from scowling at him.

I know he hates my company. He'd rather break his favorite hockey stick in two than spend one measly dinner sitting across from me.

But does he have to make it so obvious?

Carol and Victoria are watching our every move. We need to sell that we're in a relationship or Carol's going to see right through us.

"Don't be ridiculous. I already asked Rebel and she said she'd love to come," Carol pipes up.

Gunner frowns at me. I can tell he *really* doesn't want me there. Why? Does he regret claiming me as his girlfriend now that Victoria is hanging around? Does he want to get back with her?

I blink my eyelashes twice in warning. *You better play along.* He can have Victoria or any other woman he wants. *After* I've secured my place in the Society.

Is that selfish of me?

Yep.

Am I potentially standing in the way of Gunner's one true love.

Pfft, so what?

He's the one who announced we were in a relationship and convinced me to go along with it. It's too late to change his mind.

Besides, he and Victoria's family have been close since the town was founded. They're practically an arranged marriage waiting to happen. Fate itself can't stop these two distinguished families from forming an alliance.

I'm not cocky enough to think that I'll make a dent in the illustrious Kinsey history books. I'm just a tiny footnote in a chapter of Gunner's life.

"Enough chit-chat," Carol says, gesturing to the door. "We better get a move on or we'll be late. Rebel, this way."

I follow Carol, noticing how Victoria walks a little slower to keep step with Gunner. Twisting around, I watch them together and feel a pinch in my heart.

They look perfect as a couple. The tall, quiet Gunner Kinsey, the darling child of Lucky Falls. And the polite, classy Victoria—the fancy lawyer who lowered herself to come back to a small town like ours to lend her skills to our community.

Pouting, I whirl back around and make my way into the parking lot.

Carol tries to link my arm in hers. "You can ride with me, Rebel," Carol says. "And Victoria can—"

"Why would I drive with anyone other than my girlfriend, mom?" Gunner interrupts in a quiet, firm tone.

"Rebel doesn't mind, son." Carol speaks for me. "Plus, Victoria's just got back and you two need time to catch up on all her adventures. After all, Rebel's *never* left town, and you see her all the time, so you won't be missing out on much."

The dig at my lack of travel history lands where it's supposed to and I flinch. Would I like to travel more? Sure. But there was never any money for that growing up and now I have the garage to take care of, so I still don't have time to travel.

I hate that I can't snap back at Carol but, until I secure my position at the Society, I'm not getting on her bad side. Resigned, I take a step toward her car.

Suddenly, Gunner's large fingers wrap around my wrist and he tugs me behind him. I stumble, nearly slamming into his large frame.

Victoria's eyes assess Gunner's hand on mine and she frowns.

"My passenger seat belongs to Rebel," Gunner growls. "No one else can sit there but *her*."

My heart skips a beat. I sink my teeth into my bottom lip.

Without another word, the solemn hockey player tugs me to his car on the other side of the parking lot. I'm surprised when he opens the door for me, but I figure his mom or Victoria are still watching us.

Off-kilter, I scramble into the car and Gunner closes the door behind me.

When he climbs into the driver's side, I stare at his face. The street lamps above, brush his strong profile in streaks of silver. He's wearing a pair of grey sweatpants and a long, white shirt beneath a grey pullover.

On and off the ice, Gunner is a picture of the perfect male athlete, muscles hewn to perfection, chest broader than a V8 engine. From this angle, I can sorta-*maybe* get why the girls in town call him 'mouthwatering'.

He's still a cold jerk though.

His fingers are tight around the steering wheel and a muscle in his jaw is flexing.

"Are you angry?" I ask when the silence becomes unbearable.

"No."

My gaze returns to his very active jaw muscles.

Gunner Kinsey has always been a little scary to me. As a child, he'd been smiley and carefree but after we stopped hanging out, he turned extremely sullen and quiet. Everything about him was cold and heavy.

I'd resented that about him. Here was a guy who had everything. *Everything*. Money. Parents who were together and loved each other. A big, happy family. A name that could unlock every door that was closed, every loan from the bank, every opportunity—what did he have to be sad about?

I didn't understand him at all.

But I do have eyes.

And even if I don't understand Gunner Kinsey, it's very, *very* obvious that he's upset about something.

"Is it because you don't want me to come to the dinner?"

Surprise enters his gaze and he whips around to look at me.

I guess I hit the nail on the head.

"Wow. Look at us." A dry laugh bubbles free. "We are *never* going to convince your mom we're into each other if we keep going like this. Why did we agree to this arrangement when we both can't stand each other? We were setting ourselves up to fail."

Gunner turns his attention back to the road. More silence. More jaw clenching. What did I expect?

My entire life, I've struggled to be seen as more than a pretty face. I've longed for a guy who didn't make me uncomfortable by confessing his feelings. Longed for someone who didn't constantly tell me how pretty I am and how good I look on his arm, as if being eye candy is the beginning and end of my value.

Gunner fits that bill to a T, but I guess I traded one extreme for another. Not only does he *not* find me attractive, but he genuinely, truly hates me down to his bones.

"There's no way we can pretend to be in love. It's impossible." Shaking my head, I add, "Forget it. Just drop me off on the side of the road."

"No," Gunner grunts.

So he finally speaks. "April is probably out with Chance right now. I'll ask her to pick me up and you can give your mom an excuse. Tell her I have an upset stomach or something."

The jaw flexing gets worse and this time, it's joined with an aggravated swipe of his tongue across his lips.

"Gunner."

He flicks the indicator and the car screeches as he yanks the steering wheel to the left. I grip my seatbelt, my heart flying to my throat, but he parks safely on the side of the road.

I'm annoyed and frustrated, but there's also some disappointment in there too. I'm not sure what the disappointment is for, but I *do* know that I need to get out of this car.

The seatbelt whirrs as I unclip it and free myself from the passenger seat. My fingers stretch out to snap the handle.

Before I can open the door, I hear Gunner's seatbelt whirring too and a moment later, his strong fingers grip my chin, turning my head so I have to face him. Then he pushes forward with a fierce look in his eyes, sweeps his mouth over mine and kisses me.

CHAPTER
EIGHTEEN

GUNNER

The first time I ever thought of kissing Rebel Hart, I was twelve years old. Rebel came to the farm with her mom and I watched her from afar.

She played in the daisy field, stringing together a daisy chain and weaving flowers in her hair. The sky had been the exact color of her eyes and I thought she was an angel.

Her laughter had been a symphony in my ears and though I knew I couldn't talk to her anymore, I really wanted to run out and join her.

Rebel lifted one of the plucked sunflowers to her lips and kissed it, probably making a wish. I'd, desperately, made a wish of my own. It was to be the sunflower in her hands.

The next time I thought of kissing Rebel Hart wasn't so innocent.

I was eighteen years old and at Buddy White's birthday party.

Buddy had a huge crush on Rebel back then, so obviously,

she'd been invited too. After a while, Buddy suggested we all play truth, dare or kiss.

It was a childish spin on the game of 'truth or dare', and it was designed for Buddy to make a move on Rebel, one she couldn't easily back out on.

I didn't want to play, but Buddy was going to carry on with or without me. So I decided to join in, just to keep an eye on things.

We played a few rounds and every time the bottle fell on a guy and a girl, they chose to kiss.

Then it was my turn.

I spun.

And the bottle stopped on Rebel.

My eyes had fixed on her and my heart had stopped. We hadn't spoken in years. She'd never once glanced my way since her freshman days, but that wasn't the same for me.

I was very much aware of her.

Every time she walked down the hallway, her ponytail bouncing and her laughter ringing through the corridor, I looked.

Every time she worked on a car with April Brooks in the school parking lot, her hips snug in a tight pair of jeans as she bent over to inspect an engine, I looked.

And that night at Buddy's party, she was looking back at me.

Rebel was no longer the little kid in the flower field. She was every teenaged boy's dream, especially in that tight, pink T-shirt and shorts that showed off her long, long legs.

I'd hesitated, so everyone had started chanting 'kiss, kiss, kiss!'.

Their voices barely registered. In that moment, it was just me, Rebel and the bottle.

My heart had thudded in my chest as Rebel rolled her eyes and leaned forward, being a good sport about the game.

Her soft-as-rosebud pink lips were right there.

Right in front of me.

But I knew if I ever kissed her, I'd be doomed for life. So I backed away and chose truth instead. She'd flushed with embarrassment and, after that day, there was an extra chill to the cold shoulder she gave me.

I never thought I'd get another chance. Then I started dating Victoria and it became wrong of me to *want* another chance, so I pushed it to the darkest corners of my mind.

But now, many years later, there's nothing holding me back.

My hand draws Rebel's face to mine. My mouth presses into her lips like I've been waiting all my life for this moment.

She tastes incredible—a mix of candy, sugar and honey. As syrupy sweet as every pink-tinged item she owns.

It's too much and not enough all at once.

I lean forward for more.

Tilting her head so I can get a better angle, I move my mouth over hers while my heart thuds like a wild horse loose out the gate.

Is this a dream?

Am I in bed right now?

But no, I wouldn't have allowed myself to imagine a moment like this.

Especially when Rebel opens her mouth a tad wider. It's a small, unconscious invitation. But I barge in like she threw the door open wide.

I suck on her bottom lip. I nip her top lip between my teeth. I sweep my tongue against hers in a lazy swirl and she mewls.

That sound… I didn't imagine that.

I'm kissing Rebel Hart.

Have mercy.

The temperature in the car spikes.

My skin feels hot enough to burn clear off my bones.

I push further across the console, hovering over her until her head tilts back from the force of my unrelenting kisses. My fingers grip the back of her head to keep her steady and I stay right there, savoring and suckling her mouth as if I'm drawing every breath from her body, as if I'm desperate for her oxygen.

Rebel moans again. Her hand comes up to my chest.

Is it to push me away? To slow me down?

Somewhere in the back of my head, I hear a warning to ease up on her. I'm being too aggressive.

Rebel hates me. She didn't ask for a kiss, especially not one this intense. She may be uncomfortable.

The thought is a cold bucket of water over my head. I wrench back, breathing hard. It took me a lifetime to be close to Rebel and yet, here I am, trying to force an eternity of waiting into one kiss.

Rebel's chest heaves up and down. She inches back until her shoulder hits the door. I notice the fog clouding the window and wince.

"Y-you made your point," she says quietly, a hand to her mouth and a blush spreading across her cheeks.

My point?

Suddenly, two sweeping headlights pierce my back windshield. A car speeds up and then screeches to a stop beside us. The passenger window lowers and I see mom and Victoria in the dark cabin of the car.

"Why'd you park on the side of the road? Did your car break down?" mom hollers.

I start the car and it rumbles to life, purring like a well-oiled machine.

"If nothing's wrong, why'd you pull over?" Mom insists.

Rebel blinks rapidly. "We… I mean, I…"

"We were kissing," I say bluntly.

Victoria's face tightens.

Mom rears back in horror. "Gunner Kinsey—"

"We were lost," Rebel pipes up. Her laughter sounds as high pitched and screechy as a bird at dawn. "That's why we stopped. Can we follow you to the restaurant instead, Carol?"

Mom's shrewd eyes take in Rebel's face, narrowing on her mouth. Then her eyes lock in on me.

I don't move an inch, but I hear Rebel squirming around in her seat. There's no need to turn my neck for confirmation. It's clear what she's feeling right now. Waves and waves of embarrassment are wafting from her skin.

I shift forward to shield Rebel from mom's razor-sharp inspection. "Didn't you say we'd be late?"

"Stay close behind me." Mom frowns.

I dip my chin down.

"I'm assuming there will be no more…" Her nostrils flare, "unexpected stops?"

No promises.

But I know better than to say that.

I nod again and wind my window up. A moment later, mom's car zooms in front of mine and she gases it down the highway.

I move off at a more legal speed and peek at Rebel from the corner of my eye. Immediately, I notice what put mom in such a foul mood. Rebel Hart looks like a woman recently ravished. Her face is flushed pink, her hair is tousled from my fingers, and her mouth is wet and slightly swollen.

My conscience hammers into me.

You impatient, insensitive bull dog. Look at what you did to her.

Rebel clears her throat, pulls the sun visor down and starts raking her fingers through her hair to get it back in order. While it helps a bit, it'll take a lot more than her finger combing to hide the evidence of our kiss.

The caveman inside me steps up, banging his chest.

Not sorry. Mine. My woman.

I wrench my gaze away and swipe a thumb over my bottom lip.

My mouth is wet too.

Rebel clears her throat again. "S-so…"

I wait for her to say more.

She doesn't.

Awkward silence fills the car.

I don't look at her. I don't know what I'll find in her eyes when I do. Disdain? Disgust?

"Uh... y-your mouth, I mean your *mom*." She blows out a breath. I can practically hear her heart beating out of her chest. Or is that *my* heart? Rebel tries again. "Your mom probably bought that, didn't she? I mean, *I* bought it."

I arch a brow at her. *Bought what?*

"But I still don't think it's enough to convince her we're together."

So what? She wants us to do more kissing? I'm okay with that.

"I have a feeling she's going to test us during dinner." Rebel hides her face behind a curtain of blonde hair as she rummages through her purse for something.

Finally, she pulls out a bottle of pink lipgloss and uncaps it. "I'm usually good with parents, but Carol Kinsey won't be easy to fool. We, our, you and I..." Rebel blushes prettily again. "The physical part is one thing, but your mom won't respect our fake relationship if that's all we can do to prove we're together."

I'm only half-listening, stuck at the 'you and I' part of her sentence. Why did that sound so good to my ears?

Rebel coats the mouth I'd just kissed in her lipgloss and it's as if she ingested a magical elixir. Her shoulders straighten out and the confidence returns to her voice and mannerisms. "Just follow my lead later, alright?"

I nod, feeling quite certain that I'd follow Rebel Hart anywhere.

CHAPTER
NINETEEN

REBEL

When we arrive at the restaurant, I stick close to Gunner's side. However, I stop short of looping my arm around his elbow the way Carol is doing to her husband Sheriff Kinsey.

There is no way I can touch Gunner right now.

No way I can look at him.

Not with that kiss standing like a big white elephant between us. *That kiss*.

Where on earth did Gunner Kinsey learn to kiss like that? Why oh *why* was it the best kiss of my entire life?

I'm pretty sure I hate him.

I'm a thousand percent sure he hates me too.

People who hate each other should *not* kiss like their lives depend on it. It's science.

"Rebel," Sheriff Kinsey speaks, glancing at me over his shoulder, "glad you could join us. I've been waiting for a chance to chat with you. It's been so long."

I flash a grin on cue. "Thanks for inviting me."

"Have you been to this restaurant before?" Sheriff Kinsey asks.

"Humph," Carol cuts in. "Not just *anyone* can make an appointment here, you know."

Gunner stiffens beside me.

Sheriff Kinsey's smile falters for a second, but he boosts it back up. "I'm not much for fancy restaurants myself. But when my wife puts her mind to something, there's no talking her out of it. I hope you understand."

The older man places his hands on his wife's shoulders. He slides his eyes down to her and back to me in a quick apology.

I'm used to the snide comments. Carol Kinsey doesn't faze me one bit.

Her son on the other hand…

I look up at Gunner and instantly regret it. My eyes zoom to his lips, recalling the feel of them slanting over mine. Heat burns through my cheeks and I quickly avert my gaze, but it's too late. I can feel the blush spreading through my entire body.

Thankfully, we're still on the move, weaving through the restaurant. As I follow the Kinsey family and the waitress, I start to notice people staring in my direction.

But they're not looking at me.

All eyes are on Gunner.

At first, I assume it's because he's so ridiculously tall and uselessly good-looking. He stands a head and shoulders over his dad, who's close to six feet himself. Even wearing something as casual as a grey pullover and sweatpants, he looks like a model ripped out of a sports magazine.

"Good game, Kinsey!" A patron yells.

"Nice one, Kinsey!" Another table cheers.

My head swivels around in shock. We're several miles outside of Lucky Falls and this restaurant seems catered to, well, people who watch stocks over sports.

Gunner offers little more than a nod of acknowledgement.

The way he hurries ahead, as if he's afraid to be pulled into conversation, hints at his shyness.

"This way," the waitress says, pointing to a fancy glass table in the middle of a curved, velvet booth. A crystal chandelier hangs low above the table and the mantle just behind the booth is decorated with vases of fresh flowers and candles.

I hope those candles are battery powered. Something tells me Victoria is *not* above causing an 'accident' involving my hair and flames.

Gunner gestures for me to enter the booth first, his eyes cool and unaffected.

My frustration shoots up a notch. Why is he acting like nothing unusual happened?

On the highway, he casually told his mom about the kiss. Then he drove to the restaurant without saying a word to me.

Now, he's as stoic and quiet as ever.

It's driving me nuts.

Why am I the only one who's flustered? *Why* am I the only one who's freaking out?

Probably because it meant absolutely nothing to Gunner.

It meant nothing to me too. It's not like I *have feelings for* Gunner. I'm human. Excuse me for being incapable of turning my feelings on and off like a certain hockey robot.

"Do you want to sit on the end?" Gunner asks.

Seriously. He's barely looked at me since the kiss and that's the first thing he wants to know.

"Yes," I mumble.

Don't think about anything else but the Society seat, Rebel. Do it for the Society seat.

Gunner scoots in first and I take the end. The booth is fairly large, but he's such a giant that his massive shoulders brush mine.

I inch away, subtly putting space between us.

"Victoria, you go in first," Carol says, grabbing the other woman by the arm and stuffing her into the booth.

Victoria moves to the middle of the table which is, coincidentally, right beside Gunner. Not that I care. Carol sits beside Gunner's ex while Mr. Kinsey takes up the other end seat.

A new waitress approaches our table. Her eyes fall on Gunner and stay there. "Whoa, you're from the Lucky Strikers."

"Did you guys catch the game?" Sheriff Kinsey asks conversationally.

The waitress nods.

"I was surprised to hear people cheering for my son," Carol says. "I didn't know there were Lucky Strikers fans this far out."

"We don't have our own hockey team, so we've all kind of claimed the Lucky Strikers." Leaning in, she lowers her voice, "Everyone says they like Chance McLanely because he went pro. But there are a lot of us who like you too, Gunner." She blushes. "I mean, we like your playing."

With her cheeks so red and her smile so bashful, it's hard to believe that's all she likes about him.

Poor thing.

She's blinded by a handsome face. Can't she tell that Gunner Kinsey is a rotten, pain-in-the-butt who kisses women without warning and leaves them totally confused? If that's the kind of guy she likes, more power to her.

Silence falls on the table as everyone waits for Gunner to say something. We'd probably wait until we're blue in the face because the man is a steel trap. In fact, his expression hints that he hadn't heard a word of the waitress's confession.

Carol jumps in, ever the socialite. "Thank you so much." Her eyes drop to the server's name tag. "Ann. Lucky Falls is a really small, humble town. We're not famous for much."

"That won't be the case for long," Ann says, looking relieved that Carol engaged her. "Whether the Lucky Strikers go pro or not, we'll support them."

"What a sweetheart," Carol coos.

"That's mighty kind of you, Ann," Sheriff Kinsey adds.

Gunner nods at the trembling waitress. Though that's all the thanks she'll get from him, Ann still beams like he showered her in compliments.

Grinning so hard, her cheeks bunch against her eyes, she says, "Can I start you folks off with some drinks?"

Victoria decides to make herself known then. She leans toward Gunner. "Gun, do you remember that drink we used to like? The one you ordered for me when you drove out to visit me at school?"

I nearly roll my eyes. Who does she think she is trying to bring up the past?

Gunner swings his head to look at her. Since I'm sitting on the outside, I can't see his expression or Victoria's. Are they smiling sweetly at each other? Are they having fun reminiscing the past?

I mentally slam my palm on the table. *Not on my watch.*

"Why would Gunner remember that?" I pipe up, a sickly-sweet smile on my lips.

Gunner faces me, a crease between his eyebrows.

Victoria cranes her neck to watch me too.

I rub Gunner's shoulder like I'm petting a giant cat. "He can't even remember what he ate for breakfast yesterday. How's he supposed to remember ancient history?"

I have no idea if Gunner is forgetful or not. That's not the point anyway.

Victoria's eyes cut into me. I practically hear the samurai sword sound effect ringing in the background.

She flips her short hair over her shoulder only for it to come swishing back to her cheek. In a coy voice, she argues, "You know what they say. History tends to repeat itself."

My mouth trembles, but I keep smiling for all I'm worth. No way will I let Victoria win this battle. "Actually, the phrase is 'we should learn from history so it *doesn't* repeat itself'."

Victoria's jaw drops and her eyes burn with hatred for me. However, her voice is as light as a feather when she says, "I'm sorry. I must have forgotten. Did you study history in college, Rebel?"

That nasty, nasty woman.

I tilt my chin higher. "I never went to college, but there are plenty of ways to learn that don't involve spending four years earning a degree that I won't even use."

"Right, right." Victoria smiles smugly. "You're a mechanic. So… you went to *vocational* school, didn't you?"

Gunner frowns. "Victoria."

My hackles rise. "Is something wrong with vocational schools?"

"I'll have a beer!" Sheriff Kinsey blurts nervously.

"Got it." Ann scribbles something down, her eyes lowered. "A-anyone else?"

Victoria retracts her claws.

I do the same, if only to spare the waitress. Ann is innocent. She doesn't deserve to be a spectator in this bloodbath.

"I'll have a glass of red wine," Carol says, clearing her throat and slanting me a disapproving look.

"I'll have the same," Victoria says, flipping the book closed.

"I didn't get a chance to look at the drinks menu," I murmur.

Suddenly, Gunner leans over with the menu and speaks in that steady, quiet voice to me, "The Pink Moscato looks promising. So does the Strawberry Daiquiri. If you don't want alcohol," he slides his fingers down the book and it feels like he's dragging that hand over my very skin when he adds, "this Pink Lady Mocktail sounds… suitable."

I hold my breath as his cologne threatens to stall my heartbeat. It carries a hint of spice, leather and cedar. A fragrance as masculine and restrained as he is.

Am I overthinking this or was Gunner quietly perusing the menu and looking up pink drinks for me?

"You have a really nice voice," Ann gushes, looking two seconds away from melting into a puddle. "If hockey doesn't work out, you could host a late night podcast."

She has a point. Gunner could read drink names to a microphone all night long and he'd probably gain a following.

"What drink do you want? The waitress is waiting," Carol scolds.

I'm so frazzled, I don't have the presence of mind to be upset at her tone.

Gunner glances at Ann. "You don't mind giving her a minute, do you, Ann?"

Ann blasts another excited smile at him. "N-no. Take your time. I'm here to serve you."

"Then can you come back in a second?" Gunner adds.

"It's okay. I-I'll go with the mocktail," I tell Ann. The dinner's barely begun and I already feel hot and breathless. I definitely don't need to add alcohol into the mix.

Ann nods and darts off to get the order.

I lift the menu and fan my face, struggling to gain control of myself. There's too much at stake. Later tonight, when the mood is right, I intend to steer the conversation toward the Lady Luck Society and wangle an invitation to the next meeting.

Before I can find a neat way to bring it up, Gunner unfolds himself from the table and rises to his full height. I crane my neck to look at him, but what I see makes me shudder. His pale blue eyes are narrowed slightly and his usually aloof expression is marred by a dark frown.

"Son, what's wrong?" Sheriff Kinsey asks.

Carol's eyes dart all over Gunner's face. It's clear as day that she'd run into incoming traffic to protect her son.

"Mom, I forgot something in the car. Can you come with me and get it?"

"I'll come with you," Victoria blurts, reaching eagerly for her bag.

"Mom." Gunner speaks firmly.

Carol's mouth curves down in an even bigger frown, but she gestures for Sheriff Kinsey to rise. Once her husband gets up,

Gunner's mom scoots out from the table and waits for Gunner to join her in the aisle.

"Rebel," Gunner says gently to me, "can you scoot out for a second?"

The unease in the air feeds my burning curiosity. I can sense that something big is happening, but I'm not sure why.

I scramble to my feet. Gunner scoots out and towers over me.

I grab his arm and mumble just low enough that he can hear, "What are you doing?"

He looks at me determinedly, and I finally get it.

He's going to talk to his mom about me.

I worry my bottom lip between my teeth and try to stop him. "I told you to follow my lead."

There's a stiffness to his shoulders and a tension to his jaw, but when he turns to me, he plants the softest kiss on my forehead.

I blink in surprise.

Without a word, Gunner spins away and escorts his mother out of the restaurant.

CHAPTER
TWENTY

GUNNER

This dinner was a bad idea. With mom and Victoria eager to shun Rebel at all costs, it feels like I dragged Rebel into the lion's den without any weapons to defend herself.

Honestly, she shouldn't have needed a weapon in the first place.

I should have been her defense.

But because it's mom, I've been walking a tight rope, not wanting to step on any toes while watching Rebel parry countless attacks.

Rebel handled herself well, but a relationship—fake or otherwise—doesn't involve just one person. It's a team sport. If we were players on the ice, I'd be a crappy defenseman. In fact, I'd be kicked off the team. No questions asked.

Rebel doesn't seem to expect much from me, which is probably why she didn't look at me once for back up. She even tried to get me to stand down when I left the booth.

Unfortunately, I've been holding myself back all night and I can't any longer.

The doorman opens the door for mom and dips his head politely. My mother stomps past him, her eyes set on the parking lot.

I nod at the doorman and follow her into the darkness.

Mom stops a few paces from the restaurant's front door. "What exactly is it that you want to say, Gunner Kinsey?"

Her arms cross over her chest and she glares at me, while simultaneously bracing herself.

I'm not surprised that mom sniffed out my true intentions. Even Rebel sensed what this sudden trip 'to the car' was about.

"Mom, I love you, but I can't and won't sit by while you embarrass and berate my girlfriend."

"Who said I was—"

"That comment about her not being able to afford to eat at a restaurant like this one…"

Mom stutters. "It was just an observation! She clearly can't."

"… and then, a few seconds ago, when you snapped at her like she's a child…"

"I was simply pointing out how long we had the waitress waiting!"

"I love you," I say again. My father raised me to be unafraid of those words and I mean them sincerely. "But Rebel did not sign up to be dragged by my mother and my ex-girlfriend on a Saturday night. I won't ask you to like her, but I will ask you to be respectful of her."

Mom's jaw drops. "Gunner."

"If it happens one more time, mom, I'll be taking Rebel away. We will leave the table and the restaurant." My words are low and respectful but firm.

I don't want mom to think I'm joking or that I'm only saying this to intimidate her. I *will* leave if she hurts Rebel again, but I truly hope it doesn't come to that.

I think Rebel and mom have a lot in common—not that either woman will appreciate the comparison. They're both fierce, independent, brilliant women. Together, they'd be an unstoppable force.

Mom blinks rapidly. She runs her teeth over her bottom lip, back and forth. "You!" She shakes her head and starts pacing. "You've been brainwashed!"

I have no idea what to say to that because she's not wrong.

I spent my entire life pretending Rebel Hart didn't exist but, now, she's all I can see. The shift wasn't gradual at all. It's like I had control of the puck and a winger came out of nowhere, body slamming me into the boards.

I was blindsided.

"That woman...!" Mom flings a finger at the restaurant and then pulls the finger back to rub her temple. "You would *never* talk to me like this. It must be her idea."

I tilt my head back in a silent groan. Did mom completely miss my point? Or did I not say anything? Have I become so quiet, so reclusive, that when I speak, no actual words leave my lips?

"I raised you with my blood, sweat and tears," mom grinds out, "I gave birth to you and changed your diapers and ran after you every day on the farm, keeping you away from sharp objects and electrical outlets and small, digestible knickknacks that could kill you. I gave you the best education, the best hockey gear, the most expensive trips to foreign countries. I did *everything* for you and you choose that girl over me?"

"Mom—"

"Forget it! You've made yourself clear. You don't care about me or my opinion."

I heave out a sigh. Where in my entire speech did I use those words?

"I won't say anything more to her tonight. In fact, I'll pretend she's not even there." Mom stabs her finger in my chest. "But don't even *think* of sending her to the Lady Luck Society meeting tomorrow."

I grimace. *Uh-oh.*

"I know that little Jumbotron announcement was your scheme, but I will not be *bullied* into letting anyone into my sacred space. We can play nice at the table, but the Lady Luck Society is *my* jurisdiction and she is *definitely not* invited."

I grimace. "Mom, wait—"

Her phone pings.

Mom gives it an aggravated glance. "It's your father. He wants to know if everything's alright. Let's go back in before he comes out here looking for us."

I watch my mother stomp back into the restaurant. She yanks on the door before the doorman can get to it and lets it crash closed.

Oh no.

What have I done?

Rebel's only reason for going out with me is to lock in a seat inside the Lady Luck Society. I know how much joining the Ladies means to her.

And this talk with mom might have just cost her everything.

* * *

I RETURN TO THE TABLE. THE ATMOSPHERE IS TENSE. MOM IS SITTING stiffly, her mouth twisted into a hard frown and her eyes on the table. Dad has his arm around her and is rubbing a soothing circle on her shoulder.

When I look at Rebel, I find her gaze waiting.

She arches an eyebrow in silent inquiry.

I do a tiny head shake.

Rebel gives me an uncertain smile and prepares to scoot out of the bench so I can slide in. When I brush by her, I take her wrist and ask quietly, "Do you want to leave?"

"Not until I get your mom to tell me when and where the next Society meeting will be," she whispers back.

I wince.

How do I tell Rebel that's not going to happen tonight?

Thankfully, I don't have to kill her dreams because dad does it for me. He clears his throat and says, "Um, ladies, son, I think your mom's tuckered out from tonight's game. I'll cancel our order and take her back home. I'll pay for your meals on the way out. You young folks can stay and enjoy yourselves."

Rebel's eyes widen and she sends me a panicked look.

I look away. As much as I read the request in her eyes, I'm not stopping dad or trying to keep mom here.

"Carol, are you feeling unwell?" Victoria asks, half-rising out of her seat.

"I've lost my appetite," mom says weakly. "Like my husband said, you all enjoy yourselves without me."

Rebel clears her throat. I can see the desperation in her eyes. "Carol, before you go, I wanted to talk about—"

I give Rebel's jacket a tug to stop her question.

But it's too late.

Mom spins around, her eyes filleting Rebel like raw fish. "What were you going to say?"

This time, I squeeze Rebel's knee.

She brushes my hand off and keeps plowing forward. "We haven't had a chance to chat about the promise you made at the luncheon. When you're feeling better, I'd like to—"

"There must be some misunderstanding." Mom's voice is colder than the ice cubes in Rebel's mocktail. "I didn't make any promises at the luncheon."

I inhale a deep breath, filling my lungs. And then I hold that breath until it hurts.

Rebel blinks, going a shade paler. "Yes, you did. Everyone at this table was there." Her voice is laced with a hint of panic. "They even announced it on the Jumbotron."

"Yes, well, whoever did such a thing," mom's eyes flash to me and singe my skin, "was equally mistaken."

I grimace. "Mom, you said you were tired. Dad, you should take her home."

But my mother's on the hunt and she smells blood. There's no stopping her.

Shaking out of dad's grasp, mom takes a step toward the table, her eyes locked on Rebel. "As long as *I* am the chairwoman of the Lady Luck Society…"

Rebel eases back, blinking rapidly as if she knows what's coming.

"… someone like you will never be allowed to join us." Mom raises her chin a notch. "Your application is denied."

My heart slams against my chest and I look at Rebel. Despair shatters her expression. Seeing the hurt bleed through her eyes makes me feel like I've been punched in the gut.

Rebel stutters. "But—"

"But what?" Mom zeroes in on her, delivering a punishing blow. "It shouldn't matter what the Society decides. It's not like you announced you were dating my son just to get in. Because that would make you a hypocrite, wouldn't it?"

Rebel's nostrils flare like she's trying not to cry. She looks away, her lips trembling.

"You three have a good night." Mom cuts her hand through the air, returns to my father's side and allows him to escort her from the table.

The din from around the restaurant swoops back into my ears and I realize I'd tuned the entire world out for a solid three minutes.

Rebel's head sinks and her hair swishes forward to hide her face. It hurts so bad watching her defeated posture. Her devastation is palpable.

There's not much I can say that will make this better, but I wish I could find the words. Any words.

Just then, Ann bounces back to the table as chirpy as ever. "Alright, folks, I got your… oh? Where did this side of the table go?"

"Ann, we'll take those to go," I point to the food on her tray, my eyes on Rebel.

Ann's smile wanes. "Y-yeah. Sure. I'll be right back with some containers."

While Ann hustles away, Rebel grabs her purse, shoots to her feet and steps out of the booth. Her intentions to leave are clear and I'm right there with her.

"Gunner, where are you going? Who's going to take me home?" Victoria calls.

I keep following Rebel.

Rebel throws me a teary-eyed look over her shoulder. "Don't follow me."

"Let me drive you."

"I want to be alone."

"Rebel."

"Please. I just want to be alone right now." Her voice breaks on the last word and I want nothing more than to give her a hug.

But I respect her wishes and remain in place while she rushes through the restaurant, throws the door open and disappears outside.

"Gun—Mr. Kinsey," Ann appears in front of me, "your containers?" She lifts a bunch of paper boxes.

I force myself to return to the table.

Victoria stares me down. "Were you just going to leave me here?"

I don't answer her. Why should I? We're no longer dating. My priority is the woman who just stormed out of this restaurant on the verge of tears.

My chest feels tight and I rub a hand there. It was a bad decision to let Rebel leave. How is she going to get home? What if she orders a ride and the driver takes one look at her and tries to kidnap her? The world is a dangerous place.

Victoria pouts. "Your mom brought up a good point, Gunner. Did Rebel ask you to be her boyfriend so she can get into the Society? Because that's a form of manipulation and fraud. Your mom could even sue."

My mind whirrs. Is Rebel going to cry alone in the taxi? Will she spend all night, torturing herself with mom's harsh words?

"I'd be happy to represent the Kinseys. I heard Rebel's friend, April Brooks, is trying to sue your Uncle Stewart. We can even use this to counter sue—"

Abruptly, I take out my wallet and slap a hundred-dollar bill on the table. Then I turn to Victoria. "You have your license on you?"

"Yes, but Gunner, I was saying we could sue—"

I slap my car keys on the table. "Take my car back to town. I'll have one of my cousins pick it up from you later."

"What? Gunner! Where are you going? We're in the middle of a conversation!"

Her words slap my back as I sprint out of the restaurant. I don't care that everyone's watching me. I only hope that Rebel is outside when I get there.

CHAPTER
TWENTY-ONE

REBEL

I KEEP TELLING MYSELF THAT CAROL KINSEY WAS JUST REACTING OUT of spite.

I can still join the Society.

I can still make it work.

But the more I self-talk, the more cold, hard reality slams into me.

It's over.

After everything I did to make it happen…

… lowering my head….

…. accepting all her rude comments…

…agreeing to fake a relationship with my mortal enemy…

My chances have been obliterated. *Poof.* Gone.

Whatever power I thought I had, whatever delusion convinced me that I could go up against a Kinsey and win, that's done with. The rose-colored glasses have been ripped from my eyes.

I see the world with startling clarity.

I'm a Hart, born with my feet in the dirt. There's nothing I can do to change my world, nothing I can do to change my place in this town, to make a difference.

But that's not the most disappointing part.

I *already knew* I was powerless.

And yet, the moment Gunner stood behind my chair at the luncheon and declared we were dating, I started hoping for more.

Expecting more.

Why did I forget my place?

With one word from Carol Kinsey, it all came tumbling down. In a snap. *Just* like that.

As I wait for a taxi, I feel a presence behind me and glance over my shoulder. Gunner followed me out.

"Did I not speak English?" I snarl.

He stares at me with those cold, unfeeling eyes. As usual, he says nothing.

I scoff and turn my head away. "Go ahead. Walk all over me too. It's a Kinsey tradition."

"That's not why I'm here."

"Then leave."

"I will. After I see you get home safely."

"Whatever. Who am I to tell you what to do?" The car I ordered drives to a stop in front of me.

I tap on my app, double-check the license plate and get in.

To my surprise, Gunner opens the door on the other side of the car and climbs in too.

I glare at him.

He stares straight ahead, ignoring me.

I don't have any energy left to fight. My tank's on E. So I just lean my head against the window.

It starts to drizzle and fog gathers on the thick glass. I try not to think about the last time I saw fog on a window. But of course, trying not to think about it drags the memory to the forefront—Gunner leaning into me. A steady hand on my neck. A hot mouth caressing mine.

Kissing Carol Kinsey's son feels especially pathetic now that I've been banned from the Society. But in a way, I'm glad I got rejected. Now that my bid to join the Society is over, our fake relationship is over too.

It's about time this ruse was taken behind the barn and shot.

The driver glances at me in the rearview mirror. "You're heading to Lucky Falls, right?" He rattles off my home address.

Gunner sits straight up like a vampire roused out of his casket and grunts my mother's address instead.

The driver punches it in. "That Lucky Falls too?"

"Yes," Gunner says.

The driver taps the navigation app on his phone. "Okay, got it."

I pin Kinsey with my stare. "What do you think you're doing?"

He looks at me coldly. "You shouldn't be alone tonight."

"I want to be alone tonight."

"Would you prefer to sleep over at April's?"

"Gunner."

"Bell."

I stiffen.

"You're holding back tears and your voice is cracking on the end of every sentence. You either spend the night with your mom or with your best friend. Or you can spend the night with me. Take your pick."

Was Gunner hit in the head with a puck during tonight's game? He must be two forks short of a picnic basket if he thinks I'll ever spend the night with him.

I twist around, giving him my back.

The scenery outside my window shifts from skyscrapers and franchise coffee shops to flatlands.

Would I feel a bit less depressed if the view outside was filled with majestic mountains? Or a calm, still ocean biting into wet sand? Or skyscrapers with billboards blinking a commercial 24-7?

Should I just pack up and move out of Lucky Falls, go somewhere people don't know my family? Where everything is fast-paced, and everyone's too busy in their little bubble to care who my forefathers are? Somewhere neighbors haven't met in years, and the term 'community' is reserved for online forums instead of an entire town?

What if I just left it all behind instead of fighting?

A tear slips down my cheek and I brush it away. Beside me, the sound of rustling is followed by a hand appearing under my nose. Gripped in that giant hand is a thin tissue paper.

Surprised, I follow the line of Gunner's palm up to his broad shoulders, further up to a sharp jawline and finally, into a quiet pair of pale blue eyes.

"You keep tissues in your pocket?" I ask.

"In my wallet."

"I'm fine." I push his hand away.

Gunner takes both my hands, forces the tissue into my grip, and then looks away. "Be angry. Yell at me if you want. But don't cry."

I'm equal parts horrified and distraught that he saw my tear fall, so I respond with sarcasm. "Is that an order Mr. Kinsey?"

"If that's all it takes, then yeah. Consider it an order."

I bristle. "Who are you to tell me when I can and cannot cry? I don't remember selling my tear ducts to the Kinseys."

Gunner takes my berating silently.

Watching his expressionless face, I clamp my mouth shut. His willingness to be screamed at takes the pleasure out of it.

We continue riding in silence.

After a while, I turn to look at him, wondering if he's asleep. He's not.

Gunner notices my stare and looks solemnly back at me.

Caught, I have no choice but to address him. "Why did you drag your mother outside?"

He frowns as if he doesn't want to discuss it.

Great. That makes me want to discuss it more. "When she came back, she was glaring at me like I'd kicked her dog."

Gunner remains tight-lipped.

"Did you speak to her about me?"

He hesitates and then nods.

"Did you scold her for being rude to me?"

This time, there's no hesitation. He nods again.

I twist my body so I'm facing the giant hockey player. Anger churns in my voice when I say, "Why?"

He remains quiet.

I press, "Did you think I was holding back because I didn't know she was rude? Do you think I'm an idiot who can't tell when I'm being laughed at and ridiculed?"

Gunner breaks his silence, his eyes fierce. "I couldn't sit by and watch them tear you down."

"Look around, Kinsey. What do you think people see when they look at me? You think they see someone like Victoria, who wears fancy pantsuits and touts around her law degree like it's a family heirloom?"

I shake my head. "*You* and *Victoria* can demand all the respect you want. Since you were babies, you were told you were someone important and people had to treat you well. That's not true for the rest of us. We have to choose our battles because sometimes, it's a fight between respect or a job. Do you understand? It's either we get respect or we keep the lights on."

Gunner's eyes flutter and his jaw returns to flexing and unflexing as it did when we were driving to the restaurant.

"But I wouldn't expect *you* to get it, Mr. Kinsey." I flop against my seat and stare into the headrest in front of me.

"You say we're different," Gunner's voice cuts through the silence.

"We are," I clip.

"No, we're not. I don't care what your last name is, who your parents are or how much you make. You're human. Just like me.

You matter. Just like me. And if I had to do it all again, I would still choose to defend you."

My heart skips a beat, but I struggle not to let it show. "Do you expect me to thank you?"

He glances away.

"Did you think I'd be happy? You thought you 'saved' me?"

His jaw flexes. Nothing. No response.

I play the scene with Carol over in my head. Rather than sadness, now all I feel is hot, burning anger. "I didn't ask you to be my knight-in-shining armor. I wanted us to be *partners.*"

He flinches. My words, like a knife, seems to have cut something inside him. And I decide to give that knife a good twist.

"At least one decent thing came out of tonight's dinner," I mumble.

Gunner's head whips in my direction and he studies me, waiting.

"Without the Society, I don't need you. I don't have to pretend I like you. I never have to talk to you again."

For a second, I see hurt flash in his eyes. "You hate me *that* much, Rebel?"

No, I don't.

But I can't say that. No way.

Like a boulder going downhill, I let the rude, nasty part of me free. "You're a Kinsey. You're the enemy. Everything about you irritates me. Just one look at your face ruins my day."

Gunner's eyes sink to the ground and it seems like his entire being dims.

"It's not like you feel any differently," I bite out, trying to ease my own guilt.

Gunner says nothing.

Thought so.

I turn back to facing the window as my heart cracks a little. In a quiet, strained voice, I say, "We'll go back to how things were before and it'll be like none of this ever happened. From this moment," I rest my forehead against the cool glass, "you and I are *done*."

CHAPTER
TWENTY-TWO

GUNNER

Rebel stomps out of the car and storms all the way up to her mother's trailer. She wrenches the door open and disappears inside.

The door slams shut.

She's gone.

I notice the driver flashing me inquisitive looks in the rearview mirror.

I stare pointedly at him.

He clears his throat. "I, uh, need to know where I'm dropping you off, *amigo*."

I give directions. As the car takes off, I go back to stewing in frustration.

'Just one look at your face ruins my day'.

Wow. Rebel Hart sure knows where to hit where it hurts.

"Yo," the driver twists his neck to look at me, "about your girl, two things." He sticks up stubby fingers. "Roses and foot massages."

I give him a blank stare.

"Seriously. It works like a charm."

"Were you listening to our conversation?"

"Kinda hard not to. Your girl's pretty loud."

"She's not my girl." I grunt. Rebel made that fact abundantly clear.

"Nah, don't get too down about that. It's scarier if she *doesn't* blow up on you. When a girl checks out and she doesn't care anymore, that's the scary thing. If she's emotional, it means you still got a chance to make it right." He flashes me a grin. "You got this, *amigo*."

It's a bad idea to take relationship advice from a stranger, especially one who thinks an angry woman yelling 'you and I are done' is a sign of a healthy relationship. But I'm so desperate that I latch onto his encouragement.

If he saw our train wreck of a breakup—fake relationship or not, that was a breakup—and he still thinks there's a chance to turn things around, I'll take it.

The driver grins knowingly and says nothing more.

Left to my thoughts, I push aside my initial defensiveness, my hurt, and my disappointment and try to look at things from Rebel's perspective.

Everything she said was right.

No matter how noble my intentions, the fact that I'm a Kinsey will always overshadow me. It was foolish of me to think that I could be seen for who I am outside of my family. Rebel will never be able to separate one from the other.

The driver slows to a stop in front of the giant ranch sign that serves as the entrance to our property.

He whistles. "You live here or work here, *amigo*?"

I reach out to pay the fare and open the door.

"If you own this place, I'd mention that to your girl!" the driver calls.

He has no idea. This place and all it stands for is the reason Rebel will never be 'my girl'.

"She's into you, man. I can tell. Don't give up."

I pause.

Fishing out more bills from my wallet, I hand the driver a tip.

"Thanks, bro." He waves the money around with a grin. "I'll say an extra prayer for you and your girl to work things out."

I appreciate that. Divine intervention is probably the only thing that can turn this mess around.

It's quiet on the ranch, and I'm craving some alone time, so I take the long way home. Low clouds cover the stars, choking out the moon. The barn lights in the distance and my cellphone flashlight are all that illuminate my path.

Before long, the farmhouse looms ahead. A yellow light glows from the front-facing window. My parents are waiting for me to come home.

At the thought of another conversation with my mother, all my energy seeps out. I bet mom has a ton more to say about the dinner. In the time spent driving back to Lucky Falls and waiting up for me, she's probably invented ten more reasons to be angry.

I'm okay hearing about how betrayed she feels, but I don't think I can handle more cruel taunts aimed at Rebel.

It's because of that fear that I decide not to go home.

Shifting directions, I cut through the orchard, inhaling the scent of freshly overturned dirt and ripening apples. I'm not sure where I'm headed… until I arrive exactly where I'd wanted to go.

The treehouse.

The ramshackle structure looks extra rundown and lonely tonight. I grimace at the overgrown vines, weathered railings and leaves scattered by the wind. The sunken-in roof is a giant safety hazard too.

Mom's been mumbling about hacking the treehouse down and building a she-shed for years. But dad's never allowed it.

"The treehouse has a solid foundation and good bones. Who knows? Maybe one day, it can be beautiful again."

Testing dad's theory, I climb up the ladder. The boards nailed into the trunk are slimy with mold and moss. If I didn't have grip strength from years of playing hockey, I'd have slipped and probably cracked my neck.

Moving carefully, I clear the last rung and pull myself onto the small verandah. The logs dad used to form the floor of the treehouse are colored from age and neglect, but they hold my weight.

I spin in a slow circle, lost in happy memories. Like a movie—I see Rebel and I shrieking with laughter. Collapsing on our backs to find shapes in the clouds. Scooting all the way to the edge of the verandah, our bare feet hanging over while we snack on melting popsicles.

Before she was 'the Hart girl' and before I became 'a Kinsey', we were just Gunner and Bell.

I blink and the visions of the past are gone, replaced with the cold, dark present.

Was dad right? Can this abandoned, old eyesore ever be beautiful again?

Right now, it seems impossible.

Not unless someone's willing to put in the work.

I look beside me, and for a moment, the five-year-old Rebel and the seven-year-old me appear, waiting to play again.

A surge of energy pulls me forward and I start snapping pictures of the treehouse with my phone, capturing every angle from the verandah to the roof.

Slowly and methodically, I catalogue all the areas that need to be restored. The rusty hinges on the door. The overgrown canopy roof. The questionable ladder.

When that's done, I jog to the barn where dad keeps the farm pickup. The keys are always in the ignition. Dad's the sheriff and few would be bold enough to steal from him.

It's close to midnight when I drive through the dark, empty streets of Lucky Falls and head downtown.

A privilege of working at a hardware store? I have a key and the alarm code.

A privilege of being the nephew of the owner of the hardware store? I can loot the place without consequences.

I grab brand new hinges, cleaning solutions, and all the tools I need from the shelves. Stopping at the cash register, I write a note and tabulate the total of my 'shopping spree' so I can pay Uncle Robert later.

Next, I take over Uncle Robert's workshop at the back of the store and spend a few hours measuring and cutting boards.

When I'm done, I turn off all the lights, set the alarm in the store, and return to the farm.

My first task is prying off the old, mildewed boards nailed into the tree trunk. I replace them with the wood I cut in my uncle's workshop.

Next, I fix the door of the treehouse until it swings open and shut like a dream.

After that, I get to work hacking through the overgrown roof and shaping the canopy.

My phone buzzes what feels like minutes later. I pull it out of my pocket and flinch when I see the time.

It's three a.m.

My phone keeps buzzing and mom's picture fills the screen. I cut off the hacksaw, wipe the sweat from my brow and let the phone go to voicemail.

A moment later, the device chirps with a deluge of new messages.

MOM: *Where are you?*
MOM: *Why aren't you home?*
MOM: *At least let me know you're alive, Gunner.*
MOM: *Even if you're mad, you shouldn't sleep outside.*
MOM: *Come home.*
ME: *Don't worry. I'm fine. I'll talk to you tomorrow.*

My phone rings again.

I keep working.

The light of dawn touches the horizon by the time I finish fixing up the treehouse. As a soft blueish-purple hue takes over the sky, I run the broom over the balcony, sending tree leaves, bugs, worms, and decades of moss skittering.

Every bone in my body aches and I'm pretty sure there are new callouses over my old callouses.

But it's done.

I lean the broom against the railing and step back, admiring my work. I wiped or sanded down every wooden surface until it glistens. The canopy's been pruned back, leaving one half as a natural roof and the other side free of foliage. The porch has been swept and tidied.

But something's missing.

I scramble down to the ground and make a break for the daisy field. Grabbing a few of the wildflowers, I tuck them together and hold them carefully in my arms as I crawl back up to the treehouse.

Setting the bundle on the roughly hewn window, I step back and assess. The flowers add much-needed color to the dark brown of the wood.

There.

The treehouse is beautiful again.

As the sun spills over the horizon and birds trumpet to the start of a new day, a fresh resolve wells in me. With a decisive nod, I scramble back to the ground and head home so I can shower, change and make some calls.

CHAPTER
TWENTY-THREE

REBEL

"Are we really not going to talk about what happened last night?" Mom grins at me as I plod out of the bathroom with my toothbrush.

I roll my towel and dirty clothes into a ball. "What about last night?"

"I heard Carol made an announcement that you joined the Society!"

A groan builds in me. "Mom, please. Let's not."

"Let's not *what?*"

I shuffle ahead of her.

She follows me, a crease between her brow. "What's wrong, sweetie? You've been in a mood since last night." She pauses. "Did you have a fight with Gunner?"

I chew on my bottom lip and look away, so mom can't see me flinch. "How'd you find out about the Jumbotron?"

She brightens. "The video was everywhere. It was even posted on the Lucky Falls official news account."

Oh no. Even residents who've moved out of town follow those accounts.

"I wish I'd gone to the game. I would have loved to see the video in person."

"It wasn't that big of a deal," I mumble, padding over to the sofa. Mom converted my old bedroom into a storage unit, which is another term for 'junk room', so I spent the night on the couch and my back is killing me.

Mom clears her throat. "I'll be honest. I was a little nervous about you hanging out with the Ladies. Folks like Carol Kinsey and Marjorie White... they can be..."

"Judgemental? Rude? Condescending?" I offer helpfully.

Mom gives me the side-eye. "I was going to say *intimidating.*"

"Huh." I cap my toothbrush and set it on the coffee table.

"But that video proves they accept you as one of their own."

I snort.

Mom keeps gushing. "I really think the Society will take you places, Rebel. The Kinseys are the backbone of Lucky Falls..."

"You mean *tail*bone," I mumble.

"... and what with you dating Gunner and joining the Lady Luck Society, you'll be—" Mom freezes and narrows her eyes at me. "What was that, young lady?"

"Nothing." I force a grin. "Are you hungry? I'll get started on some grits."

Shuffling to the kitchen, I flare up the stove. *Poor mom.* It will really hurt when Carol Kinsey makes her clarification statement. I am *not* looking forward to that.

"By the way," mom comes into the kitchen and brushes my hand away from the cupboard, "when is Gunner coming over for dinner? I bought the ingredients for pasta. He used to love my pasta when he was little."

"He's on a diet." I reclaim the pan from her.

"Diet or not, he still has to eat, doesn't he?"

I tilt my gaze to the ceiling, searching for another excuse.

"Does he not want to meet me?" Mom looks around frantically. "It's not because the trailer's too shabby, is it? It's no three-story farmhouse like the Kinseys have—"

"There's nothing wrong with our trailer, mom. And no, that's not why he can't come. He's just… busy. Yesterday, he had the game, and I bet he had training early this morning too."

"Why is he working so hard? Don't they get a break after a win?"

"I've seen how Max cracks the whip with them. He won't let them rest until they come back with a championship."

"I guess you're right," mom mumbles, drawing away from the kitchen. "Anyway, who says he has to come to me? As his future mother-in-law, I'll bring him and his teammates some snacks this week. It'll be something that won't break his diet, of course. Perhaps some homemade granola?"

Horror drains the blood from my face. That absolutely *cannot* happen.

First of all, Gunner Kinsey doesn't deserve mom's homemade granola.

Second of all, he wouldn't appreciate it anyway.

"Mom, there's actually something I have to tell you." I squeeze my eyes shut and decide to rip the bandaid off, "Last night, Gunner and I—"

The screen door screeches and mom's voice rings out, "Gunner Kinsey, what a sight for sore eyes!"

"Mrs. Hart." A deep voice rumbles.

I whirl around. Why does that *sound* like Gunner?

"Oh, none of that. Call me Rachel."

Footsteps thud on the floor and then a giant appears, filling the doorway with his muscular frame.

I gulp. Why does that *look* like Gunner?

My mortal enemy is wearing a simple long-sleeved blue shirt, flannel and jeans. He fills the trailer and makes the entire space ten times too small.

The sight of him after our, well, *my*—because he didn't say much—fight last night pinches harder than I expected it to. I look away to the table, enduring a twinge of embarrassment.

"My, oh my. Gunner Kinsey, how you've grown! I remember when you were knee-high and now *look* at you."

I snort. Knee-high? Maybe Goliath's knee.

Gunner isn't just big physically. He's got this way of making other people feel small simply by standing next to him. It's his aura—mysterious and guarded. No, not just guarded. He's a secret vault buried under an alien research base. Everything about him is locked off, held behind a thousand door knobs and rattling chains.

"Have a seat. Let me get you some lemonade," mom chirps.

Gunner folds himself into mom's sofa, turning the average-sized loveseat into a chair fit for an elementary kid. His eyes lock on my face.

Trying to look busy, I grab the pan I'd set on the stove and then hiss in pain. The pan clatters back on the open flame. I'd forgotten that I turned the stove on.

"Ah!" I fling my hand up and down.

"Sweetie, are you alright?" Mom yells.

She hurries toward me, but a blur streaks past her. Gunner's long, loping strides eat away the distance. He's at my side in a flash. Grabbing my hand, he glares at the angry, red stain on my skin as if it did him a personal grievance.

"I-it's okay. I let the pan go quickly enough. It doesn't hurt that much." I try to tug my hand away, but he holds firm and drags me to the sink.

"I'll get an ice compress," mom says. She opens the freezer. "Oh, dear. It seems we're out of ice. I'll run to the store real quick."

The screen door shrieks open and then slams shut.

I stare at the side of Gunner's face as he concentrates on my hand. There are dark circles under his eyes and his face looks a little pale. I wonder if he'd gotten lightheaded when he jumped out of the couch to help me.

Gunner's piercing blue gaze meets mine. My heart skips a beat, and I hate myself for it.

I'm angry with him.

Aren't I angry with him?

What am I angry with him about again?

Right. He's a Kinsey. I don't need an actual reason.

My jaw clenches and I turn away, tugging my hand out of the faucet's cold spray. But Gunner doesn't allow me to budge and keeps my hand in place.

"It needs to run for at least twenty minutes," he says firmly.

I shoot him my fiercest glare.

The corner of his mouth turns up and my heart falls over itself. Why is he smiling like that? What's wrong with him? What's wrong with me?

What on earth is going on?

"D-didn't we end this last night?" I murmur, ignoring the way my stomach is doing backflips. "What are you doing here?"

"I brought breakfast."

"That's not an answer."

Gunner lifts my hand close to his face, inspecting the fading mark. His mouth is a millimeter away from mine. If I lean over, I could probably kiss him.

The thought sends a shiver down my spine.

Should I check myself into a mental health clinic? A few hours ago, I was in a cab screaming that I never want to see him again.

I must be going insane.

He turns off the faucet and cradles my hand as gently as I cradled the fluffy yellow chicks in the Kinsey's hen house when I was six.

Looking around, Gunner locates a dry towel hanging on mom's cupboard door and pats at my hand to sop up the water.

I pull away. "You still haven't told me why you're here."

His voice is velvety smooth. "You're my girlfriend."

"Fake girlfriend. And we broke up," I remind him, keeping my voice low in case mom's close by.

"Wouldn't that make it a *fake* break up?"

I narrow my eyes. Did Gunner Kinsey just… joke with me?

"I want to talk to you about something," he adds before I can answer.

"No."

He arches a brow.

"I'm not interested in any more of your schemes."

"Have you given up on the Lady Luck Society?"

"Hence our breakup. Were you not listening last night?" I scowl.

He tilts his head. "What about your plans to help people?"

I glance away.

He plants one massive hand on the counter and leans against the cupboard. The stance brings him closer to me, like he's half trapping me between him and the sink.

"Was all that fuss just to get into a club with The Davis Sisters and Marjorie White?" Gunner taunts.

I reel back. "Of course not."

Gunner's stare is intense and probing. "Then what are you going to do?"

I look up at him, see the challenge in his stare, and I lift my chin higher. "If no one else wants to help this side of town, I'll do it myself."

It was my dream to be a part of the Lady Luck Society, but the world didn't end because Carol Kinsey said no. The school still needs painting. The basketball court still needs fixing. Those wild dogs still need to be caught before they hurt someone else.

I think of poor little Rebecca Jergenson who had a run in with one of the dogs last month and got herself bitten. The sun doesn't rise and set on the Kinseys approval.

Gunner shifts a little closer to me. "How do you plan on getting it done?"

"I might not have money or connections, but if I take it little by little, I can do it."

His eyes soften from their usual, cold stare and it almost feels like Gunner Kinsey is proud of me.

Until he says, "You're only one person."

I lean toward him, feeling a familiar fire in the pit of my stomach. "I'm the *right* person."

Rebel Hart the 'pretty face' turned into Rebel Hart 'the mechanic' overnight. I didn't listen to any of the naysayers who said I couldn't fix cars because it would be a 'waste of a pretty face'. And I didn't let the auto repair instructors embarrass me out of my love for pink and fashion either.

I'm not the type to let the world define me. Every time someone pushes me into a box, I turn the box on its head.

"Watch how I change this neighborhood with my own two hands." I lift my arms to prove my point.

Gunner takes my hand again, and I inhale sharply at his touch. My eyes drop to his mouth like a magnet to steel.

"This hand is busted. You'll need some help," he says with the finality of a doctor.

"I told you. It's not that bad and even if it was, it's just a burn. I'm a mechanic. I get injuries like this all the time." I avert my gaze. "Besides, I don't need *your* help. I'll figure it out on my own."

"No."

My eyes shoot back to him. "No?"

He nods, doubling down.

I bark out a disbelieving laugh.

Gunner remains unbothered. "If you plan to do everything you listed, you'll need all the help you can get."

Just then, the screen door flings open and mom hurries inside, holding a melting bag of ice. "Um, is there a reason a food truck just drove up outside?"

I lean past Gunner's bulk to see my mom better. "What?"

A car horn blasts through the air and mom waddles back to the doorway. Whatever she sees outside makes her jaw drop.

"What is it?" I ask urgently, taking note of her expression.

"The hockey team. They're... they're outside. With paint brushes."

My eyes scurry to Gunner. I notice the confident tilt of his chin and the ghost of a smile on his lips.

I grab his arm and jerk him closer. "What's going on, Kinsey?"

"I told you." His eyes dart to my lips for a second and it makes my knees weak. "I brought breakfast."

CHAPTER
TWENTY-FOUR

GUNNER

I follow Rebel down the steps of the trailer. The bright, morning sunshine glints against a caravan of parked cars. To the side, in a grassy lot across from the mobile homes, is a bright blue food truck.

The shutter above the window is rolled all the way to the top. Two chefs wearing white hats and clear, plastic face masks wield a spatula expertly.

"Kinsey!" Theilan waves. "I want a food truck for my birthday this year!"

"It really is an entire food truck…" Rebel shakes her head. "How much did it cost?"

I keep walking.

She scrambles to keep up with me and hisses, "Gunner."

Thankfully, Watson grabs our attention by yelling loud enough for the entire neighborhood to hear, "I get first dibs!"

Theilan takes off at a breakneck speed. "Oh no, you don't!"

He and Watson start a stampede as everyone in the team hustles to the window of the food truck.

Theilan and Watson get there first, placing their orders ahead of everyone else.

By this time, the neighbors are poking their heads out of the windows and spectators are gathering on the street to watch the activity.

I push past the gathering crowd to get to the line of vehicles.

Max is on the phone a couple paces away.

Renthrow is climbing out of a pickup with Gordie in his arms. I jog toward them, surprised to see Gordie on site.

"Uncle Gunner!" Gordie fixes her tiny hands into finger-guns and makes the cutest sound effects. "Pew-pew."

I smile and return the gesture. "Pew-pew."

She spreads her arms wide, and I take her from her father, balancing her on my hip. Gordie grabs my face and gives my cheek a kiss. "When are we playing video games again?"

"I've been a little busy." I hoist her higher on my hip and promise, "But I'll swing by as soon as things calm down."

Gordie's sparkling brown eyes move past me and fasten on the woman at my side. "Hi, Rebel."

"Hi, Gordie."

"You're so pretty."

Agreed.

I take the opportunity to run my eyes over her. Rebel's hair falls around her shoulders in thick waves. She's wearing a simple pink tank top and a pair of knee-length, cream pants. Even in casual loungewear and barefaced, she looks effortlessly stunning.

"Like *really, really* pretty," Gordie adds.

From the mouth of babes.

"Thank you." Rebel grins and draws closer to Gordie, but that, effectively, brings her closer to me too. Her arm brushes mine as she rubs Gordie's back affectionately. The scent of Rebel's flowery, citrus perfume winds around me like a magic spell.

We'd been this close a second ago, but Rebel had seemed to

be on edge. With her focus on Gordie now, she's a lot more relaxed.

"Do you want to date my dad?" Gordie suddenly offers. "He's single."

I whip my head around to fix Gordie with a disapproving look. *And this is why children should be seen and not heard.*

Renthrow clears his throat and awkwardly scolds, "Gordie, I told you to stop going around saying things like that."

"But Gran said you wouldn't get me a new mommy on your own. She said you needed help."

Renthrow's face turns pink. I've never seen our winger so embarrassed.

The little girl nods as if the decision has been made. "I want Rebel. She's really pretty. All the kids at school will be jealous if she's my new mom."

"Your dad can't have Rebel," I explain as gently as I can.

"Why not?" Gordie pouts.

"Because she's mine."

Rebel's eyes widen.

"*Please.*" Gordie sticks out her bottom lip.

I shake my head.

"Pretty please with ice cream and cherries on top?" The bottom lip sticks out so far, I can use it as a shelf.

"Gordie, that's enough," Renthrow scolds.

Renthrow's daughter is adorable, but I stand firm. "I'm not giving her up for anything."

Rebel starts coughing.

Renthrow is massaging his head like he has a whopper of a headache.

But Gordie and I are two bulls in the middle of a coliseum. She takes after her dad, who's relentless on the ice. And I'm barely holding on to Rebel Hart as it is.

Neither of us budge.

Gordie's eyebrows slash over her stubborn brown eyes. "Ms. Nancy says it's nice to share."

"Toys. Not people."

"But—"

Rebel breaks us apart. "Alright, that's enough. Gordie, do you want to come with me and get a sandwich from the food truck?"

Gordie nods eagerly, her two pigtails thrashing. At this age, her priority is food over setting her dad up with a new girlfriend.

I'll take it that I won the argument.

I set Gordie on the ground and Rebel accepts the little girl's hand. Neither of them look at me as they skip toward the food truck.

The guys part to make way for Rebel and Gordie, allowing the ladies to order ahead of them. One by one, Gordie high fives the players like she's a celebrity at a sports event. And, honestly, she is. The kid's a rockstar.

"Sorry about that," Renthrow grumbles, walking over to me. "My mom's been pushier than normal lately. She's my mother and I love her, but she's a bad influence on Gordie."

I shrug. "It's fine."

Renthrow's mouth twitches. "Is it though? You seemed real insistent that I don't take Rebel from you."

I cough and glance at the food truck. Rebel is under the shade of the food truck's awning. She has Gordie hoisted up so the little girl can watch the chef work.

My heart warms when I see Rebel sharing one of her brilliant, sincere smiles with Gordie. Her entire demeanor seems softer and more approachable when she's with the little girl. I bet she'd make an amazing mom.

Even better if she was the mother of *my* future children.

Whoa. Did I really just think that?

"I guess it's serious between you two," Renthrow says, watching me and then Rebel.

Uncomfortable with where my thoughts are leading, I don't answer that and slap him on the back instead. "Fuel up. We've got a lot to do today."

I pretend not to notice his thoughtful look and walk toward Max. The team manager is finished with his phone call now and is standing with his back to the rest of the team, his shoulders slumped.

"Something wrong?" I ask Max quietly.

He flashes me a quick glance and then shakes his head. "I reached out to some of my old college buddies, hoping I could get us some more sponsors. None of them bit."

"I was thinking about our sponsorship issue. Have you ever thought of finding a sponsor in the city?"

"Of course I did. I'm not an idiot." Max's voice bristles with frustration. "I was schmoozing and dining all the usual potential sponsors before I'd taken office. No one was interested."

"Try again."

"Why?"

"Things have changed." I recall Ann's excitement while waiting on us and the way everyone had yelled out to me as I passed table after table. "Being the biggest fish in the smallest pond has its advantages. I'd reach out to the sponsors again."

"Alright. I'll give it a shot." He checks his watch. "Should we get started?"

I nod.

Max approaches the team that's gathered around the food truck, chatting, eating and drinking. He claps his hands to get their attention. Max is about the size of a bear and his paws are twice the size of my own. The clap gets *everyone's* attention.

"Pack it up, team. I didn't cancel morning practice so we could prance around eating sandwiches. We're here to sweat, burn calories and help our community." Max glances at me, indicating I should take over.

I meet Rebel's crystal blue gaze. "Rebel, what would you like us to do first?"

"Um…" Her eyes wander to the ground and I see her take a deep breath. When she lifts her head again, her stare is firm and direct.

The bold and confident Rebel is back.

"I'll need twelve guys on the school building. Two on the basketball court." She takes big strides forward, explaining what she wants to happen in each area for today's community service.

As she moves, I get the sense that this is no longer a Lucky Strikers event.

We're in Rebel Hart's garage now.

"Did you all get that?" Rebel asks, her voice strong and sure despite it originating from her delicate, beautiful frame.

"Yes, ma'am!" Theilan yells.

Watson points at me and then gestures to Rebel. "Gunner, you sure you can handle all of this!"

Rebel's lips curl up in my direction. Her eyes crinkle at the corners. It's the closest she's ever come to *really* smiling at me and my heart thuds in that strangely familiar way.

"Let's get to work!" Rebel orders.

While everyone jogs off to get to their tasks, a fancy black car drives up to the food truck. It looks completely out of place amidst all the rugged pickups and four-wheelers nearby, so I stop and take notice.

The door pops open and a frazzled voice says, "Am I late?"

My entire body goes rigid when a man hops out of the car and lopes over to Rebel. At first, I can't place him. But after a few seconds, it clicks.

It's the suit from the luncheon, the one who'd looked at Rebel like he could *also* see her as the mother of his children.

"Benji?" Rebel gasps, her eyes going wide and her smile puttering to new heights.

The guy doesn't stop moving and I wonder if he intends to plower Rebel down. But he doesn't.

Instead, the idiot wraps my girl in a hug that instantly has me seeing red.

CHAPTER
TWENTY-FIVE

REBEL

Benji's hands come up to rest on my shoulders, giving them a squeeze. His friendly smile brings out a smile of my own.

"What are you doing here?" I ask, pleased. I'd enjoyed our conversation at the Kinsey's luncheon, so it's good to see him again.

He pushes up his glasses. "I saw a video of you joining the Lady Luck Society."

"What?" I blink in confusion. "Oh, you mean the announcement on the Jumbotron?"

He nods.

"So you drove all the way here to congratulate me?" In the corner of my eye, I notice someone hovering around the food truck.

It's Gunner. His pale blue eyes are glaring at Benji's hands on my shoulders.

"I had business in town as well," Benji explains, looking in the direction of my stare. He notices Gunner and his forehead furrows slightly.

"But how did you know I was *here?*" I wonder.

"I stopped by The Pink Garage and your mechanic friend gave me directions."

That makes sense.

My eyes stray to Gunner again.

He takes the both of us looking in his direction as permission to approach because he stomps over. My heart pinches at the stormy look on his face. When he'd held Gordie, he'd been so soft and sweet. It felt like I was seeing another side of him.

But there's no sign of *that* Gunner now.

He swats Benji's hand off and drapes his arm around my shoulders, marking his territory.

Benji's lips tighten and he sizes Gunner up. He's not as broad-shouldered as Gunner, but he's fairly tall. I remember him mentioning that he played baseball in high school.

His past sports history is about as close as the two have in common. Benji has nothing on Gunner's six-five height or his muscles hewn from constant hockey training.

I step between the two men, already smelling the testosterone battle on the horizon. "Gunner, this is Benji. Benji, this is Gunner Kinsey."

"Kinsey." Benji gives Gunner a tight smile.

Gunner's hands fist at his side.

"Gunner is Carol Kinsey's son," I say. "She's the chairwoman of the Lady Luck Society."

Benji nods and immediately dismisses that information. Looking eagerly at me, he asks, "Now that you're in the Society, I'm assuming you're single?"

My eyebrows fly up.

Gunner's eyes harden.

I lick my suddenly dry lips. "How's your dad, Benji?"

"He's good," Benji says, looking like he wants to steer the conversation back to my relationship status. "My father hasn't stopped talking about what you did for Scooby's Nightmare.

Every time we meet up, he hints at inviting you out as a thank you."

"There's no need for that." I shake my head. "I was just doing my job."

"Yes, but—"

"Today's not a social event," Gunner clips. "If you haven't noticed," he gestures to the hockey players who are lifting a tall ladder out of the back of a truck, "we've got work to do."

I turn to Gunner, frowning.

He pretends not to notice and speaks to me in a dark tone. "Rebel, we need directions on where to start painting."

"Oh, right." I nod at Benji. "I'm a little tied up today, but maybe you and I can meet up afterwards?"

Gunner makes an animal-like growl behind me.

Benji smiles and undoes the button at his cuff. "Why don't I stick around?"

"Didn't you say you came to town for business?"

"I'm flexible." He rolls up the sleeve of his crisp white shirt. "You need more painters?"

"We'll need all the help we can get. By the way, Gunner, Theilan said the paint truck came all the way from the city. Who donated that much paint?"

Gunner clears his throat and glances away.

Something in his expression makes me pause. Why does he look so guilty?

"Gunner, did you—"

Benji blurts, "You should have told me about your community initiative, Rebel. I know a lot of wealthy businessmen who'd love to give to a worthy cause. Tell you what. I'll make a few calls. Just tell me what you need and they'll have it here for you by mid-afternoon."

Gunner rolls his eyes.

I nod absently at Benji. "L-let's head to the school first."

Several of the hockey players are already mounting ladders

against the school building. Max gestures to me and I'm grateful to leave Benji and Gunner behind so I can focus on the project at hand.

When I'm finished hashing out the details with Max, I get a text from April.

APRIL: *Sorry, Rebel. A client's expecting his car today and I ran a quick test and saw another problem. So sorry. I really wanted to be there by now.*

ME: *It's okay. I'm the one who's sorry for leaving you with all those cars in the bay.*

APRIL: *It's totally fine. The rest can wait. I sent Chance ahead since this will take longer than I expected. As soon as I'm done though, I'm coming straight over.*

I text my best friend a line of pink heart emojis.

The Pink Garage opens from Monday to Saturday and I hate that April is there, fixing cars alone. We really need to interview the female mechanic she mentioned and get some more help in the auto shop.

"Rebel." Mom's voice draws my attention away from my phone. My eyebrows shoot to the top of my head when I see a crowd of people from the neighborhood standing behind her. "What can *we* do to help?"

My heart squeezes in my chest. "Mom."

"This is our community too." Mom smiles gently at me. "We want to do our part to take care of it."

Emotions roll to my throat, making it hard to speak. Inhaling a few deep breaths, I regain my composure and point in the direction of the basketball court. "I need two people on the bleachers. The swings, too, could use a fresh coat of paint. Also…"

Mom takes in everything I say. She turns to our neighbors and repeats my instructions, helping to divide everyone into groups.

Time flies as I flit from one project to another, checking on progress, pitching in where I can, and running to solve problem after problem.

It's a monumental task to cover an entire neighborhood in one day, and so many things go wrong.

The water pressure slows to a creep, making it impossible to wash down the side of the school.

Pet control got all but one of the dogs and the animal ran into the park, startling one of the volunteers who turned over a paint can. The dog then ran *into* the spilled paint and left yellow paw marks all over the freshly painted basketball court.

The volunteers in charge of mowing the abandoned lots accidentally sent a stone crashing into a vehicle driving by and the owner was yelling and arguing at the top of his voice, demanding repayment.

But on the bright side, with so many hands pitching in, the school building is halfway painted. If we keep going at this pace, we'll hit every task on our list by five p.m. the latest.

"Rebel," mom calls me to the house while I'm enroute to the school for another check in, "the ladies and I packed sandwiches for the men. Can you help us share them out?"

I agree and switch routes to pick up my mom and the sandwiches instead.

Almost all the volunteers have congregated at the school along with the hockey team. Theilan and Watson are on top of ladders, painting the upper half of the building. Max and Chance are below, holding the ladders steady.

"Is anybody hungry?" I yell, lifting the bags of food.

My statement is met with cheers and a crowd quickly gathers around us.

"I'm sorry we don't have anything better than sandwiches," mom says sheepishly. "I know you just ate sandwiches for breakfast."

Theilan somehow manages to scale down the ladder in a blink and gets to her first. He accepts his sandwich with a gleeful smile. "Are you kidding? I was starving!"

Benji walks over to get a sandwich from me. "How's it looking?" He gestures to the school building.

"Great." I notice the sweat seeping into his fancy white shirt. "You're working hard."

He bobs his head and says something else, but I'm not paying attention. My eyes swoop the field, looking for a tall hockey player with dark hair, cold blue eyes, and a could-careless expression.

Gunner is nowhere to be seen.

"… anyway," Benji is saying, "I decided I didn't mind monster truck shows all along and—"

"Sorry, Benji. Can you hand the rest of these out?" I stuff the basket into his stomach. "I need to find Gunner."

He blinks.

I walk off and then abruptly turn back.

There's a hopeful look in Benji's eyes as I approach him.

Awkwardly, I snatch two sandwiches from the basket. "Forgot these," I mumble.

Weaving through the crowd, I keep looking but I can't find Gunner anywhere.

"Chance," I approach April's boyfriend, "have you seen Gunner?"

The famous hockey player glances up with a sandwich halfway to his mouth. "Yeah, I think he went that way to wash the paint off."

"Thanks." I head around the school building to the outdoor sink.

The school has a large football field for the kids to play. Like the basketball court, the net is missing from the goal posts. I make a mental note to buy some new nets for the kids.

As I near the outdoor sinks, a tall, muscular figure comes into view and my entire body goes still.

Oh my gosh.

Gunner.

Kinsey.

Is.

Shirtless.

Gunner cups his hands under the faucet and splashes his face. Droplets of water flicker across his shoulder to his cut bicep and slide down to his chiseled torso. The tattoos that he normally keeps under a respectful, long-sleeved exercise shirt are on full display, wrapping around his pale skin like he's a Viking ripped straight out of a storybook.

Prickles pop on the back of my neck as my skin starts overheating.

There's no way I should be looking at Gunner in this state. That dark hair, those tattoos, those muscles—it's a testament to raw, powerful masculinity.

Maybe a little *too* raw.

Maybe a little *too* masculine.

I should definitely look away.

But my feet are frozen on the ground and my head refuses to turn.

Breathe, Rebel. I remind myself when I start feeling lightheaded.

Gunner startles and his head twists to me. I blush, realizing I've been caught drooling over my mortal enemy.

Propriety takes control again. I force my gaze to the sky. "I-I brought you some sandwiches. Theilan and the t-team didn't seem like they'd leave any leftovers."

Why am I stuttering? It's not like I've never seen a shirtless man before. They're at the beach. And at the pool. And I've seen homeless men shirtless too. Sure, the homeless guys on the street do *not* look like Gunner but…

Suddenly, the stream of water pouring into the sink shifts to silence.

Gunner's boots crunch against sand and loose stones.

He's walking over.

Nerves tangle in my stomach and I chew on my bottom lip, struggling to breathe evenly. My heart is hammering so hard against my ribs, there's a real possibility it breaks out and starts flopping around in my stomach.

I can't help it. My gaze darts to Gunner's torso for one more peek.

Ugh! It's disgusting how beautiful he is. The man might be arrogant, cold, and impossible to understand, but his body is a work of art, from the muscled arms to his six pack abs.

Wait. Are those only six? I'm sure I counted more than six earlier.

In a single step, Gunner closes the distance between us, taking my chin in his hands and tilting my head. "My eyes are up here, Rebel."

Heat washes through my entire body. I wrench my chin out of his grip. "I wasn't looking."

A corner of his mouth curves up.

Am I insane? Are Gunner's half grins somehow hotter to me now that I've seen him shirtless? What is *wrong* with me?

A drop of water plops from Gunner's hair which, unfairly, makes him look like a vampire prince who got caught in the rain.

He leans in, his blue eyes scorching. He whispers over my lips. "Do you want it?"

"Want…" I sway forward slightly. "Want what?"

"My sandwich?" He looks down at my hands and I do too, realizing that I'm gripping his sandwich so hard, I punctured the plastic wrapping over it and I'm squeezing out all the tuna.

I release the sandwiches and they almost tumble to the ground. Gunner and his quick reflexes snatch them out of the air instead.

"P-put a shirt on," I snap, averting my gaze and preparing to stomp away.

But Gunner grabs my hand and tugs me toward him.

I stumble into his firm chest, gasping as the sweat and water on his skin seeps into mine. Heat engulfs me like I stepped into an erupting volcano.

"What are you doing?" I squirm. "Let me go."

"I can't."

I freeze. My eyes flit to his.

Gunner slides his fingers down the curve of my cheek. "I can't let you go, Rebel."

CHAPTER
TWENTY-SIX

GUNNER

I COULD EASILY LEAN DOWN AND KISS REBEL.

Right here. Right now.

And a part of me thinks she'd want that too.

But I stand firm, refusing to slam my lips on hers despite the tension pulling us forward.

There's a thin line between hate and love and I don't want Rebel to be confused about which side of the line she's standing on.

If I thought taking her sweet lips between mine could convince her to give me a chance, I would. But I'm too realistic to let myself get carried away.

Kissing her in the car hadn't fixed anything or brought any sort of understanding between us. In fact, directly after the kiss, everything fell apart.

So for now, I just hold her.

Rebel's hair is coming loose out of her ponytail and the strand I just tucked behind her ear comes free again, dancing in the wind. How is it that she smells so good in this heat? How is it that she still *looks* so good?

I've been keeping an eye on her all day. She never sat down, not even for a second. She's been driving up and down, carrying tools, transporting people, and coordinating with different groups.

Through it all, she kept her bright smile, met the most frustrating of challenges with grace, and made it all seem easy.

"Are you tired?" I ask.

Her eyelids flutter.

I push the stubborn blonde strand behind her ear again. "Have *you* eaten?"

Her vibrant blue eyes widen in surprise. My gaze searches hers, soaking in every fleck of green and gold trapped in the pools of blue.

She's truly, *truly* magnificent to look at. It's unfortunate that that's where most people stop. If they inched a little closer, they'd see how brilliant, selfless, and capable she is too.

I take one of the two sandwiches she brought, unwrap half of it and offer it to her.

She glances at it and then back to me.

"If you go back now," I nod to the main building, "you won't eat."

Rebel considers my words, but we both know I'm right. The moment they spot her, someone will come with a problem and she'll run off to solve it. Battling that much chaos isn't sustainable. Even the best leaders need a break, just to regroup and catch their breath.

Taking her elbow, I draw her to the other side of the sink where it's dry. Not convinced that the sink is clean enough for her, I spread my flannel over the edge.

Rebel watches me, a question in her eyes.

I place my hands on her hips and hear her intake of breath when I lift her on top of the counter. Shoving the sandwich in her hand, I nod to it.

At first, I think she'll argue. But, to my surprise, Rebel nibbles on the sandwich.

"You're very stubborn," she says. "Has anyone told you that?"

I shrug and pull my shirt back on, covering up my tattoos.

We stare out over the soccer field, eating together in silence.

"Why are you doing this?" Rebel whispers.

I glance over at her.

She's not looking at me with the burning desire from a moment ago. This gaze is devoid of her usual hatred too. For the first time, she's looking at me with curiosity.

I roll up the plastic wrapping and face her, wondering how to tell her what I'm feeling when I'm not quite sure myself.

Rebel's phone rings.

"It's my mom," she says, putting the device to her ear. "Mom, what... *what?* Okay, I'll be right there."

Rebel plants her hands on the sink, intending to jump off. I stop her with a hand to her back. Smoothly, I pick her up as if she weighs nothing and set her on her feet.

"A news station is here," Rebel says excitedly. "They want to interview us about today's work."

Her excitement is contagious but, even better than that, Rebel's smiling at me.

There it is. In all its glory. The first real smile I've received from her today. It's as stunning as I expected.

She hustles toward the main building and then stops halfway and swivels around. "Gunner!"

I tilt my chin up.

"Thanks!" She points to the plastic wrapping of her sandwich.

My heart beats double time and I watch her sprint away while wondering when the sun turned so bright and the breeze started smelling so sweet.

* * *

Rebel smiles prettily at the camera. "*This was a labor of love. I have to thank the community who came out to support and, of course, I have to thank the Lucky Strikers as well. They brought glory to our town last night, but that didn't stop them from working alongside us in the sun today…*"

I rip my eyes away from Rebel and notice that I'm not the only one transfixed. The suit is sitting on a bench nearby. His eyes are locked on her like she's an angel sent straight from heaven.

A possessive grunt gets caught in my throat. I wish I could rip his eyes out and sew them in backwards.

"Do you want us to drag him to the alley and rough him up a bit?" Theilan asks, swinging the stick of a long paint brush over his shoulder.

I startle and realize that my teammates have noticed my angry stare.

"We'd need masks or something," Watson mumbles, leaning against the wall and scowling in the city slicker's direction. "That guy looks like the type who'd snitch. One hundred percent."

Chance looks astonished. "Are you guys plotting an assault when Gunner's dad is the *sheriff*?"

"Why do you think we'll wear masks?" Watson spits out of the side of his mouth and a thick glob lands in the dirt.

"You're one of us now, McLanely. You can't be so naive." Theilan shakes his head.

Chance glances at the suit, studying the man's fixation on Rebel. In a low voice, he leans toward me and says, "Want me to find out where he lives?"

"Now we're talking." Watson grins.

Theilan gives Chance a high five.

The captain juts his chin at Rebel. "If some schmuck was openly drooling over April like that, I'd put on a ski mask too."

"It's disrespect. Plain and simple," Theilan agrees.

Watson grins and rubs his hands together. "So we all agree? We're slashing his tires, dragging him to the field behind the drug store and roughing him up a bit?"

A dark voice grumbles behind us, "*No one is roughing up anyone.* Are you guys insane?"

We all whirl around to find Max glaring at us.

Theilan whistles and pumps the paintbrush handle like it's a barbell. "Oh, hey, team manager."

"Roughing up?" Watson blinks innocently. "No, you heard wrong. I said… *drinking* up."

Max glowers at him, not buying it for a second.

Watson opens his phone. "Oh, I'm getting a call." I spy him opening his calculator app a second before he puts the phone to his ear and croaks, "Hello? Yeah, this is Watson."

Theilan doesn't bother with an excuse. The guy just runs away.

Max takes a seat beside me.

"You're the captain and vice captain," he scolds. "You should know better. We can't afford a scandal in the middle of playoffs." He points a finger at Chance. "A bar brawl got this guy suspended from the league. You think the minors will play nice?"

"They were just messing around," I say.

Max snorts. "Those knuckleheads look up to you. They'd attack if you say the word and you know it." He nods at Rebel. "I don't mind if you're using us to win brownie points. The Lucky Strikers are a part of Lucky Falls and putting in time to help people is never a waste. But if you have relationship issues, solve them yourself. Don't drag the team into it."

"Who said he has relationship issues?" Chance jumps in, defending me like his life depends on it. "He and Rebel are totally in love! Why would two people who love each other have issues? It's not like they're faking a relationship or anything."

My teeth grind together and I slant Chance a punishing look.

He winces.

Max turns to me, groaning in disappointment. "Come on, man. Not you too."

Me… too?

"Was this *your* idea?" Max wields a threatening finger at our captain. "Just because you and April started that way, you want everyone to do the same?"

"It wasn't me." Chance lifts both hands.

I scrutinize our team manager. "Did you know about Chance and April?"

"Yeah, I knew." Max plucks his shirt, trying to whip up more breeze by moving the material back and forth. "I also knew it was only half-pretend. April thought he was leaving Lucky Falls eventually, but I didn't. From the start, this sap was a goner."

Chance grins from ear to ear. "Guilty."

I raise a hand and admit, "Me too."

Both men freeze, staring at me in shock.

I lower my hand.

Rebel's laughter carries on the breeze. *"You know, it wasn't easy,"* she says into the microphone. *"To tell you the truth, we had a bit of a mishap with a dog and a can of paint. But it worked out. We now have a whimsical paw trail across the basketball court, a fun design for the kids."*

She glances at me and smiles, her eyes crinkling in the corners.

My heart detaches from my body and floats all the way across the lawn to her feet.

In another lifetime, all those crinkly-eyed smiles would belong to me. In another lifetime, I wouldn't have abandoned our friendship. I would have joined her in that field of daisies and soaked in the warmth of her like sunshine. I would have kissed her at Buddy White's birthday party and confessed that I've been thinking about her for years. All those times I snuck looks at her in the school hallway, she would have been looking back.

In another lifetime…

Regret winds through my veins and my shoulders slump.
I was lying to myself earlier.
I know exactly what this feeling is.

CHAPTER
TWENTY-SEVEN

REBEL

Gunner Kinsey is staring at me.

And normally, that wouldn't do anything but annoy me. If I even noticed at all.

However, *today*, I notice.

And I force myself not to turn his way for fear of losing my train of thought. The last thing I want to do is look like an idiot on the nightly news.

Kierra Griffin, a high school classmate, conducts the interview.

Kierra's got a chirpy, upbeat personality, which wouldn't suit a metropolitan news station. However, there's something about hearing 'a chicken thief's on the loose' or 'there's flooding around the Lonely Rise Creek' with her exuberant, smiley-faced delivery.

"Okay, I think we've got enough for tonight's slot. Thanks, Rebel," Kierra says, her dark eyes glittering.

"No problem. Is that all?" I step back.

"Oh, one more thing." Kierra gestures to me. "I notice you didn't mention the Lady Luck Society at all."

"Er... no I didn't."

Her eyes sharpen and I see exactly why Kierra went into journalism.

"Was that intentional?" She shoves the mike at me as if she wants to stick it into a nostril.

"Ugh..."

Never losing the smile, she sinks her claws in, smelling blood. "Everyone in town knows about the announcement made at the game. However, Carol Kinsey—the chairwoman of the Ladies—has yet to put out a statement. Do you know why she hasn't publicly declared you as one of the Ladies?"

"Well, Carol Kinsey is busy."

"Can you clarify what your position is in the Ladies and whether they had anything to do with today's community transformation?"

I inhale deeply and my eyes stray to Gunner again. He's sitting up and leaning forward like he's ready to bolt over to me if I say the word. What does he intend to do when he gets here? Push Kierra and the camera away? Scream 'no paparazzi'?

The thought makes me smile. Mostly because I can't imagine Gunner ever raising his voice or making a scene. He's so contained, so frustratingly aloof, that it's more likely he'd just take my hand and run.

"Rebel?" Kierra insists.

It's at the tip of my tongue to admit that I'm not a part of the Society.

On the one hand, it might be better for me to see myself out than to have Carol Kinsey kick me to the curb.

However, some part of me hesitates to blurt the truth.

I glance at Gunner again.

He half-rises from his seat, his eyes intent on me.

I clear my throat. "Kierra..."

"Yes?"

I take the microphone from her, square my shoulders and look the camera dead-on. "The biggest supporter of today's event was the Lady Luck Society."

Kierra raises both eyebrows.

"For years," I say sternly, "Lucky Falls residents have felt abandoned, left out and unheard. But I came today with the Lady Luck Society's full support *and* with a message."

Kierra grins from ear to ear while ripping the mike out of my hands. "What message is that?"

"The Society is for *everyone*. No matter where you live, no matter what you do, no matter who your parents are and what they do and do not have, if you're a part of Lucky Falls, then the Ladies are a part of you. You are not forgotten. You are not abandoned. We see you and we will build with and for you."

Kierra sniffs as her eyes turn glassy. "How moving."

I lower my eyes to the ground.

"You heard it here, folks. The Lady Luck Society is at it again, being the heartbeat of our beautiful town. I'm Kierra Griffin with Lucky Falls News."

"And cut!" the cameraman yells.

Kierra shakes my hand. "Congratulations, Rebel. I'm so glad you're a part of the Ladies."

"Really?"

"I once thought the club was just a way for rich families to show off. But if *you* have a seat around the table, I know real change is going to happen."

My heart swells. Technically, I don't have a seat around the table. What I have is my pink-polished toes in the door. And barely. Each of my little piggies are probably black and blue from trying to stay there when Carol keeps closing the door on me.

But I'm hoping, after this interview airs, it'll be difficult for the matriarch of the Kinsey family to keep me out.

While Kierra and her team pack up, I return to the volunteers who have been working tirelessly all day.

I clap to get everyone's attention. "Thank you so much for

coming out today. We've accomplished so much in such a short time because we've been working together. Now that the end is in sight, let's keep pushing!"

Cheers and hoots go up from the volunteers. The crowd is much smaller now than it was before. Many of our neighbors went back home. Renthrow left with Gordie about an hour ago since she was getting tired.

However, the other members of the hockey team are still around. There's enough people that I'm confident we can hit our schedule.

"I'm here! I'm here!" a familiar voice yells breathlessly. I hear the thud of feet pounding the sand and turn to find April galloping toward me.

"Slow down." I laugh when she flops against me, breathing hard.

Her straight brown hair fans across her cheeks and the strands lift with every puff of her breath. "I saw the news van. Did you have an interview?"

"Kierra came by." I fan my best friend's face with my hand.

"Kierra's nice." April pants. "Why is it so hot? Speaking of hot…" She whips her head up. "Where's Chance?"

I roll my eyes.

"Right here." Chance opens his arms and April flings herself into them. He brushes her hair back tenderly and tilts her chin up, his eyes skating affectionately over her freckles. "Did you run all the way from the garage?"

April swats him teasingly. "You're lucky… I'm too tired… to talk."

"What was wrong with the car?" I ask distractedly while looking around for Gunner. He seems to have disappeared again.

April shakes her head and prepares to launch into an explanation, but we're interrupted by Benji.

His hair is sticking up in places and there are paint spatters all over his clothes. The skin behind his neck and on his nose are a different shade than the rest of him. I probably should have offered him sun screen earlier.

Benji draws close to me. "Rebel, you were *amazing*. You almost convinced *me* to pack up and open a firm in Lucky Falls. I was *that* moved."

"It was nothing."

Benji touches my shoulder. "I've seen lawyers twice your age choke in front of a camera. You're a natural."

"Rebel's never been afraid of the spotlight," April jumps in, her eyes darting from where Benji's touching my shoulder to my face.

I clear my throat. "April, this is Benji. His father is the owner of Scooby's Nightmare. Benji, this is my best friend and business partner, April. If you ever have car trouble, *this* is the person you should call. She's never met an auto problem she can't solve."

Benji looks impressed.

"April's a genius with cars." Chance puffs out his chest, proud as a peacock.

I can't help but snicker at him.

April gestures to me. "Rebel's a genius too. But since you saw her work on Scooby's Nightmare, I don't have to convince you."

"You two must be drowning in customers. I know *I* would love to bring my car to a shop with such beautiful mechanics." His voice softens and so does his gaze when he looks at me.

I clear my throat again.

April frowns. "It's a good thing people bring their cars to us because we can actually *fix* them and not just because we're pretty."

"Oh." Benji's eyes widen. "I didn't mean that with any disrespect. Of course, you're both extremely capable. I only meant—"

April chuckles. "Relax, Benji. I was just kidding. Any friend of Rebel's is a friend of mine. I'll second what Rebel said about bringing your car around if you have trouble. We've got a full schedule, but I'll make time for you."

Benji's grin is tinged with relief. "Thank you. I appreciate that."

Finally, I spot Gunner coming around the school building. Something's wrong. I can tell by his quick, urgent strides, stiff shoulders, and tense arms.

I lunge toward him. "Gunner, what happened?"

He careens to a stop and looks down at me. My gaze gets sucked into a pale, worried blue.

"My mother," he swallows, "she's in the hospital."

CHAPTER
TWENTY-EIGHT

GUNNER

I'M STILL NOT SURE IT'S A GOOD IDEA TO BRING REBEL TO THE hospital. Dad said that Uncle Stewart, Uncle Robert, and a bunch of other relatives are there too.

I have no idea what we'll face, and I can't promise that I'll be around to protect Rebel if mom or Uncle Stewart get nasty.

"Gunner, that's the hundredth time you've looked at me and sighed since we started driving. If it's so distracting having me here, I can just get out now and catch a cab back to the school."

I contemplate her words, torn between needing her around for my own sanity and wanting to keep her far, far away from my family drama.

However, when I think of Rebel getting hurt, it's an easy choice.

"You should go back," I say roughly.

Rebel folds her arms over her chest, a stubborn tilt to her chin. "Do you really mean that?"

I clamp my mouth shut.

She leans forward, her blue eyes searching my face. "Do you *really* want me to leave you alone right now?"

My Adam's apple bobs.

I'm not strong enough to say yes.

"I'm staying," Rebel says, wiggling further back in her chair and planting her arms over her chest like a protester with a sign that says *'we shall not be moved'*.

"I can drive if you don't think you can handle it, buddy." Benji leans forward, forcing his unwanted mug between the headrests. He smiles sweetly at Rebel. "I have my license."

"You're *not* driving," I grind out. "And I'm not your 'buddy'."

"I'd like us to be friends."

I scoff.

"We both care about, Rebel. I'd say we have that much in common, don't we?" he adds.

Did he just say he 'cares about Rebel'. To *me?*

"You can drive..." I growl. "Over my cold, dead body."

"Alright, alright. No need to get testy." Benji shrinks back like a balloon losing air.

How he managed to finagle his way into my truck is a mystery worth investigating.

All I remember is a panicked phone call with dad, informing me that mom fainted and she'd been transported to the hospital.

Next thing I knew, I was running to my truck and Rebel blocked my path. She offered to come with me and I wasn't in my right mind, so I let her.

A moment later, the city slicker wormed his way into the backseat, spouting nonsense about 'knowing a doctor friend at the hospital'.

Rebel was convinced by his words so she pleaded his case, claiming the guy could help. Help with what? I have no clue. All he's good for is making moon eyes at Rebel and ticking me off.

"Hey." Rebel puts her hand over mine. It's a brief touch, but it soothes me like a startled horse with an expert rider. "Your mom's going to be fine."

I appreciate her words, especially because I can tell she's sincere. Given how rocky her relationship is with my family, it means a lot.

"Did your dad call the... rest of your family?" Rebel asks tentatively.

I wince, hearing what she's really asking. "Uncle Stewart will be there."

She pulls her lips into her mouth and stares straight ahead. "Great."

Again, I get the feeling that I shouldn't be dragging her into this mess.

"Would you like to listen to some music?" Rebel asks.

As she extends her arm to turn the radio on, I reach out and weave my fingers into hers. Her jaw drops and she gives me a startled look.

I settle our joined hands on my leg. "I like the quiet."

Rebel's eyes dart to the stowaway in the backseat and she hisses, "Gunner."

I run my thumb over the back of her hand, taking comfort in the touch.

She squirms and tries to pull her hand away.

I don't budge.

Chewing on her bottom lip for a second, Rebel flings one more perturbed look at me before settling into her seat and accepting that my hand and hers are going to be connected for the rest of the ride.

Benji makes a couple sounds of discontent from the backseat but, since I'm driving, and he's got no good excuse to be here anyway, he doesn't say a word.

At the hospital, I release Rebel reluctantly and jog around the car to meet her on the sidewalk.

This is a really bad idea.

But Rebel isn't intimidated at all. Her hair flounces against her back as she takes the lead and walks confidently to the nurse's station.

"We're looking for Carol Kinsey?" Rebel says to the nurse.

As I watch her, I feel a presence by my side.

"She shouldn't be here," our unwelcome guest complains.

I ignore him.

"I saw the way your mom treated her at the luncheon. All you're doing is subjecting her to embarrassment and she won't be able to fight back, especially if your mom's sick. She'll just stand there and take it."

It bothers me that Benji knows Rebel that well.

Bothers me even more that he's right.

"Rebel isn't even your real girlfriend," he grumbles, brushing at a stain on his shirt.

I whirl on him, ready to grab him by the collar. "What did you say?"

"Your mom is on the second floor in a recovery room." Rebel's voice interrupts what would have been Benji the Suit getting shoved into a wall. When neither of us moves, Rebel arches a brow. "Gunner?"

Battling guilt, worry, and frustration, I grab Rebel's hand and send Benji a blistering look over my shoulder. His bottom lip trembles as if he's scared, but he meets my stare head-on.

When he makes a move to follow us, I bark, "You stay here."

"I'll call you if we need you, Benji," Rebel says, trying to smooth over the rough bite in my words.

Don't hold your breath, buck-o. She's not calling you anytime soon.

Rebel staggers behind me as I drag her to the elevator.

She wrenches her hand free as soon as we get on and the doors close in front of us. I retreat to a corner of the elevator, glaring. In the shiny chrome walls, I see my reflection. Dark hair. Blue eyes. Wicked dark scowl.

"What's your problem?" Rebel stares at me. "Why are you dragging me around?"

My chest expands on a sigh.

"I get that you're worried about your mom, but Benji's not the enemy here. And neither am I."

My head is pounding. I suck in a deep breath.

"Tell me. Honestly. Am I just an object to you?"

My expression shifts on a dime. *What is she talking about?*

"Back in the car, you held my hand to prove some stupid point to Benji. Just now, you dragged me away because you were angry with him too. I came to the hospital with you because I was worried. I didn't sign up to be a trophy you two are competing for."

I blink in surprise. Rebel is *not* a trophy to me. And I did not hold her hand in the car to 'objectify' her. I did it so I could *breathe*.

As I'm searching for a way to explain myself, the elevator doors open.

Rebel stalks out first.

I chase after her.

She picks up speed.

The woman is fast, but my legs are longer. It only takes me a moment to catch up. I stop in front of her, blocking her path.

Her frosty eyes fix on a point just over my shoulder.

I breathe out shakily. "You're not a trophy, Rebel."

She glances away.

"Look, I held your hand in the car because—"

"Gunner."

Quick footsteps thud down the hallway and all the blood drains from my face when I see Uncle Stewart.

The old man glares at Rebel, his mouth twisting into a sneer. "You sure have some nerve coming here when you're the reason my sister-in-law's in the hospital."

Instinctively, I drag Rebel behind me and stare my uncle down. "Don't talk to her."

Uncle Stewart smirks. "Don't be so dramatic, nephew. It's unlike you."

"Let's go," I whisper to Rebel. I take her hand again and circle around my uncle.

"I heard you didn't come home last night," Uncle Stewart calls.

Rebel freezes.

I stop moving and look back at my uncle.

His eyes track over to Rebel and there's a glint I don't like in them. "I can take a guess as to what you were doing all night long."

My temper spikes and I lunge forward.

Rebel grabs my hand before I can make a move against my uncle.

Uncle Stewart laughs low in his throat.

"Gunner, don't do this outside your mom's hospital room," Rebel warns quietly.

I step back, although everything in me strains to correct my uncle.

"What? Were you planning to hit me, boy?" Uncle Stewart shakes his head. "That's the problem with your generation. You have no respect."

"Respect is earned, not given," I warn him. "Talk about Rebel again and I'll show you what 'no respect' looks like."

CHAPTER
TWENTY-NINE

REBEL

Gunner pulls me into his mother's hospital room, his face flushed with anger. My heart pounds as I watch his perfectly crisp jaw line clench and unclench.

This is the second time Gunner's stood up to his uncle for me. The first was when Stewart Kinsey wrestled his way into a seat at our table that day at the Tipsy Tuna.

He's been sticking up for me in front of his mom too.

A sudden thought hits me right between the eyes. Did he not go home last night because of me?

I shift my attention to his extra pale face. After a day of hard labor, the lack of sleep is starting to show. He seems weary and gaunt.

"Son." Sheriff Kinsey's voice drags my gaze away from Gunner.

Gunner pauses a moment and I *see* him tuck on a mask to show that signature, aloof expression. He moves forward a step and then startles when he realizes he's taking me with him.

Pale blue eyes shoot down to my hand and widen. He

releases me quickly and in a flustered voice says, "If you want to leave…"

"I'll hang back here."

Relief flashes across his face and I know I made the right choice.

Gunner approaches the crowd of relatives surrounding his mother.

Carol Kinsey flops an arm over her forehead, moaning pathetically. "Son, you're here."

Robert Kinsey, the owner of the hardware store, slaps Gunner on the back.

His relatives absorb him like a giant, human-sized Venus fly trap. With so many Kinseys blocking him from sight, there's not much I can do except awkwardly hang by the door.

I kind of wish I'd brought Benji with me. At least then, we could be awkward together.

"Oh, son!" Carol Kinsey whines. "I don't know what came over me. I waited up all night, but you never came home and you didn't answer my texts—"

"I answered your text, mom," Gunner says quietly.

"… my neck started to hurt." Carol moans. "And black spots danced in front of my eyes…"

"The doctor said her blood pressure was through the roof," Sheriff Kinsey says.

"You gotta be careful with that, Carol. You know our family has a history of high blood pressure," Mayor Kinsey scolds.

"What do you mean?" Robert Kinsey grumbles. "She's our sister-in-law. Not our sister by blood. It's us who have to worry about our blood pressure."

"Oh, right. I forgot." The mayor coughs. "You see how much of a Kinsey you are, Carol?"

The conversation is nauseating and, since I don't particularly like any of the people here, I decide to leave.

But before I can, the door widens and Stewart Kinsey walks in. His scowl deepens when he sees me, however, he doesn't say a word. I give him a good, solid glare before walking out.

The elevator dings while I'm looking for a place to sit and three ladies dash through the hallway. Marjorie White is leading the charge.

Marjorie's eyes widen when she notices me. "Rebel, Rebel. Oh thank *goodness*."

My brows fly all the way up to my hairline. Did… Marjorie White just smile at me? Since when does that woman's face know such pleasant expressions?

"We just heard the news about Carol," Cecelia Davis says.

"How is she?" Rosalie Davis leans into me, her eyelids batting up a storm.

If Stewart Kinsey is a five out of ten on the creepy scale…

Marjorie White and her minions are *breaking* the scale.

"Uh, she's okay. Her family's with her now." I step aside so they can rush in.

But they don't.

"Rebel, you look absolutely drained. Let me see. I've got a bottle of iced tea in my purse." Marjorie opens her giant bag and rifles through it.

"Do you want some chocolate?" Cecelia offers.

Rosalie walks backward. "I've got nothing but mint, but I can run down to the vending machine and get you a cup of coffee."

Fear seizes my heart and my eyes dart back and forth. Marjorie and her posse must be up to something truly horrific.

"Here you go." Marjorie offers the drink.

It's probably spiked. "I'm not thirsty."

"Chocolates?"

I shake my head at Cecelia.

"Coffee, then? I'll grab a cup." Rosalie darts away.

Unnerved, I gesture to the hospital room. "I'll wait downstairs. You guys should head in."

"Wait." Marjorie slides into my path. "I have something I need to discuss with you."

"I really don't have time—"

"It's Lady Luck Society business," Marjorie tacks on.

"Lady… Luck Society?"

Marjorie nods. "You're Gunner Kinsey's girlfriend, aren't you?"

"I… am."

"We heard what Carol said about Kinsey wives and girlfriends getting legacy privileges."

Well, I'll be.

Marjorie White is having herself a mutiny. Carol Kinsey is lying in the hospital bed only a few feet away and she would *not* approve of this conversation.

"We heard what you did at the trailer park and for the school," Cecilia explains.

Marjorie takes over. "The entire town is buzzing about what you, I mean, what *we*," she gestures to herself and Rosalie who nods enthusiastically, "did for the less fortunate."

I fold my arms over my chest.

"I just got a call from a very wealthy businessman who offered to set up a meeting with five of his business colleagues. They want the Lady Luck Society to help even *more* of the folks on *that* side of town."

"He was very specific that it be for *that* side," Rosalie jumps in, bobbing her head.

"And since you're the expert on those types of neighborhoods…" Marjorie flaps her eyelashes.

Translation: Since they prefer to avoid actual people in poverty…

"… we thought you'd be the perfect candidate to meet with the donor and present a plan of action." Marjorie's grin turns strict. "Under the umbrella of the Lady Luck Society of course."

Translation: you do the hard work, but we want the credit.

I frown. "Is this how you usually discuss matters in the Society?" I arch a brow. "Haphazard meetings outside of the hospital room of the chairwoman?"

Cecilia's face reddens.

Marjorie glances away. "Consider it your last... test. If nothing goes wrong, we'll support you one hundred percent. Carol will have to acknowledge you."

A bitter laugh escapes me. "But if something *does* go wrong, you can say that I was never an official member of the Lady Luck Society and I did everything on my own."

Marjorie clears her throat. "What could possibly go wrong? It's a simple community outreach project. Very similar to what you did today."

I hesitate to agree. Marjorie White has her own agenda and I doubt she has any intentions of helping me. However, I *do* want to join the Lady Luck Society and I *do* want to help more communities like mine.

Two birds, one stone.

Isn't it worth the risk?

Just then, the door to Carol Kinsey's hospital room opens and Gunner comes sprinting out. His pale blue eyes land on the women in the corridor and jerk around until they find me. His shoulders slump in relief but, a moment later, his face pales and he stumbles backward.

I rush to him, slipping an arm around his waist. "Gunner, are you okay?"

He nods faintly, sweat populating on his forehead and neck.

"Son, you look like you need a hospital cot of your own," Marjorie White says worriedly.

Rosalie returns, balancing a cup of coffee. "Here, Rebel."

I take the coffee from Rosalie and offer it to Gunner. "Drink this. It'll wake you up."

Gunner shakes his head.

Seeing that he's being stubborn, I blindly hand the cup back to Rosalie whose smile drips into a frown before she fixes her expression.

"Let me drive you home," Gunner whispers weakly to me. "It's been a long day."

There's no way I'll let him get behind the wheel of a car in this state.

I steer Gunner down the hallway. "I think I saw a bench somewhere. You need to sit down."

Gunner doesn't argue. Not that he's the argumentative type anyway, but…

"Rebel, consider our offer and get back to me ASAP!" Marjorie calls. Her voice bounces against the walls of the hospital hallway.

I wave a hand in acknowledgement and focus on getting Gunner to a bench. He immediately leans his head against the wall and closes his eyes.

"What was that about?" he asks wearily. "Did the Ladies insult you again?"

"The opposite." I settle beside him. "Marjorie offered to support me joining the Society."

He peeks one eye open. "In exchange for what?"

"Doing more community projects like today."

He makes a disbelieving sound in his throat.

"I'll meet the donor and find out if it's legit before I agree to anything. Don't worry. I won't be led into a trap."

"Good," Gunner croaks.

"Good," I say.

His eyes fall shut again and his breathing deepens. He's asleep.

I study the way his dark hair falls against his forehead, the straight slope of his nose and his firm, pink lips—lips that, for once, aren't hardening into a scowl or tightening into a straight line.

My heart stirs strangely. When Gunner's asleep, he's way less intimidating. The hard planes of his face soften until I can see echoes of the little boy I'd been obsessed with when I was five.

My phone rings.

I jolt and answer the call, setting it against my ear. "Hello?" I whisper.

"Is anyone around? Can you talk?"

"Benji? Uh, yeah. I can talk." Gunner's out like a light, so I'm basically alone.

"Good," Benji says. "Because what I want to tell you can't be repeated."

At that moment, Gunner's head moves against the wall. It slides down, down, down… until it lands on my shoulder.

I gasp and look at his pale face.

"I've been holding myself back because it's your business and I don't want to make you uncomfortable, but I know what's going on between you and Gunner."

"W-what?" My heart jumps with guilt.

"I know he only said you two are in a relationship to get you into the Lady Luck Society."

"Benji—"

"I asked around. The whole town said that you and Gunner were like enemies. People who went to high school with you guys were surprised when you started dating."

"Yes, but—"

"It's not right that you're forced to date your enemy for the sake of joining the Ladies." Benji clears his throat. "As your friend, it bothers me a lot. So I did something about it."

My throat gets dry.

"I offered a donation to the Lady Luck Society and I specifically asked to work with you."

Marjorie's proposal echoes through my mind and it all clicks into place.

"It was *you*? You're the donor?"

"Well, mostly my dad," Benji says. "But I'm the one who convinced him to do it."

Gunner adjusts his head on my shoulder, nuzzling against my neck. Prickles of awareness skitter over my skin when his breath hits my throat.

I whisper tersely, "Why would you *do* that?"

"I'm offering you a way out, Rebel. You can help people *and* get into the Society without tying yourself to someone you don't like or respect."

"I had everything under control. You shouldn't have bothered your dad over something like this!"

There's a beat of quiet and then Benji says, "Are you... angry with me?"

"No," I snap. "It's just... I..."

I swallow hard, unable to explain myself.

He's right. I'm angry. But why? *Why* am I annoyed that he intervened?

Benji's voice cuts through the pounding of my heart. "Do you *want* to keep dating Kinsey?"

My eyes slide down to Gunner's face and my throat clamps tight.

I don't know how to answer that question.

CHAPTER
THIRTY

GUNNER

Soft fingers run through my hair and I blink my eyes open. I'm leaning sideways, my head resting on Rebel's shoulders.

At first, my heart expands happily and I smile to myself.

Then I freeze.

What if I drooled on her? I was dead-tired and I wouldn't be surprised if I did.

The potential for embarrassment wakens all my senses. I sit up so quickly that my head spins.

"Hey," a voice that is *not* Rebel's purrs, "slow down. You shouldn't move that fast when you just woke up."

I lurch backward, stunned to see Victoria occupying the seat where Rebel had been a few minutes ago.

Was it a few minutes ago?

I lift a hand to check my watch and grimace. It's been an hour.

"Where's Rebel?" I demand, my voice hoarse.

"I don't know. She wasn't here when I arrived." Victoria folds her arms over her chest, seeming annoyed that I mentioned Rebel's name.

I fumble around for my phone. "You should have woken me."

"You were sleeping so peacefully."

I clamor to my feet and pull my phone out of my pocket.

There's a message from Rebel.

REBEL: *Benji and I are catching a cab back to town. Tell your mom get well soon.*

I read and re-read the message, my heart twisting painfully. Why did she leave with Benji? I would have gladly taken her back to town.

Rubbing my forehead to clear the lingering grogginess, I start down the hallway. I'll check on mom one more time and then swing by Rebel's. Not to talk to her… just in case she hasn't made it home yet and I can see her before she goes in.

Victoria grabs hold of my T-shirt and stops me.

I look back and find her staring pleadingly into my eyes.

A deep, weary sigh slips out of me. I push her hand off.

"Gunner," Victoria stares at the ground as her hand swings limply at her sides, "I didn't come back to town to compete for you. No matter how much I like someone, I have my pride too."

I turn to her, my eyes cool and emotionless.

"I also have my own values." Victoria lifts her chin. "I respect when a man is in a relationship and I would never encroach."

I find that hard to believe. Wasn't she the one who ran her fingers through my hair a moment ago?

"But," Victoria adds stubbornly, "even if I know this is embarrassing, even if I feel like a second-grade villain, I can't stop. I like you *that* much." She pauses. "And I'm also not convinced that you're really interested in Rebel."

I stiffen at her words.

"I saw how surprised she looked at the luncheon when you told everyone you were dating. Even if I wasn't a lawyer, I would have found the timing suspicious. And last night at the restaurant, you went against your mom for her, but she was still angry with you. She didn't care about you at all."

I wince, but I can't argue with the truth.

Victoria shakes her head like a teacher disappointed in a student's failing grade. "If it were anyone else, maybe I could concede, but women like her are nightmares."

My eyes narrow and I stare down at Victoria in warning.

"It's the truth." She stands ten-toes-down on her statement. "She's used to getting her own way because she's so pretty. She knows that a guy will do anything she wants and that gives her a power trip. But she's just a girl. In the city, there are tons of girls who look just like her or even better."

Says who? Rebel Hart is the most beautiful woman in the world to me.

Victoria keeps spitting her vitriol. "Honestly, back then and now, I don't understand what men find so irresistible about her. Every guy at Cornblue acted like she was such a prize." Victoria shrugs. "Except you. You were the only one who didn't fall at her feet."

My eyes slide to the ceiling. She has no idea. It took intense restraint to act like I didn't notice every little thing that Rebel Hart did in high school.

It took even more restraint to act like I hated her when I didn't.

Victoria squeezes her eyes shut and makes a circular motion around her head. "So I kept thinking and thinking about you two. About why you would date someone like Rebel and why she would agree to date you too. And then it hit me."

I shift from one leg to the other.

"I know exactly why you're doing this." Victoria reaches out again, touching my hand. "Everyone might think you're cold and heartless, but I know you, Gunner. We dated for three years and I experienced firsthand how thoughtful, considerate, and patient you are. You don't say what's on your mind, but your actions speak so loudly—"

I pull my hand away.

Victoria winces, but keeps going. "You don't *actually* care about Rebel. You're doing this so she can join the Ladies. You just feel sorry for her and want to help."

I frown.

Her eyes search mine. "It's okay. I won't tell anyone. But Gunner, there are other ways to get Rebel into the Society. I can talk to your mom and the other Ladies. I can even talk to your uncle and get the mayor's office involved—"

"Victoria," I say gruffly.

She snaps her mouth shut.

I speak as clearly as I can. "You and I are over."

"We can be friends."

"No, we can't."

Her eyes fill with hurt. "Gunner."

"I won't be friends with someone who's doing her best to break up my relationship."

"But Rebel—"

"Is my girlfriend," I say in a tone that brooks no argument.

I'm not with her because I feel sorry for her. I'm not with her because she's pretty. And I'm not with her because she's a prize.

The words pulse through my throat, but I don't set them free. That isn't a conversation that I need to have with my ex. When I share the depth of my feelings, it'll be in front of the person to whom those feelings belong.

I turn away. "Don't waste your time on me anymore."

From the corner of my eye, I see Victoria's shoulders slump.

Though she's hurt right now, I strongly believe she'll get over me. Victoria Pierce has a lot to offer someone. But that 'someone' isn't me.

"Gunner?" My dad's voice stops me as I'm halfway to mom's hospital room.

I stop and wait for dad's long strides to catch up to me. It doesn't take long.

Dad's holding two cups of steaming hot coffee. "I was

wondering where you disappeared to. I thought you took Rebel back to town."

I shake my head.

Dad studies my face and then offers me a cup.

I accept it. "How's mom?"

"She's doing much better."

"When can she leave?" I take a sip of the strong brew. Dad likes it as black as the dirt in the orchard.

"Tomorrow. The doctor said that she needs to avoid stress and anxiety."

I tap my finger on the flimsy paper cup. That'll be a difficult task. Mom works herself into a frenzy over the tiniest details.

Comfortable silence falls between us.

"Son," dad clears his throat, "about last night, I don't blame you. It's normal for adults to want some breathing room."

I study my father's weathered face.

He rubs the back of his neck. "You don't have to tell me where you went if you don't want to…"

"I was rebuilding the treehouse," I answer bluntly.

Dad's eyes widen. Guiltily, he shifts his gaze to the coffee cup.

"I didn't stay out last night because I was mad." I consider my next words. "I did it to avoid another fight with mom."

Not that it did any good. Mom ended up in the hospital because of me.

"I feel responsible for this," dad says, setting a hand on his belt and looking off into the distance. "I'm the one who told you to go after Rebel, and yet I can't show you any support. Your mom's stubborn and she seems hell-bent on disapproving you two." Dad takes a sip. "Carol seems to be of the opinion that you want to replace her."

"That's not it." I square my shoulders and look my father in the eye. "In this world, mom has you to protect her, look after her, and worry about her. I want to be that person for Rebel."

Dad smiles behind his coffee cup. "I didn't know you were so romantic, son."

I rub the back of my neck.

A smile grows on dad's lips. "You know what I find amusing? You and Rebel were thick as thieves when you were," he taps his knee, "yay high? Then you seemed to have some sort of falling out and I barely saw her around. Now you two are together again. Isn't life funny?"

'You need to stay away from that girl, Gunner. Bad things will happen if you keep hanging around with her.'

A cold chill runs down my spine at the memory.

"Gunner?" Dad looks at me in concern. "What's wrong? You look pale."

I shake my head.

Dad gives me a nudge. "Head on home and get some rest."

"Tell mom…"

"I will." Dad shoos me away.

I stumble to the elevator, lost in the memory of that cold windy day. The hospital walls fade out, replaced with the brick of a dark church. I hear pealing church bells and loud sobs. And then the tap-tap-tap of a cane. I remember the feel of bony fingers pressing into my shoulder as if he's there in the elevator with me.

'Bad things will happen'.

To a seven year old boy who still believed in Santa Claus, those words left a deep, dark impression. By the time I was grown enough to question the warning, the damage to my relationship with Rebel was irreparable. She had already grown to hate the sight of me.

Thinking we'd be forever estranged, I never questioned the warning I was given and almost convinced myself to believe that it was my decision to abandon her.

But after only a few days in Rebel's company, there's no escaping the truth.

I should have never cut her out of my life. So why did I?

No, the better question is, why was I forced to?

As I near the hospital parking lot, I hear Uncle Stewart's familiar voice. He's speaking in low, hushed tones.

"I'm pretty sure the Hart girl don't know nothing. No, of course not. Gunner has no clue either."

At the mention of my name, I snap to attention.

"Of course. I have it all under control…" Uncle Stewart whips around and sees me. Guilt strains across his face and he hangs up.

I approach him determinedly. "Who was that?"

"I thought you left."

"Who. Was. It?"

He slips his phone into his pocket and moves past me.

I grab his upper arm. "Why did you mention Rebel's family. What did our family do to hers?"

Uncle Stewart swats my hand off. "Keep your nose out of adult business, boy."

Red fills my vision and I block his path, "Why? Because bad things will happen if I don't?"

Uncle Stewart freezes and turns slowly around to face me.

"What did we do to Rebel's family?" Those foreboding words that cast a shadow over me when I was seven return to haunt me now. An insidious fear winds its way around my spine and claws at my throat. "Tell me."

Uncle Stewart extends a hand.

I stare at his grizzly palm, my eyes narrowed.

"Give me your father's badge first," he snarls.

My eyes whip up to his.

Smugly, he pulls his hand back. "Hand over your uncle's political career. Fire your mother as chairwoman of the Society." His grin sends another chill down my spine. "Then I'll tell you."

CHAPTER
THIRTY-ONE

REBEL

I slap the radiator cap back on the car and stomp to the driver's side so I can turn on the engine.

The car rumbles to life and I listen for the high pitched noise the client complained about. I diagnosed it as a radiator leak, but if the sound continues, I need to investigate deeper.

A throaty roar erupts in the mechanic bay as the engine throttles.

The high-pitched sound is gone.

Machine, 0

Human, 1

I wait for the thrill of another victory.

But the excited gush in the pit of my stomach is missing today.

To be honest, it's been missing all week.

"If you're scowling because of the other noises rattling under the hood, I wouldn't be too hard on yourself," April says, offering me a bottle of water. "The client only asked us to diagnose *that* specific sound."

"I know." I uncap the top and guzzle the water back.

April eyes me up and down. "Then why do you look so mad? Are you okay?"

"I'm fine." I bend into the car and turn off the engine. "The high pitched noise is gone for now, but I still want to take the car on a test drive to be sure. I'll do that after our interview with the new mechanic though."

"Hm." April keeps on watching me.

I check my sparkly pink watch and notice a dirt stain on the band. Avoiding eye contact, I grab a nearby pink rag and wipe the plastic material. "Isn't she supposed to be here for the interview by now?"

Silence meets my question.

My eyes bounce up to April. She's staring at me with a crease between her eyebrows.

"What?" I ask, feeling like she can see right through my act.

"You've been extra testy since Monday."

"I have no idea what you're talking about." I pick up my work tablet and log in.

Since April and I don't have a dedicated office assistant, we've had to keep meticulous notes about the parts we order and the hours spent on the job.

"I thought you'd be happy now that everything is going your way," April says, leaning against the table and resting her chin in her hands.

"I *am* happy," I mumble, ignoring the empty pang in my chest that says otherwise.

"Fine," April waves a hand, "then I thought you'd be *super* happy."

"What do I have to be 'super happy' about?"

"You're kidding me, right?"

I shrug, looking cluelessly at her.

"Rebel, you had an incredibly successful community service day last weekend. The news practically called you the 'New Face of the Lady Luck Society'. Not to mention, the Scooby's Nightmare client believes in you so much, he donated to the Society and put *you* in charge."

"I'm not in charge. The Ladies still expect me to report to them."

"So? You did it! You're helping the very people you wanted to help and the fancy ladies at the Society all play nice with you."

"Except for Carol," I point out.

"Well, yeah, but that's a given. You and the Kinseys don't mix." April pauses. "I mean, except for you and Gunner. For some reason, you two look really good together."

I stiffen. "That name is banned from this garage."

"What? Gunner's?"

"Put two bucks in the bad word jar." I point to the empty pink mug.

April snorts.

I spin on my heels and plod to another car. "Was this the next in our lineup?"

April ignores the question and follows me closely. "Have you been sulking all week because of Gunner?"

"That's four dollars now, missy. And I have not been *sulking*."

"Is it because he left for the playoffs?"

"No. Of course not."

April bursts into belly-deep laughter.

I glare at her. "What's so funny?"

She guffaws harder. "Is this how I looked?"

"Have the car fumes been getting to your head? Do I need to drive you to the nearest hospital?"

"Give me a second." April presses her lips together and struggles to regain a semblance of composure. "The first time Chance left for an away game, I missed him so much, but I never thought *you*…" She stops so she can smack her hand on the table a few times. "This is too good."

"I'm glad you're enjoying yourself," I grumble, checking the tablet for the client's complaints.

"Oh, Rebel, I'm sorry." April rubs her eyes that had gotten glassy with tears. "I don't mean to tease. I'm just shocked. I was sure you and Gunner wouldn't actually fall for each other."

"We haven't. And we never will."

"But... you're acting like this because you miss him," she declares, like an old-timey adventurer discovering a new island.

"You're way, *waaay* wrong. I don't miss him. I'd be happy if I never saw him again."

The humor drains from April's eyes. "Did you two fight?"

"When would we have time to fight? He never talks to me."

She shrugs. "Don't you text?"

"No."

"Call?"

I bristle even further. "I haven't seen or heard from him since last Saturday. He didn't bother telling me he was leaving." The words scrape my mouth like mini-knives and I stab the tablet even harder with my finger.

Astonished silence fills the bay.

"Seriously? He didn't stop by before he left town with the team?"

"No." I inhale shakily, "I found out when I went grocery shopping and saw Gordie with her grandmother."

April shakes her head as her face twists in confusion. "But that... I mean... maybe he..."

"There's no maybe about it. In a town *this* small, there's no feasible reason for me to not even *see* He Who Shall Not Be Named around before he left. Unless he's avoiding me."

I picture the giant hockey player ducking into alleys when he saw me coming in the distance or scurrying through the back door of the Tipsy Tuna when I walked in. Or maybe he spent all his time at the stadium. Whatever he did, I didn't see so much as his shadow for days.

April blinks like her brain is short-circuiting. "Avoiding you? Are you sure?"

"Honestly, this isn't the first time." I think of those embarrassing days chasing Gunner through the Kinsey farm, only for him to act like I was dirt beneath his shoes.

Back then, I was crushed.

"I'm over it. It's my fault for expecting common decency from a Kinsey."

April's shoulders tighten and I can tell she's slipping into protective best friend mode. "I'll ask Chance to talk to him. Even if you're not in a real relationship, he should still communicate."

"Don't bother."

"But—"

Emotions roil in my chest. "He doesn't owe me anything. And it'll only embarrass me if you and Chance act like he hurt me or something."

"But he did."

"It's really not that big of a deal."

"I mean… if you didn't care, you wouldn't be so angry."

I growl out like the She-Hulk, "I'm *not* angry."

April flinches.

I stare at the tablet, the words all blurring together. "Like you said, April, I'm *suuuper* happy."

"Mm-hm."

"I'm so happy, I hope he wins all his games and comes back with an MVP trophy."

My best friend arches an eyebrow. "Really?"

I last all of three seconds.

"Nope. I hope he slips on a banana peel on the ice and goes belly up in the middle of a crowded rink."

April's eyebrows pinch together in the center of her forehead and her lips tremble.

"I hope when he bends down to do his exercises, he rips his pants and that he's wearing his most embarrassing pair of boxers and everyone films it and it goes viral and he ends up being too ashamed to leave his house."

"Ooh. Remind me not to get on *your* bad side," a raspy voice says.

April and I whirl around.

A woman with black hair cut bluntly to her chin, hazel eyes, and lips painted a bright red steps into the bay. She's dressed in motorcycle leather and has a bike helmet nestled against her hip.

My eyes skate past her to the impressive bike parked on the front lawn. There's no mistaking who that machine belongs to. Even if this woman wasn't wearing a leather jacket, leather pants and motorcycle gloves, her wild-child aura would give it away.

"You must be Cordelia?" April smiles with uncertainty and wipes her hands on her navy jumper before extending her hand to the newcomer.

Cordelia takes April's hand. "I go by Delia and yes, that's me."

I take my best friend's lead and try to act like the put-together owner of a garage and not like an uninspired shaman hurling curses around a bonfire.

"I'm Rebel Hart and this is April Brooks. We're the owners of The Pink Garage. It's nice to meet you in person."

"You too." She tips her chin up at me, and I know that I could never be that effortlessly cool in a million years.

"Should we sit?" April suggests, pointing to the contract on the table that we set aside for the interview.

"Oh?" The woman looks surprised. "Do we have more to discuss? I got the understanding that you were satisfied with my references.

April clears her throat. "We are. It's just… you and I chatted about salaries and such over the phone, but I hammered out the details with my business partner and unfortunately…"

To our surprise, Cordelia Davis takes the pen on the table and scribbles her name on the dotted line.

"Don't you want to read it first?" I ask, glancing frantically between her and the contract.

"I can tell who's good people on sight." She surveys me and then studies April. "I'd like to work with you."

April and I exchange looks.

I shrug.

My best friend's lips curl up in relief. "Well," April says, "I guess… welcome to The Pink Garage."

I hurry to the fridge. "I bought pink champagne."

Delia smirks and pulls off her motorcycle gloves. "Save the champagne for later. It's been a while since I got my hands dirty. Do me a favor and point me to a car?"

CHAPTER
THIRTY-TWO

GUNNER

The lawyers that Chance hired to investigate my uncle have no idea how small towns work.

I snarl at each of the suit-cladded, Rolex-touting schmucks, stunned that Chance's well-to-do family keeps them on retainer.

"Ooh." Chance flinches, wagging a finger. "That's his disappointed scowl."

The head of the team, a tall, thin man who looks like he should be an undertaker and not an attorney glances at me.

I shake my head.

Chance interprets. "That's his annoyed scowl now."

I clear my throat.

Chance opens his mouth to say something else.

"I can speak, Chance," I grumble.

He gestures for me to go ahead.

I slide the reports back over to the team. "How did you conduct your investigation?"

"Erm…" The undertaker looks at Chance for approval.

The captain makes a 'go on' motion.

"We compiled a list of former female employees who worked under the establishment within a ten year range."

"And how did you come up with this list?"

The attorney pulls his collar away from his throat. "We conducted a series of interviews."

"With who?" I press.

"The staff at the garage."

I snort out a laugh.

Chance raps his knuckles against the table. "Gentlemen, I'm sure I don't have to tell you that laugh has nothing to do with amusement."

The lawyers shift uncomfortably.

I grind out, "So you spoke to Stewart Kinsey's employees about matters that could possibly incriminate their boss?"

"We didn't ask any leading questions," the lawyer defends.

"You're strangers." My eyes cut through them like samurai knives. "Why would anyone from our town trust you over the man who signs their checks?"

"We didn't just speak to the mechanics. We spread our search further and went to the mayor's office."

I turn slowly in my seat and give Chance a 'you've got to be kidding me' look.

He scratches his neck. "Guys, you *do* realize the Mayor is also a Kinsey."

"We also spoke to the sheriff… who…oh." The lawyer trails off before finishing his statement.

Chance runs his fingers through his hair. "Wow."

"You got nothing from the investigation? Nothing at all?" I ask.

The lawyer's eyes shift from side to side. "Stewart Kinsey, as far as we could tell, has never committed any form of harassment, work place discrimination or—"

"What about tax fraud?"

"W-what?" The lawyer pales as if I accused *him* of shirking the government.

"Or a prior arrest?" I drum my fingers on the table. "Murder?"

Chance pats my shoulder. "O-okay, Gunner. I don't think you're talking to the right team here. These are labor rights and workplace discrimination lawyers, not private investigators or detectives."

I gesture to the reports that basically spell out the word 'angel'. At least in the eyes of the law.

But I know there's got to be more to Uncle Stewart's past.

In his smugness, he confirmed to me that the warning I received when I was seven years old wasn't an exaggeration. If I have any hope of starting a relationship with Rebel, I need to get to the bottom of the mystery first.

The lawyer points to the report. "There are no warrants out for Stewart Kinsey's arrest. He has a few parking tickets, but nothing above average. Not to mention, his family is well-respected and practically rule the town. We couldn't find anything in our initial search."

"Look again," I snap. "And this time," I scribble a name on a piece of paper and slide it over, "see if you can find any connection between them."

"Clarence Kinsey? Who's that?"

I square my shoulders. "My grandfather's brother."

If Uncle Stewart's past is squeaky clean, that tells me one thing—he's just a pawn in the game. Which makes sense. He's far too impatient and clumsy to conceive a plot against anyone. He wasn't even smart enough to deny my accusations outside the hospital.

A part of me wishes he had.

At least then, I could have run to Rebel and told her how I really feel.

But how can I hold her hand, look in her sky-blue eyes and pretend that I can protect her when my family carries such a dark secret?

The real player moving us around the chest board is someone else. And I bet *his* papers won't be as sparkly as Uncle Stewart's.

"Is this in conjunction with the workplace discrimination case?" the lawyer asks, arching an eyebrow at Chance.

"Do you have a problem with that?" our captain asks tightly. The smile on his lips fools no one.

The attorney swallows. "No, not at all, Mr. McLanely."

"We'll look forward to your call." Chance nods to the door.

I follow him out of the conference room, my boots scuffing on the shiny marble floor. The law firm sits at the top of a tall, opulent building. The vaulted ceilings, giant offices, and impressive view of the downtown area speak of immeasurable wealth.

We pass a wall filled with pictures of the firm's founders and the current and past associates.

"They're the best in the business," Chance tells me as we walk past the wall. "I'm sure they'll find something."

I grunt. "Have you noticed?"

"Noticed what?"

"For a legal team that focuses on gender equality and workplace discrimination, they don't have one female lawyer on the team."

Chance takes a look at the wall and his face blanches. "I'll hire a new firm."

"Do what you want." I pass him and head into the sunshine.

It's our last day before we head back to Lucky Falls and I still haven't done any shopping. Mom nags me if I don't bring back a souvenir for her, so it's become a habit of mine.

"How's your mom doing?" Chance asks, ignoring the whispers that follow in his wake. The fact that no one has stopped to take a picture with him is a small miracle.

"She's good," I answer dryly.

Lately, she's been hinting that Victoria is talking about moving back to the city, as if she expects me to do something about it.

She's also been complaining about the Ladies going behind

her back and giving Rebel the authority to work with Rodney Howard, a donor that asked to work exclusively with her.

When mom complains about Rebel, I usually turn the phone off or skip past that section of her voice message. At this point, I might discover gold on the moon before I find a way for mom and Rebel to get along.

"I miss April," Chance says, his voice breaking into my thoughts as we approach the crosswalk.

I miss Rebel.

But I can't say that out loud.

I don't even *deserve* to feel the way I do.

Does mom know about what our family did to Rebel's? is a question that runs circles in my mind. *Does dad know? Does Uncle Rodney? Does Uncle Kit? How many of the people I love are in on this?*

I could come right out and ask, but I don't want to tip off Uncle Stewart to my investigation. And, honestly, I'm not brave enough to ask my parents—especially my dad—about this yet. It would crush me if the two people I love and look up to the most, had anything to do with hurting Rebel Hart.

"You know," Chance says casually, "April mentioned that you were dodging Rebel before we left town."

I keep walking.

"I heard Rebel was pretty upset about it."

I stop short.

Chance smirks at me. "So that got your attention, huh?"

I lift a finger and point at a shop window.

In the display is a fluffy rug, feather boas, and a comforter set all in the same shade of bubble-gum pink. On the frosted glass, printed in a simple font, is one beautiful word—*Pinkies.*

Chance's face crumbles. "Nope. No. No way. I'm not going in there."

A group of teenagers pass by, giggling as they enter the shop.

I take a step forward.

Chance makes a run for it. "I'll meet you at the hotel."

I drag him by the elbow and pull him back. "I'm not going in there alone."

"It'll be weirder if we go in there together," Chance hisses.

"So call Renthrow. The three of us can go in."

Chance looks at me like I'm crazy. And then he gives it a second thought. "Deal."

I wait while he makes the call and, faintly, from the cell phone speaker, I hear Renthrow ask, "Think they'll have anything Hello-Kitty themed in there?"

"Uh…" Chance gives me an inquisitive look.

I nod, which could be considered a lie. But hey, if there's anywhere that Hello Kitty products would be sold, it would be in a shop called *Pinkies*.

Chance tells Renthrow confidently. "You bet."

The single dad grunts. "I'll be there in ten."

CHAPTER
THIRTY-THREE

REBEL

I ADJUST THE COLLAR OF MY PINK BUTTON DOWN SHIRT AND LOOK myself over in the mirror. I went with business casual for my nine a.m. meeting with Rodney Howard, so I'm pairing the pink shirt with a smart black pencil skirt and pink kitty pumps.

Is it too much? Not enough?

I reach for the blazer again. Holding up the jacket to my face, I debate it and then return to my original decision.

No blazer it is.

I send the jacket flying across the room and it lands on one of the many clothing heaps on the ground.

All that's left is makeup.

Nerves make my fingers shake as I apply my mascara.

"Come on. Come on," I mutter, wiggling my arm out and leaning toward the mirror to try again.

My hands still shake.

I give up on the mascara and simply coat my lips in a strawberry-scented lipgloss. It's no big loss. When it comes to business meetings, less is more anyway.

Mom shows up when I'm leaving my apartment. "Hi, honey. I brought you breakfast. I figured you'd be too busy to eat."

"Thanks, mom." I accept the plastic bag from her without looking inside. Hustling toward my car, I moan, "I'm late."

"You're early."

"Not if there's traffic."

"You'll be fine."

I freeze and jog back to the stairway. "I forgot my folder."

"You mean, that folder?" Mom points.

I look down and see the folder in my grip.

"I'm losing it."

"You're spiraling. Just slow down for a second."

I check my watch. "I don't have time."

"You have time, Rebel."

"What if I choke? I'm a mechanic, not a motivational speaker."

"Just breathe through it. Do exactly what you practiced with me and you'll have them opening their wallets faster than a tornado snatching a roof."

"Thanks, mom." I shuffle past her to my car. "And how do you know what I practiced last night? You slept through most of it."

Mom smiles guiltily. "In my defense, you practiced the same speech for two hours."

She has a point.

"But," mom adds, "if I had millions in my bank account, I would have been *riveted* by every word."

I laugh out loud.

"Remember," she smoothes down my collar with a veiny hand, "you're one of the Ladies now. That means you're a respected member of Lucky Falls. Don't let those city slickers intimidate you."

I open the door of my truck and it creaks loudly. "I'll call you when the meeting's over."

Mom makes a 'go on' gesture.

As I drive, I mentally run over my speech. This is my first official meeting on behalf of the Ladies. Though my position in the Society is still shaky, it doesn't change how important today is. I have to ace this.

April calls a few minutes later.

"Have you left yet?"

"I'm already on the freeway," I inform her, reaching across the seat to munch on mom's breakfast.

"You're early."

"There's traffic."

"You're nervous," she says with a laugh. "Breathe."

"That's an involuntary action. Give me something I can *really* do."

"Wait a second, let me think about it," April murmurs. "How about... breathe *slowly*."

I chuckle. "Thanks for allowing me another day off." Sheepishly, I admit, "I feel like I'm always working on cars after hours to make up for all these other projects."

"It's no big deal."

"I should be doing more to help run the shop."

"Hey, you still get the job done—even if it's a little later at night. And besides, you're not just a mechanic. You're, like, Joan of Arc if she wore pink jumpsuits and had blonde hair."

I bark out a laugh. "Thanks... I guess? I'm just glad we have Cordelia to fill in when I'm not there."

"Yeah, she doesn't have much experience working in a garage, but she's got lots of promise."

That's true.

Cordelia Davis came to Lucky Falls with something to prove. Every day ,she arrives early to the garage and leaves very, very late at night. And I know, because I'm right there catching up with work late at night too.

Her approach to diagnosis is totally different than mine or April's. While April uses scanners and shop manuals with intricate wiring diagrams and I use intuition and eyeballing,

Cordelia is the type who systematically fixes one area of the car, takes notes, and then fixes another area until she hits the right path.

It's a *much* longer route and less effective too. But April plans to teach her a better method for diagnosis. With Cordelia's dogged determination, she'll outpace both April and I in no time.

"I really want to do this right." I adjust my fingers on the steering wheel.

"You will. You've been working so hard on this presentation. They'll be blown away by your brilliance."

By the time I pull my car into the basement parking lot and take the elevator up to Rodney Howard's firm, I'm a lot more confident.

A receptionist greets me when I step into the lobby. She dips her chin and gestures for me to follow her down a hallway. I'm impressed that she knows who I am since I didn't give her my name and I obediently trail her through the corridor.

On the way, I mumble my speech under my breath. *"Since the drought last summer, Lucky Falls farmers have been hit the hardest..."*

"In here," the receptionist says.

I nod and push the door open.

"There she is!" Rodney Howard is seated at the head of a long, mahogany table. He pushes to his feet and rounds the desk to approach me, a warm smile on his lips.

"Mr. Rodney."

He reaches for my hand and I expect to give him a firm handshake. Instead, he claps my fingers and gives me a fatherly squeeze.

My eyes dart to his in surprise.

"Gentlemen," Rodney waves to the five older men sitting around the table in suits, "this is Rebel Hart, a female mechanic based in Lucky Falls and the woman who orchestrated one of the best days of my life—the day I got my son back."

"Oh, it's nothing so dramatic," I say nervously, glancing

around. I don't see any projectors in the room. Leaning toward Mr. Rodney, I whisper, "Do you have a projector? If not, it's okay, but I was hoping to share some pictures of the farms and communities in need."

Mr. Rodney shakes his head subtly and grins, leading me to the table of businessmen.

I find his reaction strange but, until I have a clearer picture of what's going on, I have no choice but to stumble along.

"Rebel, this is Vivesh Nandwani. He's my business partner and the man who invested in me when no one else would."

"Pleasure to meet you, Ms. Hart. I've never met a female mechanic before." He bobs his head, staring at me like I'm half fish, half woman.

"Nice to meet you."

The next man who's introduced is so big, his shirt button is holding on for dear life. At any second, that poor button will burst and smack me in the middle of my forehead.

"This is Henry Griffith," Mr. Rodney says.

"No wonder your son fell head over heels, Rod. She's a beaut!" Mr. Griffith takes my hand in his sweaty palm.

I smile in discomfort and pull my hand back.

Mr. Rodney introduces me to everyone in the room. They all grin, crack jokes or compliment my appearance.

While their overt friendliness should have set me at ease, it only confuses me. This feels more like I'm being paraded around at a family function, not a business meeting.

Did I misunderstand the assignment?

Realizing that I'll need to take control of the meeting and get us back on track, I walk to the head of the table.

"Ehem."

The men stop and stare at me.

"Your time is precious gentlemen, so I'd like to get started. I'm here on behalf of the Lady Luck Society—"

Mr. Rodney hurries around the table. "Rebel, Rebel."

I stop.

"There's no need for that. Today's meeting is simply a formality."

I blink slowly. "I don't understand."

"Rodney, I think your daughter-in-law should move here and take over the company's NGO division," Vivesh Nandwani says. "With her face, she won't even have to say a word. People will instantly throw cash at the charity."

I gawk. "I'm sorry. Did you say 'daughter-in-law'?"

"Gentlemen." Mr. Rodney flashes the room a sheepish look.

Henry Griffith guffaws. "Rod, were you boasting about it to everyone *but* her?"

My heart lurches in my chest and I feel like I'm about to throw up. "W-what do you mean?" I turn to Mr. Rodney. "What are they talking about?"

"That's enough." Mr. Rodney nods at Henry Griffith. "This is why you're on your third marriage."

Henry Griffith throws his hands up.

Mr. Rodney gestures for me to follow him outside.

My chest swells and contracts as the truth sets in.

No one wants to hear what I have to say. All the nights I stayed up working on my speech, interviewing the community, perfecting my presentation—it was all for nothing.

I stop in the middle of the hallway.

Mr. Rodney notices and turns to face me.

I inhale shakily, feeling my throat tighten with unshed tears. "Mr. Rodney, I think there's been a misunderstanding."

"Rebel, please don't let what my friends said rattle you. I admit, I went ahead of myself and shared my wishful thinking about you and Benji, but it was nothing more than the musings of an old man. We are one hundred percent making that donation to the town. It has nothing to do with… other things."

"What other things?" I demand.

"Can we talk in my office?"

"No." I stand firm. "We'll talk right here."

He sighs and gives in. "I wasn't there for my son for years.

The day I repaired things with Benji, I made a vow that I would give my son whatever he desired. That's the only way I can repay him."

"And what exactly does Benji want?" I ask, my heart in my throat.

Mr. Rodney slips a hand into his pocket and looks down at his shoes.

My heart stammers in my chest because I already know the answer. Today's meeting was never about helping Lucky Falls. All that matters to Mr. Rodney is that his son thinks I'm pretty.

Once again, that's all I amount to. It's all I'm good for.

"So you thought," my voice turns scratchy, "that you could *buy* a relationship for your son?"

"I admit, that does sound rather vulgar, but I truly don't mean any offense. I admire you greatly, Rebel. You're smart, ambitious and gifted at repairing cars. The fact that Benji cares for you is no surprise to me. I simply wanted to help you two along by showing you how... advantageous our family could be to you."

I back away from him, sick to my stomach. "I apologize for wasting your time, Mr. Rodney, but I don't date people for their money and I certainly can't be bought."

"Rebel, Rebel, please. I truly didn't mean it in that way." Mr. Rodney scrambles to keep up with me, his eyes panicked. And I know, even in this moment, he's not worried about hurting my feelings, but about how my negative reaction to this will affect Benji. "I apologize. I won't bring this up ever again."

I keep going.

He jumps in front of me, pleading. "Can you please not tell Benji about this? He would be very upset if he knew."

I fight back tears of hurt.

"Please, Rebel," Rodney Howard says.

I swallow past the lump in my throat. "I won't tell him."

"Thank you." Mr. Rodney sags with relief. "I hope you won't

hold today against me or Benji. Perhaps, as you two get to know each other naturally, you can draw closer and—"

"That isn't going to happen," I say firmly.

Rodney Howard's eyebrows shoot up. "Why not? Is there something about Benji you don't like? You can tell him and—"

"I have a boyfriend," I snap. "Let me know if that affects your donation. I'll inform the Ladies when I get back to town."

CHAPTER
THIRTY-FOUR

GUNNER

As the bus zooms past the 'Welcome to Lucky Falls' sign, I unzip the front pocket of my backpack and grab the pink velvet jewelry case. Unclasping the lock, I open the case and touch the thin silver necklace with the pink gemstone.

The moment I saw it, I knew that it belonged to Rebel. The big question is… how do I get her to accept it?

A phone rings.

I snap the jewelry box closed and search for my cell.

Renthrow's sitting next to me and he does the same.

"It's a video call." Renthrow points to his device. "Do you mind…?"

I shrug.

He swipes a thumb over the screen and smiles brightly.

It still freaks me out the way Renthrow changes on a dime when it comes to Gordie. He goes from grim and grumpy, to smiling toothily in a second.

"Hi, sweetheart," Renthrow says, throwing his daughter a wave.

"Hi, daddy." A sweet voice sings through the quiet bus.

Every head swings upward on command.

"Is that Gordie?" Theilan yells from the back of the bus. "Hey-o, Gordie!"

"Hey, Gordie!" Watson, who's sitting behind us, pops his head up to see the screen.

"This is a private conversation," Renthrow growls, but his voice lacks the bite that he intends.

"Nah, Gordie would rather talk to her favorite uncle than to boring old dad," Watson argues.

"What's up, Gordie?" Chance leans across the aisle to push a hand at the screen.

Gordie laughs sweetly and sings, "Hi, everyone!"

"Enough." Renthrow yells at the team. "Give me a second, pumpkin. Let me plug in my headphones."

Enthusastic *boos!* ring from the entire bus.

I turn my face to the window and smile softly.

"Daddy are you here yet?"

"We just rolled into town. I'll be there very soon." Renthrow's voice thickens with concern. "Why? Is something wrong?"

"Miss Candice was asking."

My ears perk up.

Chance gives Renthrow a pointed look.

Max clears his throat.

"Why was your teacher asking for me?" Renthrow asks, as clueless as a newb on his first play. "Did you get in trouble at school, pumpkin?"

"No." She giggles. "Miss Candice always asks about you. I think she likes you, daddy."

Ooohs break out next.

Twin circles of red flush across Renthrow's face and he mumbles, "I should have used the stupid headphones."

"*Gordie!*" Someone calls from the background.

"Gotta go, daddy. We're baking brownies."

"Save one for me!" Theilan yells.

"I'll see you soon, pumpkin," Renthrow says and then he ends the call.

A wolf whistle erupts from the back of the bus.

Theilan's voice rings with mischief. "Candice Pott? What does she see in the likes of you, Renthrow?"

"Maybe it's like Beauty and the Beast?" Watson teases.

"Must be," Theilan agrees, laughing loudly.

I think of the slim, cheerful kindergarten teacher. She's the polar opposite of Renthrow who's on the gruff, quiet side. However, what matters is that Candice is good with kids.

Renthrow ignores the commotion about his love life, and eventually, the bus quiets down. Theilan, especially, only pokes at people who give him a response and Renthrow's perfected the art of acting like he doesn't care.

The bus chugs to a stop in front of the arena.

Bobby swings around from the driver's seat, a smile etched into his dark face. "Alright, fellas. This is your stop. Make sure to swing by The Tipsy Tuna sometime today. Mauve's got a welcome home drink, courtesy of us."

The team cheers.

I smile and nod my thanks.

Max gets up next. He claps his hands together to bring us to attention. "Alright, guys. We got some decent momentum going, but we're still a few points short. This last game will determine whether we make it to the finals. So there will be no slacking off. I expect everyone…"

"… *at morning practice five am tomorrow*," the team finishes for him.

Max's mouth flicks up in a grin. "Exactly."

We dismount the bus.

Renthrow takes off to his truck, speeding to see his little girl.

Theilan and Watson head straight to the Tuna to soak in the local praise and grab some drinks.

"You want a ride?" Max offers me, pointing to his truck.

Chance passes us at that moment, his phone glued to his ear.

"I'm back, Tink. Are you at the garage? I'm coming over." He sees me watching and lifts a hand. "See you later, guys."

Is Chance going to the garage?

I picture Rebel working in her pink jumper, her hair pulled back into a ponytail and her blue eyes narrowed in concentration.

"Gunner?" Max says. "Car's this way."

"We're not going in the same direction," I mumble to Max and then I take off after Chance.

"What are you talking about? I live fifteen minutes away from you!" Max yells at my back.

I catch up to Chance fast. "Can I get a ride?"

He motions for me to get into his Lamborghini.

The first time I got a ride with Chance, I couldn't figure out how to open the door. Now, I easily engage the latch and slide in.

As soon as Chance starts his car, his phone connects to the speaker system and April's voice blasts through the car.

"She was *so* upset, Chance. I had to beg her not to drive. I called one of those sober-driver chauffeur services to pick her up instead."

Instantly, all my nerves tighten and I sit straight up. "Are you talking about Rebel?"

The line goes quiet.

Chance looks over at me and winces.

"Chance, is Gunner in the car with you?" April shrieks.

"Uh… yeah."

"Why didn't you *tell* me!"

"What happened to Rebel?" I demand.

"Oh. *Now* you care?"

"April."

"What?" she snaps.

"Tell me."

"Or what?"

April Brooks is a fierce little thing and she sounds like she's ready to reach through the cell phone and grab me by my collar.

"You don't intimidate me, Gunner. I don't care if you're a Kinsey. I don't answer to you."

"I'm not trying to intimidate anyone. Just... please. What happened to Rebel?" My voice breaks on the last word.

I'm already imagining the worst.

What if Uncle Stewart found out I'm investigating our family? What if he decided to make good on the threat of 'bad things' happening as a result? What if Rebel got hurt because of me?

"Tink," Chance's voice is coaxing, "Gunner's about to have a heart attack over here. I think you should tell him."

I lean forward, staring at the fancy dashboard display and waiting on pins and needles for April to speak.

She pushes the words out reluctantly, "Rebel got an opportunity to pitch her community service project to a bunch of wealthy businessmen. She stayed up late for days, practiced her speech, and put her heart and soul into doing a good job."

The knot in my chest loosens with every word from April's mouth. This has nothing to do with Uncle Stewart or my family. That's good.

Then...

Why was Rebel so distraught she couldn't even drive her car?

"Did she get rejected?" I ask, frowning.

"Not exactly," April says. "She was accepted... without having to present at all."

"I don't understand."

"That's all I'll say for now. Chance, I'll call Rebel again. It's been a while since I talked to her and I want to check in."

"I'm almost at the mechanic shop," Chance says. "I'll wait with you until Rebel comes."

Chance steps on the gas and I wish he'd go even faster.

What did April mean by that last statement? Rebel got the funding without having to do anything? That doesn't sound like something that would make her cry. Unless one of the men came on to her? Is that it? Did someone do or say something inappropriate to her?

My fingers fist at my sides.

Chance parks the car in front of the mechanic shop and I notice a motorcycle glinting in the sunshine.

That's not the only vehicle parked outside.

I recognize Benji's fancy black car from that day at the community project. He sprints out of the vehicle, hurrying into the garage.

"Isn't that…" Chance is saying.

I'm already hopping out and storming into the auto shop.

An unfamiliar woman with short black hair looks up from behind an open hood. Her eyes skate past me, flit to Benji and then widen. She ducks her head under the hood again and doesn't look up once.

I ignore her and look across the bay just in time to see April send Benji a scalding look.

"What are you doing here?" the female mechanic fumes.

Chance walks in, his eyes narrowing. "Sounds like my girlfriend wants you to leave."

The tension in the air is high.

I stand beside our team captain, my arms folded over my chest and my heart speeding up from the anticipation of a fight. I've been searching high and low for a reason to punch Benji in the face and I feel like my time might be coming.

Unfortunately, April puts her hand on Chance's arm and whispers, "It's fine."

My fists twitch in disappointment.

Benji looks haggard. "Is Rebel here?"

"No, she hasn't gotten back yet."

He runs a hand through his hair, his voice faint. "I heard what happened at the meeting. I drove straight over to clear things up."

"There's no need, Benji. Your dad made everything exceptionally clear."

"I had no idea he would pull something like this. Honestly."

"Tell that to Rebel, not to me."

Actually, I'd prefer if he kept a five mile distance from Rebel at all times.

Benji scrapes his hands through his hair again. "Rebel's not answering my calls. Can you please tell her I need to speak with her. I'll wait at the burger place. I'll wait as long as it takes."

"No need. I'm right here," an upbeat voice says.

We all turn to face the door.

Rebel strides in. She looks stunning in a pink blouse and a black skirt that shows off her long, toned legs. Her hair's twisted up into a bun, allowing my eyes to scour every inch of her face.

She's… smiling.

But those eyes… they're not crinkling at all.

"Rebel," Benji says, taking an unconscious step forward.

I slam a hand in front of him, barring his way.

The movement draws Rebel's attention to me. Her blue eyes widen and then narrow in calculation. A second later, the plastic smile on her face widens, "Baby, you're back!"

B-baby? I gawk at her.

"Did she just call him 'baby'?" April whispers to Chance.

Rebel makes a running leap toward me.

The entire world gets fuzzy at the edges except for the sight of her lean arms swinging back and forth and her heels thudding against the concrete floor.

My heart slows to match each rhythmic beat of her feet on the ground.

Thud, thud, thud.

A second later, Rebel collides into me.

I stumble back, placing both hands on her hips to steady her while fighting to keep my own balance. In a fluid motion, her arms wrap around my neck, bringing my head down just as she pulses to the tips of her toes.

Without warning, our lips crash together in a harsh, searing kiss.

CHAPTER
THIRTY-FIVE

REBEL

Act like everything's okay. Act like everything's okay.

The phrase pounds like a drumbeat in my head as I run straight to Gunner.

His look of utter confusion should have been enough warning to stop, to get ahold of myself.

But I'm not thinking straight.

My body is on autopilot and my mind is still stuck in that boardroom. Disappointment cuts me to the quick and I feel lower than dirt.

But what does it matter? I got the donation, didn't I? I won, didn't I? Marjorie White and the other ladies are going to guarantee my seat on the Society, aren't they?

My entire life, I've heard the same thing:

"There are worse things than being pretty, Rebel."

"Oh? No one listens to you because you're so pretty?"

"Oh poor, pretty Rebel. Life must be so hard for you, huh?"

No one will fully understand why this morning hurt me so much. No one, except April, will really care anyway.

Why bother explaining to them?

Why waste my breath?

It's better if I don't break down in front of them, better if I brush it off and act like the painful words and the cold dismissals don't leave a dent. At least that way, I won't be judged or told I'm superficial for wishing the world would take me seriously.

At least then, I can tell myself that they're right. That it's okay to be ignored, talked over, and misjudged because of other people's assumptions.

It's okay.

Everything's okay.

Even if it's not, I'm too pretty to be sad or upset—at least, that's what I've been told.

So I wrap my arms around the neck of a blue-eyed hockey player who hates me.

I pull his lips to mine and I seal it with a kiss.

This is the script I wrote for myself.

Rebel Hart and Gunner Kinsey. This is the lie people need to believe.

Is Benji watching?

I keep my lips pressed to Gunner's. Lifelessly, I go through the motions of the kiss and hope it's convincing enough. The best thing I can do right now is prove to Benji that I'm in a happy, committed relationship.

At least, if I have a boyfriend, he'll finally back off and I won't have to bear the humiliation of being the girl 'for sale'.

Gunner's grip on my hip tightens and he nudges me back an inch. As he pushes me away, embarrassment snatches the courage from under my feet.

My good sense returns.

What the heck am I doing?

Panic roars louder than an overheating engine and I look up at Gunner, noticing the storm in his pale blue eyes.

Is he angry?

I wince and hang my head, preparing to step back.

But Gunner stops me by framing his large hands on my face and lifting my chin. His lips descend on mine tenderly.

No chaos.

No wild, untamed emotions.

It's so, so gentle that I can barely breathe.

His mouth cups mine like a quiet symphony, as if he's tasting my pain and heartache. A rough, calloused thumb brushes across my cheek, soothing me like a warm blanket on a cold night.

You matter is what his kiss whispers to me. *You matter, Rebel.*

I might be completely delusional and reading way more into the kiss than is really there, but something inside me releases. A tear rolls down my cheek.

Before I'm ready, Gunner pulls away and wraps me in a protective hug. I melt into his massive body, clinging to him while his tree-trunk arms and brawny chest completely block out the world.

"Rebel," Benji's voice seeps in from somewhere beyond the warm cocoon.

"We're leaving," Gunner announces in his deep, intimidating voice. I feel the rumble of his words travel from his chest.

"But, I need to talk to…"

I glance up and see Gunner skewering Benji with a glare that could fillet a fish on the grill. The other man clamps his mouth shut.

My composure restored, I inhale a deep breath and turn to Benji.

In a blink, I flick my smile 'ON'. "Sorry, Benji. Now's not a good time. My *boyfriend* just came back home, so I can't talk now."

Benji swallows hard. "Rebel, I know what you're doing. I know my dad made things weird. Just five minutes. I only need five—"

"We can meet up later," I clip.

Gunner makes a growly sound in protest.

I ignore that and glance at April. "Do you mind if I…"

"Go."

I smile gratefully.

The man at April's side looks at me with concern.

I nod at him. "Welcome back, Chance."

He smiles slightly.

I throw a wave at Cordelia who's been ducking behind the hood of a truck for the entire conversation.

Satisfied that I'm giving the best performance of my life, I keep my smile in place and tug Gunner out of the garage.

Sunshine warms the top of my head and forces me to squint. Cars zip by, carrying normal people living their normal lives to normal destinations. Despite how tumultuous the past five hours have been, it calms me to see that the world is still turning. The sky isn't falling. I'll be okay.

I feel a presence beside me and then Gunner rumbles, "Where's your truck?"

"Why?"

"Keys." He holds out a hand.

I frown, but he doesn't seem like he's in the mood to argue and, since I did spring a kiss on him without permission, I figure it's fair to let him grunt and growl and throw his weight around. Just this once.

Gunner accepts my keys and surprises me by setting his hand on the small of my back. The air rushes from my lungs as he guides me to my car and opens the door for me. I recall that he did the same thing after we left the game together that night.

After I settle in, he jogs around the truck to the driver's side. The entire car rocks when he folds his giant body into the driver's seat.

Gunner drives in total silence. I twist my bracelet around and around on my wrist, unsure of what to say to him. He ignored me before he left for the playoffs, and it spoke volumes. He literally can't stand the sight of me.

And yet…

I kissed him in front of his team captain and Benji.

If the roles were reversed, and someone I despised put his lips on me without permission, I'd be furious.

I'd probably even sue.

Nerves tighten in my stomach. What if Gunner tries to sue me for harassment?

I imagine getting carted off to the station by Gunner's father.

He did kiss me back though. And he even hugged me.

So… is he angry about the kiss or not?

I stare at the side of Gunner's face, watching his jaw clench and unclench. What on earth is this man thinking? I'd drain my bank account to know.

Gunner swings the car into the parking lot of the grocery store and hops out. I scramble to open my door too, but he's already ten steps ahead of me and disappearing inside the building. It seems he doesn't require my assistance.

As I wait, I take out my phone and see messages from Marjorie White.

MARJORIE: *Rodney Howard's office just called asking for the bank account of the Lady Luck Society.*

MARJORIE: *Rodney Howard will send the money next week.*

MARJORIE: *Our next Society meeting is in three days.*

My stomach roils and I quickly shut my phone off and turn it face down.

The creaking of the driver's side door alerts me to Gunner's return. He tosses the plastic bag into the back seat before I can take a peek at what he bought.

We drive some more, following the road that leads to the Kinsey farm.

My stomach twists into knots. I don't want to go one-on-one with Carol Kinsey right now. But Gunner doesn't turn into his parents' driveway and keeps going through the orchard and toward a familiar route.

"Are we going to the treehouse?" I ask him, my heart beating wildly.

Gunner stops the car. "We'll have to walk the rest of the way."

I guess that's a 'yes'.

Throwing my door open, I prepare to jump out of the truck when Gunner appears in front of me. My heart stops beating when he bends a knee and takes my foot in his hands. His thumb brushes my ankle and a consuming heat zings straight to my heart.

I watch his shoulders, ripped with muscles, tighten as he hesitates for a second and then he slowly pulls my heels off. His eyes skip over my pink polished toenails before he sets the heels aside.

Next, Gunner reaches for something in the grocery bag and pulls out the softest pair of pink slippers I've ever seen. My nerves stretch tight as he adorns my feet with the slippers.

"Who was it?" Gunner asks in a dark voice.

I startle.

"Who made you so upset you couldn't drive back?"

"Why? Are you going to fight them?"

"Maybe." His eyes are hard as marbles and I don't have a single doubt in my mind that he'll drive all the way to the city to avenge me.

I lean forward, setting my hand on his shoulder. "No one bothered me."

"If they touched you…" His fingers curl into fists.

"They didn't. It wasn't like that. I swear."

He looks up, his blue eyes burning into me.

The tension between us snaps and crackles like an engine consuming fuel.

Does he hate me or not?

Do I hate him or not?

Nothing Gunner Kinsey does makes sense. Nothing that I feel when I'm around him makes sense either.

A blush inches across my face the longer he stares at me. To hide the reaction, I hop out of the car but, since Gunner is still kneeling and he's a giant of a man, that puts us at the same height.

We're a breath away from each other.

His lips are close.

Too close.

Because of our kisses—two and counting now—I'm hyper aware of his mouth and how soft it felt against mine.

Not that I care.

Not that it will happen again.

Gunner closes the gap between us, his eyes steady on me.

My heart ricochets with nerves, but I don't step back.

I don't cover my mouth this time either.

As he leans in, I lean forward just an inch and, to my surprise, Gunner freezes abruptly.

My eyebrows hike in a *what?*

His eyes slide down my face like a caress and then his lips tug up in a smirk. A moment later, he reaches for something behind me and pulls out my laptop bag. Then he stands to his full height.

Horrified, I step away from him, my skin buzzing as if he'd actually kissed me. "Why are you taking my laptop?"

"I want to hear it."

"Hear what?"

He hands me the laptop and tilts his head slightly. "Your presentation."

CHAPTER
THIRTY-SIX

GUNNER

"Here? Now?" Rebel asks, a question mark in her eyes.

I nod.

"That's so awkward. I can't."

"Alright then." I shrug.

"Wait." She clears her throat and worries her bottom lip for a moment.

I force my gaze to her eyes.

That mouth is dangerous territory.

But to be fair, *every* part of this woman is dangerous territory.

Didn't realize I was a feet person until about, five seconds ago, but the moment I saw Rebel's pink nail polish...

I knew I didn't need to be keeping my eyes there either.

"Okay, fine," she sighs heavily. "But only because you begged."

I watch her step back a few paces and hold the laptop up with one arm.

"Oh, keep in mind that I haven't given a presentation since high school."

I nod.

She starts her speech, and I lock in like it's the finals of the '87 Canada Cup.

Rebel is as fascinating as a televised hockey game. And I'm not just saying that because of my feelings for her.

As an athlete, the gap between professionals is hard to see because everyone at the top is separated by a tenth of a degree. But the gap between professionals and amateurs is pretty wide.

And Rebel Hart is no amateur. It's clear that she's been training for this moment.

As she presents, she doesn't stammer over her words or second-guess her points. She speaks clearly, boldly and passionately. Her love for the community she wants to serve screams from every pore and stirs the soul.

She was born to be the face of a movement.

As she brings the presentation to a close, I start clapping.

She blushes fiercely.

"That was incredible," I say.

Rebel battles a smile. "I'm sure I have a lot of room for improvement."

I shake my head, blown away. The first time I ever swung a hockey stick, I hit myself in the face. This is definitely not the equivalent of a 'first time'.

"What was the account number again?" I open my phone. "I want to donate."

A genuine smile eases across Rebel's face. She laughs and shakes her head. "Your family is the backbone of the Lady Luck Society. You're already donating tons of money. And time. And effort."

It doesn't matter. After that speech, I need to donate more.

Rebel stretches her arms over her head. Something about her seems looser, freer now. "Wow. Doing the presentation actually made me feel a lot better."

Good. That was the point.

Her eyes slide to me and, when I stare back at her, she blushes even harder.

"Um…" She hesitantly darts past me and locks her laptop back in the bag. "So, what now?"

I lean against the truck and shrug. I didn't exactly run out of The Pink Garage with a plan.

"Are the shoes comfortable?" I ask.

Rebel glances down and wiggles her toes. "Yeah. They're great."

I slip a hand into my pocket, wondering if now is the time to give her the gift but, unfortunately, Rebel scurries past me in the direction of the tree house.

"No way!" she squeals, staring in delight at the renovations.

And I can't help it.

I smile.

Watching those baby blues sparkle harder than the sunshine makes me feel like I'm walking on clouds. Her exuberance is contagious, and I'm glad to see the excitement return to her eyes. The fake smiles and forced cheerfulness she had in the garage drove me up a wall.

Rebel swings around. "The last time I was here, this thing was two seconds away from falling apart. What changed?"

"Nothing much."

"Come on, Gunner. This place was a dump."

"The foundation was always strong," I tell her. "What you see now was always there."

Rebel glances up at me, a flush rising in her face.

My heart jolts at the sight. I wanted to kiss her so badly at the truck.

I want to kiss her now.

But I made the decision to keep my distance until I figure out the truth behind our family history.

And I'm sticking to it.

No matter how tempting she is.

Keep your hands to yourself, Kinsey.

"Were you the one who worked on it?"

I nod.

"When?"

"After our last home game."

She gasps. "You didn't go home that night because you were repairing this place?"

I nod again.

"Are you crazy?" She throws her hands wide. "Why would you do that? What if you'd gotten hurt out here in the middle of the night? And why on *earth* did you come to the community clean-up after working so hard on the treehouse? No wonder you conked out at the hospital. You were running on fumes. What were you *thinking?*"

I smile harder.

Rebel plants her hands on her hips. "I'm not laughing with you, Gunner Kinsey. Don't think you're invincible because you have all those muscles. That was really dangerous."

She's worrying about me.

It's adorable.

Pleased, I jut my chin at the ladder. "Need a hoist up?"

"Absolutely not." She looks offended. "Climbing trees is like riding a bike." She taps her head. "You never really forget."

I smirk and watch her approach the ladder confidently. She plants her foot on the bottom rung and pulls herself up.

I admit. It's impressive.

The higher she climbs, however, the more her skirt bunches up, showing off more and more of her shapely calves.

I'm terminally attracted to Rebel Hart and flashing all that skin doesn't help me in my goal of keeping my hands off her. Desire rears its ugly head, demanding I drink her in. But I beat it back and force myself to be a gentleman.

I avert my gaze until she makes it to the top.

"Haha!" Rebel rejoices, pointing down at me. "Told you."

I blow out a long breath and join her on the porch.

"Wow." Rebel's eyelashes flutter and she leans against the

railing, soaking in the view. "I'd forgotten how peaceful it was out here."

I stand beside her, looking at the canopy of trees and the scattered leaves across the forest floor. The sky is a deep shade of blue that's almost as pretty as her eyes. A gentle breeze cools us down.

My pulse settles the longer we stand in silence.

Until Rebel whispers, "About what happened in the garage…"

I turn my head to her.

Rebel draws her lower lip between her teeth and the need to capture that plump lip with my own teeth awakens within me.

"…I assume April told you about what happened this morning?" she finishes.

I stare at her, waiting.

"I was upset about a few things, but that's no excuse for kissing you without… um… you know. So yeah… I'm sorry if you were upset by it."

I frown. Upset?

I'm upset that we had an audience.

I'm upset I couldn't tilt her head back and swallow her whole.

I'm upset the only reason she kissed me was because she'd had a bad day and needed another guy to take a hint.

Forcing myself to stay away from her is shredding me into ribbons, but I'll never be angry at an opportunity to taste Rebel Hart's lips.

"So yeah." She squares her shoulders. "Glad we cleared that up."

I watch her spin in her fuzzy slippers and hurry inside the treehouse.

I follow her in.

"You should have done this at the garage," I mutter, annoyed that I can't kiss her. Or tell her about my family. Or admit that I like her.

She goes still.

The frustration eases into my voice. "Be angry when you feel wronged and clear things up when you calm down."

Rebel looks at me with surprised eyes. "What are you talking about?"

"You don't owe the world a smile you don't feel."

Her eyebrows cinch tight and I can tell she's feeling exposed. And annoyed about it.

"That's rich coming from you," Rebel accuses.

I fold my arms over my chest.

"You're a Kinsey. You have the luxury of scowling at everyone and *still* being waited on hand and foot. These 'insincere smiles' you hate so much? I'm proud of them. I earned them by constantly taking the high road, by making everyone in the room comfortable despite being the most uncomfortable one there."

I blink in surprise, having never thought of it that way.

"And why are you so obsessed with my smiles anyway? What's it to you?" Her chest rises and falls as she stares me down.

I like you. "It's just… an observation."

"An observation?" She repeats the words slowly, like she's giving me time to take it back.

I want you to be happy.

"Uh-huh?" She leans back.

I wish I could protect you from anything that tries to hurt you.

I stuff my hands into my pockets. "Sometimes, it could come across as being fake."

She blanches. "Fake?"

My eyes widen. I can tell immediately that I said the wrong thing.

"Give me a break, Gunner. You have no right to judge me." Her eyebrows are two angry slashes above her seething blue eyes. "What's 'fake'," she advances in a cloud of pink fury, "is *you* making a big show of helping me at the community clean up, bringing a food truck, painting the school and then turning around and acting like I don't exist for *days*."

She sticks a finger in my chest. "'Fake' is you not calling me *once* when you were away and then showing up today and buying me slippers and taking me to the treehouse and wanting to hear my presentation and acting like you care about my feelings."

My gaze locks on the leaves in the canopy above.

"I can tell when a guy likes me on sight. But with you… I can't make up from down. You're *impossible* to figure out." Her voice crackles with frustration. "It's driving me up a wall."

Does she think she's the only one who's going insane? I'm barely holding myself together as is.

Rebel's voice whips across the treetops. "Would it kill you to be clear for *once*? Which one of those actions was real and which was fake?"

I make the mistake of looking at her again. Her eyes are firm on me, leveling a challenge that I can't ignore.

Don't do it, Kinsey.

I take a step forward.

The laser beams spitting from her gaze shifts on a dime, sputtering out. A crease forms between her eyebrows.

You promised you wouldn't touch her.

I move into Rebel's space as a thousand hockey pucks skate around in my veins. They thud against the strings of my heart, sending nerves and anticipation firing through me.

Her mouth slackens.

My gaze fastens there.

Pink, scrumptious, glorious lips.

Don't. Do. It.

I do it.

I kiss her.

My arms band around Rebel, dragging her flush against my chest. My lips seal hers and she moans softly as I do what I've been wanting to for ages—I nip her bottom lip between my teeth. She startles and I press harder against her mouth, taking another nip and then soothing the sting with my tongue.

She tastes so good.

It was stupid of me to think I could keep myself from touching her.

What an idiot.

I'm powerless against this infuriating woman.

Utterly and totally helpless.

She is everything I have ever wanted. Everything I told myself I couldn't, no that I didn't *deserve* to have.

But now that I've reached this point, there's no going back.

I've crossed the line of no return.

She's mine.

"Mm." I whisper, savoring the taste of her as I tear myself away.

Rebel pants against my mouth. Her fingers are clamped around my biceps as if she's holding onto me for dear life.

I lean back to meet her gaze. Her blue eyes are darker than normal, the electricity between us turning them a rich shade of ocean blue. Her bun comes undone, causing golden waves to spill around her shoulders.

My eyes remain steady on her. "Rebel."

Her eyelashes flutter.

I can *feel* her mind racing with a flood of panicked thoughts.

I call her name again and this time, I anchor her body to mine, forcing her to look at me. I want to make sure she hears what I say next.

"Rebel."

Her eyes meet mine and her shoulders go taut, like every muscle just tightened at once.

I say nothing and just look at her.

Can she see it? My feelings for her? The decades of yearning?

"Rebel," I call one more time.

"What?"

"That was real."

CHAPTER
THIRTY-SEVEN

REBEL

Gunner Kinsey is my mortal enemy and has been since I was six years old.

I still remember breaking my crayon in anger the day he walked past me on the swings, acting as if he hadn't seen me.

I vowed to myself that I wouldn't fall for him again. The moment I did, I'd be a *neener, neener, pumpkin eater*.

Which, apparently… I am.

That kiss set decades of effort up in flames. The ten foot walls I built, the careful life I curated that erased every hint of our past… *poof*.

Gone.

All because he said it was real.

That kiss.

The intense look in his eyes.

The heat in the air.

Gunner Kinsey has real feelings for me.

No, it's more than that.

I saw the truth flash across his face like a message written in the stars. This is more than combustible lust between two people who hate each other.

Gunner Kinsey wants me. Craves me.

And I... I...

"I have to go." I spin around like the treehouse is on fire and scramble down the ladder. One shoe falls off when I jump to the ground, but I don't stop to pick it up.

Running half-barefoot down the trail, I fling my car door open. Thankfully, Gunner left my keys in the truck. This is Kinsey land and no one in town is dumb enough to steal from the most powerful family in Lucky Falls.

Twisting the key until the car rumbles to life, I back out of the lot like a crazy woman, nearly slamming into a tree. Just then I see Gunner scaling down the ladder. He notices my slipper and picks it up, glancing at it and then at me.

Slamming my foot on the gas, I tear a path through the orchard and down the road that leads out of the Kinsey farm.

Carol Kinsey is driving up to her garage when I speed past.

Her eyes, as pale blue as Gunner's widen on impact. The confusion in her gaze shifts to disdain when she recognizes me.

How much deeper would that scowl go if she knew how badly I wanted to keep kissing her son?

My heart tumbles.

I grip the steering wheel and press harder on the gas, trying to outrun those scandalous thoughts.

Gunner Kinsey has feelings for me.

And I... I...

I slam my foot on the brakes as the adrenaline in my blood finally retreats enough for me to think.

What do I feel for Gunner?

I hate him floats through my mind on auto-pilot.

But the negative feelings have lost their sting, overshadowed by all the moments we've shared.

I think about the night his head slid on my shoulder in the hospital and about how hurt I was when he left Lucky Falls without telling me. I think about how safe I felt in his arms when he hugged me earlier and how moved I was when he arranged the community service day.

I park the car to the side, my head a mess of tangled thoughts.

Do I like Gunner? CAN I like Gunner after… everything?

I groan.

This is all so complicated. Why couldn't he keep hating me in peace?

"Stupid Gunner Kinsey," I grumble, beating the steering wheel. "Obnoxious, massive pain in the—"

Knuckles rap against my window and I jump.

Gunner is standing outside the truck. Sweat slides down his face and his chest heaves violently.

Did he… run here?

For a split second, I debate starting the car and speeding away again, but his eyes bore through the glass like a fist reaching through the air and choking me. There might as well not be a thick glass between us. He might as well be right here in the car with me, making my knees wobble from up close.

Like a coward, I drop the window a smidge. "What?"

"Get out of the car, Rebel."

"Don't tell me what to do," I grumble.

"Please get out of the car," he grinds out.

It still sounds like he's ordering me, but I give him points for saying please and ease the car door open. However, when I try to hop down, I realize that one foot is bare and I curl my toes in embarrassment.

Without a word, Gunner grips my upper arm, slips his hand beneath my knees and scoops me out of the car. He carries me to the thick wooden fence bordering the Kinsey acreage and plops me down on top of it.

I glare at him. "Rude much?"

"Rude is running away when a man confesses his feelings for you."

My heart does another running kick at my ribs, but I force myself to remain calm. "I... left my solder iron on."

He gives me a disbelieving look.

"I wasn't running away," I insist.

He holds up my abandoned shoe. "You even forgot your glass slipper, princess."

Gunner Kinsey should never be allowed to call a woman 'princess' in that deep, velvety voice of his. I should call his father and have him arrested.

"And you missed the rest of what I wanted to say," he adds.

I swallow hard. "There was more?"

Gunner bends down and slides my slipper on again. "I wasn't happy about it. I didn't want to like you."

His words take me by surprise and I jerk back.

"In fact, I wish I had feelings for anyone *but* you."

I scoff and hop off the fence. "Sorry I'm such a burden, Kinsey. How about I just leave—"

He wraps his fingers around my wrist to stop me. "Because I never in a million years thought I'd get the chance to be with you."

I spin around slowly.

"I'm not the best at explaining how I feel. The words always come out wrong so I'm going to shut up after I ask you one question."

To my surprise, Gunner takes out a velvet box from his pocket and cracks it open. I glance at him and then at the pink box in shock. Inside is a beautiful, gold necklace with a pink gemstone at the center.

"Rebel Hart," Gunner says, "will you be my girlfriend?"

My heart is training for a flash sale at my favorite boutique because it's doing all kinds of flips and one-armed handstands.

"I…" My eyelashes flutter and I look up at him in shock, "aren't I already?"

A corner of Gunner's lips hitches up. "Then I guess you don't need this." He snaps the pink box closed.

"Yes, *yes*, I'll be your girlfriend, Gunner."

He scrunches his nose. "Are you only saying that because of the necklace?"

I toss my hair over my shoulder. "What if I am?"

He thinks about it, rubbing his chin.

"You're the one who offered me a bribe. Don't judge me for accepting it," I grumble.

He chuckles.

I giggle.

Gunner takes the necklace out of the box and leans in to fasten it around my neck. He's close enough that I can inhale the woodsy scent of his cologne mixed with the fragrance of the wildflowers growing by the fence.

Gunner Kinsey likes me.

And, against all odds, I like him too.

And now we're dating.

Like… for *real*.

"How does it look?" I ask when he leans back and gives me a soft, affectionate once over.

"Beautiful."

I blush.

He cradles my face and gives me a gentle kiss on my temple.

A giddy rush of emotions flows over me and I look up at him. "When did you start liking me?"

He tucks his bottom lip into his mouth, thinking it over. "That's a secret."

I narrow my eyes.

He gives me a pleased look. "When did you start liking *me*?"

"Well, I'm not telling you now."

His laughter is soft but joyful. "Typical Rebel. Always so…"

"Petty?" I supply.

He scrubs a thumb over my cheek. "Competitive."

"Same difference."

I laugh, but then I remember how he totally abandoned me before he left for the away games and I shove him.

He stumbles back, his eyebrows raised.

"If you felt this way, why'd you ghost me before you left town?" I frown.

Gunner glances down. "I'm sorry."

"I don't need the apology. I want to understand why."

He looks at me, unrest in his eyes. "I give you my word, Rebel. I'll tell you everything when it's over but... not right now."

I blink in confusion.

Gunner takes my hand in his. "Can you give me some time?"

I glance away.

"Please." He pulls me to him and gives me a hug.

I melt completely. "How many more secrets do you have?"

"What do you mean?"

"Apart from when you started liking me and why you ghosted me." I lean back. "What else is there?"

He tilts his head.

"You don't secretly collect toenails or anything creepy like that, do you?"

He gives me a blank look. "Do I look like the kind of guy who collects toenails, Rebel?"

"No, but you can never really be sure. Guys like that don't walk around with a sign." *Usually.* Although I'm sure I could find a toenail collection convention if I looked hard enough online.

He shakes his head in a silent 'what have I gotten myself into'.

"You're regretting this already, aren't you?"

"Never."

"Are you sure?"

He nods.

"Even though your mom still hates me and I still can't stand your family and things are only going to get tougher and weirder from here?"

I expect Gunner to laugh, but he doesn't.

Instead, he gets very, very serious and says, "No matter how tough it gets, the one thing I will never, ever regret for the rest of my days is being with you."

CHAPTER
THIRTY-EIGHT

GUNNER

I SEE REBEL OFF, HIDING MY SMILE THE ENTIRE TIME.

The moment her truck zooms off the property, I let loose the sappy grin that's been tugging on my mouth.

Rebel Hart is my girlfriend.

How did I get so lucky?

As I near the house, Mom throws the front door open and launches down the stairs.

"I saw the Hart girl leave in her truck. Were you two on the farm?"

I don't answer, but mom reads my face and her mouth twists into a scowl. "How *could* you bring that woman here?"

"She's my girlfriend and this is where I live."

"Yes, but it's where *I* live too. She shouldn't be here when she's trying to take over the Society!"

As usual, mom is being dramatic.

"Don't give me that look, Gunner Kinsey. Marjorie and the girls went *behind* my back and gave the Hart girl access to one of our biggest donors. Rodney Howard won't even pick up my calls anymore. He had his secretary send me an email saying he'll only work with Rebel now."

I frown. Rodney Howard isn't high on my list of favorite people at the moment.

"Maybe you shouldn't accept his money then."

"I can't do that!" Mom shrieks.

"Why not?"

"Do you know how many teachers from the school stopped by to thank me? Whether I like that girl or not, it's true that we haven't been as... dedicated to her side of town as we could have been. I don't want the Society's power struggle to affect the people who need help the most."

I study her, pleased to hear that her heart is still to help the town.

Mom rolls her eyes. "Oh, don't look at me like that. Even if I've changed my mind a little bit, I still don't approve of that girl."

Sure, but she respects Rebel's cause now and that's a step in the right direction.

I lean down and give mom a hug.

She grouchily smacks my shoulder. "Harumph. You haven't been back for a proper hour yet and you've already ticked me off. And where are your bags?" Mom nudges me away to look around.

"In Chance's convertible. I'll get them from him later."

She motions me inside. "I made your favorite, mashed potatoes and steak. And there's pie in the fridge."

My stomach grumbles. I skipped breakfast so I could be early for the meeting with the lawyers—a meeting that went as well as a defenseman wearing two left skates on the ice. It looks like the only way to get the information I seek is by digging around myself.

Mom hums as she fixes a plate and sets it in front of me. When she sees me looking at her, she stops. "Is something on my face?"

I shake my head.

"I'm almost done here. Go wash up and I'll have the table set."

"Mom?"

"Mm?" She continues stirring the gravy.

I'm not sure how to ask what I need to and the silence lengthens.

Mom lets out a nervous laugh. "What's the big announcement, Gunner?"

I look down, trying to find a way to interrogate my own mother.

Mom goes pale. "You didn't... you didn't propose to that girl, did you?"

I shake my head.

She folds forward, her shoulders sagging in relief.

"But someday..."

Mom's eyes zing to me. "Someday what?"

"Someday I'd like to."

"Gunner."

"Is there a reason I shouldn't?" I ask, watching every twitch of her face. "A good reason?"

"If you're asking my opinion, you know what I'll say. I don't think she's the right girl for you. She and I don't get along."

"Why not?"

"Because she stood in front of *everyone* at the charity luncheon and said terrible things about the Lady Luck Society. Why, she basically accused us of being *useless!* After all I've given to this community..." Mom shakes her head, aggravated. "And she's not humble at all. She goes out of her way to have the last word. *Very* argumentative girl. I can't imagine spending Thanksgiving and birthdays with someone who's so unpleasant."

Rebel and mom share the same spit-fire, outspoken personalities. If mom finds Rebel 'unpleasant', it might be because she reminds her of herself.

"Is that the *only* reason, mom?"

Mom furiously stirs the gravy. "What other reason could there be?"

"Did we…" I lick my lips, "did our family ever do something to Rebel or her mom that we shouldn't have?"

Mom looks baffled. "Gunner, what kind of question is that?"

"Did we hurt them in any way?"

"Is that what Rebel said?"

"I'm just asking a question."

"Well, it's a dumb question. When Ms. Hart was our cleaner, I treated her with respect. So did your dad."

Mom's voice is high pitched with annoyance, but that's on brand for her. She's maintaining eye contact the entire way through her speech too, all signs that she's not lying.

I breathe easier. "What about Mrs. Hart's relationship with the rest of our family?"

"What do you mean?"

"Did she ever date Uncle Stewart?"

Mom snorts. "Now that would be something? As far as I can tell, they never had that sort of relationship."

"What about one of my other uncles?"

"Where is all this coming from?" Mom winds her wooden spoon around in the air.

"I heard rumors."

Mom scoffs. "Rumors are nothing but idle talk. Why, Mrs. Hart was cleaning this house since your grandaddy was alive! At one point, folks thought she was his secret daughter."

Now that I think about it, my grandfather had always treated the Harts like family. I remember him handing out pocket money to both me and Rebel equally when we were kids.

"My disapproval has nothing to do with her mother being a cleaner. I don't hate families like the Harts. They're good, hard-working folks." She humphs. "If that girl wasn't so outspoken and determined to have you, I wouldn't have a fuss with her."

I cringe. *It was going so well, mom.*

"I'm the one who's determined to have Rebel. Not the other way around," I correct her.

"Yes, well…" Mom's brain audibly whirrs as she cooks up a way to pin this on Rebel, "you wouldn't have thought you had a chance if she didn't give you that impression. So it's still her fault."

The conversation is turning into a mess, so I focus on setting the table instead of arguing.

After dinner, I wash the dishes and head up to my apartment so I can grab my laptop and start some work for Uncle Robert. He emailed me with business questions while I was on the road and I promised him I'd take a look at it the moment I got back.

The task is more complicated than I expected and, by the time I come up for air, it's nightfall.

I lift my arms over my head in a stretch and my thoughts instantly go to Rebel.

A smile works its way over my face. I pick up my phone and type out a message.

Hey.

I stare at the three letters.

Then I hit the backspace until they're gone.

Hi, Rebel.

I erase that too.

Cracking my knuckles, I stare at the phone and think for a minute.

Suddenly, I get a notification.

It's Rebel.

REBEL: *What are you up to tonight?*

I feel my lips pulling up into a foolish grin and smack my cheek a couple times. Unfortunately, the warmth spreading in my chest isn't so easy to disguise. It's like I'm being buried in the middle of a supernova, one that's been hidden in ice and set to hibernate for centuries. But now the ice is thawing and there's no containing the pure, nuclear energy that's about to crack out of the ice.

I type back immediately.

ME: *Nothing much. You?*

I let my phone clatter back to the table and spin my chair around as I wait for her response. It takes fifteen minutes for the phone to buzz and I launch at the device immediately.

REBEL: *I'm out with April, May and Delia.*

ME: *The Tuna?*

REBEL: *The mall. April's idea.*

ME: *Having fun?*

REBEL: *Me and May? Yeah. April and Delia? Not so much.*

ME: *??*

REBEL: *I think April's trying to cheer me up after what happened this morning. Poor thing. But she's miserable.*

ME: *She's a good friend.*

REBEL: *She's suffering for no reason. I'm in a great mood even without the mall.*

The grin is back on my face.

ME: *Does your good mood have anything to do with me?*

REBEL: *We'll never know…*

I run a hand down my face, massaging my cheeks that are spasming from holding a smile for this long.

ME: *I'll take that as a yes.*

REBEL: *I neither confirm nor deny those allegations.*

I laugh.

REBEL: *Do you have practice tomorrow?*

ME: *Bright and early. Max has no off-switch.*

REBEL: *You should get some rest then.*

ME: *I'll be up a little longer. Text me when you get home safe.*

REBEL: *I will. Goodnight, Gunner.*

ME: *Goodnight, Rebel.*

I toss the phone and flop against the mattress.

Something bright and warm hums in my veins.

It's hard to explain…

I've only felt this type of rush on the ice.

And it's usually seconds before I hit the puck straight into the net and hear the crowd roar in the stadium.

But there's no crowd here.

It's just me.

Alone.

In my bedroom.

Texting back and forth with my dream girl.

The girl I've been silently in love with for decades.

I get up to pace around my bed, too amped to go back to work on Uncle Robert's finances. Instead, my thoughts are filled with all the ways I can make Rebel happy tomorrow, the day after that, and a million days after that.

I've waited my whole life for this moment.

Even with all the obstacles coming at us, I'll throw my heart and soul into showing Rebel Hart she made the right decision to be mine.

CHAPTER
THIRTY-NINE

REBEL

"What's got you smiling?" May asks, wiggling her eyebrows. She sings, "Is it your *boyfriend?*"

"Mm-hm," I answer frankly, pocketing my phone and taking a sip of my strawberry smoothie.

May grins from ear to ear while April looks like she's about to fall out of her chair.

Delia stirs her straw around her drink, brown eyes drooping with boredom.

We're sitting at the food court after April all but begged us for a break from shopping. It's so loud that I can barely hear myself think. The crowds have thickened since we first arrived. It's mostly young couples on dates and teenagers traveling in packs to the arcade on the second floor.

May points to Delia. "Does she know?"

Delia awakens from her stupor.

"About you and Gunner?" May adds with an eyebrow wiggle.

"May!" April hisses, giving her sister a warning look.

"I didn't mean anything else!" May raises two hands up as if to say '*I wasn't trying to spill your fake dating secret*'.

"It's okay." I calm May with a smile. "No, I don't think Delia knows."

It hasn't been long since Delia started at The Pink Garage and she's kept mostly to herself.

I doubt it's because she's shy. Delia rides a tricked-out Harley, dresses in leather, and is strikingly beautiful in a 'sultry assassin' kind of way. The woman is no wallflower and doesn't seem like the type who'd be intimidated by a conversation.

Instead, I get the sense that Delia doesn't want to ask us any personal questions because then we'd have the license to ask her personal questions in return. She's dodged every attempt at getting to know her better.

April and I haven't pressed. Delia does her work spectacularly and is pleasant to us and the customers.

It's not like we can force her to be friends.

Although we've tried and failed multiple times.

It's a miracle she's at the mall with us tonight. Turns out, May's bubbly insistence is a force that not even a leather-clad, motorcycle-riding mechanic can resist.

"May is asking if you've met my boyfriend," I explain to Delia… and to April, who breathes out in relief.

"Yeah." May grins a little harder. "Delia wasn't in town when they got together."

"I've seen him." Delia shrugs.

May looks intrigued. "Where?"

"At the garage. Today. I got an eyeful."

May leans forward. "An eyeful of what?"

Delia stiffens as if she hadn't meant to say those words out loud.

"An eyeful of *what?*" May insists.

Delia points at me. "Them kissing."

I choke on my fruit punch.

April guffaws.

"Okay, now you *have* to tell me everything," May says, snickering. "Were they going at it thinking no one was around?"

I cover my face. "Delia, don't say another word."

Delia makes a zipping motion over her face.

"*Come* on," May whines. "You can't stop there."

"She's the boss," Delia says.

"I'm the other boss and you have my permission to keep going," April says with a mischievous grin.

I shoot my best friend an angry scowl for betraying me.

April scrunches her nose, unrepentant.

Delia's expression remains passive, but I can see a little sparkle in her eyes like she's enjoying this. "She ran up, jumped on him, and basically attacked his mouth. It was very dramatic."

My eyes widen.

May barks out a laugh.

April hides her giggle behind her smoothie.

"I did not 'attack him'." I glare at Delia. "Is that what it looked like?"

Delia shrugs. "Yeah, it looked kind of painful."

"I'll admit, I… wasn't gentle. But it's not like I meant to hurt him."

"I'm sure I saw bruises," Delia says in that dry tone.

I kind of miss when she was keeping her distance from us.

"Rebel, you're blushing," April says, awestruck.

I fan my face and explain myself. "I was excited. He's been gone for a long time."

"I didn't say anything." Delia stirs her drink again.

"You've got a way with words, newbie," I sputter, embarrassment sweeping through my chest. To cool down, I gulp the rest of my drink and crunch on the ice cubes.

April observes me with her eyes narrowing.

"I've never seen Rebel so flustered before," May points out, still laughing at my reaction.

"Me either," April agrees studiously. "What's going on?"

"Gunner and I..."

April leans forward. "You what?"

"We're going steady."

"You and Gunner?" April balks.

"Yes."

A heavy silence falls on our table.

"You're *dating*-dating?" May says at last.

"For real?" April stares at me with shocked eyes.

I nod.

May screeches so loudly that the entire mall comes to a standstill. "I knew it! I know chemistry when I see it. I saw this coming a mile away."

Delia glances between us. "I'm confused. Aren't they dating already?"

"We're just really happy for her," April beams and gives me a quiet arm squeeze that conveys her approval. "I've seen how well Gunner takes care of you. He's very earnest." Then she pauses. "Does this mean you've figured things out with his mother?"

"Uh, no. She still hates me."

"What about the feud between your shop and Stewart Kinsey's?" May spits out Stewart's name.

"Uh, yeah, that's still happening."

The celebratory energy around the table dies like a balloon losing air.

"Are you guys dating without figuring those things out?" April asks, gnawing on her bottom lip.

I shrug and nod.

April scrubs a finger over an eyebrow, her concern expanding so far it threatens to snowball the entire building.

"You know," May stabs her drink with a straw, attempting to lighten the mood, "I'm *so* curious about how Gunner is as a boyfriend. He's so quiet and he looks angry all the time. I'd be scared to even talk to him."

"I'm used to dating guys who love hearing themselves talk,

so being with someone quiet is a nice change of pace. Gunner's really sweet once you get to know him." I stroke my pink gemstone necklace, remembering how his hands had trembled as he put it on for me.

"*Gunner?*" May's mouth opens in surprise. "*Sweet?*"

I bob my head unable to stop grinning.

"Are we talking about the hockey player? The giant one with the black hair and the dark eyes who grunts like a caveman in after-game interviews? *That* guy?" At my insistent nod, May shakes her head slowly. "I can't imagine it."

I pop another ice cube into my mouth. "He's not sweet to everyone only to me, but that's what I like about him."

April and May look eager to ask me more questions, but I notice Delia checking her watch and tapping her nails on the table. Rather than let the conversation drag on, I suggest we call it a night.

On the way to the escalator, a little boy streaks past us.

"Mommy!" the child says, crying big, desperate tears. "Mommy!"

Immediately, my head swivels around.

As one, May, April and I head right over.

April kneels in front of the little boy while I pluck out my pack of pink tissues. She accepts them from me and wipes the child's ruddy face.

"Don't cry, sweetie," May says in a gentle voice.

The little boy cries harder.

"*Phillip!*" A woman's harried voice bounces around the mall and, a second later, she bursts into sight.

The moment the little boy sees her, his tears dry up. "Mommy!"

"Oh, sweetheart. I told you not to take off like that." The woman scoops him into her arms and looks at us with a harried smile. "Thank you so much. I took my eyes off him for one second and he got lost in the crowd."

"It's okay." May gives her a reassuring nod.

"We're glad that he got back to you safe and sound," I tell her.

"Phillip, say goodbye to the nice ladies," the mother says.

Phillip waves with tears still dangling from his lashes and is carted off happily in his mother's arms.

"What a cutie," I say, grinning.

April glances around. "Where's Delia?"

"She was right behind…" May's voice drifts off. "Hey, where'd she go?"

I search the crowd until I find Delia hiding behind a nearby column.

"Delia?" Confusion laces my tone.

Delia adjusts her motorcycle jacket and approaches us with a strong, confident stride. If not for the sheepish tilt of her chin, I wouldn't believe she'd been hiding.

"What happened? Why were you all the way over there?" April asks.

"I… had to answer a phone call."

I study her keenly. Something about her answer doesn't ring true, but May starts chatting and I let the matter go.

"Oh, I can't *wait* until you two get married and start having kids," May chirps, dreamily clasping her hands and pressing them under her cheek. "I want to be an aunt *so* badly."

"Hold your horses, squirt. *I'm* not in a rush for marriage or a baby," April says.

"Me either." I agree.

"But don't you want your own adorable, little Phillip?" May makes a squishy-squishy gesture with her fingers. "Did you see those chunky cheeks?"

"Right now, the garage is my Phillip," April says.

I point at May, "That means you're already a proud aunt. Congratulations."

April laughs.

May sticks out her tongue in disgust. "You guys are no fun. Hey, Delia?"

"Hm?" The mechanic turns around, her black bob swishing with the movement.

"Do you like kids?"

"Kids?" She looks off to the side. "Er…"

May's smile drops. "I guess you don't."

"It's not that I hate kids," Delia says, stepping off the escalator. "But they're so small and fragile. They make me nervous."

"That's fair," May says. "I once babysat for the Elmers and their one-year-old pushed her finger into an electric socket the moment I looked away. I almost had a heart attack."

Delia forces a smile, looking uncomfortable.

I watch her, trying to figure her out. I'm getting very curious about our new hire. What did she do before this? What drove her to a town as small as Lucky Falls? What exactly is she running from?

"I'll see you guys later," Delia says, hurrying away from us in the parking lot as if we've got a contagious disease.

"Did I say something offensive?" May wonders. "I hope she doesn't think I'm judging her over not liking kids. I really meant it when I said I understood."

April rubs her sister's shoulder, ever the voice of reason. "It's okay, May. Delia will open up when she's ready. But what I *really* want to know…" My best friend turns her eyes on me, "is what happened between Rebel and Gunner after they left the garage this morning."

"Ooh, yes! I want all the juicy details! How did he ask you out?"

I shake my head. "I'll tell you next time. I need to head home too."

"Why?" April asks.

"My boyfriend has an early practice and he won't sleep until he hears I got home safely."

"Blegh." May pretends to throw up.

April looks squeamish. "Is this how I am with Chance? Please tell me it's not!"

I bark out a laugh. "Goodnight, ladies!"

I throw a backward wave and sashay to my car, hearing the scrape of April's jaw hit the concrete.

CHAPTER FORTY

GUNNER

The next morning, I wake before dawn and send Rebel a good morning text.

Birds aren't even singing yet when I lock my front door, so I don't expect an answer right away. But I'm still happy to send it.

I wonder if Rebel still sleeps with her mouth sprawling open and her golden hair sprawled around her like she did when we were kids?

I'd give anything to see that.

Actually, I'd give anything to lie next to her and wake up to her beautiful face every morning.

But I'm getting ahead of myself.

Today is our first official day as a couple.

I want to make the most of it. Both our schedules are bound to get busier with the last game of the playoffs right around the corner and construction work soon to be done on The Pink Garage.

A few minutes later, I cruise through empty streets, headed to the arena. The donut shop catches my eye and I make a mental note to swing by after practice. I'll get Rebel her favorite pink frosted doughnuts and bestow her with a strawberry smoothie as an excuse to see her…

A loud *vrooom* echoes across the quiet road.

Surprised, I check the rearview mirror.

Chance's flashy convertible roars into sight and then it zips past me on the way to the arena. My annoying teammate honks and waves from the front seat as he overtakes me and screams past my truck.

Oh, it's on.

I step on the gas.

Chance and I are neck and neck.

Then I pull slightly ahead.

I blaze through the gates of the stadium, yanking the steering wheel and bringing my car to an abrupt stop as close to the arena's front doors as I can manage.

Chance jumps out of his Lambo first.

I'm right behind him.

Breaking into an all-out dash, I gain ground until I sprint past Chance. His eyes widen when I crash through the doors and stumble into the arena first.

It's a narrow victory.

But hey, a win's a win.

"Did Rebel juice your truck engine? How'd you pass me back there?" Chance grumbles, catching up to me as I stow away my gym bag in the lockers.

"Losers ask how. Winners just win," I grunt.

"I was barely jogging, but you're about to pass out. If I'd put in a little more energy, you'd be eating dust, Kinsey," Chance mocks.

I tuck my exhaustion away, hoping that I'm not as red-faced as I feel. "Try harder next time, McLanely. You're just too slow," I taunt.

Chance scowls and that expression alone was worth exerting so much energy.

He struts past me to his locker. "I got to the parking lot first. So technically, I was here before you."

I shrug out of my hoodie and stuff it into my locker, shaking my head.

"By the way, April told me about you and Rebel making things official." He slaps me on the back. "That's great, but I'm obligated as Rebel's honorary brother-in-law to warn you…"

My eyebrows raise at that self-appointed title.

"… if you hurt her, my girlfriend knows how to use a wrench."

I smirk. "Noted."

Chance smacks me once more on the back and we head to the ice together. The two of us do drills until coach arrives. Then we spend hours sweating through a series of plays we're perfecting for the game.

After practice, the team peels away their sweaty hockey gear and hit the showers, but I go straight to my locker. Once I've freed my phone from my gym bag, I notice a new notification on the screen.

REBEL: *Good morning.*

There's a smiley face emoji, a heart emoji (pink of course) and a sunshine emoji.

I grin as I touch the heart emoji.

My own heart is ramming against my ribs with the force of a defenseman slamming into the boards.

You know what's crazy?

Even Rebel's texts are pretty.

I tap the emoji button and a billion emojis pop up. Which one do I use? Why are there so many of them, dang it?

Before I can decide on one, another text comes in.

REBEL: *Is practice over?*

ME: *Yeah. Are you at the garage yet?*

REBEL: *Heading there in a few.*

ME: *Hungry?*

REBEL: *Starving.*

ME: *Doughnuts?*

REBEL: *Only if you want my undying love and devotion.*

My mouth trembles.

Don't do it.

My lips inch upward.

Don't. Be a man, Gunner.

A soft, pleased smile pops free before I can restrain myself. Rebel's undying love and devotion sounds like a sweet reward to me.

"Gah! My eyes! My eyes!" A commotion erupts next to me.

I turn to find Renthrow, Theilan, Watson and Chance staring me down.

Renthrow is studying me like I sprouted antennas.

Watson is cringing.

Chance is smiling knowingly.

Theilan is writhing on the bench. He points an accusing finger. "What was that…?" Theilan gestures to my face. "That sappy expression?"

I grunt and slam my locker door closed.

"What's wrong with you?" Theilan yells. "Are you sick or something?"

Watson looks me up and down, suspiciously.

"Must be because of his girlfriend," Renthrow says.

"No way. Gunner's been dating Rebel for a while and I've never seen him smile like that," Watson argues.

Theilen smacks his hand on the bench and then lifts that very hand to point at me. "Are you seeing someone else?"

I slant him a cutting look.

Immediately, Theilan shirks back. "Uh, has anyone seen my stick tape?"

While Theilan avoids my stare, my phone vibrates with a new voice message.

I press play and put the cell phone to my ears.

Rebel's silky-smooth tone caresses my ear drums. "Thank you in advance, *boyfriend.*"

After a few seconds of debate, I decide that I don't care about my audience and press the button to answer Rebel's voice message with my own.

"You're welcome, *girlfriend*."

"Ah!" Watson roars in pain.

Renthrow shudders and quickly makes his exit, yanking his Hello Kitty gym bag over his shoulder.

Chance is laughing so hard he's red in the face.

Theilan shudders. "I need to bleach my ears."

Face a mask of utter apathy, I tuck my phone back into my locker and hit the showers.

Most of my teammates are gone by the time I step out in a towel. They must have cleared out to avoid me.

Unbothered, I drive to the doughnut shop.

"Hey, Phil." I nod stiffly when I get to the counter. "I'd like…"

"Three pink frosted donuts, three chocolate donuts and a strawberry smoothie?"

I blink twice.

Phil leans over the counter and whispers, "It's Rebel's usual order."

I blink.

"My chocolate donuts sell out quickly, but I always keep a few in the back for her."

I nod again. "Thanks."

He boxes up the pastries. "I never do this for customers, but when a man comes face to face with a woman that pretty, well… it's hard to resist." He closes the lid of the box. "I hope you know how lucky you are, son. Why, if I were a few years younger, I would've…"

My eyes laser into his, daring him to finish that sentence.

Phil gulps and slides the box over the counter. "You and Rebel enjoy."

"Thanks." I snatch the donuts and stomp to my car.

Inside my truck, I take a few deep breaths.

Before Rebel and I were officially together, it bothered me to see other guys sniffing around her. However, I managed to tamp those feelings down as, rightfully, I didn't have any right to be upset.

But now…

Dating Rebel hasn't cured the problem.

In fact—I set a hand on my chest and feel the unease swirling inside—I think making things official worsened my condition.

I sigh. Why did my girlfriend have to be so breath-taking?

It's not just her face—as stunning as every inch of it is. It's the way she laughs, melodious and joyful. It's the way she smells—like the very essence of sweet strawberries and fresh cherries. It's the way she looks you right in the eyes and makes it hard to breathe.

It's only natural for Rebel to have plenty of admirers.

Like me, other men have eyes.

I won't get any closer to sorting myself out here in the parking lot, so I make my way to Rebel instead and deliver the donuts—minus Phil's compliments—into her outstretched, pink-gloved hands.

"You really brought them." Rebel looks up at me with a sultry smile. Her ponytail slides down the shoulder of her pink mechanic jumpsuit and her blue eyes sparkle like the pink gemstone necklace clasped around her neck.

I notice a streak of dirt on her face and wipe it with my thumb. "Busy?"

"Always. I'll be *so* relieved when we start construction next month. We need somewhere to keep all these cars."

"Don't overwork yourself. Make sure to take breaks when you need them."

Rebel salutes. "Yes, sir. Any other instructions, sir?"

I smile at her teasing and rest my hands on her shoulders. "That's it for now. You're busy, so I won't stay long."

She pouts. "You really only came to give me doughnuts?"

I nod.

Her bottom lip sticks out even further.

"And…" I admit. "I wanted to see you."

Rebel's expression softens with another brilliant smile. She wraps both arms around my neck. "Look as much as you want." She twists her head from side to side, showing off her stunning cheekbones and the sweet curve of her chin. "Had enough yet?"

Never. I grab her hips and pull her forward. She lets out a little gasp when our bodies collide. Her skin is soft to the touch and the curve of her waist feels like heaven against my palm.

Leaning forward so I'm inches away from her face, I gaze at her softly. "I could spend all day looking at you and it wouldn't be enough."

Rebel's eyelashes flutter.

Her gaze darts to my lips.

"That's so *sweet*," a voice chimes.

I startle and Rebel does too.

We both turn to take in April who's hovering over the donut container.

"I meant the donuts." April blushes.

"I bought enough for everyone."

"You're such a gentleman," April says. Scooping up the container, she makes a run for it. "Delia! Look! Donuts!" She waves to the quiet, dark-haired mechanic who's half-buried inside a car.

I reluctantly let Rebel go. "What are you doing tonight?"

"I'm working late as always. Gotta keep up with the demand here at the garage. And then I'll be planning the first of the sponsored community service activities. Why?"

I step back, astonished. "You're going to keep working with Rodney Howard?"

"His money didn't do anything wrong and besides, I don't want my personal issues getting in the way of helping people. That's the whole reason I started this."

Mom said something similar yesterday but, somehow, the

thought of Rebel continuing to get involved with Rodney Howard and Benji makes me uneasy.

The wealthy business owner was willing to drop a *significant* amount of cash for Rebel to consider dating his son. I've been around determined businessmen like Rodney Howard before. They don't stop because they hit a challenge.

"What's with that face?" Rebel tilts her head.

I glance at the floor, saying nothing. I'm already awful with words and if I try to explain myself now, it'll sound like I'm a dangerous, controlling guy. It's better if I don't say anything at all rather than start a fight.

A brief smile flits across my face and I jut my chin at where April and Delia are devouring the doughnuts.

"You should get over there before there's none left."

"They wouldn't!" Rebel twists, her eyes trained on April. "Hey! Save a few for me!"

"You better hurry up then," April warns.

Rebel takes a few steps toward her friends and then she turns back. "Do you want to come over tonight?"

"Come... over."

"Yeah." She tosses me a distracted smile. "I'll wrap up everything I need to do around eight. Is that too late or...?"

I shake my head so hard if I were a bobblehead, my springs would have popped out. "No."

"Great." Her eyes sparkle. "It's a date."

Instantly, all my unease about Rodney Howard and Benji melt away like they never even existed.

I walk out of the garage and let my smile loose again.

Softly, victoriously, I whisper to myself, "It's a date."

CHAPTER
FORTY-ONE

REBEL

A knock on my door sends my head shooting up from my computer and papers fluttering all over my thrift-store coffee table.

Gunner's deep voice vibrates through solid wood and concrete. "Rebel?"

Anticipation and surprise whips my heart into a gallop. *He's early!*

I throw my front door open. Gunner appears, wearing a simple white button down shirt and a pair of dark jeans. His hair hangs low, hiding his pale blue eyes and giving him a menacing air.

If I didn't know what a softie he is under that intimidating stare and those broad-as-a-building shoulders, I'd probably slam the door and run to hide under my bed.

He greets me with a nod and lifts his arm to wave. It's then that I hear plastic rustling and realize that he's holding a grocery bag filled with giant leafy stems. In his other hand, he's holding a case of my favorite pink lemonade.

"You're early," I say, pushing the door open wider and flattening my back against it so he can step inside.

Gunner's so powerfully built that even though I give him plenty of space, his shoulder still brushes against me as he passes by.

"I'm right on time," he says.

My eyes bulge. "Is it eight already?" I stampede to the couch where I set up my temporary 'office' and push aside folders, documents and my clipboard to locate my phone.

Once I press the button, the screen lights up and reveals the time in giant, neon-pink numbers.

"Oh my gosh. I can't believe it's eight already. I didn't even notice."

Gunner's lips inch up ever so slightly and I can tell he doesn't mind how scatterbrained I'm being about our date.

His gaze meanders slowly down my tank top, shorts and pink bunny slippers. A blush steals across my face. I originally planned on taking a shower, blowing out my hair and wearing something nice before Gunner arrived.

This is not how I planned to look on our first official date.

"Don't watch me." I pounce on him and set my hand over his eyes. "I need to get ready."

Gunner grips my wrist and lowers my hand, shaking his head.

"I haven't showered since I came back from the garage," I argue. "I still smell like engine oil and exhaust. I'll be quick." I turn to walk away when I feel a tug on my wrist—which is still in Gunner's grip.

He yanks me back to him using only a smidge of his strength and I go stumbling into his chest.

Gunner steadies my chin beneath his giant hands.

I catch a whiff of his light cologne mixed with the fragrance of fresh mint. *De-licious*. I want to bottle up his fragrance and sell it as a car freshener to all The Pink Garage customers. It would fly off the shelves.

Gunner presses closer to me, the warmth of him a magnetic pull that I can't resist. Like spark to an ignition, I lean in too, gasping softly when he bypasses my lips and instead keeps going past my cheek to my neck.

I freeze, every nerve alight as he inhales deeply.

My heart stutters like a car with a bad starter.

"You smell… amazing," he murmurs in that deep, gravelly voice.

My knees betray me, buckling wildly like I'm standing in the middle of an earthquake. His scent, his voice, his words—they're intoxicating.

Out of sheer necessity, I dig my fingers into the collar of his shirt to keep myself steady.

Gunner steps back and taps my nose. "Keep working. I'll let you know when dinner's ready."

He retreats into the kitchen and I follow him in a daze. "W-what…" I clear my throat and do my best to hide the tremble in my voice, "you're making dinner?"

He nods.

"Why?"

"Why not?" He opens a cupboard and then closes it.

It's a fair argument. "What are you making? Spaghetti?" I try to peer into the bags.

"Risotto with fresh salmon and—"

"You're cooking *salmon?*"

Gunner grunts the affirmative and continues hunting through my cupboard for pans.

"Since when do you know how to cook salmon? Actually, since when do you know how to cook *period?*" I ask, reaching past him and finding the pan that he needs.

"My mother believes every man should know how to cook, clean and fold his own laundry."

"Stop." I lift a hand. "If you keep going, I'll start fangirling over Carol and that'll be uncomfortable for the both of us."

He leaks a smile. Gunner doesn't smile often and, even when

he does, it's just tiny smiles like this one, yet it makes his face ten times more appealing.

I want to stay and stare at his face, but I tear myself away from the kitchen and take a quick shower.

Since I don't have time to blow-dry, I run a towel over my hair, throw on lip gloss and one of my favorite pink dresses and head back outside.

Gunner gives me a once-over and a corner of his lips inches up in a stamp of approval.

"See," I call him out, breezing to the living room, "I look better now, don't I?"

"You looked nice before too," he assures me. "I liked the bunny slippers."

I grin and sink into the couch, setting the laptop into my lap. "Did your Uncle Robert keep you busy today?"

Gunner grunts. "He uses my away games as an excuse to double my workload."

"You *could* say no."

"It's fine. It works for us."

Smiling, I grab my fuzzy pink pen.

For the next thirty minutes, Gunner quietly takes over my kitchen. Except for the sizzle of oil in the pan and the slight crackle of the salmon skin crisping, I wouldn't even know he was there.

Part of his silence, I'm sure, is a by-product of his reserved nature, but I also get the sense that he's intentionally being as quiet as he can to allow me to concentrate.

Unfortunately, it isn't working at all.

Instead of calculating the estimates for our senior citizen outreach gift baskets, I keep getting distracted by Gunner's bulging biceps.

Ugh. Does he *have* to sauté vegetables so sexily? Does he realize how charming he looks filleting a salmon? What if my smoke alarms go off from how hot he is stirring the rice?

I force my eyes back to the data I collected.

But those pesky orbs bounce back to the kitchen minutes later as if they're dogs hopping back to their owner.

Gunner rolled the sleeve of his shirt up to his elbows and I get an eyeful of his impressive tattoos. They're so intricate and well done. And manly. I love the way they add character to his otherwise stoic personality, as if hinting at the rebel underneath the mask of the perfect Kinsey prince.

"It's almost ready," Gunner says, misinterpreting my frequent looks in his direction.

I give up on work and wander back to the kitchen. "On a scale of one to ten, how clingy can I be in this relationship?"

Gunner arches a brow.

"Seeing you cook makes me want to hug you from behind." I press my hands flat on the counter. "But this is just our first date and I'm not sure if you're ready for Clingy Rebel."

Gunner blinks slowly, looking pleased. A little shell-shocked too, but mostly pleased. "I don't mind."

"No." I back off. "I change my mind. A woman should be a little mysterious or things will get boring fast. Would you like me to do the salad?" I point to the lettuce leaves near his elbow.

His gaze becomes unsteady as if he can't keep up with the speed of my conversation.

I laugh as I peel the skin of the carrots. "Am I intimidating you, Gunner? You look scared."

"I'm impressed."

"Impressed?"

"At how easily you say what's on your mind."

"Some people would call that annoying." His mom, being one of them, but I choose not to speak that part out loud.

"Not me."

"Then maybe *you're* the strange one," I tease.

He grunts and shrugs as if to say 'maybe'.

I finish my salad preparations and pull out a beautiful glass bowl from my bottom cupboard. Gunner stops to stare at it.

I answer the question in his eyes. "Do you remember the

glass blowing exhibition the art committee hosted a few years back?"

He nods.

I rinse the bowl and then scrape my chopped lettuce, carrots and tomatoes into it. "The featured artist gifted me this after I took his class. It was so strange. He pulled me to the front of the class and I thought he was going to scold me for my awful glass blowing skills, but he gave me this instead. It had his number taped to the bottom of it, but obviously I threw that away."

There's no overt shift in Gunner's expression. But I sense his energy tilting away from light and playful to guarded and uneasy.

However, in usual, Gunner fashion, he says nothing and sets the table with smooth, patient movements. I follow with the salad bowl, staring at his back and wondering what I said wrong. Should I not have mentioned another man during our date?

Gunner pulls out my chair for me, still quiet as ever. I notice he's not looking me quite in the eyes.

"Gunner?"

He finally looks at me, seems to think about saying something and then snaps his mouth closed. I watch it all play out in real time and heaviness lands in my stomach, making me lose my appetite.

Whoa.

What is this new feeling?

I normally don't let a man's mood affect me or my voracious appetite, even if he *is* my boyfriend.

But tonight…

The thought that I might have upset Gunner makes me slightly panicked.

Which means…

I like Gunner Kinsey, way, *waay* more than I thought.

CHAPTER
FORTY-TWO

GUNNER

Great. I made it awkward.

I see the light draining from Rebel's eyes like a dial winding down from a hundred to zero.

What is wrong with me?

She mentioned some other guy giving her his number and dark flames ripped at my chest again. The expression I made must have scared her.

Or did it?

I was *extra* careful not to show any outward signs of frustration.

Maybe it's something else?

The scrape of forks against the plates is louder than my roaring heartbeat. Salmon risotto is one of my specialities, but I can't taste a thing and it's hard to say if that's because I did a poor job or because my tongue's too dry to enjoy it.

Rebel sits across from me, her head tucked against her chest, her eyes locked on her plate. A curtain of hair hides her face from sight. She hasn't said a word since we started eating.

I beat my head against a proverbial wall, searching for something to say that will put the smile back on her lips and the sunshine back in her eyes.

"Is it good?" I ask, but my voice comes out a little too gruffly and I see her flinch.

"Uh, yeah. Yeah, it's great." She pushes the rice from one side of her plate to the other, making her statement less convincing.

I scratch the back of my head, at an utter loss on how to save this.

I'm sure that Rebel is upset.

I'm sure that I'm the reason why.

What escapes me is how I should go about rectifying my wrongs.

"Uh," I reach for the soda and gesture to her cup, "would you like some more?"

"I'm good. Thank you," she says, as if I'm an overeager waiter who's visiting the table a little too much.

Hesitantly, I put the drink down.

Silence swirls around us, making it hard to breathe.

Should I just apologize and figure out what I'm apologizing for later?

The plan resonates with me and I open my mouth but before I can say anything, Rebel blurts, "Are you upset with me because I said that guy gave me his number?"

My brows shoot up and my gaze locks on hers in disbelief.

She leans forward, earnestly making her case. "To be honest, I don't even remember that guy. It happened so long ago. But I know for sure that I wasn't interested in him at all. Lots of guys give me their numbers, but I never text them back *or* encourage them."

"Rebel—"

"I will admit that I *might* be accused of flirting to get my way sometimes, but that's only in extreme situations when nothing else has worked and I use that sparingly."

"Rebel..." I try again.

"I wouldn't do that *now* of course. I'm very loyal once I'm in a relationship and I won't disrespect you or our relationship by doing anything you—"

I reach out, my index finger brushing her lips, the contact gentle yet electrifying. My eyes lock on hers, pinning her in place and dissolving the remainder of her frantic confession.

"I'm the one who needs to apologize," I say. And when I'm sure that she won't interrupt me, I remove my finger from her lips and take her hand instead. "You've done nothing wrong. I'm the one with the problem."

"What do you mean?"

"I've liked you for a long time," I admit. "And I've watched a lot of guys hit on you. Heard even more of them discussing how much they like you and how much they want to be with you. It bothered me a lot, but I couldn't say anything because…" I gesture to her hand in my mine. "Well, because I couldn't."

She nods slowly.

"I thought that, dating you, those feelings would be like a switch I could turn off. I thought other men being interested in you would suddenly not bother me. But that's not how it's working out." I stumble over my words. "I-it still gets to me."

"Oh, Gunner. I'm not interested in other guys," Rebel says gently. "You can trust that."

"I trust *you*. It's *them* I don't trust." I glare a hole in the wall, imagining Rodney Howard and Benji making another play for Rebel's affections. "Even men twice your age talk about wanting you. Phil went on and on this morning."

Her entire expression brightens with awareness. "I knew I sensed something off when you brought donuts this morning. It was because of Phil?"

"It's not Phil. It's me. This is my problem. Not yours. I promise I'll deal with it on my own. I won't let something like this stop me from becoming the man you deserve."

The smile in her eyes falters, melting into a startled vulnerability. "You say the sweetest things, Gunner Kinsey."

I give her hand a squeeze.

"But," Rebel continues in a firm voice, "you don't have to handle this alone. If something bothers you, I want to know. I want us to work through it together. The more you keep it to yourself, the more it festers. A small misunderstanding might turn into a big deal if you don't talk to me about it. I can't read your mind."

"Understood." I smile slightly. "But I disagree. You seem to understand me without me saying a word."

She picks up her fork and finally starts eating with gusto. "Well, yeah. I've been around you enough that I can pick up on a few things. Like tonight, I sensed you were upset right away, but I didn't know what you were angry about and it drove me nuts."

"I'll work on that too."

"And I'll make it abundantly clear that I have a boyfriend. No matter where I am."

"What if that doesn't stop them?" I ask with a frown.

"I'll…" Her eyes roll to the top of her head in thought, "I'll bark at them or something." She shrugs. "I'll figure it out."

I chuckle.

Rebel laughs too.

Once she's finished eating, I clear the plates from the table and set them on the counter. Then I let the basin fill with water while I arrange all the dirty plates, pans, utensils and cups.

"You don't have to wash the dishes. You can leave them there. I'll get to it later."

"I got it," I grunt. Honestly, I feel relieved after our heart-to-heart around the table. I wouldn't have blamed Rebel for thinking the worst of me when she heard I was struggling with the attention she gets. Her understanding and gentleness makes me want to do more for her.

"Let me help then," Rebel says. And I expect her to pull on the pink rubber gloves at the side of the sink and rinse.

But instead, her soft arms slide around my waist and she plasters herself to my back.

I look down at where her hands are locked around me and smile, melting like butter in her palm.

"This is how you'll help?" I ask, twisting around to look at her.

"It's called 'moral support'. I can stop if you want…" She starts to unwind her hands and I quickly touch her wrist to stop her.

Rebel settles against me again. As she hides her face in my back, I feel the indent of her smile.

"Sit when you get tired," I say as gently as I can.

"Mm-hm."

I get started on the cups first. Rebel's body is soft against mine and her shampoo fills my nose with pleasant notes of cherries. The thunk of cups hitting the sudsy water and the swish of the cloth is all that can be heard for a few moments.

I feel full enough to burst. With Rebel, I feel extremely happy doing something as ordinary as washing dishes.

"Gunner," Rebel says.

I look back at her.

"You said you've liked me for a long time. How long is that?"

"Still can't tell you, Bell."

"Oh, come on," she whines. "Why is it such a big secret?"

Among all the secrets I'm keeping from her, the exact timeline of my feelings is probably the least complicated. But I still don't want to reveal it.

"You're just keeping me in suspense to be dramatic," Rebel says, sliding away and leaning against the counter. "I'm going to take a guess. Since you said it was a long time, could it be that you liked me the day you asked me to be your fake girlfriend? No, you couldn't have. We barely spoke to each other then."

I finish washing the last of the dishes and twist my body toward hers. Arms out, I trap her against the counter.

Rebel backs up, watching me with eyes crinkling at the corners.

"I'll give you a hint."

She nods eagerly.

I tilt my head and lean in, stopping a breath away from her lips. "It was before then."

Her blue eyes, alive with shock, are the last things I see before I swoop in and take control of her mouth. She's as sweet as the dessert I have stowed away in the fridge and I just can't get enough.

The angle of the kiss changes and I sense Rebel rising on the tips of her toes to kiss me back passionately. My vision blurs, the edges of the kitchen melting into oblivion as my pulse roars in my ears.

After a while, we both ease away.

Rebel's breathing hard.

I'm barely breathing.

The air feels heavier, my limbs light enough to float me straight to the ceiling, untethered and lost in the moment.

I rest my forehead against Rebel's, my heart beating fast.

"Gunner?"

I look at her.

"I really, *really* like you. And I have for a long time too."

CHAPTER
FORTY-THREE

REBEL

The next morning, I float to work, still high from my date with Gunner. *I can't wait to see him again.*

There's so much more to the quiet hockey player than meets the eye and the more I discover of him, the more I want.

"Good morning," I coo, nodding at Delia and April who are already there.

April smirks over at me as I skip to my workstation and pull on my gloves.

"Someone's in a good mood." Leaning against the car I'm diagnosing, she asks, "How was your date last night."

"Incredible. He cooked dinner. Salmon."

Her eyes widen. "Gunner can cook?"

"That's what *I* said!" I laugh.

"Huh. I guess you really can't judge a book by its cover."

"You should know that by now, with how many books you read," I tease, shooing her away from the car so I can get started. I have a feeling I'm close to discovering what the problem is with this car, and then I can start doing my favorite part—sketching and creating the part it's missing.

A little later, April leaves the garage to go visit her dad and I continue with Delia, getting lost in time while doing what I love.

From somewhere outside my happy, little bubble of focus, I hear a shout.

And then I hear the thud of boots on the floor.

I flip my welding mask up and look over at the door.

There are five people in hazmat suits descending on the garage like a horde of puffy-white locusts. I've never seen people in actual hazmats suits outside of those alien takeover movies and they look extra menacing in real life.

I'm so startled, I nearly drop my torch. Thankfully, I have the good sense to turn the machine off.

Snapping my welding mask up, I stare at the men in horror. "What's going on here?"

Delia stops too, her eyes as wide as my fists.

"We received reports of a safety violation."

The voice coming from the hazmat suit is muffled so, at first, I'm not certain that I heard correctly.

But somehow Delia has superhuman hearing because she understood the man from all the way across the room and yells "What do you mean a safety violation?"

"Time is of the essence, ma'am." The little display window on his hazmat suit fogs up as he speaks. "We need you to vacate the premises for your own safety."

The hazmat suit grabs my arm and starts dragging me to the door. Delia throws me a confused look as she, too, is aggressively escorted out. I'm so stunned that I don't even fight the hand dragging me outside.

When I finally get a grip on myself, it's too late. They're already invading like cockroaches, spreading out everywhere inside the auto shop.

I can see exactly what they're doing as all our shutters are rolled up today. We have four giant doors acting like floor-to-ceiling windows to the chaos inside the shop.

"Hey, don't touch that!" I yell when one of the hazmat suits start jimmying our exhaust extraction hose.

Another one starts taking pictures.

I turn frantic eyes on Cordelia. "What are they saying?"

"I think they found something wrong with the exhaust hose."

My face pales. "That's impossible."

Ever since our huge scare with April, we've been extra careful about poisonous gases. Chance, out of fear, installed three different poisonous gas alarms.

I've been extra careful too. Seeing my best friend get carted to the hospital once was enough to scar me for life.

I look around, searching for the key to stopping this madness. There's a smug-looking man in a suit standing on the lawn, tapping notes on a tablet. He's the only one not wearing a hazmat suit.

Stalking to the guy who looks like he's in charge, I demand, "How dare you? This is private property. You can't just come in here and mess with our things."

"We're here on behalf of the County's Safety Committee, Ms. Hart. You have been found in violation of several safety codes. Under county law, we have the right to shut this place down until the completion of a thorough investigation."

Those were a lot of snooty words, but my brain stops functioning at the phrase 'shut' and 'down'.

"What do you mean shut down? You can't do that!" I yell.

"We can." He nods to the hazmats who start rolling yellow 'KEEP OUT' tape all along the shop. "And we will."

My bones feel hollow. My muscles twitch. For a second, it feels like the sky turns completely black above my head.

Panicked, I whirl around to find that the hazmats have successfully blocked off our garage like it's the scene of a crime.

A crowd is gathering to watch and some of them have their phones out to record. This will be all over the neighborhood chat by evening. There's a big possibility it might even get picked up by the evening news.

Delia touches my arm gently. "Should I grab my wrench and start swinging?"

My mind is spiraling with a million thoughts, but the comment makes me smile. She looks dead serious too.

"No." I shake my head and take a few, calming breaths.

Think, Rebel. Think.

The Safety Committee swarmed the shop because someone made a complaint. But how did they know to go straight for the exhaust hose—the one safety hazard April and I had trouble with before, as if they knew they could use that fact against us.

Today's rampage was instigated by someone with a plan.

I turn slightly. "Delia, call April and tell her what's going on."

The mechanic nods and taps on her cell phone.

I march back to the Safety Committee member. "I'm Rebel Hart, co-owner of The Pink Garage. Who issued a complaint against our auto shop?"

"I can't tell you that, ma'am. We on the Safety Committee accept anonymous complaints." He shakes his head. "And we can't go around exposing our sources."

What a perfect answer.

"I at least deserve to know what the next steps are to sort this out. I assure you that we run our shop with safety in mind. I'm very certain this is all a big misunderstanding."

"The investigation will determine that," he says, looking over at me with disapproval.

I fight an eye roll and keep my tone civil. "How long will an investigation take?"

"It depends." He taps something on his tablet. "It could take a few weeks or a few months. Depending on the schedule of the lab."

His words twist me inside out. "I'm sorry. Did you say it could take *months?*"

He ignores me and motions to the hazmats. "You boys about finished?"

"Yes, boss!" The hazmat-men shout.

Turning away, the boss walks to his truck as if I'm nothing but a buzzing mosquito in his ears.

I keep step with him, pleading my case. "So you're saying… we won't be able to use our garage for months?"

"Ma'am," he tucks the tablet under his arm and reaches for a clipboard, "your garage is officially under investigation and, according to state laws, you are not allowed to resume business here until our investigation is complete." With a flourish, he snatches out a piece of paper and shoves it at me. "That's your official notice. If you have any complaints, you can send them to the address written there. Have a good day."

"But…" I reach out to him with the arm holding the paper.

The man climbs into his truck and slams the door, nearly whacking my finger off in the process. The hazmat men dive into their vans, pulling away from the garage like clouds getting swallowed up by the night. Trucks rumble and the men leave tire tracks on our grass as they peel out of the parking lot.

Whispers float from the crowd. Their eyes watch me to see what I'll do next. I'm so shocked, that I can't even form a sentence.

Delia clears her throat. "Wish you'd thrown a punch or two now, don't you?"

I glance at her.

She winces. "Sorry. I, uh, I'll keep my mouth shut."

My lips twitch. "It's fine. You're right. I do want to throw a punch. But not at them."

"At who?"

"At the man responsible for this mess."

Stewart Kinsey.

This has his grimy paw prints all over it.

While Carol Kinsey hates me, it's not her style to send men to do her dirty work. She likes watching the life drain out of her opponent's eyes herself.

Stewart, on the other hand, is underhanded and slimy.

"I came to tell you that I'm not getting through to April," Delia says worriedly.

Oh right. April usually puts her volume low when she's with her dad so the phone doesn't disturb him if he's trying to sleep.

"Keep trying. Tell her I'll meet her back here later." I pull my keys from my jumpsuit pocket.

"I'll stay here and keep guard," Delia says, lifting her chin up like a warrior about to be stationed on night duty.

I shake my head, eyeing the yellow tape tensely. "Go home."

"Where are you going?"

"To find the man responsible for this mess."

Delia takes one look at my determined face and says, "Do you have a wrench?"

I snort out a laugh. "Yeah, it's in the tool box in the truck bed. But I won't need it where I'm going. Violence isn't going to solve this one."

"Always good to have a plan B."

I throw a smile over my shoulder. "I'm sorry you're caught up in this mess, Delia. And don't worry. No matter what happens, April and I will make sure to compensate you for the work you've done and help you find a new job if…" A lump forms in my throat and I can't finish the words.

"I'm not going anywhere, Rebel." Delia speaks with conviction. "I signed the contract with The Pink Garage and I'm a part of the team, for better or worse." She pauses. "But, hopefully, we don't have to live through 'worse' because I do need to pay rent."

Fear chokes me up and I can't laugh again, so all I can do is offer a watery smile and send Delia a wave.

As I drive to Stewart Kinsey's garage, I force myself not to think about what will happen if we can't operate out of the garage. Where will we go? How will we accept our clients' cars and keep them safe?

Instead, I turn on a rock song and hike the volume all the way up. I can't leave room for doubts. To handle a slippery snake like Stewart Kinsey, I'll need every one of my senses.

Stewart's garage rises into view and I'm instantly hit with a flood of memories. Mom would bring me here after school and I'd work on my coloring book in the corner while she cleaned around the auto bays and washed the cars.

It was here that the seed of my love for auto repair was planted.

So I guess it's ironic that it's here I'm running back to now that my shop is in trouble.

I storm past the technicians who gasp when they see me walking in.

Stewart's receptionist shoots to her feet, her chair skittering across the room and smashing against the wall.

"Rebel, you can't go in there."

I stomp past her.

She bounces in front of me, her bleached hair teased into a giant bun on the top of her head. "He's with someone."

"I don't care." I sidestep her and wrench Stewart's office door open, yelling, "Kinsey, how dare you—"

The words get stuck in my throat when the man sitting across from Stewart Kinsey turns and a familiar pair of eyes meet mine.

Gunner?

CHAPTER
FORTY-FOUR

GUNNER
Thirty Minutes Earlier...

MOM'S ON THE PHONE WHEN I PASS THE LIVING ROOM ON MY WAY to practice.

"Say that again?" Mom screeches. "The Safety Committee is doing *what* to The Pink Garage?"

I stop in my tracks. *Did something happen to Rebel?*

Mom's leaning forward in the love seat, her cell phone to her ear.

"Put it on speaker," I mouth, gesturing to the phone.

She taps a button. "Go ahead, Janice. What did you hear?"

"I found out from Courtney's daughter. She's the Committee's new receptionist. She's also working with the law firm. She said they've been scrambling to find another lawyer now that Victoria changed her mind and left Lucky Falls—"

"The garage, Janice," I cut in impatiently. "What happened to Rebel's garage?"

"Hi, Gunner!"

I rub my temple, fighting for patience. "Yes, hi Janice."

Janice makes a smacking sound as if she's eating and talking at the same time. "So Courtney's daughter told her that Stewart stormed in there asking to make a report. Apparently, the garage is not up to code, and they don't have proper safety measures in place. He said someone got hurt and was rushed to the hospital because of the poor conditions..."

I'm on the move before she's finished her statement.

"Gunner, where are you going?" Mom yells at my back.

I crash through the screen door, whip out my cell phone and dial Uncle Stewart's number.

The line connects.

"What?" Uncle Stewart grunts.

"Where are you?" I growl. "We need to talk. *Now.*"

CHAPTER
FORTY-FIVE

GUNNER

The Present

The moment Rebel Hart bursts into my uncle's office in her pink mechanic jumper, an unsettled feeling lands in my stomach.

I rushed over here to protect her.

But the optics...

Will she jump to conclusions and assume I've been plotting with Uncle Stewart against her and the garage?

The fire in Rebel's eyes blazes brighter when she looks at me and the knot in my gut twists even more.

"Rebel." Uncle Stewart's lips curl up in a menacing smile. "I heard there was trouble today. Everything alright?"

I press my lips together as my gaze sweeps to the floor.

"You know..." Uncle Stewart hisses, "the inspector is a really close friend of mine. I *could* be convinced to talk to him on your behalf."

Rebel makes a disgusted sound. "I doubt you'd be so generous as to offer that for free."

"My terms are simple. Call off Chance McLanely's lawyers and I'll make all the bad things…" Uncle Stewart waves both hands, "*poof.* Go away."

The old man looks back at me, his smile tinged with victory.

Bad things will happen…

I realize that whatever he's doing to attack The Pink Garage isn't only to put Rebel and April in their places. It's also a warning for me.

And it's a warning I hear loud and clear.

Rebel advances, nostrils flaring. "Listen here, Stewart Kinsey, because I'm only going to say this once." Her hair bounces against her back and the sparkly clip she keeps at the front slides down to her ears. "You made a big mistake going after my garage and my people. I planned to leave you alone because I thought you were pathetic enough without any help from us…"

Uncle Stewart's mouth slacks. "Pathetic?"

"… but now I don't have a shred of care left." Rebel points at him. "I'm coming for you, Kinsey. So sit back and enjoy. I'll show you why you were right to be scared of us."

Uncle Stewart charges to his feet and lurches forward threateningly.

I'm on the move in the blink of an eye. Standing so fast the chair I was sitting in topples over, I take big strides until I'm standing in front of Rebel. My expression darkens with a menacing scowl. I silently dare my uncle to take a step toward her.

He comes to a screeching halt, amusement glinting in his eyes.

I hope he's not assuming that I wouldn't hurt him.

I wouldn't *want* to.

But I also won't allow one hair on Rebel's head to be harmed. Not on my watch.

Rebel takes my hand and I spin to look at her. She juts her chin at the door in a silent 'let's get out of here'. I follow her, eager to whisk her as far away from my uncle as possible.

"Ms. Hart." Uncle Stewart's stern voice halts our exit.

Rebel stops.

I freeze.

"That hand you're holding… how long do you think you can keep holding on to it?"

Fear crawls over my throat and the world spins like a ride I desperately want to get off.

Uncle Stewart digs his fingers in the wound deep inside me by adding, "Your looks can do a lot for you, but it can't change objective truths. And the truth is, no matter how much my nephew loves you, no matter how much he cares, at the end of the day blood is blood. Gunner will *always* be a Kinsey."

The swirling storm in the pit of my stomach rages, making me nauseous. I hear what Uncle Stewart *isn't* saying. As a Kinsey, even the sins that aren't mine are still mine to bear. I'll always represent the best and the worst of my family.

To the world.

And to Rebel.

Especially to Rebel.

Rebel tugs me out of the room while Uncle Stewart cackles behind us. We pass my uncle's workmen and keep going until we get outside.

"Oooh!" Rebel shudders. "That man is *awful*! Does he really think I'll strike a deal with him after what he did? Typical Kinsey! So full of himself." Rebel realizes what she's said and her face stamps with guilt. "I didn't mean—"

I give her a tight-lipped smile.

"Don't let what he said bother you. You're nothing like your uncle."

I don't respond. Mostly because I'm having a hard time breathing.

"Gunner? Are you okay? You're so pale." Rebel dabs at my temple with the heel of her hand. "And you're sweating."

"Are *you* okay?" I ask tightly.

"Yeah, for now." Rebel steps into me, her eyes cautious. "Did your uncle call you over today?"

I can tell she's putting great effort into not accusing me of anything.

"I heard he was stirring things up at the Safety Committee."

"Yeah, your uncle managed to shut down our garage."

Surprise ripples across my chest, temporarily stealing my breath. "What?"

"Just a sec, Gunner. April is calling. Hello?" Rebel walks away with her cell phone to her ear. While she updates her business partner, I wilt against my truck, sucking in deep breaths.

Uncle Stewart is boldly making moves, which means that whoever is behind him is ready to clear the board. The timing couldn't be worse. I've yet to find any concrete evidence of what my family did or a way to gain the upper hand.

To make matters worse, Rebel and I are at the beginning stages of our relationship. I doubt we'll be able to survive a 'my family might have ruined yours' conversation this early on.

I hear Rebel's footsteps approaching and straighten.

She pockets her phone, her sky-blue eyes glued to me. "Gunner, you really don't look well."

I shake my head. "Are you going home now?"

"Yeah, April and Chance are going to meet me there so we can strategize on what to do next." She offers a brave smile. "It'll work out somehow."

Not if my uncle has his way.

I nod to my truck. "I'll come with you."

She holds up a hand. "I don't think that's a good idea."

The hitch in her voice makes me stop and look down at her.

"This is a little complicated given… I mean… he's your uncle."

I step back.

Rebel winces. "I'm not blaming you at all, Gunner. It's just that April and I probably won't have any nice things to say right now, and I don't want you to feel uncomfortable. The last thing I want is to put you in an awkward position."

It's not that *I'll* be uncomfortable. It's that *she'll* be uncomfortable.

I guess Uncle Stewart was right.

In her eyes, I'll always be a Kinsey.

I take another step back. "Go have your meeting with April and Chance."

"Gunner…"

"Let me walk you to your car."

Rebel gnaws on her bottom lip as I escort her to the pink truck.

She sneaks a peek at me. "Are you angry?"

"I'm not angry."

"You look angry."

"I'm not."

"Would you tell me if you were?" She pouts. "You wouldn't."

I open the door for her. "Call me if you need me. I'll come running."

"I know." She offers me a sad smile.

After she drives off, I return to my truck and release a weary sigh.

What do I do now?

Uncle Stewart attacked The Pink Garage and he may have another bomb to drop to make sure they *stay* down. The situation is quickly getting out of control. How do I put an end to this before it escalates any further?

Lost in my thoughts, I hear a knock on my window.

It's Rebel.

Her eyes are burning blue jewels in her face and she flaps her hands, indicating that I should lower the window. I do, my gaze wide and questioning.

"I thought you'd left," I say.

"I came back to tell you something," she replies, sounding winded.

I brush a lock of her hair away from her cheeks, waiting.

"We are *not* on opposite sides of this fight," she says, her voice low and earnest. "I trust you, Gunner. But I'm not ready to ask you to choose me over your family." Rebel licks her lips. "Maybe it's because I'm afraid of the choice you'd make…" Her eyes dart away. "Or maybe it's because I don't think I'm deserving of being chosen either."

My gaze snaps to hers and, for a fleeting moment, I feel the weight of those words like an anchor driving me deep into the core of the earth.

"It took a lot of courage to come back and tell you that, but we promised we'd be honest with each other. And that's honestly how I feel."

"I understand," I say, wishing I could give her the assurance she needs.

But I can't say more.

I don't dare to.

Because she's mistaken.

The choice that will determine our future isn't one I'll make between my family and Rebel.

It's a choice Rebel will have to make between my family… and me.

True terror seeps through me when I think of her *not* choosing us. It's so real, that I push out of the window, cradle her chin in my palm and kiss her while I still can.

The touch of my lips on hers is featherlight, the faintest whisper, a question rather than a claim. My fingers slide over her neck and tangle in her long, blonde hair. I tilt my head, slowing the pace of my strokes and letting my eyes squeeze shut.

I want to remember everything about her, about this moment.

The slight hitch of her breath as my mouth grazes across her strawberry-sweet lips.

The citrusy scent of her carried on the breeze.

The way her hair falls like a silky waterfall over my knuckles.

Rebel kisses me back, balancing herself on the running board and wrapping her arms around the back of my neck.

I stroke her mouth with mine and tilt her head to sip from her one more time before backing off. Not too far though. My breath mingles with hers, the connection between us fragile but achingly real.

Rebel pulls her lips into her mouth as if to savor the lingering buzz of the kiss.

I could sit here, staring at her through the window, all day. But a whistle erupts behind us. A few mechanics are gathered at the door of the garage and they're staring our way.

I scowl and Rebel ducks her head self-consciously.

"Call me," I demand gruffly.

"I will."

"I'll bring lunch after your meeting."

That earns me a bigger smile.

Rebel hops off the running board and sends me a tiny wave before hurtling back to her truck.

The tightness in my chest fades a bit as I watch her back out of the lot.

Maybe there's hope for us.

Maybe we really *can* get through this with our relationship intact.

Just then, my phone chirps.

I answer distractedly. "Hello?"

"Gunner," my mom sounds excited, "get home quick. You won't believe who just rolled into town!"

There's a rustling sound, as if mom's handing over the phone and then a dark voice croaks...

"Hello, Gunner."

Ice runs through my veins.

That voice instantly carries me back to my grandfather's

funeral and the instruction that changed the course of my life forever.

"It's been a while, hasn't it?"

My mind whirs with chaos.

My stomach roils threatening to bring back everything I had for breakfast this morning.

"I think," the throaty voice whispers, *"you and I need to have a chat."*

CHAPTER
FORTY-SIX

REBEL

April and I discuss damage control while Chance calls his lawyers.

The McLanely wealth isn't something I think about much, but I'm *extremely* grateful for Chance's connections now.

"Our lawyers will submit an injunction," Chance says, walking back to us with a frown. "But we won't know what we're really fighting against until the investigation concludes and a report is submitted."

"Let me guess. The 'investigation' can take as long as Stewart Kinsey wants?" I mumble.

"That jerk!" April scowls. "I thought he couldn't get any lower, but I was wrong. He's lower than scum." April spins around to glare at Chance. "This is ridiculous! Do we really have to close our shop because Stewart said so?"

"Not because Stewart said so but... yeah. You do."

April scoffs.

I loosen my ponytail because I'm getting a massive headache.

Chance taps his cell phone in his palm, his eyes on April. "It's unfortunate, but legal."

"Great," April grouses.

"The lawyers said Plan B is to countersue. They'll prepare the documents and get back to me in twenty-four hours, but there are no guarantees. So in the meantime…"

"We wait?" I supply, finishing his sentence.

Chance takes one look at April's aggrieved expression and says, "We don't have to. I can find a way to make Stewart's life miserable right now."

"How?" April leans forward eagerly.

Chance arches a brow. "It depends on how angry you are."

April's lips form somewhat of a smile. "Very."

"I'll give Theilan a call. I know he won't ask questions if I ask him to bring a shovel and a large duffel bag."

April considers it and then shakes her head. "It's not worth it. Besides, I don't want to get you and the team in trouble. Especially before the last game of the season."

Chance puts his phone away.

"What are we going to do about the expansion?" April groans and sinks into my sofa. "We've already paid for the preliminaries and gotten the bank loan approvals. This will ruin everything."

"You know I'm always here to help, Tink," Chance says. "I'm not hurting financially."

"No way," April says.

"I'll take that deal." I lift a hand.

April frowns at me.

"We're in emergency mode. This is no time to be coy. Let's call on the power of #Chapril and find a way to solve this."

My best friend springs to her feet again, her eyes dark and wary. "This is all Stewart Kinsey's fault. I should have kicked him in the shins when I had the chance."

I chuckle.

Then I feel guilty for laughing when I think of how Gunner would have felt hearing that.

This is exactly why I didn't want him around. The feud between me and his family is reaching a boiling point and I don't want him caught in the middle of it.

"Is it possible to rent another garage until we sort this all out?" Chance asks, rubbing his chin in thought.

"Where would we find another garage in Lucky Falls?" I wonder.

"Maybe you could convert a factory or some other building? Then you can take the bank's money and build a new garage somewhere else, can't you?"

"That's a great idea." I look to April.

She shakes her head. "The bank is issuing the money out in phases. We have to prove we did phase one to get phase two's cash. We can't reroute it or we'll be in even bigger trouble."

My shoulders droop as what I *thought* was a great idea goes swirling down the toilet.

April reclaims her seat beside Chance and buries her face in her hands. "It was difficult enough to get the approval for this loan. I can't imagine going back to the loan officers. And what are we going to do about Delia? She uprooted her entire life and came to Lucky Falls because of us. Are we going to kick her out on her own after less than a month?"

"My money is still on the table."

"Chance McLanely, put your wallet away. I'm venting."

April's boyfriend pins his lips together and reduces his role to that of a silent back-rubber.

I dig a toe into my fuzzy pink rug. "Something about this doesn't feel right."

"Yeah, it feels pretty dang awful," April grumbles.

"I don't understand why Stewart's trying so hard to shut us down."

"It's because he hates us," April says tersely. "He has ever since I turned down his proposal to merge our two garages."

I scrunch my lips. "Why do I get the feeling it's more than that?"

"What do you mean?"

"When I went to confront him, Stewart said that he'd help us out if we stopped Chance's investigation."

Chance narrows his eyes. "Was he messing with you or was he serious?"

"He was serious. Gunner and I both heard him."

April flinches. "Is it a coincidence that all this started happening *right after* you officially started dating Gunner?"

I fold my arms over my chest, on the defensive.

"Tink, what are you saying?" Chance asks worriedly.

"I don't know." April throws her hands high. "That maybe Gunner's been planning this all along? Rebel, you said it was strange when he called you his girlfriend in front of the Lady Luck Society."

"Gunner has nothing to do with this."

"Even if he doesn't mean to, it's more likely that he'll side with his family than with us."

April's words echo what Stewart Kinsey said today and my hackles rise. "So what? What do you expect him to do? Cut off everyone in his family because his uncle's a creep?"

April's mouth falls open and I realize that I'm yelling.

"I trust Gunner," I say with a little less 'shrieking banshee' in my tone.

"So do I," Chance agrees. "If you knew how invested Gunner has been in this investigation, you wouldn't even question him."

I stop in my tracks, my eyes fastened on Chance. "Gunner's been helping you investigate his uncle?"

"Yeah. I remember him asking them to investigate a connection between Stewart and some guy… what was his name…" Chance scratches the back of his neck. "Clarence Kinsey."

"Clarence Kinsey?" I gasp.

April winces.

Chance frowns. "I'm guessing you know the guy?"

"Clarence Kinsey is Gunner's granduncle," I explain. "He's the brother of Gunner's grandfather."

I don't remember much of him from my days playing on the Kinsey farm, but I do remember seeing him at the funeral for Gunner's grandaddy.

Clarence had tapped into town with a walking cane, a large black fedora on his head and a three-piece suit wrapped around his scrawny body. I remember thinking he looked a little too happy when all the other Kinseys were sad.

Clarence Kinsey did not live in Lucky Falls. When I asked about him after the funeral, mom said Clarence's personality was too big for a town as small as ours.

He'd stayed in Lucky Falls for a few days after the funeral. I have a faint memory of being at the wake and seeing a whole lot of angry stares when he walked in the room. He was like a black cloud that spread gloom over everyone he touched.

Including Gunner.

Come to think of it, Gunner stopped talking to me shortly after his Uncle Clarence rolled into town.

To be fair, I hadn't noticed the timing. Back then, I assumed Gunner pulled away because he was sad about his grandfather's passing. To my five-year-old brain, everything would go back to normal eventually.

But of course, it never did.

Gunner avoided me staunchly for years, and I chalked it up to him flipping a switch and turning into the cold, arrogant Kinsey he was always meant to be.

But now, after hearing that he's investigating Stewart *and* Clarence, I can't help thinking that there's something more to the story.

"He lives in the city and he's extra, *extra* rich. Legend says the Kinseys have held on to power for so long because Clarence Kinsey funds all their businesses, investments, college education, everything."

"I thought the Kinseys were rich on their own," Chance says, his nose scrunching. "Don't they own almost every store on Main Street?"

"I said it was a legend." April shrugs. "I don't know when it started, but we've all kind of known that Clarence Kinsey was the one who held the purse strings ever since his brother, Clay, died. I think only the Kinseys would know the details though."

A sense of foreboding falls over me and I quietly ingest Chance's revelation.

Suddenly, Chance's phone rings loudly.

I jump.

April shrieks.

Chance gives us an apologetic look and goes to answer the call in the other room. When he returns, he looks somber.

"What?" April scrambles to her feet.

"The lawyers found bank transactions between Clarence and Stewart. *Big* transactions. Stewart's been selling off a *lot* of Kinsey land lately."

April's brows knit in the center of her forehead. "Do they know why?"

Chance pulls out his fidget spinner and gives it a flick. "No, but maybe Gunner does."

"What do you mean?"

"Now that I think about it, he seemed a little frantic during our last meeting with the lawyers."

Those words drop in the center of the room and stare at us like a hissing mountain lion. Gunner is many things but 'frantic' isn't one of them.

"Land and money," April shudders. "People do a lot of terrible things for them."

Chance braces himself. "Why do I feel like we're stepping into a minefield here?"

I rub my necklace. "Because whatever Gunner knows about Stewart and Clarence has him going against his entire family.

And his family just so happens to be *the* most powerful one in Lucky Falls."

"I think you should call Gunner," April squeaks.

"Yeah." I pick up my phone that suddenly feels as heavy as a rock. "That's probably a good idea."

CHAPTER
FORTY-SEVEN

GUNNER

My phone rings from my back pocket, but I ignore it and stare at the man in mom's living room.

Uncle Clarence, or 'Uncle Clancy' to most of us, still uses a cane and the way it *tap-tap-taps* on the polished wooden floors makes me clench my fists and brace myself for a fight.

His hair is just as grey as it was that day outside the church. His eyes are just as sharp and piercing, bracketed by the very same wrinkles that deepen when he flashes a deceptively serene smile.

It shocks me that he hasn't aged a day. He might as well have walked right out of my worst memories.

"Gunner. Let me give you a hug." Uncle Clancy wraps his arms around me like a snake engulfing its prey in a lethal hug.

I stiffen in his arms, holding myself still.

He leans back, glancing over at my mother who's beaming at us as if Uncle Clancy hangs the moon.

"How many years has it been, Clancy?" Mom asks.

"Long enough that I almost didn't recognize Gunner. Your

son got so big, Carol!" Uncle Clancy wags a wrinkled finger in my face. "Looking at him, you wouldn't believe he was ever small enough for me to pick up and carry around."

My mother laughs.

Uncle Clancy joins her.

The harmony of their voices suffocates me.

Mom grins. "How long are you going to be in town, Clancy? Does anyone else know you're here?"

"Not yet," Uncle Clancy says, tapping his way to the chair and sitting down gingerly. "I thought it would be a nice surprise if I showed up unannounced."

"I'm honored that we're the first house you came to. Stewart and the rest will be so jealous when they hear." Mom preens.

I growl at my uncle, "Why the sudden visit?"

Mom's eyes whip to me, blazing with silent disapproval. "Excuse him, Clancy. Gunner's not one for mincing words, but his bark is worse than his bite."

Mom finishes off the excuse with another, pointed look at me.

Behave, her eyes convey.

Uncle Clancy grips the top of his cane and swivels to face me. "I was finishing up a very important deal close by and I figured, since I'm here, I might as well come down to Lucky Falls and see the old haunts."

"You've been gone since the funeral, haven't you?" Mom taps her chin. "Wow. How many years has it been?"

"Too long," Uncle Clancy says wearily. "I stopped by the cemetery on my way in."

Mom turns sober. "Did you visit Clay's grave? We keep it clean and I regularly change the flowers."

"I appreciate that." Clancy smiles sadly. "It's been so long, but the pain of losing him is still fresh. Between the two of us, Clay was the dreamer."

"He contributed so much to Lucky Falls," mom says, dabbing at the corner of her eyes. "I'll never forget how nervous I was when I got married and he spoke to me so kindly and made me feel welcome. He was the kindest man I've ever met."

"Maybe a little too kind." Clancy's eyes turn strained. "If I wasn't there to stop him, our family would have gone broke a long time ago."

Mom straightens her shoulders. "Well, there's a time for kindness and a time for business. You need both to survive. That's why you were such a great team. It's thanks to you and Clay investing in Lucky Falls that our family was able to thrive here."

"Clay was the one who saw what this town could be. I was just along for the ride."

Mom smiles.

"Carol, you wouldn't happen to have something warm I could drink, do you?" Clancy rubs his throat. "I'm feeling a bit under the weather."

"Of course. Of course. I'll be back in a jiffy. Gunner, you should update your uncle on everything you and the team have accomplished this season. Did you hear that *the* Chance McLanely joined our local hockey team?"

"That I did." Uncle Clancy lets out a rusty laugh. "Very impressive."

Mom beams from ear to ear. "I'll be right back." On her way past me, mom stops and gives me a pointed look.

I hold myself still until she disappears.

The moment her footsteps recede, all the warmth in the room leaves with her.

"Gunner, sit, sit. Why are you standing there? You look uncomfortable."

I remain standing, on edge.

Uncle Clancy laughs at my face and then he looks past me, sighing heavily. "My brother had a soft spot for this backward town." His eyes pierce through the window. "I never understood what he found so magical about this tiny place. My whole life, I knew I was destined for bigger things, but Clay never seemed to get it. You can't go big in a town this small."

Uncle Clancy's posturing is fooling no one. It was Grampa Clay's investments in this 'tiny' town that gave him the seed capital to start his business back in the city. Everything he has now... is because of this town.

"You never answered my question," I say darkly. "Why are you *really* here?"

"You know..." He pushes to his feet. "That deep voice of yours makes everything you say sound like a threat."

I watch him, silently measuring his movements as he gets closer.

The day of the funeral, Uncle Clancy was wearing a three piece suit along with the cane. Today, he's dressed in a more simple shirt and khakis but, somehow, he still carries the same subtly dangerous air as he did in flashy funeral clothes.

"Why do I get the feeling you're angry with me, Gunner?"

I hold still.

Uncle Clancy feigns a smile. "You're not still upset about what I told you after the funeral?"

'You need to stay away from that girl, Gunner.'

'Our family did something really, really bad to hers.'

'And if that girl ever finds out, bad things will happen to our family. Or to her. Do you understand?'

"So you *do* remember," I growl.

His pleasant facade drops and he stops beside me, staring in the opposite direction. Voice low and dark, he says, "I thought *you* were the one who forgot."

Never.

I still remember the way he loomed over me with his dark scowl.

The way his fingers clawed into my shoulder, hard enough to hurt.

The way his voice thickened with a threat because—even as a naive and relatively innocent child—I knew he meant it when he said; that Rebel would be hurt if I kept being her friend.

"Here you go." Mom re-enters the living room with a tray of drinks. "What were you two chatting so seriously about?"

"Oh, nothing. Just taking a walk down memory lane," Uncle Clancy says, backing away from me. "Thank you, Carol. Why, this drink looks lovely."

"It was nothing." Mom blushes and waves away his compliment.

Uncle Clancy takes a sip. His eyes slam into mine over the rim of the cup. "Gunner and I were talking about his memories from the funeral."

"He was so young then," mom says, a note of surprise in her voice. "I doubt he remembers much."

"I remember everything," I reveal coldly.

"After the funeral, I gave him a little talk about making good choices and watching out for bad folks who want to destroy his future."

My back goes ramrod straight.

His eyes train on me unflinchingly. "You were such a good boy, very obedient. Your mother taught you well."

I clench my jaw.

"He's still a good boy." My uncle releases me from his firm look and points a calculated smile at my mother. "Isn't he, Carol?"

"Er…" My mother looks between me and Uncle Clancy as if she can sense something is wrong about this conversation, but she can't put her finger on it. "Since you're here, Clancy, why don't I call the rest of the family over? Rather than visiting them one by one, they can come here instead. It'll be a nice little gathering."

My uncle and I are eyeing each other like gunslingers in a western. I doubt either of us are hearing a word of mom's nervous spiel.

I size my uncle up. If we were on the ice and someone came

onto my turf, taunting me like this, I'd slam them into the boards and take my chances in the sin bin. But this game we're playing still hasn't been defined yet. I don't know the rules and I don't know how to win.

My phone buzzes again. Someone's desperately trying to reach me.

I check my phone and notice I have several missed calls from Rebel.

Then I notice a text from Chance.

CHANCE: *The firm called. They found evidence of your Uncle Stewart selling off land and sharing the profits with Clarence Kinsey.*

There's another text with a pdf attachment of the documents.

Bingo.

I open the documents and read through quickly, glad that I have my experience in finance which makes the accounting clear. The story these numbers paint shakes loose in front of my eyes in high definition.

My gaze lifts from my phone to my uncle. Whatever he's hiding has something to do with the land he's selling off.

How nice of him to come back to Lucky Falls so I can confront him on my turf.

Just as my confidence rises, a needling voice in the back of my head holds me back. *'Don't do it, Gunner. Think of your parents. What if this secret hurts them?'*

I remember Uncle Stewart's warning. *'Give me your father's badge first. Hand over your uncle's political career. Fire your mother as chairwoman of the Society. Then I'll tell you.'*

What if exposing this secret destroys the happiness of my entire family? Would it still be worth the price?

I trust you, Gunner.

Rebel's words from earlier fill me with a quiet determination.

At seven years old, I had no choice but to cower in front of my uncle. At fifteen, I watched Rebel from afar, missing her like crazy and burning with longing. At eighteen, I ripped her heart out when I held myself back from kissing her. And again, as adults, it took faking a relationship to finally get close.

I kept my distance for *decades*. I spent my entire life, bowing to the whims of my family, carrying the burden of being a Kinsey, of protecting my family from the consequences of their sins, because I felt I had no other choice.

But now a choice is in front of me.

Will I still be that scared little seven year old, shaking and panicking because of his uncle's grave words?

I look at the ground, contemplating.

And then my eyes snap up, burning with determination.

The decision I need to make isn't easy, but it *is* simple.

My family shaped my past, but Rebel is my future. The girl I turned my back on all those years ago is the woman I now need to protect.

My lips curl up in a cold smile and I don't take my eyes off the old man when I say, "Mom, I'd like to show Uncle Clancy the apple orchard."

"All of a sudden?" Mom's voice warbles. "Why?"

I tilt my head, daring my uncle to make a move.

I've been tiptoeing around this matter long enough. If he pushes me, I'll crack the whole thing wide open, right here in front of my mom.

Clancy's smile drops and he grits his teeth.

The tension in the room pulls taut, threatening to snap and sting someone hard enough to draw blood.

"I'd love to see the apple orchard. Excuse us, Carol."

My heart burning a hole in my chest, I stalk through the door and hear the *tap-tap-tap* of Uncle Clancy's cane behind me.

CHAPTER
FORTY-EIGHT

GUNNER

On the way to the orchard, my phone rings again.

REBEL: *I texted Max and he said you aren't at the stadium.*

REBEL: *You aren't at your uncle's hardware store either. Is everything okay?*

REBEL: *Call me when you get this.*

My chest tightens.

I text her back.

ME: *I'm okay. I'll stop by your house when I'm done here.*

I hesitate and then send one more text.

ME: *There's something I need to tell you.*

I dig my fingers into the phone, take a deep breath and then shut it off.

In this moment, I can't afford to get distracted.

We keep going until we arrive at the orchard.

The neatly lined trees go on as far as the eye can see. A cool breeze tickles the leaves and draws the eye to the branches heavy with apples. The scent of the coming harvest fills my nose and reminds me of simpler times. Sitting beside dad on the tractor. Climbing rickety ladders to pluck the juiciest apples. Running behind a much smaller Rebel with a basket. Canning apples in jars of syrup and honey with Mrs. Hart.

A long, long time ago, before secrets and threats invaded my life, my world was sweet and ordinary.

I come to an abrupt stop in the middle of the orchard, but Uncle Clancy keeps going. The grass swallows the sound of his cane as he marches closer to me.

"Seems you're a man now, Gunny. Calling your uncle outside like that."

"I thought this way would be more comfortable. But we can have this conversation later. In front of everyone. I don't mind."

Uncle Clancy tips his head back and laughs. The sound booms around the treetops. Nearby birds take off in flight.

Their black wings flap against the clear blue sky. A bad omen.

"I know you've been selling off the family's land," I say simply.

Uncle Clancy tilts his head, watching me without a hint of surprise. "I'm in charge of the family portfolio. Nothing wrong with that."

"The money from the land didn't go back into the family portfolio, did it?"

His upper lip stiffens.

"It went into Uncle Stewart's 'garage'," I accuse, recalling the numbers I saw in the spreadsheet. "He was acting as a shell company for the funds. But the moment he stopped getting customers and the numbers for his shop dwindled, the harder it was to hide where all that money was coming from. Your cover was about to be blown."

Uncle Clancy speaks through gritted teeth, his voice low and taut with anger. "Those are big allegations, boy."

"I'm stating the facts," I say calmly.

"You should stick to hockey. You're jumping to conclusions when you don't even understand—"

"I have a business degree. I understand plenty."

"Everything I have ever done, I've done for this family. Your dad and your uncles aren't investors. They're not businessmen who can see the bigger picture. If they were, they wouldn't stay in a good-for-nothing town like Lucky Falls. They wouldn't be satisfied with this drivel, with the crumbs of what being a Kinsey can offer them. And still, I respect their choices. I slave away for them, securing our future and the future of this *entire* family. *I'm* the reason the Kinsey name is respected in this town. I'm the one who keeps everything together."

"No, you're not, Uncle Clancy," I say calmly.

He seethes.

"Grampa Clay is the reason the Kinseys are respected. The way he treated people, cared for them and served them is why our name is worth its weight in gold. You? You didn't do anything for us. You're a liar and a thief."

I notice a truck winding down the dirt road. It's Uncle Robert's vehicle.

"Clay's bleeding heart would have run this family straight into the ground. Do you think farms like this can exist without money?" Uncle Clancy sneers. "Who do you think pays for all this? Who do you think funds your uncle's campaigns? Pays for all your mama's charity work? Donates all those cruisers to the police station? You, *boy*, with your snobbery and your moral grandstanding have benefited from everything this family has to offer. You and the rest of the Kinseys have wanted for *nothing* all because I made it so!"

His spittle flies and lands against my face.

I wipe it off with a stiff hand.

"The only thing that gains respect is money. Everything the Kinseys have, everything we stand for, you owe to *me.*"

"Then maybe we stand for the wrong things," I clip, my voice low with unrestrained fury.

His eyes narrow. "Would the rest of them agree with you?" Uncle Clancy points in the direction of the house.

More cars are winding down the road.

More of my family members are gathering to see him.

"Sure, they may have sided with Clay at first. No one welcomed me when I came back for Clay's funeral, but is it the same now?" He walks around me in a circle, a predator sizing up it's next target. "It's been many, *many* years since I became the head of the Kinseys. Do you think any of them want to give up their comfortable lives all because I took a little bit," he clips his fingers together, "off the top?"

My heart thuds against my chest.

But I push the conversation where it really needs to go. "If this was only about you siphoning the funds, why did you tell me to stay away from Rebel?"

A barely perceptible twitch in his right eye alerts me to his unease.

"My dad wouldn't have to give up his badge and mom wouldn't lose her honor just because a crooked family member sold off land that belongs to us."

He takes a step back.

My nostrils flare.

My heart beats faster and faster.

"This is far more than you laundering money off our land, isn't it?"

He backpedals and tries to laugh me off, but his bottom lip trembles.

"You stole from someone else." The words saw at my throat as they escape into the air. "You stole from Rebel's family."

CHAPTER
FORTY-NINE

REBEL

Gunner isn't picking up and I'm too restless to stay at home, so I go for a drive.

I'm a few meters away from The Pink Garage before I realize I drove to work on autopilot. As the night sprawls before me and stars glisten overhead, I stop the car and stare at the giant, yellow 'KEEP OUT' caution tape.

April said the garage is her baby and, honestly, I feel the same. We put our blood, sweat and tears into this place. We took a huge gamble just to bet on ourselves.

It can't crumble to dust like this.

At this point, The Pink Garage's future looks grim. Before she left my apartment, April said she would talk to May about putting a notice on our website. The customers won't be happy about the delay and I can just imagine all the angry comments we'll be slammed with.

With a sigh, I put my truck in gear and head to my mother's.

"Rebel!" Mom greets me with an excited smile. "Hey, baby."

"Hi, mom." I slip into the mobile home and kick my shoes off at the door. The weight of the day crashes into me and I wrap my arms around my mother, burying my face in her neck. I'm taller than her and she buckles a little.

"What's wrong?" Mom asks, stroking my shoulder.

"Nothing," I mumble into her freckled skin.

Mom's voice holds a hint of laughter, "Then why are you acting like a baby?" She tries to pry me off.

I hold tighter. "Mm-mm."

Mom's laughter vibrates her entire body. "Let's sit down."

Still hugging her, I follow her to the sofa.

Mom sits down and I immediately fold into her side. Taking her weathered hand in mine, I stare at the callouses, nicks and marks from her many years of hard labor.

"You want to tell me what's going on?"

"I don't really want to talk about it."

She nods and strokes my hair. "You know how proud I am of you, don't you, Rebel?"

"Because I'm dating a Kinsey?" I ask dryly.

She flicks my forehead.

"Ow!" I exclaim.

"I'm proud of how smart, brave, and kind you are." Mom's eyes glitter like the stars I saw twinkling above the garage. "Look at what you did for the school."

"It wasn't a one-man job."

"True, but it was *your* vision. Your drive. By stepping up, you gave us the chance to show up for ourselves and for each other."

After all the losses I took today, mom's encouragement is like rain to a dry, deserted land.

Burrowing closer to her, I mumble, "Mom?"

"Mm?"

"What would life be like if we were rich like the Kinseys?"

"What?" Mom jerks a little.

"Imagine," I whisper, "if you owned the orchard and all the Kinsey land. Imagine," I gently caress her worn hands, "that you hired *them* to clean your houses and your businesses. Imagine you could rearrange *their* lives with just one word?"

Mom's other hand closes around mine. "Rebel, it's no good to imagine those things. Look at all we *do* have. Health. Strength." She touches my cheek gently. "Each other."

I smile.

Mom closes her eyes peacefully. "I wouldn't trade the life I have now for anything."

"How can you be so sure?"

"Because I am." Mom sounds resolute. "Money is useful, but it's not everything. I'm happy and content. There's nothing else in this world I need."

Something inside me cracks open and I let loose a sigh of relief.

All day, I've been panicking about the unfairness of the world and fending off anxiety for the future. The garage could very well end up closing its doors for good and all our hard work could go down the drain, but mom's words give me a much needed perspective shift.

The best thing about coming from nothing is that I'm no stranger to starting from the bottom. Having wealthy parents or lots of valuable land to my name didn't bring me to where I am and I don't need those things to get to where I need to go either.

My mood picks up and all the despondency that had sent me crying into my mother's arms clears away. I'm ready to take on Stewart Kinsey and whatever else might come at me. *Bring it on, sucker.*

I give her hand a squeeze. "Do you have any ice cream?"

"I'm not sure, why?"

"I'm suddenly in the mood for it." I patter to the fridge and throw the door open. Cold air blasts my face and I lean in, eyes searching the shelves. "Looks like you're out."

"Let me run to the store and get some." Mom starts to get up.

"I'll go." I put my slippers on at the door. "I'll be right back."

"Get some popcorn too," mom says. "We can watch a movie."

I give her an 'okay' gesture and drive to the store.

Inside, I grab a basket and begin perusing when I hear my name.

"Rebel?" Sheriff Kinsey hurries toward me. He's not in uniform today and is simply dressed in a T-shirt and jeans. "I thought that was you."

"Sheriff." My lips tilt up in a wary smile.

"Please. Call me Dan."

My smile turns even more awkward. Sheriff Kinsey represents the law around Lucky Falls and people from my side of town don't have the greatest relationship with the police. Because of it, I've kept my distance from him. I can count the number of times we've talked on one hand.

"Is Gunner with you?" His eyes dart past me as if his giant son will come bounding down the aisle at any second.

"No, he's not."

"Oh." The sheriff looks down thoughtfully. "I was sure he told his mother that he was going to see you."

"Maybe he got caught up on his way."

"Maybe," the Sheriff muses, rubbing his mustache.

"You know how the Lucky Strikers are when they get together," I add, throwing in a little laugh.

The Sheriff pauses and gives me an uncertain look. "Rebel, has anything been going on with Gunner lately? Anything strange?"

"Something like what?" I gulp.

"He's been asking his mother some strange questions…" The Sheriff's words trail. "Perhaps I'm overthinking it. Gunner's not the type to share his true thoughts and sometimes it's hard for me to understand him."

Unsure of how to answer that, I nod to his basket instead. "That's a lot of ice."

The Sheriff lifts the basket high. "My uncle came down for a visit and the entire family's at the house. Carol sent me to pick up a few things." He checks his watch. "I better run before the ice melts and I get in trouble with my wife."

"See yah." I smile as he passes me by. But when his words register, I call out, "Sheriff?"

He spins, his brows tightening in a way that reminds me of Gunner during an intense play. It's like his mind is already ten steps ahead of the moment.

My heart humming with quiet dread, I ask, "Who came down to visit again?"

"Uncle Clarence. My dad's older brother. I'm not sure if you've ever met him."

The blood drains from my face and I struggle to hide how shaken I am. "Uncle Clarence. Yeah, yeah, I've heard of him."

Water drips on his shoes and the Sheriff winces. "This ice is about to melt completely. Let's talk again soon, Rebel."

The sheriff rushes to the counter to pay for his items while I frantically process the news.

Clarence Kinsey is here. In Lucky Falls.

After everything that happened today, that *can't be* a coincidence.

I run to find the nearest clerk, who so happens to be one of the little girls I babysat as a kid.

"Rebel!" Britney brightens when she sees me.

"Brit, I'm so sorry. Can you put this back for me?" I hand over the basket with the ice cream and popcorn kernels.

Hurrying out of the mart, I climb into my truck and dial Gunner's number.

He doesn't pick up.

I call Chance next. "Hey, have you heard from Gunner?"

"No," Chance says. "Why? What happened?"

"He's here," I relay in a frantic rush. Throwing my seatbelt on, I back out of the parking lot and speed down the road to the Kinsey farm.

"Who's here?"

"Clarence Kinsey."

Chance leaks a stunned breath.

"What happened?" April's voice echoes in the background.

"Clarence Kinsey is here in Lucky Falls," Chance tells her.

I can picture my best friend's eyes double in sizing.

"I'm going over there."

"Where? The Kinsey farm?" April yells and I realize that Chance must have put me on speaker.

Chance throws in his own protests. "Are you sure that's a good idea? What if you run into Clarence? We don't know what we're up against here. He could be dangerous."

"He's not going to try anything with the entire family there. And I doubt I'll run into him. I have an idea of where Gunner is right now."

"Just… be careful," April stresses.

"I will."

I hang up and focus on the dark road. Since I know the Sheriff will be right behind me, I take a detour that leads to the back of the Kinsey property, and closer to the treehouse.

After parking the car, I throw the door open and hike on foot until I see the platform built on long, winding tree branches. Hiking up my pants, I scale the ladder quickly and just as I'm about to pull myself up, a hand appears in front of me.

My eyes collide with Gunner's as he leans down, his hair blowing gently in the breeze and tugging on his shirt.

Heart bursting with relief, I take Gunner's hand and let him pull me to the top of the treehouse.

CHAPTER
FIFTY

GUNNER

I'm not surprised to see Rebel at the treehouse. But deep inside... I was hoping that my hunch was wrong and she wouldn't show. Or at least that, when she did, I'd have found a way to tell her the truth.

As soon as I hear her footsteps trudging down the path, I have a moment of panic. I've felt this adrenaline rush before. But it's usually during a game, when it's down to the wire, I'm fighting for control of the puck, and there's no one around to make the pass.

With a deep breath, I look over the railing and see Rebel climbing up the ladder. Her blonde hair dangles all the way to her back and her bangles clang musically as they crash down her arm to her elbow.

My mind is rushing with a million thoughts, but not even Uncle Clarence's damaging revelation can stand up to Rebel's beauty.

In another world, one where fairytales are reality, she'd be a mesmerizing woodland fairy. And she probably wouldn't need to climb up here because she'd be able to fly.

What on earth am I thinking?

Rebel's almost at the top of the ladder now. I allow myself the luxury of holding her hand to help her to the platform.

Her fingers are warm against mine and it truly feels like home.

How much longer can you hold on to that hand? Uncle Stewart's words echo in my mind, a foreboding warning.

The world might say I'm too good for Rebel.

But I've always known it's the opposite.

Rebel Hart is way classier than all the Kinseys combined. And when she finds out the truth, her small, delicate hand will never, ever reach for mine again.

When Rebel's on steady ground, I remove my hand from hers and take a few steps back. My eyes dart to the shadowy treetops below us, marking a clear path over everything but her face.

The darkness of the night surrounds me. I thought the world would be brighter this high up. Up here, we should be closer to the sky. But the silver streaks from the moon are choked to death by the forest around us and the stars cower behind dark clouds.

"Hey," Rebel says.

I look at her and my chest squeezes tightly.

"Are you…" She nibbles on her bottom lip. "I won't even ask. I can see you're not okay."

This is it.

Whether I like it or not, the moment has come.

I need to tell her.

I open my mouth, but the words won't shake loose. My tongue is heavier than the stones on the forest floor and my brain screeches to a halt.

Rebel walks over to me. I hear her footsteps thudding and my heartbeat slows to match the rhythm of her steps.

"You want to count the stars with me?" Rebel asks in a quiet hush.

My eyes lift to hers and fall into liquid blues that were plucked straight out of heaven.

She smiles encouragingly and leads me further into the treehouse where there are less branches obstructing the view. Stooping down, she yanks on my hand until I join her on the floor. The planks are hard against my back and the earthy scent of wood and moss overwhelms me.

"Look at how many stars are out tonight," Rebel observes, her voice low and filled with awe.

I let my hands relax at my sides, staring at the constellations. The truth still looms over me but, having Rebel here, I feel I can breathe for a moment.

"Want to know a fun fact I learned about stars lately?" Rebel asks.

I grunt.

Her shirt rustles as she moves. I sense her watching me, but I don't look her way. Instead, I train my eyes on the scattered lights suspended through the night.

"At the last home game, Gordie and I were talking about stars. She said they're constantly in motion. I said they weren't. Then I looked it up and, turns out, a first grader is smarter than me."

"I wouldn't recommend getting into a trivia fight with her, especially when it comes to space. Or hockey." Whatever Renthrow feeds Gordie makes her brain ten times bigger than the average kid.

Rebel chuckles and returns her attention to the night sky. "Stars are kind of sad, aren't they? So pretty and bright, but in reality, they don't choose where they want to go. They're just caught in the riptide of a giant, cosmic wave."

I make a low sound in my throat.

"We might not be as brilliant as the stars," Rebel says thoughtfully, "but at least we can choose our own direction."

"Keep your mouth shut and nothing has to change," Uncle Clarence growled after telling me everything in the orchard

today. *"You really want to see the Kinseys crumble? You really want to be the reason your family suffers?"*

"Even if, in the moment, the waves are bigger than we are and we're being ripped apart by the tide…"

"Think of all your father's done for this town. Think of all your mother's accomplished. Everything you have, everything you are, you owe to them."

"We have the power to change course. I think… I think that's the way *we* shine in the greatest darkness," Rebel finishes.

My fingers curl into fists. The truth is going to rip the rug out from under my entire family. There will be no taking it back. The moment I pull the trigger, everything goes boom.

It's the right thing to do.

But that doesn't make it easy.

Suddenly, Rebel rolls closer. My breath hitches as she props her arm up and rests her chin against her fist, looking at me beneath thick lashes. The gemstone necklace I gifted her dangles from her neck and swings like a pendulum trying to hypnotize me. But I don't need a swinging motion to be put under Rebel's spell.

I'm already there.

I'm already hers.

"You don't have to tell me anything, Gunner. Not if it tears you up this much. I truly don't ever need to know."

My eyebrows climb to the top of my head and I stare at her. She's giving me a way out, a free pass, a ticket to easy street. Keeping this truth to myself is a much smoother road than the one I'm preparing myself to take.

"I'm happy, right here. Right now. With you. I don't need anything else," she promises.

Moved, I slide my fingers over the back of her neck and pull her down for a kiss. Our lips move in tandem, tender yet urgent. I slip my other hand over her back, losing half my mind when she mewls and arches into me.

I kiss her harder.

Faster.

Because this might be the last time I ever get to taste her lips.

Rebel tilts her head, inching down a bit as she matches the rhythm of my kisses. I realize the way she's angling her head down to meet me is uncomfortable. Without removing my lips from hers, I roll her over me and wrap both arms around her waist.

She's so soft it's enough to send my pulse into overdrive. My heart beats fast enough to rocket straight through my ribs, past my skin, and spark fireworks in the night sky.

The franticness of my touch doesn't seem to bother her, so I don't hold back. I nip at her full bottom lip, skate my tongue across the inner lining of her mouth and kiss her like I'll die if I have to stop.

Briiiing!

The sharp tone of her phone going off fills the night air.

Our lips rip apart with a pop.

"*Your* phone?" Rebel pants, her eyes a bit glazed.

If the truth wasn't looming over our heads like an ancient guillotine, seeing that dazed expression would fill me with a great deal of satisfaction.

But as I lose the warmth of her lips, cold reality quickly chases away the fire of her touch.

"It's mine," Rebel says, touching her pocket.

She plants her hands on either side of my body and tries to push herself up, but I grip her wrist to keep her lying on top of me. She flashes me a confused look, shakes her head and then an indulgent smile teases over her face.

"Answer it later," I demand.

I'm not ready to let her go yet.

My fingers stroke the curve of her cheek and the shape of her ear. I push aside her hair, tucking it behind her ear, and the strands that spilled against my shirt like golden fabric shift away.

Briiiing!

With a groan, Rebel sits up. "Let me check just in case."

I allow her to sit up and I sit up too.

"It's mom." Her hooded eyes suddenly fling open. "Oh my gosh. I told her I was going to the store and I'd be right back."

Rebel clears her throat a few times and then picks up the call. In a forced, casual voice, she coos, "Hey, mom."

"Where are you? What on earth happened? I was this close to calling the police, Rebel!" Mrs. Hart's voice is so loud that I can hear her through the phone's tiny speakers.

Rebel winces and looks over at me helplessly.

I shrug and shake my head.

She scrunches her nose, waits a beat for her mother to calm down and then says, "Sorry, mom. I, uh, got lost in the grocery store."

"Lost!" Mrs. Hart rails. *"For two hours, Rebel?"*

"Sorry, mom. We'll have movie night another time. I promise I'll make it up to you. Bye, love you!" Without giving her mother room to cut in, Rebel ends the call. "Whew." She sighs. "I completely forgot about movie night."

"If you were with your mom, why did you come looking for me?" I ask. My hand moves to the side of her neck, stroking along her jawline.

"Because I heard your Uncle Clarence was in town."

My thumb freezes on her.

Rebel looks up beneath a fringe of thick lashes. "I have a confession to make. I, uh, already know what you're so nervous to tell me. I already know what he did."

My hand falls away from her.

No, she doesn't.

She has no idea.

"It's okay, Gunner." She takes my hand in hers. "I'm not saying we should write off what happened. Your uncles are shady. That's undeniable, but honestly, I feel relieved that it wasn't anything worse."

I blink slowly.

I have never, and *will never*, love anyone the way I love Rebel Hart.

She'll be my one and only until the day I die.

But I can't keep hiding the truth just so I can keep her in my life.

I need to tell her.

Slowly, I pull my hand away from hers and admit, "It is."

She looks flustered by me pulling away and asks distractedly, "It is… what?"

"Something worse."

CHAPTER
FIFTY-ONE

REBEL

My skin is still buzzing from Gunner's kiss.

Every inch of me is begging to give him a hug.

But I know he'd push me away again.

I stare at the hand Gunner let go of and then back up to the light blue eyes swimming in agony. Deep shadows play across his inky black hair and sharp jawline. He looks like a dangerous, fairy prince. Or a vampire teetering on the edge of sanity, fangs bared to suck my blood.

Except the big secret on the tip of Gunner's tongue is the one sucking the life out of *him*.

"When my grandfather died, he left a will. And you and your mother were in it," Gunner says bluntly.

"What?" The word escapes on a puff of air. It mingles with the throaty croak of toads and the shrill cry of cicadas.

"My uncle stole the land my grandfather left for you and your mom."

Gunner's words are firm, almost harsh, but from the way he's staring at the ground and the way his hand shakes slightly, I can tell that the coldness wrapped around his words is not because he's unfeeling.

It's that he's feeling *too much*, and he's trying his best to repress it the way he always has. To remain in control. To look like nothing bothers him when, in truth, he's the most sensitive soul I've ever met. It's been that way since we were kids.

I blink slowly. "W-what do you mean?" My brows knit together. "W-what land?"

Gunner glances to the side, his face tightening. "I made a call to Victoria and asked for a favor."

My eyebrows hike at the mention of his ex-girlfriend.

"She still had access to the law firm's database in Lucky Falls. She sent me these."

He turns his phone over and swipes through photos.

Something tells me that Victoria isn't supposed to be sharing sensitive information like this, but I don't question it too deeply.

"What is all this?" I ask, swiping through images of documents, land titles, and estate listings.

"Evidence. The one I was looking for, except I didn't know exactly where to look until now."

I'm looking at a list of the Kinsey assets along with a handwritten will determining how the assets are to be divided.

"If you look at the original will and the one submitted to the public, you'll see the dates are mismatched," Gunner points out.

I look carefully. He's right. The dates don't match on some of the pages.

"Look again and you'll see there's a page missing from the original will."

I swipe back and forth. The weathered, handwritten will has a section torn from the bottom of the third page. The tampered page is less than a quarter of the document and I could see how an official would be persuaded—financially or otherwise—not to investigate why.

"What about the notary?" I ask, looking up. I don't know

much about wills, but there's a notary sign on the original paperwork. "Who was the witness?"

"Chuck Princeton."

My shoulders slump. "Chuck got sick and died a few years after your grandfather did."

"Given what I know of my uncle's tactics, I believe Chuck was pressured to take this secret to his grave."

"But... why would your grandfather leave anything to my mother? She was just his cleaner."

"I don't know."

"Then how are you so sure that missing page named us?"

"Because the person who tore the page confessed it today." He takes the phone from me and presses a button.

Gunner's deep, gravelly voice rings out. *"You stole from someone else. You stole from Rebel's family."*

Another voice chuckles cruelly. *"So what? There's no proof. No witnesses. No one knows but you. Do you want to turn our entire family upside down for a truth you'll never be able to prove?"*

I scramble off Gunner's lap and step away from him.

Poor, poor, mom.

Even a tiny portion of the Kinsey wealth would have been life changing for her. Mom and I could have moved out of the trailer park and had a much better life.

My eyes fill with tears as the unfairness of it all sets in. "Why would Clarence Kinsey *do* that?" I rage. "Was he so greedy for money that he couldn't stand to see someone outside of the family benefit even a little?"

Gunner remains quiet.

My eyelashes flutter as I recognize the quiet shame in his face. "What?"

"I'll be right back." He moves purposefully down the ladder.

As I wait for him to return, I go through his phone, scouring the pictures he took from Victoria.

Gunner returns to the treehouse a few minutes later, his arms laden with documents and what looks like a map. He spreads everything on the ground in front of me.

"I found the piece of land my grandfather left your family." He takes a few small stones and uses them as paper weights.

"How?"

"By cross-referencing the land that the will explicitly shares out between Uncle Clancy, my dad, my uncles and all the other relatives."

I pick up a Lucky Falls Re-Zoning document that has his notes all over it and my heart hurts for him. He put so much effort into unearthing the truth.

"What land was it?" I whisper.

Gunner hesitates before admitting, "The one near Darkwell Ridge."

Every inch of me stiffens.

Everyone in Lucky Falls knows about that particular Kinsey land. A few weeks after Clay Kinsey passed, there was a thorough survey of all the properties in his portfolio. Surprisingly, oil was found in Darkwell Ridge and the discovery was even mentioned in the national news.

"Your grandfather… left the land at Darkwell Ridge to us?" My heart wallops my ribs and I can hardly believe I'm saying that.

Gunner nods.

"The one with the…" I can't even finish it.

"The oil," Gunner does it for me. "Although he didn't know it at the time, he gave your family the most valuable property in Lucky Falls."

I rock back as if someone swung a bat at my face. Gunner's beside me in a flash, putting a steadying hand on my elbow. I barely register his touch because my head is about to explode. My eyes dart from side to side as I try to compute everything that's happening right now.

I don't believe it.

I can't.

My brain is about to melt into a puddle of goo.

This…

This can't be…

Clay Kinsey didn't leave my mom land out on the edge of town that nobody would miss. He gave us the land by Darkwell Ridge. The land that allowed the Kinseys to buy all the storefronts on Main Street and establish themselves as *the* family in Lucky Falls.

"I can't believe this," I wheeze.

"Put your head between your legs and breathe," Gunner commands.

I follow his instructions and keep breathing until my chest doesn't feel as tight.

At last, I look up at him and croak, "Have you told anyone?"

He shakes his head. "I will. I just haven't figured out a way yet."

I stop freaking out long enough to think about this from Gunner's perspective. Once this matter is taken to the law, the Kinsey businesses and assets will be stripped away. Not only that, but everyone will know that the Kinseys built their entire legacy on theft and fraud.

The Lady Luck Society, as superficial as they are, won't allow Carol to continue being the chairwoman.

The Sherriff will have to arrest his own uncle, if he manages to keep being the sheriff at all. Lucky Falls folks forgive, but they don't do the forgetting part that easily.

Everything in Gunner's world will change. All the people he loves will be affected—and not for the better.

Gunner stares at the floor while I stare at his clenching jaw.

"Hey."

He tilts his head in my direction.

"I'm sorry." I lick my lips. "It would be easier if we just ignored this, wouldn't it? But…" I inhale sharply, "I don't think I can ignore this, Gunner, even for you."

"I know."

"Just because my mom's a cleaner, just because she's not a Kinsey, that doesn't make stealing from her okay."

He nods, jaw clenching and unclenching.

"What… happens to us now?" I croak.

Gunner jolts like I hit him. "I need to tell my parents—"

"I meant *us*, Gunner. What happens to us if we follow this to the end?"

He takes a deep breath again. "I don't know, princess."

My stomach tightens with agony and confusion. The thoughts in my head are swirling too fast and I don't think I can say the right thing in this moment, even if I try my hardest.

"Maybe… we should…"

Gunner winces before I've even completed the thought.

His jaw keeps flexing. In and out. In and out.

His Adam's apple bobs.

"I… don't think we should be naive just because we want to be together."

He turns his head slightly away, bracing for my next statement.

"I think we should take a few days apart to think about what this means." I blink back tears. "For you, for me and… for us."

CHAPTER
FIFTY-TWO

GUNNER

In that moment, it's not my family's potential doom that shreds my heart to pieces.

It's not the thought of my father's crushing disappointment.

Or my mother's tears.

Or the inevitable shunning that will come from every Kinsey alive.

What kills me is Rebel Hart's defeated posture.

My whole life, Rebel was something like a mirage in the distance, a shining jewel I could never, ever touch. She breezed through the world with her shoulders straight, her smile brilliant and her steps so light she was almost floating.

But tonight, her shoulders slump and she doesn't lift her head once as she plods down the ladder.

She didn't break up with me.

At least not yet.

The thought of losing Rebel makes it hurt to breathe, but I knew the risks when I told her.

Whatever happens next, I'll accept.

With a shaky sigh, I prepare myself for the next challenge—letting my parents in on the secret. That task is going to be difficult in a completely different way.

The wind turns chilly and I shiver in my thin T-shirt. It'll be warm in the house, but I linger in the treehouse, procrastinating for as long as I can stand it.

After a few deep breaths, I bite the bullet and head to my family home.

The porch lights are on and a warm yellow hue beams on the steps. The wind stirs the wind chimes and they sing to me, doing their best to calm me down.

From here, I can hear mom's laughter. She's probably on a high after the family gathering. Mom loves having the people over. She was born to be a good host.

Heart hammering inside my chest, I take the steps one at a time.

Mom and dad are in the kitchen.

Dad's at the sink, wearing pink rubber gloves as he washes all the dirty dishes and wine glasses. Mom's sitting on one of the barstools, chattering excitedly.

"And that's when Clarence said… oh! Gunner, *where* have you been? We were calling you. You missed your uncle's welcome home party."

"It wasn't an official party," dad says, giving mom an indulgent smile.

"*Everyone* was here. The only person missing was you."

"He was busy with his friends." Dad smiles at me, the crow's feet around his eyes deepening. "Did you end up seeing Rebel? I ran into her at the grocery store and had a quick chat."

Mom pokes dad in the arm. "You were talking to *her*? You're supposed to be on my side."

"It was just a polite conversation. I am still, very much, on your side."

Dad and mom smile at each other.

I battle the urge to run out the door, find Rebel and beg her to keep this secret buried forever. Is it too late to take it all back?

"Gunner?" Mom's voice rings with concern. She pushes off the stool and patters over to me. Lifting a hand to my face, she breathes, "What's wrong?"

"There's something I need to tell you," I announce gravely.

Dad stares at me with the eyes of someone who's put many a criminal in the back of his cruiser. Soberly, he slaps the faucet down and snaps his rubber gloves off completely.

"Gunner, you're scaring me," mom says weakly. She sits down again, mumbling, "I have a feeling I should be seated for whatever this is."

Dad places a supporting hand on her shoulder.

"Go ahead, son," he says, his gaze steady on me. "We're listening."

I force the words out, starting from my encounter with Uncle Clarence after Grampa Clay's funeral and ending with my discoveries about the land that really belongs to Rebel and her mom.

The revelation sits in the air, swirling like an ice cloud.

Mom blinks as she absorbs my words.

Dad's arm drops away from mom's back.

I rub my hands over my face frantically, rubbing until it hurts and my cheeks turn red. "That conversation after the funeral, all the harassment Uncle Stewart has done to Rebel and her garage, the sudden visit from Uncle Clancy, it's all to keep that truth from getting out. Our entire family profited from Uncle Uncle Clancy's fraud. We built everything we have on stolen money."

"That-that's ridiculous!" Mom stammers. "I know Rebel resents our family, but this is taking it too far!"

"Mom…"

"Why are you putting your entire inheritance at risk for a girl you won't even be with in two months time? Can you *for once* think with your brain instead of your—"

"Do you have evidence?" Dad asks.

"Darling, you're not taking this *seriously*, are you? Why… surely if this were truth, someone would have flagged it a long time ago?"

"I have evidence," I say quietly. "But more importantly, Rebel has evidence."

Mom goes very, very still. "Are you saying that girl… *who hates the Kinsey name*… might go around telling people about this nonsense?"

"I don't know what Rebel will do now…" My breath hitches because after giving it thought, Rebel might decide a relationship with me is too complicated and that scares me to my bones. "But is that really important right now? Shouldn't we be more concerned about how to make this right?"

Mom suddenly grabs her head and moans.

"Carol!" Dad yells.

"Dan." Mom squeezes his hand, her eyes pulled shut with lines of distress running across her forehead. "This can't be right. He must be mistaken. Tell me he's mistaken."

"I'll look into it. Let me help you to bed first."

"Take me to the sofa instead. I want to see this so called 'evidence' too."

Once mom is settled, dad grabs the laptop he uses for work and accepts all the documents I'd gathered, including the voice recording of Uncle Clancy.

After checking through them, he hands them to mom who looks it over as well. The rustle of documents and the clack of fingers over the laptop keyboard resounds for a long time.

Both my parents get very sullen when they hear Uncle Clancy recording.

Mom groans and buries her face in the couch.

Dad just blinks rapidly.

As my parents visibly lose their minds, I feel strangely relieved. The matter is far from resolved, but at least the most important people in my life know the truth.

Mom grabs my phone again and swipes through all the

photos. Then she sets the phone down as a numb expression crosses her face.

Dad's hands shake slightly, but he sounds more put together when he says, "This needs to be properly investigated but, from what I can see… you're right, son. The will *was* tampered with. Your uncle confessed as much. But whether the will ever involved the Harts, there isn't evidence here to say."

My eyebrows draw close together. "But you heard what Uncle Clancy said."

"Recordings that the other party aren't aware of can't be used in court and Clarence might argue that he never said these words or that he was misunderstood."

I frown.

Dad gathers all the maps together neatly. "You'll need the torn half of the original will or some other key evidence before you have a case."

"And if he finds that evidence?" Mom trembles. "Then what?"

Dad sets his glasses down and rubs at the little imprints they left in his nose. "Then that would mean the Kinseys, every one of us, would become penniless in an instant."

"P-penniless?"

"This isn't a small sum, Carol. Everything we have would need to be transferred to Rebel and her mother. At best, we can hire a lawyer and work out a settlement out of court. At worst…" Dad blanches. "We can only pray Rebel and her mother don't press charges because if they do, plausible deniability or not, it's not going to end well. For any of us."

Mom's eyes dart back and forth. "If it's that bad then… what if we never find the evidence?"

"Carol."

"Don't look at me like that, Dan. Our entire world is going to crash around us if we lose this house. And the farm! Do we give up the farm?"

"Are you suggesting we ignore this, Carol?"

"Yes! *We're* not the ones who lied and stole. We didn't deceive anyone. This isn't our fault! Why do we have to suffer for something we had no part of?"

"Can you live with yourself if you did nothing?" Dad challenges.

"Can you live with yourself if we lose everything!" Mom shrieks.

"I can't believe you're saying this." Dad's voice is hard as granite and he draws away from mom.

Tears cropping in her eyes, mom sobs. "I am *not* the bad guy here, Dan. I'm thinking about my family. Is it wrong for me to want to protect them?"

Dad looks away.

Mom runs, crying to her room. The door slams shut a moment later.

Bitter silence falls on the living room and makes me squirm.

That… did not go well.

Mom and dad have only sat with the truth for a little over ten minutes and they're already tearing at each other's throats. If the evidence we need is never found and the truth stays buried with us, then all I did tonight was drag my parents into my own personal hell with nothing to show for it.

"I'm sorry, dad," I say hoarsely.

"You did the right thing, Gunner," dad says, squeezing my shoulder. "You did the right thing."

But it doesn't feel that way. As I watch my father trudge up the stairs, looking just as defeated as Rebel did at the treehouse, it starts to feel like I sent the puck hurtling in the wrong direction at the final moments of the game.

CHAPTER
FIFTY-THREE

REBEL

It's been two days since Gunner told me about his grandfather's will and I still haven't talked to my mother about it.

I'm hesitant to bring it up with her for two reasons.

First, mom's conversation about being content the other night felt so real and vulnerable. Until I know that we're the recipients of the will for *sure*, I don't want to unearth her entire life in pursuit of an inheritance she doesn't even know about.

Second, I'm concerned about putting mom in danger. Money can turn people into very evil, dangerous creatures.

Stewart went as far as to shut our garage down.

I don't think Clarence Kinsey is going to be much nicer.

Putting mom in danger is an absolute no-go. If it comes down to protecting her or making a stink about the inheritance, I'd rather keep my mother and let them have the money.

A beeping sound draws me out of my thoughts.

I glance at the scanner, noticing that the report has been completed.

Chance generously allowed us to work on the acreage he bought for his future with April. He and Max rigged up three giant tents that act as temporary 'bays' to protect us and the cars from the unforgiving sun.

It's not the best set up—for us and the client's cars, but it's better than halting production completely.

"Delia, can I get a second opinion on this waveform?" I bring the recording of the car's throttle position sensor readings to her. "I tried to compare it to one of the recordings I have on hand, but it's hard to say."

Delia hunches over the little plastic table that April borrowed from one of the Lucky Strikers. Planting one hand on the table, she squints. "I think the TPS is fine. You might need to check somewhere else. Maybe the timing?"

"Yeah, I suspected that."

Delia glances past me. Something beyond my shoulders makes her stiffen. I look that way too and notice two bulky shadows hiding behind a tree trunk.

"Rebel," Delia says in a cautious tone, "I think those guys are watching you."

I shrug and keep my attention on the scanner readings. "I'll test the sensor one more time before I—"

"Shouldn't we call the police?" Delia hisses.

"It's fine." I whirl around, my mind already on the next test. "I know those knuckleheads."

Delia grabs my arm. "Even the people you think you know aren't always what they seem. If they're following you around at work, that's crossing a line. I highly recommend that you report them."

The intensity of her stare coupled with her firm grip takes me by surprise. Why is Delia being so insistent?

"It's okay, Delia. Really." My gaze moves to the bulky shoulders of the hockey players crouched behind the tree. "They're harmless."

"Why are they stalking you then?"

"You could say they're… my babysitters."

Perplexity knits her eyebrows together.

April walks closer to the tree and whistles. "Theilan, Watson. Get over here. You're scaring the newbie!"

The bulky young athletes scramble into the open.

Theilan sheepishly waves. "Hey, ladies."

April ushers them closer to our 'garage'. "If you're sticking around, make yourselves useful and help me pry something off. My high-strength wrench is still trapped at the garage and I'm having a hard time without my tools."

"On it!" Theilan saunters toward us and throws Delia a wink. "Hey."

Watson rolls his T-shirt sleeves up, eyes on Delia. "Hey, if you need help after we get through with April, we can…"

Suddenly, there's a loud *pop*.

April raises a valve high. "Oops. Looks like I got it myself. Thanks anyway, boys."

Theilan immediately pins all his attention on Delia. "Great. So back to you and me…"

"April, I've finished with the Chevy. I'll take a look at the Nissan next," Delia says in a bored tone. She walks right past the boys and gets back to work.

I snort at their disappointed expressions. "Don't you guys have practice today?"

"Max is meeting a sponsor at the arena. They wanted a tour of the stadium so he ended practice early and kicked us out," Theilan explains.

Watson frowns. "How'd you know it was us today?"

"Um…" I wrap two wires together, "your heads were sticking out from the tree. But honestly, I noticed you guys since yesterday."

"Yesterday?" Watson's jaw drops.

Theilan mumbles to him, "I told you we should've followed her on our bikes instead." To me, the young hockey player says,

"Anyway, do you know why Gunner has us watching you and your mom?"

I stop working. "You're watching my mom too?"

"Uh… no?"

"Theilan," I say in a warning tone.

Watson shoves Theilan in the back. "We gotta go."

"Yeah, we have a… thing."

"Later, Rebel."

"Watson! Theilan!" I yell, taking a few steps forward.

Watson backpedals faster than I can run facing forward.

"Hey, don't tell Gunner you found out about us, 'kay? Thanks!" Theilan yells over his shoulder as he runs off like an Olympic sprinter.

I'm left in stunned silence.

If Gunner has his teammates watching my mom too, that means he has the same safety concerns that I do.

Worried, I remove my pink work gloves, walk away from the 'garage' for privacy and give mom a call.

"Hi, Rebel," mom says cheerfully. "I was just about to call you."

"Is everything okay?"

"About that movie night we missed, are you free this Sunday?" Mom sounds upbeat and relaxed. "I was thinking of setting it up for Saturday, but I remembered the final game of the playoffs is this weekend and we've got to support Gunner."

She laughs so happily that it makes my chest tighten. "Yeah, Sunday sounds great, mom." I scuff my pink work boots into the sand. "What are you up to?"

"I'm at home."

I check my watch. "Why so early?"

"It was the strangest thing. Sheriff Kinsey very sincerely thanked me for taking care of him and his family and then he gave me a few days off."

Why would he do that unless…

Did Gunner tell his parents already? I wonder what they said and how they responded. Is he okay?

My heart hurts for him and I wish I could give him a hug right now.

"I really felt that Sheriff Kinsey appreciated my work and it reminded me that no job is too small. The officers and the Sheriff do their part by keeping Lucky Falls safe, and I do my part too."

Sometimes, I wonder if my mom is the wisest woman in the world or the most naive. "Are you really that happy, mom?"

"Of course I am. I'll take this opportunity to rest so I can go back and work even harder."

I play with my necklace, battling if I should say something about the will now.

"Rebel! Rebel!"

A new voice calls my attention to the street.

Marjorie White slows her turquoise blue Cadillac in front of our makeshift garage. "Rebel!"

"Who is that?" Mom asks.

"Marjorie White."

"She probably wants to discuss Society business. Don't let me keep you from your important duties." Mom blows kisses into the phone and hangs up.

With a sigh, I trudge over to Marjorie.

She hops out of the car and slams the door shut. "Rebel, what's going on? I thought you and Rodney Howard had a deal? Why did his secretary just call saying he changed his mind about the donation?"

"What?"

"I thought the matter was decided!"

"I-it was!"

"Not according to her." Marjorie slides dark sunshades down her nose and pins me with a dirty look. "Miss Hart, what exactly happened at that meeting with Rodney Howard?"

"It was… a regular meeting," I lie, glancing away.

Marjorie gleefully informs me, "Well, there's a nasty rumor

going around that you flirted with Rodney's son to get the donation, but it backfired and now Rodney's taking his anger out on the whole town."

Indignation swells in my chest. "Who said that?"

She primps her hair. "A reputable source."

I bet her 'reputable source' is one or both of the conniving Davis sisters. They smiled so brightly at me when they thought the donation was coming through. But they didn't waste any time gossiping about me as soon as the deal fell apart.

"I'll call Rodney and sort this out."

"I tried that. His office keeps saying he's busy," Marjorie tells me.

Rather than take her word for it, I call the office myself, but I meet the same resistance. The secretary won't even tell me when Mr. Rodney will be back.

"Why don't you call the son?" Marjorie suggests. "Since you two are so close."

I give her a chilly glare.

"These are desperate times, Rebel. What will we do about the senior citizen care packages? The after-school library initiative? Will you tell all the grannies who signed up to our program to buy their own groceries? Or will it be the dear children who get cut from the budget?"

My breathing turns shallow and my chest squeezes painfully.

Marjorie steps closer to me. "You wanted to be a part of the Society so badly." She aims a disdainful look at my ponytail. "Time to prove you deserve it."

CHAPTER
FIFTY-FOUR

REBEL

I promised Gunner I wouldn't flirt my way out of a problem.

But some promises are made to be broken.

Or so I keep telling myself as I fluff my hair and rifle through my closet for the perfect outfit, one that screams 'be kind and don't let your dad take his money back pretty please with sprinkles on top'.

It's not like dressing up for the occasion is *wrong*.

I plan to have a professional conversation on behalf of the Lady Luck Society. So what if I look extra nice in the process? I'm in charge of this project, and it's my job to fix the problem by any means necessary.

'I thought other men being interested in you would suddenly not bother me. But that's not how it's working out'.

I stop, mid-brush and stare unseeingly at the mirror.

Gunner was vulnerable with me, and in return, I promised him I wouldn't use my looks or flirt my way out of a situation.

I chew my bottom lip until my lipstick wipes clear off.

Gunner and I are taking a break. Technically, we're not

together right now. Dressing nicely for a meeting with Benji is a relationship grey area, but Gunner's *entire family* stole the land that belongs to my mother so...

That makes us even.

I get all the way to the door before my conscience hits me with a whispered *'if the shoe were on the other foot, Gunner would NEVER. He'd walk over hot coals barefoot than do anything that you clearly told him made you uncomfortable.'*

I change out of my daring pink dress and into a button-down blouse and wide-legged pants.

But I keep my hair down and my makeup the same.

It is the twenty first flipping century.

And women have rights.

Just then, I hear a knock. I'm surprised to see Benji standing outside with a bouquet of red roses.

"B-Benji, what are you doing here? I said I'd meet you at the restaurant."

Benji offers me the flowers. "I couldn't wait."

The scent of roses overwhelms me. I blink rapidly. "You shouldn't have."

"It's a token of my apology. Dad was truly out of line. I'm sorry, Rebel."

"You had nothing to do with it."

"I was worried that I made things weird and you'd never reach out again."

"Benji, you and I are friends. There's no need for all this," I say firmly, trying to give him the flowers back.

He grins and shoves his glasses up his nose. "Come on. There's a limo downstairs."

"A *limo?*"

"It's *my* apology. Don't fight me on this or I'll live with crippling guilt for the rest of my life." He makes a sweeping gesture. "After you."

I'm no stranger to men ignoring my words and being pushy. Since Rodney Howard truly thought he could 'buy' his son a relationship, I sense that Benji—as sweet and polite as he is—may be used to things going his way.

On any other day, I'd shut him down and draw my lines clearly. But I need to talk to Benji about getting the Lady Luck Society back in his dad's good graces.

"Rebel?"

"Give me a sec. I'll put these in water and be right out."

I slam the door in Benji's face and grab a vase. While the water is filling up, I pull out my phone and search through the contacts.

Benji's pushing my boundaries a little too much. To get him back on task without offending him will require backup. Preferably someone no-nonsense but well-versed in stroking the egos of obnoxious, rich people.

Someone like…

Carol Kinsey.

I groan, shaking my head. "Anyone but her."

There's another knock on the door.

"Rebel? Do you need help?"

"I'm almost done!" I yell.

Water sloshes over the rim of the vase and I turn the faucet off. Flicking out my wet fingers, I worry my bottom lip.

What other choice do you have?

Hating every second of it, I dial Carol.

"What do *you* want?" Carol Kinsey says without so much as a 'how do you do'.

"I need your help," I grind out.

She remains silent.

"I'm sure you've heard about Rodney Howard by now."

She sniffs haughtily. "I told the girls that they made a bad decision trusting you. And it turns out I was right."

Annoyance hisses through my veins, but I keep my tone even. "We can play the blame game later. Benji's at my apartment and I need your help convincing him to take the Lady Luck Society back."

"Aren't you the one accusing our family of theft and fraud? Why do you want to work with me?"

"Because this isn't about you and me, or about the Kinseys and the Harts. It's about the community we swore we'd help. The children and the senior citizens are more important than our feud." I pause. "Unless you disagree?"

There's a beat of silence and then Carol Kinsey grumbles, "The son alone won't help our case. We need to meet with his father."

"Rodney Howard isn't answering my phone calls."

"Where's the son taking you?"

"I don't know." I talk fast in case Benji knocks on the door again. "A restaurant?"

"Find a way to get him to bring me along. I'll handle it from there."

"Great. Tha—"

Carol Kinsey hangs up in the middle of me talking.

I mime a punch at the phone.

Ugh. That woman is a menace.

After taking a deep breath, I open the door again.

Benji was mid-knock. "Hey, is everything okay?"

"Yeah, but uh… change of plans. I forgot that I had a meeting with Carol Kinsey."

"Can you reschedule?" Benji asks, looking disappointed.

"I'm afraid I can't. But the good news is, she's willing to come with us."

"She… is?"

"Yup." I hurry past him. "You said the limo was downstairs? Lead the way."

* * *

I'M CERTAIN THAT BENJI WON'T ENTERTAIN CAROL KINSEY'S REQUEST for us to meet his father.

But I'm proven wrong.

After a whole lot of chatting, compliments, eyelash-batting and a few too many 'of course, darlin!'s, Benji agrees to call his father over to the restaurant.

When Rodney Howard arrives, questions well in my throat and ache to spring out. But Carol squeezes my knee and takes over, leading the conversation away from the Lady Luck Society case.

Instead, she asks about Benji's work, engages Rodney about his latest travels and keeps the conversation going. If I didn't know what she was doing, I'd be fooled by her frequent smiles and fake ditziness. By the time she *does* bring up the donation, both father and son have been completely disarmed.

"By the way, we were so *very* stunned hearing there were issues with the donation," Carol says, flapping her thick eyelashes.

Rodney Howard stops with food midway to his mouth.

Carol beams. "I've known Rodney to be very kind and very fair. So I just knew once we sat down together, we could sort all this out."

Rodney Howard clears his throat.

"You don't have to explain, Rodney. I *know* you are not the type of man who'd go back on his word. So this doesn't need to be discussed at all."

I hide my smirk by taking a drink of my soda.

Benji squirms.

If Rodney Howard had a tail, it would be between his legs.

"Dad, apologize." Benji elbows his father.

"I'm… sorry," Rodney Howard says, glancing at me and then looking away. "Not only for today, but for putting you in an uncomfortable position the last time we met, Miss Hart. Benji scolded me greatly for what I did. I assure you the next time you have a presentation, my colleagues and I won't waste your efforts. We will sit and listen."

"I appreciate that," I say with a small smile.

Carol Kinsey looks surprised by Rodney's comment. I

wonder if she'd blindly believed all the rumors about me flirting with Benji to get the donation. I'm glad that Rodney Howard's comment cleared *that* up.

"There was a mix-up with my secretary," the businessman explains. While I don't exactly believe that, it's what he says next that matters. "I'll speak to her and have the money wired first thing tomorrow."

"I expected nothing less of a man of esteemed character like yourself, Rodney. Now, would anyone like dessert? I heard this restaurant makes a *fine* pecan pie."

The rest of the dinner goes smoothly and Benji leaves to pay the bill.

Carol excuses herself to the restroom and it's just me and Rodney Howard at the table.

As awkwardness sets in, I fidget with my napkin, stare at the restaurant's low-hanging chandeliers and adjust the candles flickering on the table.

Benji chose an incredibly… non-business-meeting-like place for us to discuss business today.

Rodney Howard is in no rush to start a conversation so, rather than let the awkward silence drone on, I offer an olive branch.

"Mr. Howard, thank you again for your donation."

He lifts a hand. "No need for that."

Taking notes from what I saw of Carol today, I steer the conversation in the direction I want it to go. "I brought an updated proposal. Would you like to hear a quick rundown of the outreach programs we're launching?"

"Sure. Why not?" He takes a sip of his wine.

With the help of the slides on my phone, I launch into a summary of the projects, the budget, and the potential impact on the community. Even though it's a sped-up version of the presentation I was meant to give him, I still get excited talking about how many people we're going to help.

Rodney Howard listens without interrupting. It's only when

Benji returns to the table that I realize I've been talking non-stop for a few minutes.

"I was rambling, wasn't I?"

"No, that was very inspiring." Rodney Howard wipes his mouth with a napkin and watches me thoughtfully. After a breath, he says, "Miss Hart, have you heard the term 'looks can be deceiving'?"

"Of course." I laugh nervously. "I hope you're not insinuating that I've deceived you in some way, Mr. Howard?"

Just then, Carol Kinsey returns to the table.

"No," Rodney says, shaking his head. "It's quite the opposite. When it comes to you, Miss Hart," he gestures to my body, "your inside is just as beautiful as your outside."

"Thank you," I gasp, truly touched.

Carol Kinsey slips back into the booth.

Rodney Howard turns to her. "You know, Carol, Rebel reminds me of you from back in the day. You had this light in your eyes when you spoke about helping people. Felt like you were on a one-woman mission to eradicate all the wrongs in the world."

My eyebrows fly up.

Is he talking about *Carol* Kinsey? The woman who spent the last few years of the Lady Luck Society agenda 'beautifying' the already beautiful side of town?

"Unfortunately, the real world isn't so kind to bleeding hearts. After doing this for so long, you start to get a little burnt out." Carol glances at me reluctantly. "She's got a lot to learn, but… I know what you mean, Rodney. I see it too."

Stunned, I look at Carol Kinsey with new eyes. I see the makeup and powder seeping into the fine lines around her eyes and mouth. I see the hands that are perfectly manicured and the bold red lipstick that she probably reapplied in the bathroom.

For the first time ever, I push aside my innate hatred for the Kinseys to see the woman beneath the coiffed hair and the overblown status.

Carol Kinsey started the Lady Luck Society wanting to help people and—even if we disagree on the specific type of people who need the help—community service is something we have in common.

"I knew Rebel was special the moment I saw her," Benji says, his eyes glistening as he looks at me.

I shift uncomfortably.

Carol Kinsey clears her throat and mumbles, "It's probably why *my son* is so crazy about her."

I look up in shock. Did Carol Kinsey just put Benji in his place?

Benji shirks back as if he's been spanked and Rodney quickly steps in. To me, he says, "Do you like being a member of the Lady Luck Society, Rebel?"

I feel Carol staring at me.

"There's a lot about the Society that I like and other things I don't," I admit honestly. "No organization is perfect but…"

I feel rather than see Carol hold her breath.

"… we're on the same team. And yeah. Carol is amazing at what she does and there's a lot I can learn from her."

I mean that sincerely. The way she handled this discussion with the donor today is undeniable. She was classy, calm, and kept her control. I don't have that level of finesse nor the experience that she does.

Rather than fight her, which will only waste energy that could be used to serve more people, if I study her instead, there's no telling how many families can be impacted for good.

Slowly, Carol's lips curl upward. "I'll drink to that."

I lift my own glass in her direction and empty every last drop.

CHAPTER
FIFTY-FIVE

GUNNER

A LONE CABIN SITS AT THE END OF A TRAIL DEEP IN THE WOODS. I'm parked in a conveniently well-hidden grove, waiting for any signs of Uncle Clancy sneaking around, and so far, nothing seems out of the ordinary.

Not that I'm fooled.

Uncle Clancy's land is farther from town than all the others in the Kinsey portfolio and, back when the assets were being divided, everyone applauded him for choosing this less valuable estate.

But I know different.

Shadowy trees and thick foliage make this the perfect place to hide a body.

Or bury the contents of a will.

"How much longer do we stay out here staring at nothing?" Renthrow grumbles.

I put the binoculars down. "You're the one who volunteered to come."

"Because I've always wanted to be part of a stakeout," he mumbles. "But now I regret it."

I survey the woods around the cabin. "Are you worried about Gordie?"

"I'm always worried about Gordie," he grumbles to the window.

I whip around. "You didn't leave her home alone, did you?"

Renthrow scoffs. "Of course not. I asked the babysitter to come over in case Gordie wakes up. Do you think I'd be out here if my baby girl was home alone?"

I grunt my understanding and peer at Uncle Clancy's cabin for another quick sweep.

After meeting with a few old timers in town, visiting the grocery store to buy some supplies, and heading out to his cabin, he hasn't moved since. Seems he's settled in for the night.

It's been the same routine for the past two days.

Uncle Clancy has been so careful that he hasn't even met with Uncle Stewart publicly, although I'd bet my entire hockey career that they're communicating. Just not in a way that would tip me off.

Does Uncle Clancy know I'm watching him?

It's a possibility. It didn't take Rebel long to figure out Theilan and Watson were checking up on her. Thankfully, mom was with Rebel all evening doing Lady Luck Society business, and I convinced April to get Rebel to sleep over tonight. Chance is keeping an eye on April's place until morning.

Dad reached out to his law enforcement network to have Grampa Clay's will verified by actual experts, but I can't twiddle my thumbs until we hear back from them. Protecting Rebel and all the people who are important to her is my main priority.

Suddenly, my stomach growls.

Renthrow glances at me.

I pretend not to notice and bring the binoculars to my face. Something rustles in the passenger seat and then Renthrow tosses an object at me. I look down to find a Ziplock bag holding a sandwich, neatly cut into triangles.

I lift the bag, incredulous.

"Don't want it?" Renthrow tries to take it back.

I muscle his arm away and pop the triangle into my mouth. It's not the best sandwich I've ever had, but at least I can put something on my stomach.

"I got grapes and apple juice too," he offers reluctantly.

I scarf down the rest of the sandwich. While I'm slurping on the juice box, I glance at Renthrow. "You handling everything okay? With Gordie?"

He stares straight ahead. "Yeah."

I choose my words carefully. "Does she ask about her mom a lot?"

Renthrow blows out a breath. He's a big guy but, in the moment, he seems to shrink inside himself. "Yeah. It was easier when she was younger."

"Let me know if..." Just then, I hear the squawk of a radio.

I look to the center console where the police scanner is cradled amidst hockey tape, old hockey gloves that I keep for emergencies, and a bunch of loose change. I 'borrowed' the scanner from dad as a precaution, but Lucky Falls is such a safe place to live that the radio hasn't made a sound until tonight. I'd honestly forgotten it was there.

"Psssh!" The radio noise fills the car. "There's a reported fire at 114 Willow Lane."

Willow Lane?

Rebel's apartment is there.

But Rebel is with April, so everything is fine.

One of dad's deputies responds to the call, so I turn the radio all the way down. I don't want to hear the back and forth while I'm trying to focus on the current stakeout.

However, an odd feeling keeps niggling at me and I decide to call April just in case. Once I hear that Rebel's enjoying their girl's night in, I'll be able to breathe easily.

"Oh, I forgot to tell you," April says. "Rebel went home."

I jerk upright. "She went *home?* To her apartment?" *The one that's currently on fire?*

"Is something wrong?" April asks, picking up on my panic right away.

Even Renthrow is staring at me like I've gone crazy.

I grunt out a thanks and hang up on April. Without warning, I ram the car into gear and reverse out of the woods while the engine growls noisily.

"Hey, hey, hey! Slow down!" Renthrow yells, grabbing at his seatbelt.

I wrench the steering wheel to the left, but we're going at top speed and the car over steers.

"Watch out for that tree!" Renthrow bellows.

I yank the wheel the other direction and narrowly miss crashing into the tree. Renthrow flings curses at me, but I ignore him and keep my sights on the road.

The only thing I care about is getting to Rebel as fast as possible.

"You want to explain why you're trying to kill me?" Renthrow hisses.

"Rebel's apartment is on fire!"

He keeps his mouth shut for the rest of the ride. Not that I would have heard a word he had to say. My blood is roaring in my ears and I can barely see the road ahead.

What if I'm too late? What if Rebel's hurt? What if I never get the chance to make up with her? To wrap her in my arms. To see her smile at me?

What if I can't tell her that I'll do anything to protect her, even if it means going against my entire family. What if she never hears the truth of how many years I've been in love with her?

Time moves slowly until I get to Rebel's apartment. The first thing I notice is that the building is intact and undamaged. There are no orange flames crawling up the brick walls. No police cars. No firemen.

"Looks like a false alarm," Renthrow croaks. He's bowled over, his face slightly green. "I'm…" He makes a retching sound and pins his mouth shut. "I'm… heading home now."

"Thanks, Renthrow."

He stumbles like a drunken hockey fan in the opposite direction while I pound up the stairs to Rebel's apartment.

CHAPTER
FIFTY-SIX

GUNNER

All seemed calm downstairs, but once I'm on the second floor, I smell the distinct scent of smoke.

Breaking into a full-on sprint, I pound on Rebel's door.

"Rebel, open up!" I bark.

I press my ear to the door.

There's no sound.

I imagine Rebel sprawled on the floor, knocked unconscious by Uncle Stewart or tied up and gagged by masked cronies that Uncle Clarence hired.

My mind about to split open, I ram my shoulders against Rebel's door.

"Rebel! Can you hear me!"

The door in the neighboring apartment cracks open and an old woman croaks, "Who's making all that racket... Gunner Kinsey? Is that you?"

A moment later, a beautiful voice sounds from inside Mrs. Reynold's apartment.

"Remember not to light your granddaughter's scented candles with *the windows closed. It sets off the smoke detector and makes everyone really worried."*

"Yes, yes, I understand," the older woman replies impatiently.

I almost fall to my knees with relief when Rebel walks out. She's dressed in a soft pink tank top, white shorts, and the bunny slippers from last time.

Rebel notices me. "Gunner? What are you doing here?"

I move on autopilot. In three steps, I'm in front of her. Then I wrap her in my arms and bury my face in the crook of her neck and shoulder. "Thank God you're okay."

Rebel melts against me. As her hand settles on my back, my chest loosens and I take my first real breath in what feels like days. *Finally.* I squeeze my eyes shut, bundling her closer, closer, closer. Like I'll never get enough.

Because I won't.

"Oh, oh my," a thin voice warbles. "Gunner Kinsey, how dare you rub your love in the face of an old, single woman! Go! Hug it out elsewhere. Shoo!"

Rebel laughs when the door slams shut behind the old woman.

I stare at her.

She blushes slightly. "What?"

"You're beautiful," I say simply.

The blush gets a little brighter as she rubs at a stain on my collar. "My lipstick got on your shirt."

I swoop in and give her a quick peck.

Rebel blinks, stunned.

I pull back. "Fixed it."

"Huh?"

"Now my lips match my shirt."

Rebel swats at me, laughing softly. "Gunner Kinsey."

Man, I love when Rebel says my name.

I take her hand and lead the way to her apartment.

Rebel swings my hand back and forth, her eyes sparkling.

"Why are you here? Did Theilan and Watson tell you I was in trouble or something?"

"Something like that."

"Well, I wasn't."

I grunt.

"You need more reliable spies, Gunner."

To be fair, we're good at hockey, not security. I wanted dad to put a protective detail on Rebel, but he can't legally dispatch officers until my uncles threaten or actually hurt Rebel.

Ridiculous.

I, legally, have to wait until the woman I love gets hurt before doing anything about it? Not a pig's chance in a frying pan. The Lucky Strikers were not the best option, but they were the *only* option.

I take my shoes off at her door and trek in socks through her pink living room.

"I was going to call you tomorrow," Rebel says, sitting in the couch.

Unfortunately, her seat of choice is not on my lap.

But at least she hasn't released my hand yet.

"You should have called."

"With the last game of the playoffs right around the corner, I wasn't sure it was a good idea. And looking at you now..." Rebel scoots closer and my heart picks up speed. "You seem tired."

I've been stalking my uncle every night.

But I'm not telling her that.

"The coach worked us extra hard today since Max cancelled practice yesterday."

"I heard about that." Rebel tucks one leg underneath her. It's crazy the way she looks ready to pose for a photoshoot when all she's doing is getting comfortable. She runs her fingers through her hair and the strands fall perfectly over her shoulder again. "I heard Max was meeting with a new sponsor."

I nod. Max dragged Chance and I along to a few potential

sponsorship meetings while we were away from Lucky Falls. The sponsor he ended up connecting with seemed like the eccentric type, but Max was convinced by her offer and took the investment.

I'm happy if it'll work out for him and for the team.

"What were you planning on talking about tomorrow?" I ask.

Since she's holding my hand, it wasn't to break up with me. I don't think.

Rebel straightens her shoulders and looks at me head-on. "I asked you for a few days so we can think about us."

I dip my chin slowly.

"I've done enough thinking and I wanted to know if you were done thinking too."

"What was your conclusion after thinking about it?" I prod.

She scrunches her nose. "You first."

"I'll be honest… I made up my mind the moment I put this around your neck." I swipe my thumb over the pink gemstone.

"Seriously?"

I nod.

She looks away guiltily.

I grip her chin and turn her face back to me. "I don't mind that you needed space. I want you to make the decision that's right for you, that makes you happy. More than anything, Rebel, I just want you to be happy."

"And I want *you* to be happy," she says earnestly.

I open my mouth to say that I will be, but she speaks first.

"Do you know how difficult it'll be for you to date the girl who ruined your family? Can you imagine the awkwardness at family gatherings? The disdain on everyone's faces? You'll see the ugliest side of people you've known all your life, people you cherish. People you respect. It'll be uncomfortable for me, but it might *destroy* you."

"Then I'll be destroyed."

"Gunner…"

"No matter what I lose, if I have you, then I have everything."

Rebel's mouth parts on a stunned gasp.

I brush my thumb over her soft-as-lilies skin. "I'm ready to tell you now."

She blinks in confusion. "Tell me what?"

"The answer."

It takes a minute but realization soon dawns. "How long?"

"Since I was seven."

She jerks back and away from my hands. "But… we stopped being friends when you were seven."

I tell her about Uncle Clancy's warning.

Color rises in her cheeks and she spits irritably, "That awful man! So that's why you started treating me like I was invisible?"

"I was young, but I knew I had to protect you."

"Gunner, I had no idea."

My lips curl up at her big reaction. I knew she'd be surprised. "I stopped talking to you, but I never stopped watching you. I have a clear memory of finding you at the daisy field. I hid from you when every part of me wanted to run over."

Her eyes turn red with unshed tears. "I wish you had."

"I couldn't. Not then." I smile sadly.

She smiles back. "What about now?"

"Now… I'm not that little boy, hanging in the shadows, watching you weave daisy chains. I'm not afraid anymore, Rebel." I take her hand. "Home for me is wherever you are."

Her bottom lip trembles. "It's the same for me, Gunner. I've never felt more safe, more heard, more respected in my life. You are…" She dabs at the corner of her eyes, "the ultimate pink flag."

I laugh. "A pink flag?"

"Yeah. That's my version of a green flag."

"Isn't pink just red mixed with white?"

"So?"

"Isn't that… kind of still a red flag?"

"Don't ruin my speech, Kinsey. You know what I mean."

I bite back a laugh.

"I've thought a lot about it, and honestly, I don't know how we're going to solve this problem with the will. What I do know is that wherever things end up, I want to be with you. You're more important to me than the money, than revenge, than any bad blood between me and the Kinseys."

"I love you, Rebel," I say, leaning forward. "I mean that from the bottom of my heart."

"I love you too, Gunner."

My heart explodes with fireworks and I can't hold back. Her pink lips curling up in a smile is the last thing I see before I close my eyes and kiss her. She kisses me back, wrapping her arms around my neck.

I pull her into my lap and keep kissing my sweet, sweet first love.

Rebel Hart has always been the girl for me.

And all I ever want to be is the daisy in her hands.

CHAPTER
FIFTY-SEVEN

REBEL

APRIL IS ALREADY AT THE MAKESHIFT GARAGE WHEN I ARRIVE THE next morning. Chance and his expensive lawyers are still working to undo Stewart's attempt to shut us down.

Turns out, lawsuits aren't as cut and dry as they appear in the movies. They can take weeks or months or even years if there's no settlement.

On the bright side, being outdoors isn't so bad now that we've rigged up a generator and attached giant standing fans to chase away the severe, late morning heat.

The scent of engine oil wafts from a car's rusty gears.

Ah. Smells like home.

April's bent over the open hood of a truck, eyes locked on a tablet screen that's spitting engine readings via waveforms.

"Morning!" I sing.

"Morning. You're in a good mood."

"It's good to be outside. 'Touch grass' as they say." I grin as I set my pink tool box on a plastic table that Mauve allowed us to sneak away from the Tuna. Then I set my surprise down on top of the tool box.

April notices what I brought. "Ooh! Donuts. Phil's?"

I pause for dramatic effect and then say slowly, "Marnie's."

April doesn't drop the tablet. She *throws* it on the table and flies over to me. "Phil's mom? *The* original donut queen? The legend who came up with the recipe for Phil's chocolate donuts? I thought she retired after handing the shop over to Phil?"

"Marnie still bakes, but only for a select clientele aka the Kinseys."

When Gunner showed up with the box this morning and acted like getting Marnie to bake him donuts was no big deal, I was torn between being extremely touched and extremely irritated.

Sure, I knew the Kinseys have wealth, deep connections and the respect of the entire town, but I thought doughnuts were safe. Turns out, there's still a difference between the social classes even with sugary treats.

April rushes to wash her hands and sinks her teeth into a doughnut. The moment she takes that first bite, her eyes roll back and she groans, "Man, it must be good to be a Kinsey."

"If Gunner wasn't my boyfriend, I'd probably stage a one-woman protest over this," I murmur, taking a more polite bite.

"Oh? Are you and Gunner okay now?"

I blink innocently. "We were always okay."

"Is that why you were walking around on auto-pilot for the last couple days?"

"Was I?"

"Sometimes, you worked like a monster on steroids. Other times, you'd just be staring into space." April dusts her hands on her navy jumpsuit. "Chance said that Gunner was the same at practice. What happened?"

"A… lot."

"Oy."

Leaning closer to my best friend, I share everything about the will, Clarence Kinsey, and my agreement with Gunner to give ourselves some space to think.

"Last night," I continue, "Gunner and I had a long conversation and we decided to protect each other no matter what happens." I smile sappily as I remember his romantic words in the couch, followed by his big hands grabbing my hips and putting me on his lap while he gave me a kiss that set my entire body on fire.

"I'm *sorry*," April says, looking dumbfounded. "I'm still stuck at the part where you and your mom could be literal millionaires and you haven't told her yet."

"We still need evidence."

"*She* could have the evidence. Have you ever thought of that?" April points out.

"Of course I've thought of that." I throw my hands wide. "But…"

"April! Rebel!" A sweet voice interrupts. We both turn to find a little girl streaming out of a car and running to us.

"Gordie, be careful!" I call, noticing her going full sprint. There are many dangerous, sharp items in a mechanic shop—even an unofficial one like this—and I don't want her to get hurt.

"Wow!" Gordie's eyes dart back and forth. "Is this an outdoor garage? This is so cool."

I place my hands on my hips, smiling proudly. "It is, isn't it?"

"She's so fast," an elderly woman mumbles, waddling up to us.

"Do you want to sit down?" I gesture to a plastic chair. "You look a little pale."

"It's alright, dear." The woman gives me a weak smile. "We won't stay long. Gordie just has a question for you ladies before she goes to school."

"It's career week and I have to write a report about a cool career. I wanted to write about astronauts, but we don't have astronauts in Lucky Falls. So I wanted to write about mechanics."

"We're honored that you'd think of us, Gordie," April says, bending down to get on Gordie's level.

Just then, a loud rumble fills the air. Delia brings her bike to a stop on the grassy lawn. I'm used to the full, throaty roar of Delia's bike so I only spare our new technician a quick glance and look to Gordie to continue the conversation.

But the little girl is no longer beside me.

She is floating forward, her eyes locked on Delia and her jaw dragging on the floor.

Delia pops the shade of her helmet up and, a moment later, she pulls the entire helmet off. She is one of those rare, impressive people who don't get helmet hair so her silky black bob swishes right back into place with just a toss of her head.

"Excuse me," Gordie's nanny taps my hand, "I'm not feeling too well."

"Oh no. Do you need something?"

"I'm okay." She sniffs. "I'll rest after I take Gordie to school. Could you watch her for a moment while I take my medication? It's in the car."

"Of course. Take your time."

Delia walks into the garage and I know the moment she realizes a child is present because she jumps right out of her skin.

Gordie beams and waves at her. "Hi."

"Hello… tiny human," Delia says. Her eyes dart to me and April and she makes a subtle gesture towards Gordie.

April, knowing Delia's discomfort around kids, steers a very excited Gordie toward the furthest tent while I approach Delia.

"Ready for another busy day?" I smile. "Seems like people still trust us with their cars even if our mechanic bay has…" I gesture to the trees around us, "a more woodsy aesthetic."

She keeps a cautious eye on Gordie. "Where's the convertible I was working on? I don't see it?"

I point her to the back tent. "Chance helped April move the cars, but he isn't a mechanic so he didn't park them in the best places."

"It's alright. I'll figure it out," Delia says.

I turn in Gordie and April's direction, intending on chatting with the little girl a bit.

Just then, my phone rings.

It's mom.

A chill goes down my spine.

My shoulders tighten as if my body senses bad news.

No, everything is fine. Gunner has the team watching mom.

Then I realize the team is at early morning practice.

Uneasy, I pick up mom's call.

"Hey, mom. Is everything okay?"

"Rebel?" Mom's voice sounds thin.

"Mom?" I grip the phone tighter, my stomach churning.

"Can you come over for a minute?"

"Of course, mom. Where are you? Are you okay? Do I need to call the police?"

"No... it's..." She's breathing hard.

"Mom? *Mom?*"

There's a thud and then the line goes dead.

I'm sprinting to the door before I remember that my keys are in my purse and my purse is in the locker where I keep my casual clothes. Panicked, I change directions and head to the locker.

"What's wrong?" April asks, her eyes wide and frightened.

"My mom. Something is... I have to get to her."

I keep searching through my purse until I locate the keys. But the moment I get my hands on them, they're snatched away.

April's stare is firm. "I can't let you drive in this state. I'm coming with you. Delia, can you watch Gordie until her nanny comes back?"

Gordie's eyes light up.

Delia has the opposite reaction. Face pooling with dread, the mechanic squeals, "You're leaving a vulnerable human being with *me?*"

I rush to my truck.

"Thanks, Delia," April says in a whir as she follows me.

I'm about to dial the police and call an ambulance for my mom when her number lights up on my screen. My heart jumps all the way up my throat as I answer.

"Mom, are you okay? What happened?"

"Nothing. I just got a little frightened and dropped the phone. I'm fine now."

Something's off with her voice. I can feel it. "Who's there, mom?"

"S-Stewart Kinsey?"

My heart swells with panic and I taste bile when I swallow. "I'm calling the police. And I'll be there in, like, ten minutes."

"Rebel, don't be so dramatic. I don't need the police."

"Mom," I hiss, "Stewart is a dangerous guy. Who knows what he'll do to you?"

"He's *not* dangerous."

I lean forward, wishing I could sprout wings and fly to her. "You have no idea. Mom, I haven't told you anything about what's been going on, but the truth is—"

"He asked me to marry him."

I flop back in shock.

April glances over, a deep line marking her forehead.

I shake my head. "W-what did you say?"

"Stewart Kinsey just asked for my hand in marriage."

CHAPTER
FIFTY-EIGHT

GUNNER

After practice, I hit the shower and mentally prepare for another, exhausting stakeout.

Rebel and I have decided not to let the outside pressure get to us, but it's still my job to keep her safe. The only way I can give her the life she deserves is to resolve this matter between my family and hers.

I just hope Uncle Clancy makes a move soon.

We can't keep living in limbo.

"Gunner!" Thielan yells loud enough that I can hear over the hiss of the shower. "Your phone's been ringing off the hook."

I'm instantly on hyper alert and my first thought is: *Rebel's in trouble.*

I wrap a towel around myself and skate out of the shower so fast I almost fall. Windmilling my hands to catch my balance, I keep running and wrench my locker door open.

My phone goes silent as I reach inside my duffel. Out of breath, I tap on the recent call logs.

The number on the screen isn't Rebel's.

It's my dad.

I call back. "Hey, dad."

"Son, I just heard back from my colleagues at forensics. We got a hit."

My entire body turns rigid. "What did they find?"

"Uncle Clarence's fingerprints."

"Are they sure?" I already know Uncle Clancy will deny being involved until he's blue in the face. There can't be any room for error.

"Thankfully, your grandfather's will was kept in a safety deposit box and rarely touched all these years."

"Is that enough to end this?"

"No, but it'll help build a strong case." The sound of a harsh breeze fills my ears and robs some of dad's words. A moment later, I hear a door slam open and shut. It gets quiet in the background again. "By cross-checking court records and legal document transfers, I spotted a 24-hour gap in the will's chain of custody."

I stare unseeingly at my locker and grunt, "What does that mean?"

"It means we have motive and *opportunity*. Clarence had unauthorized access to the document before it was submitted for probate. I requested the security tapes from the city council and went through hours of footage. A few hours ago, I found a video of Uncle Clancy entering the file room after hours. There's no camera inside the room, but it's enough to bring this matter to the light."

"Where are you heading now?" I grab clothes and start dressing. It's tricky since I'm still dripping wet, but I don't care. I hold the phone with my cheek and my shoulder. "I'll meet you."

"This is police business. I'll bring in Uncle Clarence. Tell Rebel to stay at the garage. Right now, he and Stewart are probably panicking. Desperate people do desperate things, and I don't want the situation to escalate."

"Dad." I blurt.

He pauses.

I swallow hard. "Are you... going to be okay...?"

Okay arresting your own family?

Okay losing your good name?

Okay giving up the farm?

"Son," my dad says in a grave voice, "there comes a moment in every father's life when he realizes what kind of human being he raised." He pauses. "Because of you, I can say I raised a good one."

Something odd lodges in my throat.

"Your grandfather started out with nothing. We can do the same. The Kinseys are more than their money."

I rub my chest to stave off the burning there. "Stay safe."

Dad hangs up and my hand falls to my side.

"Everything okay?" Watson asks.

Renthrow's observing me too, his arms folded over his chest.

For once, Theilan isn't cracking jokes or grinning mischievously.

I grunt.

"What does that mean?" Theilan whispers.

While they discuss amongst each other, I send Rebel a text.

ME: *Hey, are you still at the garage?*

I take big, loping strides to the exits when Chance grabs my shoulder. Behind him, Renthrow, Theilan and Watson are standing close.

"Do you need backup?" Chance asks.

I look at my team members. Their eyes are set, arms tense, bodies braced for action. This entire week, they've been watching over Rebel and her mom and accompanying me on stakeouts while asking no questions.

A realization comes to me at that moment. I might get kicked out of the Kinsey clan after this, but I know that I'll still have a family.

"I've got it." I take a moment to look at each of their faces. "Thank you."

Chance steps back.

Renthrow turns away with a small smile.

Theilan looks shocked. "Did he just… smile at us?"

I leave the team behind and hustle to my car. Before driving, I check my phone to see that Rebel hasn't answered my message yet.

On the way to the garage, I call her.

She doesn't answer.

Alarmed, I call again.

Every ring echoes in my ears and sends my pulse clamoring.

The moment I hang up, my phone gets an incoming call and I answer urgently, "Rebel?"

"It's Chance. April just called to tell me they're heading to Rebel's mom right now."

I slam on the brakes. "Now?"

"Yeah. She didn't say much, but I could hear in her voice she was flustered."

I barely hear anything else that Chance says. Hands firm on the steering wheel, I slam my foot on the gas and U-turn so hard the vehicle almost teeters over on its side. Once it rights itself again, I floor it and fly to the trailer park. I spot Rebel's truck right away and come to an abrupt stop.

Running across to the mobile home, I launch up the stairs and throw the door open.

Rebel's standing in front of her mom, one arm extended protectively while Mrs. Hart trembles behind her. April is standing in front of them both, waving her phone around.

"You should be ashamed of yourself! Trying to scam this woman into marriage to cover your tracks!"

I stop short.

M-marriage?

Uncle Stewart's brilliant plan was to *marry* into the Hart family?

Somehow, that doesn't surprise me. It's just the sort of

desperate, hare-brained plan only someone like Uncle Stewart would come up with.

"Put that down, girl or…"

"Or what, Stewart? I'm on a live call with the nursing home group chat. Try anything funny, everyone will see."

"Put that phone down," Uncle Stewart growls.

April continues filming.

Uncle Stewart swipes at her device, and April jumps out of reach but she almost loses her balance in the process.

I see my uncle gearing up to get more violent with her and step inside.

"Uncle Stewart!" I yell so loud that the entire house trembles.

April, Rebel and her mom swivel to look at me.

My eyes collide with Rebel's baby blue gaze. *I'm here.*

She sighs in relief.

That same relief is echoing in my heart. Rebel's hair is mussed and she's breathing hard but, other than that, she looks unharmed.

I'll make sure it stays that way.

"*You!*" Uncle Stewart points a stubby finger. He stomps over and grabs me by the collar. "This is all *your* fault."

"Gunner!" Concern carved into her beautiful face, Rebel moves toward me.

I shake my head at her.

She stops abruptly, chewing on her bottom lip.

"You're right. It is all my fault. Let's talk about it outside." I lift both hands in surrender. Right now, all I want is for my uncle to get as far away from Rebel as possible.

Uncle Stewart follows the direction of my gaze to Rebel and his mouth twists into a sneer. "You idiot! We tried so hard to keep you away from this girl, tried to keep you from finding out and you still went ahead anyway. And for what?" He gestures to Rebel. "She's nothing but a pretty face from the trailer park. Girls like her are dirt cheap; I could buy 'em for a dollar."

My nostrils flare and I grab Uncle Stewart by the throat. Trembling with rage, I growl, "Watch. Your. Mouth."

"Or what? You'll hit me? You'll hang me out to dry? For *her*." He shoves me against the frame of the door. His elbow digs into my neck. "We're the ones who come pick you up in the dead of night when you've got a blown wheel and no one else to call. We're the ones who taught you how to drive and shoot a gun. We're the ones who share the same blood. You're turning on your own family. Making enemies of your own people. Some juicy lips and a nice rack will keep you warm at night, but is that anything compared to family?"

My face twists and anger surges through my veins. I ram Uncle Stewart in the jaw. The clash of my knuckles to his jawline hurts the both of us, but Uncle Stewart makes a garbled sound, eyes clouding in surprise, pain and shock. His entire body stumbles to the side as if he's being dragged by an invisible hand.

While the punch was deserved, it was the wrong move.

An already tense situation escalates fast.

Uncle Stewart lunges to the left. I jump on him, but a damaging blow to the head knocks me to my knee.

Mrs. Hart screams.

Rebel shrieks, "Gunner!"

I lift a hand to my hair, stars dancing around my eyes. And then I look at Uncle Stewart. He's holding a bat—something Mrs. Hart probably kept close by the door for self-defense—and is gearing up to swing again.

Pushing to my feet, I run deeper into the living room and stand in front of Rebel. "Get behind me!" I roar. "April, get back!"

April drops her phone as she races to join the other ladies. When she stops as if she'll pick it up, Rebel grabs her arm and yanks her behind me, wrapping an arm around the shorter woman protectively.

"I know why you're here! I know what you're trying to do!"

Uncle Stewart swings the bat like a drunk. His eyes dart back and forth like a cornered animal.

Desperate men do desperate things. Dad's warning from earlier rings like a church bell in my head.

"Clarence said he'd pin this on me and you're falling right into his trap!"

I hold out a hand and take a step forward. "Dad's heading to pick up Uncle Clarence as we speak. You're *both* going to pay for what you did."

"You think that slimy fox will be so easy to catch? He left town hours ago."

My eyes widen. *Does dad know about this?*

"I've been framed, Gunner. I swear to you. Clarence is the one behind all of this." Uncle Stewart swings the bat in a giant arc. "You think I know anything about shell corporations and paper companies? I'm just a mechanic. All I know is cars. He put the money in my account and told me what land to sell. That's all I did."

"What about the will?" Rebel snaps. "Didn't you know about that too?"

I glance over my shoulder and find my girlfriend glaring a hole into Uncle Stewart. My uncle better hope Rebel doesn't get ahold of that bat because I have no idea what damage she'll inflict on him.

"The will… he-he never told me about that. I have no idea." My uncle's eyes dart to the side.

"Yeah, right!"

Mrs. Hart looks very confused. "What will? What are you talking about?"

"Rebel," I hiss.

But the train is rolling down the hill and there's no stopping her now that she's off.

"Clay Kinsey left a plot of land for you in his will," Rebel blurts, her eyes as hot as the bluest flames.

Mrs. Hart's eyebrows fly to the top of her head.

"And Stewart here saw it as another opportunity to manipulate and use you."

"That's not true! I've had feelings for your mother for a long time."

"Oh please! You were planning to marry her and then pocket all the money once it comes rolling over to her."

"And you think you're any better? Didn't you date Gunner just to get into the Society?"

I freeze.

April covers her mouth.

Mrs. Hart glances between me and Rebel.

Uncle Stewart preens. "You and your mother are nothing but the help. You should be *thrilled* you get the chance to marry a Kinsey. Everyone in town respects us. But you? You're just trailer trash. You and your mother should be thanking *me* for—"

Her face a flaming red, Rebel surges forward. I catch her by the mid-section before she can fly into Uncle Stewart's bat.

"You want to see trailer trash? Fine, I'll give you trailer trash! Gunner, put me down!"

I keep her airborne as her legs scramble several inches off the floor.

At that moment, the door bursts open and dad barrels in. He's wearing his sheriff's uniform and has his two deputies with him.

"Dan!" Uncle Stewart's eyes widen.

My dad doesn't break his stride. He storms over to his brother, yanks the bat away and slaps handcuffs on him.

"Dan, what are you doing? I'm your *brother?* Get these off me."

"Stewart Kinsey, you are under arrest…"

As dad rattles off Uncle Stewart's crimes, I stare at him and a memory snaps into my brain. It was all the way back in kindergarten and dad came to present for career day. I watched him in his uniform, talking in front of my entire class and I felt a sense of awe.

That's my dad, I thought proudly that day.

The remnants of that same pride echo now.

That's my dad.

"You'd turn on your own family, Dan! You'd really do that?" Uncle Stewart squirms as dad hauls him upright.

"I'm doing what's right as an officer of the law and a servant of my community."

"You'll have nothing after this, Dan. You'll *be* nothing!"

Uncle Stewart's yelling gets fainter and fainter as the deputies cart him off.

"Oh my goodness," Mrs. Hart mumbles.

I rush to catch her as her legs give out. "Are you okay, ma'am?"

"Lewis, call the ambulance," dad says into his walkie.

"I'm fine. I'm fine. I just need to sit down," Mrs. Hart says. I lead her to the couch and Rebel pushes pillows behind her back to make her comfortable.

"I'll get you some water, mom."

"Let me." I go to the kitchen and grab three cups, handing all the ladies one.

"Are you okay?" I ask Rebel when I give her the water.

She nods and squeezes my hand.

I brush her hair away from her face tenderly. The adrenaline rush is starting to fade.

"Is it over now?" Rebel whispers.

"Yeah." I rest my forehead against hers while still cradling her cheek. "It's over princess."

Now, it's time to pick up the pieces that Uncle Stewart and Uncle Clancy left behind and give Rebel the happily ever after she deserves.

CHAPTER
FIFTY-NINE

REBEL

Gunner's thumb moves back and forth over my cheek and I nuzzle into the touch.

The moment he swept into the house with his dark hair, pale blue eyes, and dark, intimidating presence, I knew that everything would be okay.

"April!" Chance appears in the doorway out of breath.

"Chance!" My best friend flies into her boyfriend's arms.

"I was so worried. I heard everything." Chance twists her head gently up and down. "Are you okay? You didn't get hit by the bat, did you?"

"No, but... how do you know Stewart had a bat?"

"What do you mean? I heard everything," Chance says.

I straighten away from Gunner, stunned. "How did you hear... oh?" My eyes stray to the cell phone that April dropped earlier.

"Oh no!" April breaks away from Chance and picks the device off the floor. "Guys! I think my phone was still on the video chat." She shows us the screen where several rows of elderly faces are looking at us.

April taps a button.

Immediately, an elderly voice croaks. "April, is everything okay? We called the police."

"Everything's fine, guys. Thanks for staying on."

"What happened?" Another voice warbles.

April steps away to assure her audience. Chance slaps Gunner on the back, smiles at me and follows April through the side door.

Mom blows out a breath and I immediately go into panic mode. "Are you okay? Are you hurt anywhere? Do we need to go to the hospital now?"

"I just don't understand." Mom lifts her hands and then drops them into her lap. "Why would Clay Kinsey leave anything for me? All I did was clean his house for a few years."

"We don't know why he did it, but it would really help if we could prove that he did," Sheriff Kinsey says, stepping back into the trailer. "Stewart is talking, but his insight is limited. He's not the mastermind here."

Gunner's expression tightens. "They haven't found Uncle Clancy? Even with all the checkpoints?"

"He was last spotted near the pier. We think he might have gotten away by boat."

Gunner's nostrils flare. "So he's still out there?"

"We'll find him, son."

I scramble to my feet. "Sherriff, thank you. For everything."

He could have easily brushed this under the rug, but he investigated the case and even arrested his own brother.

Stewart Kinsey is absolutely awful.

But I have to admit. The Kinseys aren't *all* bad.

Though it doesn't surprise me that Gunner's parents are so incredible given how wonderful Gunner turned out.

"I'm just doing my job, Ms. Hart." Sheriff Kinsey glances at mom. "On behalf of the entire Kinsey family, I apologize to you and your daughter. Not just for what happened today but also for what happened in the past."

Mom looks horrified. "Sheriff Kinsey, there's no need to apologize. I truly think you're mistaken. I was nothing important to your father. Truly. All I did was work for him."

I take her hand gently, hating that she's downplaying how incredible she is. "Mom, you inspire me with your hard work and cheerful attitude every day. I bet you inspired Clay Kinsey too."

Mom still looks flabbergasted. "Still... a land is too much. The only thing I ever got from Mr. Clay was bonuses for Christmas and a key chain with a rusty old key still on it."

I feel Gunner's energy shift and look up at him. He glances at his father and the two share a meaningful look.

A moment later, Sheriff Kinsey approaches mom carefully. "Mrs. Hart, do you still have that key?"

* * *

MOM AND I ARE *NOT* RICH ENOUGH TO EVEN KNOW WHAT SAFETY deposit boxes are, so I don't blame her for not recognizing what the key was for. However, the moment Sheriff Kinsey sees it, he tells us that we need to go to the bank.

When we arrive, we're treated like VIPs and taken straight to a private office where we're offered tea while we wait for the manager.

A distinguished man wearing white gloves arrives and leads us through a heavily secured door, down some stairs and into a fancy room filled with bright lights and rich velvet, black boxes. The private room looks as fancy as a hotel. Mom and I both gawk at the high ceilings and fancy glass finishings.

"Did you know something like this was in Lucky Falls?" Mom asks, nudging me with her elbow.

"No ma'am," I whisper back, in awe.

The bank manager pulls out the box with his gloved hands

and sets it on the table in front of my mother. The entire process looks important and official, yet Gunner and Sheriff Kinsey remain completely unfazed.

Mom stares at the object and then at the clerk. "Am I supposed to…"

"Yes. The box is registered to you so only you can open it."

I gasp in surprise.

"That's probably why Clarence and Stewart never knew about it," Sheriff Kinsey says, rubbing his chin.

"Go on. Open it," I encourage.

Mom takes a deep breath and slowly fits the key into the lock.

She turns it.

There's a *click* sound.

Gunner, Sheriff Kinsey and I press in as mom stands on the other side of the table and lifts the lid. The creak the box makes as it pops open is the loudest I've ever heard.

"What's in it?" Sheriff Kinsey asks, his voice subdued.

Gunner says nothing, but I can feel his curiosity building too.

Mom spins the box around and takes out the contents. Inside, there are formal tax documents, printed emails, and a folded letter.

"The emails aren't addressed to me," mom says. "It's to someone named Amir O'Neil. I'm not sure who that is."

"It's the owner of dad's tax accounting firm in the city." Sheriff Kinsey's eyes dip to his shoes and he takes a deep breath before looking at mom again. "I recognize my father's hand writing in the letter. May I?"

Mom nods.

Sheriff Kinsey unfolds the letter and flips to the page that was torn from the version Clarence Kinsey tampered with. He reads quietly and then his hand falls limp. "Dad knew this would happen."

"What do you mean? What does it say?" I ask.

Sherriff Kinsey hands me the letter but, when he speaks, it's to Gunner. "You were right. He gave the Harts the property near Darkwell Ridge."

"*Darkwell Ridge?*" Mom croaks. "The place where they found oil?"

Gunner places both hands on the table, his head hanging low.

Sheriff Kinsey is sober enough for a funeral.

While I wrap my arms around mom who's trembling with shock, I can't help but feel burdened when I look at Gunner. He and his dad must have prepared for this moment, but it probably still feels like a rock landed on them knowing that it's official.

Mom and I are rich.

And the Kinseys owe us everything.

A few months ago, I'd have been whooping and hollering and celebrating the fairness of life. After all, I've hated the Kinseys for so long.

But after everything, this is no victory.

"I can't believe this," mom says, cupping her chin and staring off into the distance. "I can't believe this."

"We're going to give you two some privacy." Sheriff Kinsey gestures to Gunner. The giant hockey player catches my eye. We share a silent look before he disappears.

"What do the emails say, Rebel?"

I look through them, my voice trembling. "It… seems like Clay Kinsey was discussing taxes with the accounting firm." I run my fingers over a line of text and read, "*'The current estate qualifies for the highest tax bracket, but there is a loophole to remain in a lower bracket and relieve the tax burden on your family after your passing'.*"

"What does *that* mean?" Mom hyperventilates. "Why are those emails in the box? It doesn't make sense."

I read through the rest of the correspondence quickly. "They're referring to inheritance taxes, mom." My eyes catch on my mother's name and I linger there. "I think you should read this."

Mom accepts the email from me and reads in a wispy voice, "'I've taken your advice into consideration and would like to avoid entering the higher tax bracket, thus, I've chosen to leave the property near Darkwell Ridge to a non-family member, my cleaner...'" My mother's knees buckle. She hands the letter to me. "Rebel, w-what does this mean for us now?"

"It means..." I blow out a breath, "that the Kinseys owe us the Darkwell Ridge property. And all the money they made from the oil there."

"W-what?"

"It wasn't their oil to begin with," I explain. "They'll have to give it back."

"How much is that going to cost them?"

The question surprises me. "Are you worried about the Kinseys right now?"

Mom glances at the will and then up at me. "It's not just them. The whole town will point fingers at us. No one will think we deserve this money."

I'm so shocked by her words, I can't even think of a response.

Mom keeps shaking her head. "Mr. Clay only gave that property to me so his kids wouldn't have to pay a lot in taxes. If not for that, he would have wanted them to have it."

"Mom, you didn't read the rest of the email." I lift the paper up and continue where she left off, "'*She*—Clay Kinsey's talking about *you*, mom—*is small of frame but large in heart. It is no easy feat to dedicate your time and effort to someone else's comfort, and yet, she's done so with unwavering kindness and diligence. Her hard work often puts mine to shame. If someone outside of my blood relatives must be a benefactor, I can choose no one but her'*."

I hand mom the email so she can drink in the words for herself. "You deserve this money and more. Clay Kinsey gave you the land and it rightfully belongs to you."

"Aren't you worried about you and Gunner?" Mom asks, peering up at me. "This may make things very complicated for you two."

"Gunner and I will get through this. Don't worry about anything else but *you*."

Mom pats my hand twice and then she heads to the door. "Gunner, Sheriff?"

Both men return to the room, looking somber and thoughtful.

Sheriff Kinsey clears his throat. "Mrs. Hart, I—uh—I know words won't fix this, but I assure you that, on behalf of the Kinsey family, I will do everything to make this right."

Gunner nods along.

"We," his throat bobs, "we'll return the land to you immediately. Now, about the matter of the oil and the repayment for that, if you could give us some time…"

"It's alright, Sheriff."

My eyes widen.

Gunner's head whips up.

Mom smiles and loops her arm around mine. "I'm not the type who needs a lot. Rebel knows this. My heart's full because I get to live in this beautiful town filled with lovely people. I'm rich with a nice home, a beautiful daughter, dear friends, and kind bosses." She glances with a fond smile at the box. "Some would say too kind. I don't need anything more."

"Mom…" I whisper.

Gunner steps forward. "Mrs. Hart, we can't let this pass by without paying you back. That's not right or fair."

"I agree," Sheriff Kinsey says in a deep, firm voice. "Stewart knew about what Clarence had done and he kept you close in his shop to keep an eye on you. The harm done by our family can't be swept under the rug. A crime was done. There are consequences for that. We're willing to pay for our sins."

"But it's really fine."

"Mrs. Hart," Gunner declares, "my dad and I have discussed it and, while we don't have all the money now, we'd like to propose a payment agreement."

Mom gasps. "A what?"

"We'd like to sign a settlement," Sheriff Kinsey says. "The

Kinseys will repay you the oil in perpetuity until every cent is paid. In a sense," Gunner's dad blushes, "you can say that the entire Kinsey family now works for you."

Mom swallows hard, dumbstruck.

"Would that be okay with you?" Gunner asks mom.

"Um… I… I guess," mom stammers, looking at me.

"Then let's head outside and set up a meeting with the lawyers," Sheriff Kinsey says, gesturing for my mom to leave first.

As their voices get fainter, I walk over to Gunner. "Was the settlement your idea?"

"This way, your mom gets what's owed to her, but my family doesn't have to lose everything all at once. What do you think?"

"I think…" I glance at his grandfather's will and then wrap my arms around his neck, "that I'll enjoy bossing you around."

He laughs softly and nuzzles his nose against mine, "Any time, princess. I'm at your service."

CHAPTER SIXTY

GUNNER

Turns out, if you post a dramatic family showdown live on the retirement group home chat, it takes half a day for the rest of the town to hear about it.

In detail.

And then in exaggerated detail.

And then in details that never actually happened.

By evening's end, without dad having to call anyone over, the entire family floods my parent's home to discuss the matter.

At first, there's a lot of shouting and demands. Some family members insist that only Uncle Clarence and Uncle Stewart should pay for the damages. Others suggest we should find a lawyer and counter-sue so we don't have to pay a cent.

Dad spells out what losing a court case will mean for us—filing for bankruptcy, losing our retirement accounts and houses, giving up all gold, jewelry, and even the furniture and clothes we own.

My uncles and aunts flinch.

"Carol, what do you think of this?" Uncle Robert asks, looking at my mother with desperation in his eyes.

The rest of the family turn to mom too. She's been silent through most of the chaos. In fact, ever since Uncle Stewart was transported to the county jail and Uncle Clancy became the first Kinsey to have a wanted notice publicized on the nightly news, she hasn't said much at all.

"I'm just observing who my real friends are," mom told me when I asked her if she was okay.

Marjorie White's been noticeably keeping her distance from the house, and mom missed the last Lady Luck Society meeting. I'm considering whether I should ask Rebel, the new face of the Society, to help mom out.

"I think a settlement is a great idea," mom says, stunning the room into silence.

"But Carol!"

"Whoever would like to take this to court, can do so. After you lose everything, I will be sure to share canned food with you and you may use the wooden shed at the back of the property until you get back on your feet."

Everyone flinches.

Mom smiles tightly. "Cake anyone?"

* * *

Later that evening, I head to the ladies' outdoor garage. With Uncle Stewart behind bars, the Safety Committee should be scrambling to give April and Rebel their shop back but, instead, they're doubling down.

Chance's lawyers have officially sued the organization. I don't know much about law but, from what Chance has explained to me, his lawyers are confident that the Safety Committee is about to get creamed. At least those lawyers are finally good for something.

Rebel's bent over the open hood of a car, looking utterly

angelic while fiddling around with the engine. A pink bandana is tied around her forehead and a ponytail dangles over the shoulder of her pink jumper.

Blue eyes flit to me and then crinkle with a warm, genuine smile. "Gunner, you're early."

I wave in a silent instruction *take your time*. Then I take a seat around the table, watching her work. She moves with confidence, putting wires together, staring at waveforms on her laptop and cleaning car parts that I probably couldn't name if my life was on the line. It's the sexiest thing I've ever seen in my life.

"Huh." April's voice makes me jump. I look over my shoulder at Chance's girlfriend as she takes a can of soda from the fridge. "Chance was right. You do melt."

I arch a brow.

She smirks at me and then at Rebel. "I'm glad you know how lucky you are, Kinsey. Never forget it."

"I won't," I respond. I'm no idiot. I was lucky enough to gain Rebel's heart but, more importantly, I was lucky enough to gain Rebel's trust. Life will change and the both of us might change with it, but my adoration of Rebel Hart will always be the same.

Oblivious to our conversation, Rebel runs around the hood of the car, takes her place in the driver's seat and turns the key. The engine rumbles to life and she throws her hands up.

"Success!"

I applaud, "Nice shot."

Rebel rolls her eyes. "Calm down, hockey boy. I only fixed one problem out of many. The game's not over yet."

I walk over to her and slip my arm around her waist. "But you'll take a break now, right? Because…" I lean in and whisper in her ear, "I'm hungry."

She laughs and tilts her head up to kiss me.

"Rebel! Yoo-hoo!"

Marjorie White saunters into the garage. Rosalie and Cecelia

Davis wobble behind her. The ladies are carrying an extremely large vase.

Seeing them struggle, I take the heavy burden from them.

"Rebel, we saw this *beautiful* flower vase while we were shopping and just *had* to bring it over to you." Marjorie waves a hand at me and says disdainfully, "Put it there, Gunner. And watch it. That vase costs a lot of money. I know you can't afford to buy it back if you break it."

I almost drop the vase out of spite.

Marjorie takes out a twenty and pats it against my chest. "Here you go, sweetie. A little goes a long way."

I glare at her and let the twenty plummet to the ground, untouched.

Rebel snaps, "Give the vase back, Gunner."

I happily set the vase down and back away from it.

Rebel marches forward. "Marjorie, what are you doing here?"

"I came to brighten up your beautiful, outdoor workspace and offer my help." Marjorie puts on a Cheshire-cat smile and takes Rebel's hand, barely hiding her flinch when she realizes Rebel's gloves are dirty.

"What exactly do you want to help me with?" Rebel asks, folding her arms over her chest.

"As the most influential and wealthy young woman in town, there's a certain expectation upon you that might be overwhelming."

Rosalie and Cecilia Davis nod like the parrots that they are.

"We know you're not used to how things in our circle work, so," Marjorie sprawls her hands out dramatically, "as your Lady Luck Society sisters, we're here to teach you all you need to know."

"What a… thoughtful offer." Rebel loops her hand around my arm. The smile on her face does not reach her eyes and I hide my smirk because I know what's coming next won't be pretty. "Since you're here, Marjorie, now is the perfect time to inform you that I will no longer be a part of the Lady Luck Society."

"What?" Marjorie White gasps dramatically.

"Why?" Rosalie whines.

"I'll be starting my *own* association."

"Well," Marjorie grapples to salvage the conversation, "how does one join this association of yours?"

"If you're interested in joining, you'll have to speak to Carol."

Marjorie's cheeks turn red and her lips tighten as if she's just tasted something bitter.

Rebel leans her head against my shoulder. "Thank you for the flowers, but I'm afraid we don't have space to accommodate them." Rebel gestures to the very spacious outdoor garage. "I'll have to ask you to take them back. Now, if you'll excuse me, I have a date with my boyfriend. April!"

"Yeah!" April pops her head out of a car hood.

"I'm done for the day!"

"Got it!" April says.

Rebel leaves Marjorie gaping at her and tugs me to the sink where she disposes of her pink gloves and washes her hands.

I lean one hand against the wall, looking down at her with a pleased smile. "Are you really going to invite my mom to your association?"

"I thought I wanted to join the Lady Luck Society to help people, but really, I just wanted to prove I belonged. Now that I've tasted what it feels like to really help people though, I don't want to stop. The Lady Luck Society was nice, but it's too superficial now. It's gotten rotten. I want to build something from the ground up that's meant to help and that *continues* to help the people who need it most."

"Where does my mom come in?" I wonder.

Rebel's pretty pink lips inch upward. "Your mom is a force to be reckoned with and if the Lady Luck Society is dumb enough to ostracize her, I'm taking the opportunity to steal her away."

Delia comes to the sink too and rinses something under the faucet. She looks closely at Rebel. "Did you kick those rich ladies out?"

"Sort of," Rebel says with a shrug.

"Cool." With that, the mechanic moves away and returns to her work.

I look down at Rebel and find her eyes sparkling. "Why are you so happy?"

"Delia just called me cool," she gushes. "Do you know what a compliment that is?"

"You don't get that excited when *I* give you compliments."

Rebel scrunches her nose. "Yeah, well, you don't ride a Harley or know how to diagnose a faulty timing belt. It's different." She pulls the clip out of her ponytail and her blonde hair spills around her shoulders, turning her from astoundingly beautiful to jaw-droppingly gorgeous. "Besides, you're my boyfriend. You say nice things all the time."

I frown because it sounds like she's saying my compliments aren't as genuine.

Rebel flicks me with water and laughs softly. "Your expression just got really intense. I'm afraid to know what you're thinking."

I gravitate closer to her, still leaving one hand on the wall and the other in my pocket. Rebel inches back, her eyes widening. The superpower I've honed after years of quietly watching Rebel Hart is that I can read her better than she can read me. At least for now. And I like what I see.

A lot.

"Do you know… you only get self-conscious around me?" I whisper.

"I am not self-conscious," Rebel says, fiddling with a wisp of her hair.

I gather her by the small of her back, pulling her closer to me and staring intently into her eyes. "Shyness looks good on you."

"I am *not* shy."

That gets a smile out of me.

"Oh my gosh, Gunner. Do *not* smile at me in here. This is a no kissing zone."

I tilt my head and keep watching her.

She stares back at me.

And my heart thumps just like it always does. Just like it will for the rest of my life.

I whisper reverently, "Sometimes, Rebel Hart, you're so beautiful that I wonder if you're real."

Rebel's nostrils flare and her crystal blue eyes become more black than blue.

I take in that mesmerizing expression for a glorious moment. Then, I let her go and step back. With a satisfied grunt, I mutter, "It's settled. I give the better compliments."

She flicks me with more water and grumbles under her breath, stomping away.

I don't suppress my grin as I follow her out to the car and take my kind, beautiful, accomplished, intelligent girlfriend on a date.

EPILOGUE

It's the final minutes of the playoffs and my heart is at my throat.

Shouts erupt from the entire stadium. The noise so deafening that I'll be hearing a ringing in my ears for the next two weeks.

But none of that matters.

The clock is ticking.

The game is tied.

This is the Lucky Striker's last chance to take the number one spot on the leader board.

I can't breathe.

Gunner cuts across the ice, speeding ahead of the other team's defense. Beside me, April is screaming for Chance, who currently has control of the puck, but my eyes are on my boyfriend as the defense descend on Chance in a frenzy.

Chance sends the puck skating across the ice.

Come on, Gunner. Come on.

Gunner takes control of the puck in the blink of an eye and skates like a madman to the goal. If I thought it was loud before, the shouts in the stadium are about to tear the *roof* off this place.

I'm on my feet and screaming my head off along with

everyone else. To my left, there's a voice only slightly louder than mine and, suddenly, a warm hand wraps around mine.

I look over to Carol, who's got her eyes locked on her son. I doubt she even recognizes that she's holding me. I bet she'd be horrified. Sure, she agreed to join my association (and even took all her contacts and sponsors—including Rodney Howard—with her), but Carol still acts a little snooty around me.

It's in her blood, I guess.

Mom and the Kinseys have come to a settlement agreement, and the Kinseys have already started making payments.

Mom moved out of the trailer and into a small but more expensive home in a modest area of Lucky Falls. She also met with an architect to build an apartment on the property near Darkwell Ridge, which I recently found out has always been a dream of hers.

Gunner and I are happily dating.

Mom never has to work another day in her life.

And I no longer need to suck up to the Lady Luck Society to make real change in Lucky Falls.

The only thing we need now is for the Lucky Strikers to win this game and walk away as the champions of the season.

But that last part is easier said than done.

The opposing team swarms around Gunner like a pack of hungry wolves, doing their best to tear him to pieces. He weaves through them like a ghost. Fakes a pass and turns instead. But they're just as desperate to be number one and he can't get past.

A slick pass to Theilan is the best decision in that moment and I watch, heart in my throat until the moment the puck is back in his possession.

Eight seconds.

"Go, Gunner! You got this!" I scream, knowing my voice is being drowned out by the multitudes in the stadium.

Gunner lifts his stick and, without hesitation, he goes for it.

The puck sails through the air.

I hear every distinct beat of my heart. Every hiss of sweat

rolling down my face. Every thud of my feet jumping up and down on the bleachers.

Time slows until…

The puck soars past the goalie's glove in a lighting flash and rams into the back of the net.

Score!

Lucky Falls goes wild in the stands. I hug Carol and then I hug April and Delia. Tears are running down Carol's face and I feel a few tears pressing against the back of my eyes too.

It's the first time Lucky Falls has won a championship in *years*. A lot of that is owed to Chance, the indisputable ace of the team. But I know how hard Gunner and the other members have been working, toiling, and *yearning* for this win.

And it's finally here.

Gunner rips his helmet off and tosses it while his teammates descend on him, knocking him to the ice in celebration. The celebrating dog pile breaks and Gunner pushes to his feet, his head immediately swiveling to our side of the bleachers.

His eyes find mine and his lips twitch upward, leaking that pleased, half-smile that's just for me.

I blow him a kiss.

The smile on his face gets bigger.

"I've never seen my son smile like that," Carol says, sniffing. "I've never seen him so happy."

I hug her again, soothing her back as she loses it.

By the time I return my attention to the ice, Gunner is gone.

He has interviews and fan signing with the rest of the team, so April, Delia, and I hang out in the administration building until the players emerge.

"That was crazy," Delia says, running her fingers through her silky, black hair. "I don't know much about hockey, but I feel *pumped*."

I wrap an arm around her shoulder. "Welcome to Lucky Falls. You'll get sucked in and become a hardcore hockey fan eventually."

April nods in agreement. "It really sneaks up on you."

We hear footsteps. Chance, Theilan, Renthrow, Watson and Gunner walk toward us.

My heart skips a beat when I spot Gunner. His jersey hugs his broad shoulders and hints at the impressive muscles coiled beneath the sleeves. His hair is still damp and slightly curly over his forehead. As always, his resting face is an intimidating one—focused and dangerous.

But, when his eyes meet mine, he softens in a way that only happens when he's with me.

"Whoo! Congratulations, guys!" April says as she flies into her boyfriend's arms and gives him a sweet kiss.

"Congratulations," I murmur, moving into Gunner's arms.

He hugs me and kisses my forehead. "Thanks, princess." He eases back. "I like your jacket."

"Yeah?" I do a little spin so he can admire my pink bedazzled 'KINSEY' jacket that I had custom-made for tonight.

The last time I wore his name on a jacket, I wanted to take it off and burn it. But now, not only am I rocking Gunner's jersey number with pride… I bedazzled the heck out of it.

"You look amazing." He pulls me close again.

I grin from ear to ear. "I was hoping you'd say that. I have a pink jacket with my name bedazzled on it in the car for you."

He gives me a quick, horrified look. "Really?"

"No, I'm just joking." I laugh and cuddle closer to his chest.

"Hey, guys!" Max says, calling our attention to him.

The bear-sized team manager is not alone. A trim, older woman struts beside him. The woman is wearing red leather pants, bold red lipstick and has cutting, dark brown eyes. She's far, *far* tinier than Max, but I sense that she has a personality twice his size.

Gunner sees me watching the woman closely and whispers, "Do you know her?"

"Something about her seems familiar."

"Everyone," Max grins, "I'd like you to meet our new sponsor, Mrs.—"

"Mom!" A voice shrieks.

"Mom?" Max finishes his announcement and then his forehead creases as if he hadn't meant to say 'Mrs. Mom' at all.

"Cordelia," the woman says in a cultured voice. Her red lips inch up in a sly smile.

"Mom?" I ask, pointing between Delia and the new sponsor.

The usually cool and unflappable Delia looks ready to bolt for the doors. She eyes the exits for a second and then her head whips around like she's searching desperately for something. Suddenly, she latches onto Renthrow. Wrapping her hand around his bicep, Delia forces a smile and says in a firm tone. "Mom."

The sponsor's eyebrows tighten and there's a warning in her voice when she responds, "*Cor*-delia."

The two stare each other down and it feels like a heated but silent conversation.

Renthrow tries to wrench his arm away. "What are you doing?" he hisses.

Delia holds fast, her teeth gritted. "Mom, I'd like to introduce you to my…"

"*Daddy!*"

Delia's entire face turns pale as Gordie flings herself at Renthrow's leg.

"Oh. It's the cool lady!" Gordie points up at Delia with a giant smile. She bounces up and down. "Daddy, it's the lady I told you about!"

Delia's eyes dart between Renthrow and Gordie as if someone's pulled a sick prank on her. "D-daddy?"

The new sponsor scrunches her nose. "Really, Cordelia?"

I glance at Gunner.

He looks at me and shakes his head slowly.

Something tells me that life in Lucky Falls is about to get a lot more interesting.

* * *

Thank you for reading *Ice Princess*. Want more of Gunner and Rebel? Read a deleted scene that will have you giggling and kicking your feet.

Get exclusive access to the deleted scene *and* be the first to know when Delia's book is available, by signing up to my newsletter at www.liabevans.com

Enjoy!
Love and blessings,
Lia

ICE MECHANIC

SNEAK PEEK! ICE MECHANIC CHAPTER ONE

CHANCE

My veins buzz the moment I step into the rundown stadium. One-by-one, the lights thud on. Some of them flicker a few times in silent protest, reluctant to shine on me.

That's a metaphor for my life if I've ever seen one.

I take a big sniff, the scents both foreign and familiar. Nothing beats the dry, crisp air in the stadium. The perfect circumference of the rink. The way the lights bounce against the ice. The way the seats smell like varnish and W-D40...

I wrinkle my nose.

Actually, that smell is new.

"Ack!" A thin black man wearing a jumper streaked in oil explodes into my line of vision. Sharp brown eyes land on me, narrow slightly and then widen. "Well I'll be."

"Hey." I slip right into my people-greeting persona, tucking away my fidget spinner and reaching out for a handshake.

"Oh, I..." He swipes his hands on the sides of his pants and then hesitates. "I'm Bobby Hewitt. I'm a huge fan and I really want to shake that hand, but you mind saving it for later?"

"I'll save it with interest."

His smile widens a tad. "Wow." His eyes gleam. "Chance McLanely. The Clairvoyant in the flesh."

I rub the back of my neck. "The Clairvoyant. Haven't heard that name in a while."

Bobby laughs and mimics the movement of a skater on the ice. "Man, you knew where the puck was going ten years before it got there. You were on a roll before the…" His eyes shift away. "Uh, before everything."

Something sharp pierces my heart.

Before you got suspended…

Before…

It's agony to know that my plummet from the top is the marker of my life.

Before the league.

After the league.

But my chapter isn't done. I'll walk through hot stones in flowing lava to reclaim what's mine.

Joining The Lucky Strikers is my first lava-soaked step.

"Uh," Bobby's eyes dart to the ground and he chuckles awkwardly, "Look at me yapping. You must be here to see Max."

I nod and notice his oil-stained hands. "Were you fixing something?"

"No, no. Well, kinda. I'm the Zamboni driver, but the stupid machine's been breaking down left and right and the mechanics haven't been able to find the problem so I'm here reading up on engines like I know anything about, oh… here I go talking too much again. Let me show you to the office."

"I know where it is," I assure him.

His eyebrows hike. "Then why'd you come this way?"

I glance at the rink.

"Ah." He lifts an oil-stained finger. "Gotta make your introduction to the lady."

I chuckle. "I'll see you around, Bobby."

He waves and goes back to his Zamboni-fixing research. I continue to the admin area.

You got this, Chance. Go get 'em.

Despite the self-talk, my nerves attack me like those defensemen at last year's Halloween charity game.

Heart? Palpitating.

Lips? Trembling.

Fingers? Fidget-spinning.

After one more tug, I shove the fidget spinner back into my pocket, paste on my don't-care smile and blow open the door marked 'TEAM MANAGER'.

"McLanely!" A man twice the size of a defenseman in the Canadian league lights up at the sight of me.

"Max." I smirk.

Max Mahoney springs out of his chair so fast, it spins like a top before careening into the glass window facing the arena. He launches at me, grabs my arm and pulls me in for a bear hug.

I'm 6'4" and used to towering over people, so it's an odd sensation to be looking up at anyone but I do have to tilt my chin up to grin at Max.

"I thought you got lost in traffic!" Max bellows.

"What traffic? I didn't even see a single traffic light driving down here."

"We have a traffic light," Max says haughtily, like it's some kind of flex. "It's over on Howard and Green." He pats me on the back. "Have you settled in yet?"

"Yeah, man. Don't worry about me."

"Worrying about you is kinda my job." He smirks. "By the way, where are you staying?"

"Somewhere with an elevator and housekeeping."

"Long term, that's going to get old. If you haven't found any rentals yet, you can always room with me."

"Once in this lifetime was more than enough, buddy."

"Door's always open as they say." He laughs. "I know you

didn't have much time to prepare for the season, but I have all confidence in your skills."

"Is that my official welcome?"

"Wasn't good enough?" Max coughs and then spreads his hands wide. "We're over-the-moon that you chose to join the Lucky Strikers, Chance."

"He didn't *choose* us. He had nowhere else to go," someone mumbles.

The smile freezes on my face, and I glance over my shoulder. I was told I'd only be meeting the manager today, but I'm not surprised to see a few guys from the team lined up and waiting for me. Their faces are tense, frowns hard as the puck that makes or breaks our game.

Max coughs, "Chance, meet the, uh, the Welcoming Committee."

I hope this Welcoming Committee also serves death penalty inmates their last meal. They'd do a bang-up job.

Facing my teammates fully, I tip my chin up in greeting.

No one returns it.

Max points to a man wearing multiple gold chains and a gold ring on his finger. "That's Cooper Theilan. The guy in the Hello Kitty Crocs beside him is Viking Renthrow. They're our two best forwards."

I'd have guessed by their confident stance. Charging in to retake possession of the puck takes a certain level of daring. You can't be afraid of making mistakes or second guess yourself on the ice. From their haircuts to their style choices, it's clear Theilan and Renthrow are daring both inside and outside of the stadium.

"Ren Watson, our goalie," Max continues, nodding to two bulky men wearing gym clothes. "And that's Gunner Kinsey."

"Center," I say before Max can explain.

"Yeah." Max blinks in surprise.

I'd have known Gunner was the center even if I hadn't

studied every game the Lucky Strikers played last season. Out of all my new teammates, he's the one staring at me like he wants me to fall into an open manhole walking down Main Street.

"Hey." My wave encompasses them all. "I'm Chance McLanely, your new captain."

Theilan, the guy dripping in gold, snorts.

Renthrow, Mr. Hello Kitty, rolls his eyes.

Watson, the goalie, folds his arms over his chest, showing enough muscle to prove he doesn't skimp on the protein shakes.

Gunner sneers. "A reject from the league gets team captain just by showing up?"

"Well…" Max begins.

"If the former team captain had done a better job, it wouldn't have been so easy to take the position."

Max coughs. "Ch-Chance, why don't you—"

"You want to take this outside, McLanely?" Gunner stalks toward me, his face reddening.

"No, there will be no fighting." Max waves his tree-trunk arms.

I flick my fingers at the window overlooking the arena. "We can talk on the ice."

"One on one, I'm going to chew you up and spit you out," Gunner hisses.

"No, no, no." I point to the others. "You need at least three of you guys if you want to do that."

Max smacks his forehead.

The other men get very tense.

Gunner scoffs. "You sure that big mouth of yours can survive outside the penalty box, McLanely?"

I stiffen.

Watson snorts out a laugh.

Renthrow and Theilan smirk.

Fingers fisting, I lunge forward. Max tries to wedge himself in front of me, but I sidestep him so I'm facing off with Gunner.

"You wanna know why I'm captain, Kinsey? Your center is putting up more of a fight here than on the ice." I point to Theilan. "Your right winger is your only defense." To Renthrow. "Your left winger is right-handed and his back hand is insanely weak. So like I said, it'll take all three of you—"

"Alright, that's enough on the introductions for now. I need to speak with Chance privately."

No one moves because they're all too busy glaring a hole into my skull. Thankfully, eyeballs can't turn into jackhammers or my skull would be shattered on the floor.

"Ehem, gentlemen?" Max's voice turns firm. "You're dismissed."

Gunner stares me down. "See you on the ice."

"Looking forward to it."

The rest of the guys file out after Gunner.

The door clicks shut, and the silence that falls is so thick, it's suffocating.

"Make friends, I said." Max sinks into his chair and covers his face with his hands. "Be nice, I said. Why'd I waste my breath?"

"Putting it all out in the open is better for everyone. At least now we know where we stand."

"Did you *have* to antagonize the wingers too?"

I shrug. "You called me here to stir the pot, didn't you?"

"I didn't ask you to turn the pot over and dance on the chicken bones."

That's a vivid image.

"Gunner's got a grip on this team and you know it. You're in as shaky a position as I am."

"Oh, no, McLanely. After all that," he gestures to the door where my new teammates stormed out, "you're in a much, *much* worse place than me."

Maybe so.

But the thing is, I'm not here to make friends. I'm here to

claw my way back to the league and nothing in this Podunk town of Lucky Falls, USA can stop me.

***

To grab the rest of April and Chance's love story, visit www.liabevans.com

ALSO BY LIA BEVANS

The Lucky Strikers Series
Ice Mechanic
Ice Princess

Cool M Ranch Series
The Cowboy's Fake Wife
The Cowboy's Temporary Marriage